The
of Forever

"Withholding love will bring the worst pain and suffering that you will ever carry throughout your life"

– Dan Graham –

First published in Great Britain as a softback original in 2013

Copyright © Dan Graham 2013

The moral right of this author has been asserted.

Typeset in ITC New Baskerville by Consilience Media

Proofreading, design and publishing by Consilience Media
www.consil.co.uk

J~~████████~~

enjoy the read.

Don Graham

Thank you.

Credits

After lots of deliberation and countless months of dogged research I finally got round to penning this story. It was largely produced from the comfort of my garden shed whilst overlooking the River Stour at my home in Suffolk. At times my mind wandered like the river and at times was just as muddy. But when I needed the inspiration, the calmness and freedom to think which would set my mind to work, the river was always there for me. So my first thank you goes to the River Stour for providing that. Who needs trendy Soho cafés and cappuccino jazz for inspiration – give me Suffolk mud any day.

In addition I also need to say a big thank you to a couple of important people in my life. Firstly to my wife who has helped in more ways than she would ever know and secondly to my bendy friend who appears on every page even though her name is never mentioned. I couldn't have done all of this without either of you. So thanks for the idea that you gave me and the platform upon which to build it from, indirectly or otherwise. It's been a great journey and I am and will always be truly grateful.

A big thank you also has to go to my friend Theresa who helped me through the early days of this story and also to Jill who had the medical insight to put me right with orbital shakers and other medical toys. Thank you for the use of your eyes.

For the avoidance of doubt I should point out that this story is fictional of course. It has little factual content other than what has been quoted from the public domain and is not representative of any persons or places to which it may seem to relate in any way. I accept that in places it is not without similarity to persons or places but essentially I have made it all up.

Introduction

Have you ever fallen in love with somebody and never had the opportunity to tell them how you feel? Or perhaps you did have the opportunity but for some reason you didn't take it. Maybe something got in the way, or perhaps your heart was not aligned with your head, or simply the moment wasn't quite right. These things can happen to us all. Then before you know where you are events have overtaken themselves and the opportunity you had has gone, simply changing everything, possibly forever. It's probably a place where many of us have been, possibly more than once if truth be told. The emotion you are rewarded with for this moment of say hesitation or madness can lead to a lifetime of regret. It is the sort of regret that we can carry with us in our hearts for a long, long time. To be honest, some people could possibly end up carrying the pain of a situation like this with them for all of their lives. And it will always be the greatest pain of all.

If this has happened to you can I please ask you to answer a question honestly?

"If you were given a second chance to tell that person how you felt, to be able to almost wind the clock back, to be able to bury all of those years of sadness and hurt, to get your life on track and be in exactly the place that your heart really wants to be – would you be brave enough and committed enough to take that second chance, no matter how radical the process was?

I guess the answer and how much time you spend thinking about the answer depends on the level of regret you have suffered. It's a big question for some I suppose and not so big for others; agreed. Either way deep down most of us know that we wouldn't want to repeat the mistake of all of those years again. Life's too short right, it hurts too much – and so the scales of probability tip. And I can hear you asking in the background about this radical leap of faith that was mentioned: "Just exactly how radical is that and what does it involve?"

This is a love story which tells of exactly that; it answers the question and establishes the value in this case of radical. Two people who traded the very dreams they cared about, kidded themselves that it didn't quite matter or that it would all come good in the end. They fell in love but never had the courage or took the opportunity to tell each other how they felt and eventually they went their separate ways. They put it all off until tomorrow. It's probably a common enough story up to that point except that this couple did get a second chance, where as many don't. The second chance took many years before it came and was only made possible due to their flame never quite extinguishing itself and a miraculous development in medical science. When the opportunity presented itself the realisation that the level of pain from years of regret was so much that it was grabbed unconditionally with both hands and of course a full heart. And guess what? It worked. It worked because somebody wasn't going to make the same mistake again.

The 'radical' element that made it all happen is a process known now as transhumanisation. It's a process based on gene regeneration which was created by a miraculous yet simple sort of genetic marriage of one or more sets of genes from completely different but ultimately compatible sources. Simple as that really. This process helped two people to extend and live their lives, to transcend generations and be in total control of their destiny. They got that golden chance to do it all again and more importantly to do it differently. For how long? Well possibly another 100 years or so, even 100 to 200 years could be possible – at the moment we just don't know.

Due to the unstoppable advancing powers of medical sciences, one day this fascinating and compelling option could be there for all of us – surely it's just a matter of time for fiction to be transformed to fact. "Banzai…"

Chapter 1

It was June 7th 2007, Blake was just back in London after working in North Africa for the first five months or so of the year. He had been missing the social life that he had become so used to before he left and was now back in London needing desperately to catch up with some old friends. It was a warm day, the time was somewhere near 11.30 am and Blake was walking slowly along on the north side of Embankment heading west towards Westminster, Big Ben and the area of Millbank. The plan was to do a catch up over a beer with friends in a pub that was frequented in the area – one of the more regular old watering holes. Blake was looking forward to seeing them as they hadn't been out together now for a long time. Too long in fact.

Blake remembered the day well as he wandered along. A thin canopy of leaves gave some protection from the streaming sunlight that was burning through the London sky as he made his way along the streets. Moving shadows on the limestone pavement provided by the canopies above flickered and created what must have been London's latest West End play, live before his very feet as he passed over the aged pavement and its induced cracks. It felt good to be back.

Blake's appointment was for 12.00 midday and he hadn't really been following the time. All of a sudden he realised that he was running a bit late. He blamed the cock up that faced him when he tried to 'log off' from his computer at the office as he was leaving. That probably cost him a good five minutes without realising it. So now he had better step up the pace a little basically to avoid being late; he didn't want to disappoint after so many months away. It all seemed under control though; he checked his watch again – he still had fifteen minutes or so, plenty of time. He should still be able to make it in time. The increase in Blake's step soon made him more aware of how busy City life was, which he hadn't experienced for a few months, since he had been spending most of his time in the desert. Motorbikes and cars were speeding past in one direction and lots of busy people all of a sudden were passing in the other direction on the pavement next to him. It was one clash or side step after the other. Blake seemed to be perpetually apologising or saying excuse me. Then as if all of this swerving and so on wasn't enough there were the "works" as they are affectionately labelled.

Some things never really change do they and sure enough the London streets were still being littered with "works", or basically holes that are dug in the road or pavement for means of investigation or to allow repairs of some sort or another to be carried out – supposedly. One thing that they did do for sure though was to inflict as much grief and pain as they could onto the general public. For as long as Blake could remember the streets were always being dug up for one thing or another. They would say it was for the installation of cables or water pipes or whatever, but very little evidence was seen as to what was really going on. Anyway, like it or not, you were forced to fall in line with the flow controls that are put in place and prepare to get herded through a slalom course of plastic cones, fencing, bollards and safety panels to somewhere near where you need to go – it's unavoidable. In the end you can easily start to feel like a racing driver who is careering out of control through a chicane on a race track at 200mph with the fear of losing a wheel.

Eventually free from "the works" Blake crossed

Westminster Bridge – taking his chances with the numerous couriers on push bikes (big hairy knees) and huge volumes of tourists, coaches, various buses and the like, finally he made it to the other side of the road. At the time he clearly recollected that Big Ben was striking quarter to the hour of twelve. So this gave him fifteen minutes to go as he rounded the bend towards Westminster Abbey. He set his stare onwards toward Millbank. He only needed to dodge a few more zillion Japanese tourists who were grouped around the entrance to the Abbey, taking and posing for an endless stream of photos. Then the route should be clear. He marched swiftly on.

As he left the various tourists in his speeding wake he picked up the pace a bit more. It was at this point that Blake started to feel a little unwell; it was as though he was experiencing some sort of anxiety attack. An irregular flutter or possibly minor palpitations of some sort were beginning to occur in his chest. It was something new, not experienced before. Blake didn't feel it was enough to cause any great amount of pain or anything but he could sense an emphasised pounding in his chest. It just didn't make sense. Blake slowed his pace to see if things eased but didn't stop totally; there didn't seem to be a need to stop. Then in an instant stronger pains in his chest kicked in. Initially they were irritable more than anything and Blake figured it was probably more of an anxiety style of attack that he was experiencing. He couldn't be totally sure though since he had not experienced an anxiety attack or otherwise before. So now he was totally confused; certainly something sinister and more serious seemed to be happening but he wasn't sure what it was exactly. On the other hand of course it could simply be just a bit of indigestion?

It was becoming more and more difficult but he continued to try and not let it bother him too much. His focus was on not being late for his appointment with his friends and so he kept on walking as quickly as he could. Blake had no idea that he was on the edge of something that was about to change his life forever. The situation he was finding himself in was about to reach extreme on anybody's Richter Scale.

He had probably only managed to walk another 25 yards or so when he was suddenly winded by a swift, powerful and fiercely intense pain. It pole-axed him instantly and stopped him immediately and totally in his tracks. It felt like he had been speared in the chest by a searing hot lance which must have been fired at him from some sort of powerful cannon or medieval mechanical launching device. Blake crashed instantly to his knees; his mouth wide open he looked to the sky and gasped for air. His right hand reached out randomly for something that he could grab hold of in an attempt to stop himself from collapsing totally onto the pavement below him. His eyes had been jacked open wide by the reaction from the adrenalin as he stared up at the sky. His brain was frantically shouting instructions for him to get to his feet, wave for help, breathe deeply, try and calm yourself but some sort of evil had entered his body and not all of the messages were coherent enough to be understood and obeyed. At this point he was floundering and in serious pain, stuck fast to the ropes like a desperately losing prize fighter and rapidly losing the round. It was as though his brain was his corner team in this boxing match, its distant voice continuing to repeatedly shout to him with instructions to cling on, get up, breathe.

CHAPTER 1

Blake realised he was drowning in a lethal cocktail of
both pain and fear. He was in absolute agony; in addition
he was shocked and as confused as hell. Pouring into the
mix was the probability that what was happening to him was
possibly going to take his life. He felt helpless and at that
point he began to cry. Possibly it was a combination of hope,
desperation or a subconscious decision that he had made to
live rather than to die but Blake somehow decided that he
was not going to just roll over. He had to fight this evil, this
thing that was taking control. He needed to get help and
for the first time he looked towards his corner for one last
grasp of strength before it was probably too late. His corner
was manned by the people that he loved most in the world.
He could hear them crying out "fight Blake fight". At that
moment the choice was made to try with all of his strength to
do as his corner wanted;, he needed to fight and hang on to
his life; this was not a good day to die.

People passed by, blind to what was happening to Blake
as he struggled on the pavement. Everybody had already
made up their own minds without even asking as to what was
really wrong with him and sadly nobody chose to investigate
or help. Blake leaned on a wall to steady himself. His pulse
raced. He now started to sweat like an arsonist in a match
factory. He felt sick. At that point and for the first time he
suspected he was having a heart attack. His instincts were still
to collapse in a heap on the floor but his corner continued to
shout instruction, telling him to hold on, get and stay on your
feet and breathe deeply, big breaths.

Blake continued to reach for help from the passers-by
who continued to stare at this mad man who was possibly at
best having a fit or was maybe even a drunken nuisance. But

5

he must have been invisible because they continued to be oblivious to him, to his suffering and his desperate situation. After a couple of minutes more the pain had now reached a level that was beyond intolerance, and the shaking started. On a scale of 1 to 10 (1 being low and 10 being high), the pain was a 20.

Blake was still listening to his corner. He had to; he wasn't sure what to do next. He had to let somebody know what was happening to him before it was all too late. He decided that he would try to call his ex-wife. Hands trembling he reached into his pocket for his phone. He lifted it in front of his face and squinted through the sweat running from his forehead on to the controls. The sweat still ran down and onto the keypad but by some miracle he managed to quickly get the number. With most calls that Blake made to his ex-wife she always had to have the first five minutes of conversation which usually revolved around mundane matters such as the postman being late and was he eating OK, where she was going on her holiday and so on. Well not this time: this time the sequence went just a little bit differently. On this occasion he spoke, she screamed and then he hung up. And that was that.

Once that little task was over with Blake staggered to the edge of the pavement and with as much strength as he could muster he raised an arm as best as he could and hailed a taxi cab.

Good old London – it must have been only seconds and a black cab swung around in the street and pulled up beside him. Almost blinded by pain, sweat and fear of what was happening to him, he eased open the door and dragged himself inside.

"Where to guv?" asked the cab driver looking at him through his rear-view mirror.

Blake winced and croaked to the taxi driver, "Nearest hospital, soon as you can mate." It even hurt for him to speak.

"OK, no worries, get you there in a jiffy, one over the river there guv."

The cab indicated, pulled out into the street and sped off. The journey was a bit of a blur. They crossed Lambeth Bridge and turned left towards Guy's and St Thomas' hospitals. It was seconds later when the cab headed up the ramp and stopped outside A&E. Blake felt that the journey was quick although he couldn't say for sure. His focus stayed always on listening to his corner and his breathing. This didn't make the pain go away; in fact it was just as bad as ever and the shaking continued. Blake was getting concerned that he might pass out. He felt as though he was going to be tipped out of a big wheel fairground ride and was preparing to freefall towards hell with absolutely no control over himself at all.

Unbeknown to Blake, during the journey the cab driver had called in to his office via his radio and had explained to them the state that Blake was in and where he was taking him. The office must have then made the call to the hospital and told them because a crash team were standing at the A&E arrival bay when the cab pulled up in readiness to help Blake. But this is where the good neighbour routine ended, sadly.

The cab pulled up slowly and stopped in the allocated bay. The driver applied the handbrake and turned to Blake: "That will be £4 guv please." As is the way with London taxis the doors were still locked closed at this point.

There was a bit of a commotion going on outside the cab and Blake looked up and saw a small group of people, presumably nurses and doctors waiting outside the taxi. They were staring in at him and gesturing for him to get out. Everybody seemed to be trying to get the taxi door open. The next thing was that a trolley appeared and the crowd grew in size. The taxi door stayed locked.

The cabby repeated his demands: "That'll be £4 guv please." The doors still remained locked.

Blake began to search through his pockets for cash. The problem was his hands were numb and he could feel very little. Frantically he ripped at his jacket and trouser pockets for the cash he thought he had. He couldn't find it. He thought perhaps speaking to the cabby might help as he continued to worm his way through his pockets without success. As hard as he tried he couldn't find the money.

Blake sweating profusely, his back was like a lake, said, "Please I have money, I just can't find it, I need to get out."

The relenting cabby replied: "I need paying first, can't let you out till I get paid, sorry guv."

"Would you rather I croak it in the back of your cab?"

The cab driver clearly didn't give a damn. The medical team outside could obviously see what was happening inside the taxi. The next moment somebody waved a £5 note outside the cab immediately in front of the side window to attract the attention of the cabby. Blake remembered hearing the winding sound of the window opening and through blurred vision he saw a hand pass a Five Pound note through the frame to the driver which coincided with the clunk of a door – presumably the cab was being unlocked. The door just flung open in front of Blake, he didn't need to touch a thing. God knows which one of the medical team paid the miserable bastard; Blake would have done if only he was in a better state of mind.

Blake would never forget the cab driver's parting words; they ran around and around in his head for many years to come. "Hope you get better guv," then he drove off – keeping the change. If ever there was a reason to live Blake knew that this was it.

Blake was barely out of the taxi when he was grabbed and devoured by the goodness of the waiting medical team who lifted him onto the prepared trolley. Once safely loaded onto the trolley he was delivered at speed into the A&E reception area. He remembered thinking how relieved he was that he was able to make it that far; on the other hand he wasn't sure if he was already dead and was possibly now witnessing it all from some corner in the room. Momentarily he got a sobering glimpse of what was actually going on. This brief window of realism scared him even more. Blake became increasingly frightened. It was all too surreal to comprehend. He was exhausted; he had fought with demon after demon until too tired to fight anymore. He just felt sick and lifeless. Once again he was beginning to feel spaced out as though his body and mind were being separated for fun by some unexplainable and spiteful force. It was a really strange sensation. Physically he was numb and he couldn't function very well; mentally he was drifting off, a bit like a helium balloon up and up, just drifting along in a light breeze into a big and empty sky.

This emotion didn't last for long and in a flash he felt as though he was heading for the ground at speed, simply accelerating and sinking. Faster and faster. It wasn't good.

This mixed roller-coaster ride had convinced him that his life had ended or was about to end. Shame really because that would mean he would never be able to repay the taxi driver.

This didn't feel right to Blake and not for the first time he found himself fighting it with what little strength he had left in him. Again he listened to his corner and decided that all he could do was simply to keep breathing, slow and deep, trying not to panic. All the time he tried to breathe rhythmically, nice and easy, nice and slow, one after the other and then more deep deep breaths.

Then all of a sudden out of nowhere all of this emotional turmoil was interrupted by an outstretched neck and a face which appeared above him. It could have been an angel for all he knew as he had never seen one before.

The face spoke to him, "Hello, can you hear me?" The nurse ran the back of her hand softly down the side of his face. "We are going to give you something for the pain OK? How are you feeling?"

With that the nurse disappeared. Blake wondered if he would ever see her again. He didn't have to wait very long to find out. With all the style and swiftness of a Las Vegas croupier the nurse was back and standing by his bedside with what appeared to be a large needle in her hand; she was tantricly poised, pouting morphine and ready to strike.

Blake didn't feel a thing as the needle was plunged into him. He couldn't even tell you where they put it; it could have been in his eyeballs for all he knew – he had no idea and actually didn't care. Within a nanosecond he had drifted off down another hazy tunnel.

For a brief period of time a number of hazy faces, possibly all different, continued to appear above him, each trying to strike up conversation of some sort or other. He had no idea then who these people were, nor would he know afterwards.

"How does it feel now?"

"How is the pain in terms of 1 to 10 if 1 is low and 10 is high?"

"What's your name?" Over and over again the same questions. Nothing really registered.

Blake couldn't quite understand why the same questions were being repeated over and over. He had already answered them more than once and he didn't think that he was getting it all wrong or maybe they just weren't convincing enough answers, hence the relentless badgering for a proper answer. Could have been a possibility...

Hands began to appear from everywhere; they moved frenetically up and down his body, covering his legs, feet, arms, chest, shoulders and bits of his neck. In no time at all the hands had removed the vast majority of his clothing, and were sticking pads and wires onto his chest and on any other bits of free skin. Everything was carried out at such a pace. Blake didn't know how many people were busy with all of this but if he could have counted the hands and then divided by two he would probably come up with about 50 nurses. They were just amazing, quick and efficient.

By this time Blake obviously looked like shit. To add to all of this misery his clothes were absolutely soaking and were sticking fast to his body like some kind of shrink wrap. He must have looked more like a drowning man than somebody having a heart attack. Hopefully they had seen worse but he doubted it somehow. At this point he had figured out that he wasn't dead but very much alive and that these people were trying hard to keep it that way. He thought carefully and came to the conclusion that it was probably best not to piss them off by slipping away.

He reached deep inside and mustered the strength to speak to himself one more time, "So come on listen to the corner, breathe, that's it, nice and deep, nice and slow."

It is usually a good thing when pain eases and especially good if it is a good thing that causes the pain to ease. In this case Blake had seen enough evidence to be sure that it was the morphine which had been injected into him that was causing the pain to back off and he was reasonably confident that it had nothing to do with the grim reaper possibly winning the fight. Hooray for a drop of morphine. It felt like party time at last. Life was still fuzzy but it didn't hurt quite so much.

In a flash the brakes were taken off the trolley and he was on the move. The trolley screamed down the corridor towards a set of lift doors and he was on his way to theatre.

The corridor lights flashed across Blake's face; how many – he couldn't count. He likened the experience to having your face jammed under the lid of a photocopier and somebody had pressed for 100 copies. The lights flew back and forth over his face like tracer bullets fired from a big fast and powerful gun. He felt like he was being pushed by nurses and doctors wearing jet trainers at about 40 or 50 miles an hour. He was convinced he had landed the 'university pram race champions' which was lucky for him.

The corridors were populated by medical staff going about their duties as well as members of the public going to and from various wards for visiting. Instruction to 'move aside' was given by the lead member of the pram race team and the crowds in the corridors parted like something from a scene in a biblical story – peeling away from the oncoming high speed vehicle and voluntarily pinning themselves against the walls to avoid injury or bruising from what must have looked like a runaway train. Hooked up to monitors, drips and potentially still on the cusp of crossing the threshold to the pearly gates, Blake just tried to relax and breathe. One thing was for sure he was now in very good hands; it was an enormous relief to him. He just hoped they could operate as well as they could push prams.

Then all of a sudden, like a ghost train ends its ride on the fun fair, the trolley burst through a set of heavy rubberised doors and it galactically exploded into a very brightly lit and spacious room. This was a moment when Blake thought that the next person to greet him could be St Peter but in fact it turned out to be Dr Joseph Singh instead.

The doctor said: "OK, get this guy ready for theatre, come on, let's move it." He stared over Blake, wearing a face mask and surgical gloves. At long last he spoke the words Blake had longed to hear, "It's OK, you are going to be OK, you have my word – as long as you have signed the consent forms." Blake cried again. Yes, that was the second time in the same day: not a good look.

The next part can only be described as the most surreal moment in Blake's life and potentially the most embarrassing. Dr Singh was about to find out that Blake still had his shorts on and they needed to be removed so that he could be fully prepped for the angiogram procedure. In layman's terms it is when a stent (a piece of cylindrical tubing with an internal spring) is fitted. An incision is usually made into the groin area at the top of the right leg to access the main artery and using keyhole surgery techniques the artery to the heart is ballooned at the place of the blockage. The stent is then pushed carefully into the damaged area and keeps the artery open to the flow of blood. Sounds plausible and should be straightforward enough.

Scalpel in hand and with a focused stare on his face Dr Singh pulled back the sheet that covered Blake's modesty, only to be confronted by a pair of Burberry checked cotton boxer shorts.

There was a flurry of panic as Dr Singh called one of the nurses over, "Nurse, nurse, quickly, he still has his boxer shorts on and obviously he needs to be shaved, god he hasn't been prepped."

Dr Singh looked over to face Blake. "Sorry for this Blake, we will get this sorted out and get on with the op in no time at all."

He turned to the nurse who was rushing over brandishing a razor in her right hand – but no aftershave hopefully.

Dr Singh said: "Come on Nurse, let's hurry, this man is in a lot of pain."

Well the doctor was right of course, Blake was in pain or had been in pain but he had a funny feeling that it was about to pale into insignificance and be replaced by copious amounts of embarrassment that ounce for ounce could be potentially worse than the pain.

Very quickly Nurse Watkins arrived with the tools that she needed for the job, namely the battery operated razor. She placed the tray on the mobile cabinet which was located next to the operating table and then proceeded to remove Blake's shorts, tugging nice and gently so as not to shock him too much. Unbeknown to his saviours, Blake had already started to laugh, albeit just a little. He couldn't help himself. Blake just couldn't believe what was happening. Here he was at the centre of a near-to-death experience as he had ever been and ever wanted to be again and he was actually starting to giggle, potentially uncontrollably. With his shorts now removed Dr Singh and the nurse looked down at Blake's already shaven groin area.

Doctor Singh spoke first. "So Nurse, he has been shaved. Who the hell did this? And why shave him and then put his shorts back on him? It doesn't make sense. Nurse, did you already do this?"

Nurse Watkins replied: "No I didn't, maybe one of the other sisters did it."

The whole medical team stared down at the fully shaven groin area in disbelief.

"But I only needed a small area to be removed," Dr Singh said as he pointed to the right hand side of the groin in question. "Over here, some of it removed over here," he puffed out his cheeks and exhaled, "but this, this is a bit over the top."

As amusing as the moment was Blake thought it best to come clean so to speak so that things could move on. He raised his right arm, tears running down his face.

The doctor thought that Blake may be experiencing some pain and went over. In a calming voice he leaned over and said to Blake, "How are you – do you need more morphine? I am sorry for the hold-up but somebody got a bit carried away with the razor and was a bit severe in prepping you for theatre which kind of shocked us and caused some commotion."

Blake needed to clear this little anomaly up so that things could move on and so he paused for a moment and tried to put on a straight face hoping it would help him find the strength to utter the words which could break the deadlock on the mystery of how his pubic hair had been totally removed to provide the perfect smooth operating surface that was every surgeon's dream.

"It was me."

Dr Singh asked, "What was you?"

Blake pointed down towards the area in question as best he could.

It didn't take long before a light went on in Dr Singh's head; his face lit up and his eyebrows raised to form startled peaks. A bit shocked, he spoke to Blake: "What? You did it?" He looked confused and needed to get more confirmation.

He continued: "When, why, how, you're kidding, the nurses downstairs did it right when you were admitted?"

Blake interrupted him: "Please doc, no I did it – believe me, before I came in, a few days ago."

"Oh I see, but why?"

"Well let's just say I had a funny feeling that something bad was going to happen to me today and I just needed to be ready."

"As your mum always says – right?"

"That's right doc, as my mum always says."

With that Dr Singh made the incision and got to work.

Chapter 2

Blake's recovery period at St Thomas' lasted about eight days after the operation. The first two or three days were soaked up with trying to work out exactly what happened and why. He hoped that if he had the answers to these questions he would be able to make the necessary huge adjustments needed in his life. Some bits and pieces of what happened on that day crept back into his memory, oddly enough not all of them at the same time. As he grew stronger and stronger each day then the events of the day would unfold more frequently and become more vivid in his mind.

The ward was a happy place for Blake to be since he knew that he was getting better but on the other hand it was also a sad place as day by day he saw more and more people admitted for the same and similar treatment. The span of the ages shocked him. He never in his wildest dreams expected to see children being treated along with adults. Clearly the causes of this type of heart trouble are varied and sit somewhere between genetics and over indulgence, even probably a combination of both. There was certainly a lot to learn, a) about himself and b) the condition.

Blake had no real recollection of where the hospital was. He could remember a bit about the commotion surrounding the taxi but since the A&E entrance was at the back of the hospital he wasn't sure exactly which area of London he was in or the street name for example. For the first three days or so Blake lay fairly motionless in his bed, most of the time sleeping, and when he wasn't he was squinting out of one eye at the nurses. He had had visitors but they hadn't really registered with him. No detail of conversation could really be recalled; he sort of knew they were there though. Peace and quiet were definitely the order of the day initially. His cat napping would mostly be disturbed by routine visits from doctors and nurses, the catering people and the cleaners. He seemed to be easily woken by the interference of a noisy mop being brandished around under his bed as the lady cleaned the floor.

After about three days of being in this semi-comatose state and lying around, Blake was told that he would be able to get up and shower.

This was such a relief. No more bed pans, blanket baths and having help brushing his teeth. He was becoming independent again and was now about to be deemed capable of being able to do it for himself. He thought that he may get some help initially from a couple of the nurses but sadly it didn't materialise. He would just have to take his time and learn to take care of himself. It wasn't so much of a problem washing his body; no, what made it difficult was being hooked up to drip systems and so on, still having all of those pads for monitoring stuck all over him, that's what made it a bit tricky.

At the end of the day, although things would be a bit tender he was glad of the challenge. He accepted it as progress and decided to just get on with it.

The first shower experience went reasonably well. It was a bit slow but that's to be expected, soaping up felt a bit strange as it was the first time he had seen the enormous bruising around his right thigh and groin area. It was huge and covered more area than he expected. It seemed to cover the whole area between his navel and his right knee. He couldn't help wondering if it would go away and how long it would take – or maybe it wouldn't; he didn't know for sure. It looked

horrible though. But again bruising is part of the healing
process that the body enters into so eventually he began to
not worry about it and saw it as a good thing.

But what a relief it was to Blake to be able to get back to
being able to carry out some normal human and dignified
functions again. Rejoice! The wrapped shackles of tubes,
cables and armies of monitors had finally been removed
– albeit temporarily – and he no longer looked like a
puppeteer's plaything. He couldn't quite believe it. From
feeling like he was going to die just a few days ago to being
here now, standing in the shower and just simply getting wet
lifted his heart to the outer limits of the galaxy. He stood
for a moment and looked into the partially steamed-up
mirror which was mounted on the wall, next to the cord for
the emergency alarm and stared at his beaten up body. As
bad as it was he had a grin from ear to ear – my goodness it
was a happy feeling. Even though physically he resembled a
complete train wreck, inside he was feeling happier at that
moment than he had ever, ever done in his life. From that
moment on every bit of progress he made just increased the
good feeling that was being generated and growing inside of
him. Even everyday simple things started to cheer him up like
putting one leg in front of the other and being able to take
basic steps across the ward. It was wonderful.

As the days went by Blake's appetite to engage in
conversation returned. Conversation was always something
he enjoyed but since the heart attack he rarely found himself
in the mood. But now that was changing. He found himself
passing the time of day with the cleaning staff, the nurses
of course and even people visiting other patients in other
wards. In addition as he became more mobile he was able to

wander around the common areas in the hospital which he particularly enjoyed doing. This allowed him to chat to some of the other patients.

One late morning Blake was heading out towards the communal gardens when he bumped into Dr Singh. He introduced himself.

"Hello Mr Brown, I'm Dr Singh."

Dr Singh was a tall, slimish man of Indian decent. He wore spectacles and was clean shaven apart from his tiny goatee beard. He was wearing his white coat over his day clothes and looked very important and official; Blake thought he was probably on his way to a seminar or something. "Dr Joseph Singh, remember me? How are you doing?"

Blake wasn't totally sure which, from the look on his face, was probably obvious to Dr Singh.

Dr Singh smiled and reached out his hand. "I am the surgeon that worked on you when you were admitted, so that probably explains your vacant stare."

"Oh that Dr Singh, that's fantastic, so pleased to meet you …again. Yes thanks I am doing much better now, thanks to you of course Doctor."

"You know the staff told me of that taxi story, quite remarkable really. Even on your part to make sure that you got yourself here."

"Well it's not something I do every day but when the effort is needed it's nice to be able to give it. I had some help though from my trainers in my corner." Blake grinned. Dr Singh wasn't quite sure as to the reference but it didn't matter so much.

Blake continued, "Mmm talking about giving Doctor, since you mention the taxi incident, you don't happen to know who paid the fare do you?"

Dr Singh replied, "Didn't you?"

"No it wasn't me, somebody else did it and I would like to know."

"Sorry, can't help you there, Mr Brown. So where are you going now anyway? You seem to be a long way from the ward."

"Well I was heading to the gardens. It's such a sunny day and I haven't felt the sun on my face for a while now. Thought it would do me some good. And you?"

"Oh people to see, places to go. Well it was nice catching up with you. Maybe I will pop up to the ward one of these afternoons just to see how you are doing."

"OK that would be nice," Blake said.

"Oh by the way if you like music there is a piano recital in about ten minutes in the great hall, just left down that corridor," Dr Singh pointed Blake towards the general direction.

"Thanks Doctor, thank you."

Dr Singh waved, turned and went on his way.

Blake acknowledged his kindness with a smile and a nod of his head. What a nice guy he thought to himself, a really nice guy. One to which he would be eternally grateful. At that exact moment though Blake had absolutely no idea as to just how much.

It was nearing the seventh day in hospital for Blake. It was again a sunny afternoon and Blake was staring out of the window on the ward towards Waterloo Station, being mesmerised by the many, many fully laden trains that rolled in and out. Some would have been heading to France since the Eurostar train went in and out of there as well as local places like Twickenham or Staines or even maybe mysterious places like Strawberry Hill. Strawberry Hill, now there was an unusual name. Somewhere in the deep crevices of his mind he seemed to remember a link between the place called Strawberry Hill, a man called Horace Walpole and a book called "The Three Princes of Serendip". Horace Walpole was a famous letter writer apparently, did he live in Strawberry Hill? He wasn't sure; some things were still a bit foggy. Unfortunately he didn't have the strength to ponder over it all for much longer than thirty seconds; it would have to go onto the list of things to do that would keep him busy when he got home. Strawberry Hill – sounds exotic though.

Blake was standing at the window on the ward and just about to see the Eurostar train for Paris pull out of the station when he got a tap on the shoulder. It was Dr Joseph Singh. "Hi Blake, how are you? How is it going?"

"Hello doctor – I am OK, I think. It's good to see you again. I was just idly staring out and gazing at life passing me by."

"Did you make it to the piano recital the other day?"

"I did. I managed to get a seat there and sat and listened for a few moments before going into the garden, it was lovely. That said I couldn't tell you which piece it was that he was playing."

"I think I saw that it was a summary of compilations from Bach. I might be wrong."

"Oh well, I appreciated it anyway, no matter what it was, it sounded very nice, well played but just technically wasted on me, I am afraid. Sounds terrible, I know. Maybe as part of my lifestyle changes, Doctor, I can build in the time to study music, or learn to even play something. Saxophone maybe, that would be nice."

Dr Singh said: "Sounds good to me, lovely instrument the saxophone. I tried to play a trumpet once, back in my med school days. Bloody disaster. Mind you I had had a bit of a drink at the time."

"Oh, a true student then."

"Could say, most of the time it was hard work but occasionally tradition dictates. So what now Blake, are you actually train spotting?"

"It looks that way, doesn't it? I just find it quite fascinating really. When you get on a train and then go to the station and get off it you are just a small part of what really goes on at a station. You don't really have much of an idea of the changing faces of a station until you can get this helicopter view which lets you see what really goes on. I find the perpetual comings and goings amazing. Just hundreds, probably thousands of people, just in and out all of the time, in and out. Incredible really. Life just passes by, oblivious; they are all oblivious, just like I was."

"Come on Blake, that's the one thing we saved you from, so that you never have to let life pass you by, never."

"I would like to think so Doctor, I really would."

"Blake, you will soon be well enough to get out there and take it all on again, just like before."

"Possibly easier said than done, when you have just been through what I have, Doctor. The problem is you never know what life is going to throw at you, what cards you will be dealt. That much I have learned."

"That's true Blake, but for everybody, all of us. We are all the same. Anyway look on the bright side, due to continuing advances in medical science we were able to save your life. That's how it is, and in tomorrow's world we will be able to do even more extraordinary things for people, so keep living Blake, who knows what is around the corner."

"I guess you are right. Stay positive, that's the least we can all do." Blake seemed to take on board the doctor's words.

"We will talk again Blake. I will pop up tomorrow as I would like to see you before you go home and before I go off for my long weekend."

Blake was aware that Friday could be the day he would get discharged from the hospital. Frankly he was ready to go home now. He didn't have answers to all of his questions but the Indians were definitely circling the wagons. He wasn't sure what he would do when he got home but nonetheless he now felt ready to go.

Dr Singh left Blake at the window. It wasn't long before afternoon tea arrived which was always nice. Can't beat a cup of tea and a biscuit as one of his friends used to say, solves everything that does.

So the last day at St Thomas' had arrived. This of course all depended on being given the all clear by the Cardiology consultant, then there was the discussion with the dietician and the logistics of how he would get home to be worked out. If that plan all came together then Blake looked like he would be going home today.

It was mid-morning on the last day when Dr Singh came to visit Blake. The Cardiology consultant and the dietary specialists had been and gone already. Blake was waiting only for results of some blood tests and then he was expecting to go home. The logistics though were not quite fixed but Blake was working on it.

A slightly forlorn Blake sat on the side of the bed with his regular clothes back on. His locker was now empty and his personal things were in a small canvas bag at his side. His clothes, the ones he had been wearing when he was admitted to the hospital had been laundered and made presentable to him again. He had forgotten that he even owned the suit and shirt. It just seemed to belong elsewhere, not with him. It felt a bit spooky putting them back on, but at the end of the day Blake had no real choice. One very noticeable thing that pleased him was that he had lost weight over the last week or so and the belt on the trousers had to be hitched up another couple of notches. He told himself that it could only be a good thing.

Dr Singh said, "Hi Blake, how are you? Got the all clear and ready to go?"

"Just need some blood test results and then yes I am on my way. Subject to the final touches to my transport, of course."

"That's good news Blake, good news. Now Blake please don't take this the wrong way but I hope, for all the right reasons that I don't see you again – if you know what I mean."

"I do know what you mean Doctor and believe me I wish for exactly the same. Again, thank you for everything you have done for me."

"OK then, so how are you getting home, somebody coming to pick you up?"

"Well no, not as yet. I have contacted somebody I know in the village but they weren't in so I left a message; other than that it will be taxi to Liverpool Street station and get the train to Manningtree."

"Manningtree? You live up in Manningtree?"

Blake replied, "Well in that general area, a small place you may have heard of called Dedham."

"Heard of it? I live next door in Langham."

"So that is a coincidence, blimey, small world!"

"You may not recall but this is my long weekend and in about two hours I am heading home." Dr Singh raised his eyebrows and nodded his head in a suggestive tease towards Blake, who eventually understood the rules of engagement.

Blake responded, "You wouldn't be going anywhere near Dedham then, would you Doctor?"

"Well as it happens I might be. Who wants to know?"

It was obvious to Blake that Dr Singh and he were going to be friends for a long time to come.

Two hours or so later they were both in Dr Singh's car and heading up the A12 towards north Essex. They chatted about sports, mostly rugby and football. Dr Singh told Blake about his love of cycling. Some of his favourite routes twist and turn across the Box and Stour valleys. It all sounded far too energetic for Blake but now that he was embarking upon a different lifestyle maybe it was something he should not easily dismiss as part of his long term recovery plan.

The journey in the car would take them approximately two hours depending upon traffic and eventually the conversation got around to hospitals, medical conditions and treatments, and a number of general illnesses. After all Dr Singh had seen most things.

Blake said, "So Doctor…"

Dr Singh interrupted: "Please call me Joseph from now on, if that's OK with you."

"OK Joseph, tell me have you ever thought what it could be like to live forever? A lot of people probably flirt with the idea from time to time but the reality of it is that it's as scary as the thought of dying so we don't go there that often. Do you have any views?"

Joseph looked curiously at Blake for a moment, and wondered where that question had come from.

"Well Blake, there could be a solution, one that is achievable."

"Really? What's that?"

"Well it's not to be able to live forever but to be able to live an extended and healthier life – perhaps the compromise that would suit most of us."

"Such as?"

"Well what if we were able to pick and choose from some sort of menu which allowed us to balance a selected lifestyle with the longevity we seek? This needs to be balanced of course with risks but possibly in the future advanced medicine will allow us to achieve this. Effectively we could be able to choose our own lifestyle and choose exactly for how long we want to own it."

"Do you really believe that?" Blake asked.

"Why not? I see advances in medical science every day and I can't see, in time, why it won't become possible one day – it's just a matter of time, Blake, just a matter of time."

"Intriguing thought, Joseph, it's an amazing theory."

"But it's a viable theory, Blake. Let's look at it another way. If you had lived life in Tudor or Victorian times with what was less than basic medical knowledge then, you would have said without doubt that things we take for granted in our lives today would have been absolutely impossible at any time in future. Things like heart transplants, having new faces and replacement of multiple organs would have been as laughable as putting a man on the moon. And that's all perfectly understandable. Even having stents fitted in half an hour would have been unbelievable not so many years ago. You have to accept that the basics of medical practice during any of those historical periods were vastly different from the way it is today. Don't you agree?"

"Oh yes of course. But they had had so much scope to improve on then though, didn't they?"

"But that's my point: they didn't know that at the time; it has just continued to evolve. So my point is that this progression must be evidence to support the fact that the world of medical science is unstoppable. On this basis, Blake, at least you have to accept that it is highly plausible that it will continue to get better and more and more advanced."

Blake looked perplexed. "It sounds plausible I suppose, but I am not too sure – it's all a bit Star-Treckish to me!"

"Look Blake, answer me honestly – have you ever been sick, felt like shit and would have given anything for a miracle cure? This being the case then you have to accept that what I am about to tell you has every chance of becoming a true story one day. It's just a matter of when, thanks to something which I call 'Transhumanisation'."

"Trans what?" struggling to take it all in. Joseph tried again, "Transhumanisation."

Blake became a bit more intrigued. "So what is Transhumanisation exactly?"

"Transhumanisation, Blake, is basically the transcending of human generations. It would be achievable by gene rejuvenation. The gene rejuvenation process could be possible by either finding or creating a gene or genes that continue to reinvent themselves rather than dying, which is what they do currently of course; right."

Joseph added, "Just let me overtake this truck," as the

28

car pulled out into the outside carriageway its speed was increased to 80mph to put some distance between them and the other traffic.

Joseph went on: "That's better, I can see the road a bit better now. Look Blake, scientists today are busy with developing rejuvenation therapies that I believe will, over the next decade or so, be able to restore people to a much younger biological age. Let's say you are now forty. In twenty years' time the advances in genetic science are expected to be able to push your expected date of departure from this world from sixty to say one hundred and forty years. By the time you reach one hundred and twenty they will have probably advanced the process even more and will be able to get you back to being forty again. Funny really. Suddenly your life expectancy has rocketed to being four hundred years old and maybe more. That's Transhumanisation."

Blake's head was in a spin. "I am amazed; I am still figuring out how to work the microwave at home and you are involved in all of this!"

"It's not all good news as yet and of course it won't suit everybody. I mean some will have to ask themselves the niggly question of what is the point of living forever if there isn't a purpose? Most people will appreciate that it isn't going to be much fun just dragging things out for the sake of it."

"You would think that most people could have a purpose. I wonder if the question isn't more like – 'so what's the downside?'."

Joseph looked at Blake and laughed, "Well it will screw up inheritance tax for sure."

"So truly doc, how possible is all of this and how far away is it in reality?"

"Well at the moment it's just a theory that gets bandied about in various medical journals every so often, but for my money it will happen. It's so strong, Blake, that it will power medical science forward. You can see evidence and signs in people of natural longevity existing and so it's a case of taking what is happening to us naturally and bottling it into a serum form that can be either injected or fed into our system somehow. Yes Blake, it is coming, it's just a matter of time. People will be able to live longer, say from one hundred to two hundred years old, without loss of major body tissue through gene rejuvenation. OK it's not around the corner, Blake, but who knows, it could be with us in ten or twenty years' time. Anyway start the process and by the time you have reached one hundred and forty they will have found a way to get you to two hundred and fifty."

"How fantastic is that, possibly still playing football at one hundred and ten!"

"We are nearly there, only about six miles or so to go. Won't be long now, it was a decent run up, no real traffic issues to worry about."

A few moments later the car pulled up outside Blake's house in Dedham. Blake was grateful for the ride home. He asked, "So Joseph, what are you up to at the weekend then?"

"Well if the weather stays nice I plan to go out on my bicycle. A bit of cycling along the Box Valley would be nice."

"No family to entertain then?"

"No not at home anyway. And you, no family either?"

Blake replied, "No, divorced, just myself and the children of course when I see them, which I hope will be more often than it was before."

Joseph nodded as if he understood. "I have a sister who

lives in London and that's about it. I don't see her very often. No it's just me which is the way that I like it at the moment. Oh, here is my card Blake – call me if you need anything."

"I was thinking, maybe you would like to pop around sometime and we can continue the conversation about transhumanisation over a glass of wine and some supper."

"Sounds great Blake. Give me a call when you have settled in and have the strength to pull the cork from that bottle."

Blake and Joseph stayed in regular contact with each other over the coming years. Their friendship grew and grew. They both shared the love of Argentian Malbec and so, with every bottle consumed so their friendship developed. Sharing life's experiences and aspirations was always a good thing for Blake. He liked Joseph as a friend but also he knew that he would always be indebted to him for saving his life. It was a bond that was special to both of them and one that would always remain.

Chapter 3

Now let's rewind a little bit. Blake was born in a small Suffolk seaside town in 1964 called Pakefield to an English father and Scottish mother. Pakefield sits just to the south of nearby Lowestoft with its run down fishing industry, various boat yards for building and repair as well as a couple of food processing factories which in the good old days could freeze peas so fast you thought they had just been picked from the fields. You know the one. In the mid 1960s and even on through the seventies it was a reasonably thriving area although things did start to change and go downhill a bit shortly after that with the closure of one or two large businesses in the town.

As is usual with coastal towns, the beaches around Pakefield, being no different from others, attracted many fishermen on a regular basis. Well, when you have just lost your job and need to eat, catching fish seems as good a way as any to try and bag a meal for you and the family. Small tatty wooden huts bound only by time itself lined a stretch of the cliff top at Pakefield. Lovingly constructed from scavenged sheets of rusting corrugated iron for roofs and walls clad with semi-rotten, washed up, salty ship lap panelling, they creaked in the breeze as though they were joined at the hip. In fact come to think of it they creaked all the time, even when you walked past them.

Shabby chic doesn't even come close to describing these work houses. Blake would always remember the curtains in the windows; they reminded him of pairs of his old grannie's knickers that he saw as a lad, stretched out on her washing line, bless her. Just large pieces of faded cloth really, not particularly exciting. In fact they could have been used for a number of things. The beach huts were an odd mishmash of colours and shapes, some bigger than others. He had seen a few cowboy films in his time and to him they resembled a group of men staked out in the desert, having been captured and laid out as a form of torture. They would be ridiculously stretched across the four corners of the window to try and cover the shed's modesty. God only knows what they made the elastic out of in those days. OK so the huts weren't pretty to look at, but what they didn't have in grand design, feng-shui interior or Southwold 'je-ne-sais-quoi', these beach huts made up for in sheer stubbornness in resisting the cruellest of weather that mother nature regularly threw at them. This was all that mattered to the people of Pakefield who used them. 'Functional' – I think is the proper term that fits their description.

The huts were where local traders sold their freshly caught fish which they caught from either their rods placed down on the beach or from their inshore fishing boats.

A relatively interesting and picturesque spot, it was always busy with buyers, walkers and disapproving veggie types as well as the pure carnivore. You know the type who wouldn't eat fish, even if it had antlers and ran around a field all day. Sundays were usually the busiest day of the week for selling fish as families regularly stretched their legs along the coastal paths and picked up fish as they went.

Blake's mum and dad both worked hard to send Blake to good schools. His education started with Blake going to a private all-girls Catholic boarding school would you believe, although they also took male day students. It was a relief for most of the boys that the uniform was then extended beyond skirts and blouses to include shorts and shirts for boy day students, although there were one or two boys who clearly wouldn't have minded wearing skirts. This period of Blake's life went reasonably well. There was plenty of fighting and plenty of praying. So it was a proper Catholic education really.

Later, at the age of 12, Blake was accepted at and moved on to a local Grammar school where he studied with a bunch of posh kids. This pleased mum and dad but didn't have much of an impact on Blake. At times the learning was tough and wearing. Like most lads in his early teens the main source of enjoyment came from football and watching the girls play netball. Amazing how that fascination still remains the same today for many. Academically Blake achieved reasonable results with enough good grades to get him in to upper college and later to university.

With his qualifications in engineering and his proximity to the coast it was a pretty natural step for Blake to progress a career in some form of marine activity.

In 1985 Blake qualified as a Marine Engineer, initially working for a local company in the servicing of coastal vessels.

During his younger student days Blake had no real girlfriends to speak of. He was too busy studying and swatting for his exams. There was always the popular village girl of course who facilitated most of the local lads for half a pint of lager but that was about it. Well OK, four pints of lager to be precise. It seemed a good investment at the time. So it was inevitable that on meeting Rachael, who was as pure as a scoop of Parovani's ice cream, Blake would be bewitched, fall in love, get her pregnant and marry her. The last bit (getting married), although it was initially her father's idea, Blake was still more than happy to go along with. All in the space of seven months.

Rachael was gorgeous and Blake idolised her. She came from the same town as Blake and was just a couple of months older than him. She had attended an all-girls school in the town and at the time of meeting Blake was just a young lady enjoying life. They met one night at a local nightclub. He asked her to dance: she said no. This was always a good start. Later on that evening he asked her again and his persistence was to pay off as eventually she caved in and agreed. That was the beginning of life for Blake and Rachael. They grew close very quickly. Blake was smitten by her. If she wasn't around then it was a grey day.

Rachael was blessed with some real girly features such as long strawberry blonde hair and lovely pale blue eyes. To Blake she was everything that the cliff top huts were not. She looked good, smelt good and didn't taste a bit salty. She had a style, charm and legs that only Jerry Hall came close to matching on a good day – naturally if you know what I mean. Blake really was on the hook and besotted by her.

Blake and Rachael married in January 1987. They were married locally in St Margaret's church – in fact it was the same church that Rachael's sister and mother and her mother and her mother before that had all been married in. In total some six or seven generations had married there. Later in years to come their daughter would also get married at the same church.

The wedding day itself, although bright and sunny, was absolutely freezing. Everybody had turned out to see the shock family event of the century and bag some free booze and food into the bargain. It has to be said that it all made a nice change after being stuck in the house all over Christmas and New Year with nowhere to go. That entire numb bum suffering was finally over – we can get out, whoopee! How pleased they all were to see each other. The day went off quite well apart from when the car bringing Rachael to the church spilled fuel from its tank onto the road which meant that the fire brigade were called out to hose the road down, delaying the bride from getting to the church on time.

Blake and Rachael grew into married life very quickly and in the beginning it was very exciting; they were lucky enough to be able to buy a small house locally where they could raise a family.

Their first child, Sarah, was born in June the same year. James their son was born three years later in 1990. The kids grew up happy, living near the beach, learning how to play and live in a simple, innocent and unfussy way.

Rachael was a good mum to the children. She was so natural with the kids and did everything for them. They were cared for and loved. They were raised on eating plenty of good vegetables and fruit with their dinners.

Blake was working hard; he could sometimes be criticised for doing too much but he was young and had a beautiful wife and family – all he wanted to do was to provide the best he could for them. As far as he was concerned he had all the bases covered and the future looked ideal in many ways. He was not a person without ambition either and hoped one day that he would have his own business in something – not quite sure what. Primarily his main aim was always security for him and his family. This though is where Blake probably started to go wrong. The emphasis had shifted arguably more to the security of a lifestyle and possibly he wasn't considering the other important aspects to family life such as love, parental care, even having fun. He was missing the real reason for being a dad and sadly it had become the norm around the Brown household.

Things didn't get any better over the coming years for Blake and Rachael. Blake became more involved with his career and more detached from his family. When business opportunities came his way Blake took them in his stride and as a result financially he did reasonably well. His career continued to develop and he began to travel more. This spiralling trend started to have a negative effect on his family life. To be honest Blake hadn't noticed it as much as Rachael had.

Like too many young men Blake had an unhealthy and disproportionate balance between his work and family life. It was about to cost him his marriage.

Chapter 4

Time spent with Rachael and the children was not as frequent as it should have been. Sarah and James were in their early teens now with friends and hobbies of their own, which was probably making things worse for Rachael. It soon became very obvious that she had more time on her hands than she would have liked. Rachael found that spending more and more time on her own wasn't helping things; she became lonely and fed up. Her husband was never home from work, always travelling and the kids were out having fun. But what about poor old Rachael?

It was all Blake's fault of course. This wasn't what she had signed up for. She wanted to be loved and taken care of; she had done her share of taking care of others and now it was time for somebody to take care of her. She had had more than enough of the single parent lifestyle created by Blake's blinkered view of what he should provide as a husband and father. Ultimately it wasn't what she wanted but she knew Blake wasn't going to change; anyway, who was he now? She didn't even think she knew him anymore really. It was probably a better option for Rachael to leave him and try and find happiness for herself. Blake probably wouldn't even notice that she was gone.

Rachael initially met Tony at one of those parents' evenings organised at the children's school; it was towards the end of the Easter term. Tony had been widowed some four years earlier, his then wife having died in a fatal car accident. He was a really nice guy, good looking, tallish and a bit boyish in his dress sense. This dress sense was no doubt influenced by his daughter Claire. Tony and Rachael found plenty to talk about. It wasn't long before Rachael was seeing more and more of Tony, either by accident or design. They seemed to either conveniently bump into each other or were arranging to bump into each other. Either way it happened. She was now seeing more of Tony than she was of Blake – which wasn't too difficult if we are to be honest. There was always the added bonus of the kids being friends at school, making liaisons and sleepovers that bit easier.

So it wasn't long before the early morning waves at the school drop-off spot turned to an occasional herbal tea together and to dinner and so on. Before you knew it they were at it like wild hogs.

It was a bit like giving whisky to red Indians: they just went mad for it – an intoxicating and fierce cocktail of passion and bone bashing. Rachael was certainly enjoying the new found attention – over the years with Blake she had forgotten how fantastic it felt. It wasn't long before she realised that life was getting good again, just like it used to be with Blake and she had missed it. And the love making, oh my god, it was brilliant. She enjoyed it more than when she used to make love to Blake. It wasn't that Blake was a bad lover; no, in fact he was a very sensitive, caring and gentle lover – no real complaints in that department. It was just that Tony was – well bigger. Yup, definitely bigger. It excited Rachael and after being ignored for a long enough period of time she wanted to make up for lost time. And who could blame her really?

The problem now was that Rachael had fallen in love with Tony and was going to have to deliver what would be a very painful blow to Blake. Look, there were a thousand good reasons why she should leave him for another bloke, but on the other hand there was one really good reason why she shouldn't – and that wasn't enough to tip the balance. Blake was away in Amsterdam and she had decided to tell him as soon as he got home.

Blake didn't have a horrible, nasty or selfish bone in his body; he was just guilty of being a provider. It had developed when the children were young and he wasn't any different now. It was typical of him to go on one of those trips where he could so easily have delegated it to somebody else – but had decided to go himself. He had absolutely no idea as to how Rachael was feeling; there had been no indication that his wife was planning to leave him for another man. The trouble with Blake was that even if he had slightly suspected it he would probably have still gone to Amsterdam anyway. That's not out of disrespect for Rachael but just because he thought their love for each other was strong enough for this sort of thing. It was always going to be Blake and Rachael – as far as he was concerned it was written in the stars.

The flight back to London was nicely on time for a change and Blake had it in his mind to call Rachael as soon as he had cleared customs – he wanted to suggest that they go out for dinner.

He rang but nobody answered so he left a message.

"Damn answer machine, why is nobody ever there?" He was prompted to leave his message once the beep had stopped. Blake muttered, "Hi Rachael, how are you? I just got in to Stansted and am making my way straight home – thought we could do dinner out tonight for a change. Love you and see you soonish, should be home in one and half hours or so, bye darling."

Blake shut down his mobile and ran for the train. The train journey home seemed to go well. No major on-track incidents to slow things down as does happen from time to time – like signal failure or the suicides that were a regular occurrence on this line out of town. This could easily hold you up for another hour or so if it happened, so nobody wanted that. It was 7.00 pm when the train pulled in to Manningtree station. Now it was only a short ride home across some of the most beautiful countryside that this part of the world could offer. Twisting, undulating country roads that were lined with a thick continuous smearing of mixed hedgerows and ancient oak trees which provided the shelter from the bright sunset now setting over Dedham countryside. This, capped off with the waft of heavenly blended froth of summer scents from fresh cut grass and honeysuckle, must surely be one of nature's most scrumptious cappuccinos. En route the road was littered with old churches whose spires, visible from the road, offered occasional shade. God it was good to be home. Five minutes flat was all it would take him. The old MG purred along the country lanes like a kitten being cupped in the safe and secure bosom of its new mum. That's the benefit of regular servicing.

Blake pulled onto the gravel drive at the front of the house. The last two feet of the stopping distance were greeted with the car sliding and grinding to a halt as it partially buried itself in the small now scattered stones, spraying a few of them around as he went. He quickly gathered his briefcase from the trunk as well as the obligatory Swiss chocolates he had bought for Rachael at the airport. That ought to do it, he thought. He opened the door and entered the house.

Rachael sat in the sitting room waiting for Blake. She had planned what she was going to say; she would tell him about Tony – well not everything of course. She was also going to tell him that she was going to leave him. As always Blake called out to Rachael, as he came in; creatures of habit can be so boring at times.

"Hi Rachael it's me darling, I am home."

Rachael called back, greeting him with a cool response from the comfort of the sofa. "Blake, I'm in the sitting room."

From the tone of her voice Blake detected that something didn't sound right. He was worried because she sounded upset. Normally Rachael would come to greet him with at least a peck on the cheek and the offer of 'you must be exhausted – cup of tea?', but not this time. He sensed something was up.

He quickly made his way in to the sitting room to see her. The room was a cozy family room, nicely furnished in a contemporary style with a large open fireplace made from black granite. Original works of art by local artists hung from the walls – a mix of charcoal sketches and watercolours that reflected life in the area.

Two large Georgian windows let in a stream of light which penetrated through a large fresh display of Arum lilies arranged on the table nearby. It welcomed him home, it felt good to be back – almost. His curiosity regarding Rachael's mood was slowly getting the better of him.

Blake reached out with both arms to gently hold her on the shoulders. He spoke first: "So Rachael, what's up, are you OK? You sounded a bit offish earlier."

Rachael silhouetted and now standing against the granite hearth hung her head down slightly and answered him. "Blake, we need to talk, can you please sit down."

No way was this the Rachael that Blake had known and loved for all of these years. Here she was holding court over him; this must be serious and he instinctively braced himself for what was about to come. His mind was racing – was it the kids, was it one of the parents, what has happened, could it be that she had crashed the tractor mower again? Whatever it was it was about to be delivered with a hammer blow; he had never seen her this way.

"Blake, there is no easy way to say this other than come right out and say exactly how it is."

"OK, go on then."

"I am sorry Blake." Rachael paused, the room tense with the waiting.

"And –" Blake prompted.

"I'm leaving you Blake, it's over. You're, you're never around, you don't show me any affection, you never want to share things with me anymore, I am sick of waiting around for the old Blake that I knew to come through that door back to me. I know it's never going to happen, so it's over." She turned away.

Blake reeled in desperation, surprise and shock. "Rachael, for god's sake, this just can't be true, everything I do is for you and the kids, for us. Rachael, we can sort this out, please don't jump to a decision like this. Come on, let's talk it through, for Christ's sake you owe me that much."

"I don't care anymore Blake. It's over, it's gone too far, the damage is well and truly done." Her anger was driving the adrenalin to a fever pitch and she screamed at him: "If you must bloody know I have met somebody else and I have decided to move out and live with him."

Blake was absolutely shell-shocked. Momentarily he found it difficult to breathe and could feel himself starting to shake, almost like the onset of a fit or something.

"Rachael," he blurted in desperation, "don't do this. I have given most of my life to working for us."

"Yes Blake, that's right, bloody working. For what eh? For us? That's bullshit and you know it. It's for you, all for you; you are totally blinkered, always were and always will be. When the kids were young it didn't matter so much as they were still close in those days, but now even they are distant. It's over Blake. Don't try to stop me – my mind is made up."

Blake watched helplessly as Rachael started to gather her belongings. Altogether it took her about another fifteen to twenty minutes of door slamming and stomping around the house as bags of clothing and personal effects were packed and the bags taken from the house and loaded into the car – then it was all over. The house fell silent. She had moved out. Rachael got in her car and drove off. She had actually left him, moved out, Rachael was gone.

Blake was numb, speechless; he felt like a man hopelessly drowning. He was screaming so loud for help that his glands stood proud on each side of his neck, but nobody heard him.

Some 10 months later they were divorced. Blake increased his mortgage so he could keep the house and tried to continue with his life.

As for Rachael and Tony, well it all worked out for them which is nice. They got a dog and probably did lots of hand-holding during their country walks and fireside lunches at the village pub. Blake had no idea how long the hot rampant sex lasted for though. For all he knew they were probably still going at it like rabbits. The children lived mainly with Rachael and Tony in their new home but whenever they felt the need to visit dad they simply rocked up at their old home. It was an easy relationship with simple rules, 'home was wherever they wanted it to be'. In fact it was questionable if they were ever really seeing less of each other now than before the divorce.

As for Blake and Rachael, well in the beginning they would see each other occasionally but since she was loved up with Tony it didn't happen very often and usually involved something to do with the children. As time continued they saw less and less of each other and began to communicate solely through the children. This was always sad but probably inevitable and for the best – well for Rachael anyway. Eventually Rachael and Tony did the decent thing and got married. Blake remembered staring at some of the wedding photographs for longer than he probably should have done. It was all so surreal seeing his ex-wife smiling and oozing happiness with another guy. He had to admit that Rachael looked amazing as always, definitely the right side of fabulous. While Blake was very sad himself, he was of course very happy for her. After all it was the grown up thing to do. He had been a complete ass and he knew it.

Chapter 5

The year is 2012, September. To be honest for a long time after breaking up with Rachael Blake was still hurting. Being alone in life wasn't something that he found he could adjust to very easily – especially when he knew that she had actually left him and was still with this other man. Obviously this other man wasn't a proper man like Blake. No, of course not, how could he be? Although all true Blake realised that it wasn't helping matters much either.

The added stress that came with having had both a heart attack and a divorce was a real setback for Blake. At times it seemed as though life would never be normal again. He wasn't even sure if he knew how to start a normal life or what normal was anymore. So many years of putting it all in to the one and only relationship that he had had and needed had failed miserably. He had failed himself and his family, or so he thought. Getting back to a normal life was a constant struggle that he didn't think he could win. He desperately needed to find a way to get his life back on track. If only he had paid more attention to the real needs of his family and not been such a workaholic – but that was all too late now. He always seemed to suffer the most on the occasions that he went back home to an empty house. The deep and extensive loneliness merely facilitated joining the dark start of the day to what was becoming an even darker end of the day. It was a painful existence.

One morning out of the blue Blake realised that he had been in a routine state of self-pity for far too long. He needed to make changes. He figured out that yes, a guy could probably get quite used to the life of the antisocial and unwashed but in the long term it wasn't for him. He had always been a fighter and if he ever needed to fight again the time was now. In the long term he was better off out of the mess he had got himself into and he was going to pull himself together. First things first: do what you do best, which was get back to work.

For some years now he had set his sights on developing a small consultancy business. The idea was to get together a core team of specialists and try and present a niche service within the Energy industry. Slowly, if the business grew, he would be able to add a mix of other disciplines that would broaden the skill base of the company. Other than a small bit of start-up capital and some running costs to be covered the main ingredient would be hard work and dedication. Blake was used to hard work – long days and short nights had become the norm in his life.

Blake raised some start-up capital by remortgaging his home in Dedham; he sold his car and his small collection of art work to help support some of the initial running costs. Within a month of kicking things off Blake had leased an office in the City area of London. It meant regular commuting which at times was troublesome but there was such a powerful buzz about being back in town that it was far too difficult to ignore. Blake was starting to feel alive again and he liked it. The business grew slowly at first but, once it had established itself with a good track record, things went from strength to strength. On the back of a good reputation and sound advice the business started to develop a reasonable turnover. It had all the signs of becoming quite successful and the future looked bright.

Blake had a habit of trying to do too much of the work

himself. In the beginning this multitasking was okay but now that things were getting really busy it was becoming increasingly difficult for him to keep up with everything. He came to realise that he needed some administrative and accounting help so that he could focus more on driving the business forward. Up until now he had just muddled along for most of the time doing all of the admin support and accounts work himself. Sometimes, when he was desperate, he would get some ad-hoc help from an outside agency so that he could still find some time for the important stuff in life – like networking. Some people call it going to the pub – to Blake that would be unprofessional.

He had promised himself that before the end of the week he would contact the agency previously used to see if they could send him somebody on more of a permanent basis. He found it hard to believe that there could be people out there that would enjoy that type of work, but that was just the view of an engineer. He thought that most people would probably rather stick pins in their eyes than do accounts and admin work which probably explained why his paperwork was so messy.

It had been a particularly busy morning with various enquiries coming in unexpectedly and Blake hadn't completed the task he set himself at the start of the day which was to enquire about getting some accounting help. The agency which he had used previously, World Temp, was next on the list. It was a London business located in Paddington. Blake picked up the phone and called them. A nicely spoken young lady answered. It was always somebody different, which to Blake seemed odd.

"Good morning, this is World Temp, my name is Sally –

how can I help you?"

"Oh hi Sally, my name is Blake Brown from a company called Energy Consultants, based in the City. I am calling to find out if you may have somebody on your books who could help me set up and run a small accounting and admin department."

"You've come to the right place Mr Brown, this is an area we specialise in. Can I ask what sort of accounts system you are running at present and what type of assistance you require."

"Well the accounting system is a mixture of basic, less than basic and then non-existent; oh, sometimes, when we get outside help, we get a bit of Sage thrown in for good measure. Basically the focus to date has been on growing the business, sadly to the detriment of the admin and accounting side of things. The whole area needs a clean sweep, a fresh start. It needs a review of how we operate our business and then to develop an accounting and admin model to meet that."

Sally said, "Oh, sounds serious."

"It is, so I really would like somebody who can take control of all of this. Set it up and get things rolling. It's not a job for a prima donna, if you don't mind me saying, but somebody who has some vision, is more practical, sensible, with the knowledge of setting up and managing these systems. Could you help with that do you think?"

Blake took a deep breath; it was as though he had been talking for 20 minutes or so without coming up for air. He had posed the question and could hear Sally mulling this one over in her mind. The phone was quiet for only a few seconds.

"Mr Brown, let me have your contact details and I will get back to you as soon as I have trawled the database for a suitable candidate – is that all right?"

"Yes OK, but they are on your system as I have had ad-hoc services from you before."

"Best take them again, Mr Brown, just to be doubly sure." It was, as always, frustrating but she sounded nice and so without further discussion Blake handed over the information that Sally had asked for. It was all of the usual stuff like his office and mobile phone numbers and his e-mail address. After the conversation he hung up the phone and was even more convinced that he would never hear from World Temp ever again. Even if they had CVs from people looking for work he felt sure that this type of work was too much like real work in fact to be of interest to anybody. He tried to console himself with the fact that he would just have to soldier on and do it for himself, possibly even indefinitely.

Each working day got busier and busier for Blake. One project rolled into another and Blake continued to do the best he could with the never-ending pile of paper on his desk, all between doing what he called his proper day job and the networking of course.

A week or so had passed by from his initial contact with World Temp and he had still not received a single call. He began to think that he should really have called around three, possibly four or more agencies. But as usual it all took time which was the one thing Blake was most short of. He decided to give them a few more days before spreading his enquiry further afield, probably to the middle of the following week and that would have to be that.

Out of the blue on the following Tuesday morning an e-mail popped up in Blake's virtual inbox. He couldn't believe what he was seeing, just at the death, when time was about to run out an e-mail had arrived from Sally. What a surprise, Sally at World Temp – could she have found somebody after all?

Blake frantically clicked his mouse and opened it.

It read "*Mr Brown. Sorry for the delay in responding to your enquiry but we wanted to be sure we offered the right candidate for the job rather than just bombard you with CVs for your consideration. I hope you understand and we apologise if you were feeling abandoned.*"

It went on – "*I have attached the CV of a Miss Marci Watkins who we believe would be very suited to the position and personality-wise we think she could be the right type of person you are looking for. Marci is from New Zealand and she has recently arrived in London. She is looking for work and so is immediately available for work, if acceptable to yourselves.*

"*We have spoken with her, just yesterday in fact and believe she has just the right level of experience and capability, having carried out something similar for a consultancy company based in her home town of Wellington and more recently in Sydney. She is immediately available for interview should you wish to speak to her. Could I ask you to please review the CV and get back to me if you would like to meet with Marci. I can then make the necessary arrangements.*"

"*Regards, Sally, at World Temp.*"

Despite drowning in work Blake welcomed the light relief guaranteed from flicking open the attachment to the e-mail. His first thoughts were that Sally was actually right with her synopsis. The experience was there, the synergies with other consulting companies in New Zealand and Oz were interesting; she certainly demonstrated (on paper) the right level of capability. Plus the bills, invoices and expense sheets were out of control and just piling up again. He would have hired her right there and then but for his uncertainty over her level of commitment and possibly her attitude to work. He felt that in order to get a feel for these things he had to meet her. From the tempo of the e-mail he felt that an appointment to see Marci in the next day or so would be doable. He discussed it all briefly in the office with a couple of the other guys who agreed. Everybody knew that help was needed; it was as simple as that.

About an hour after receipt of the e-mail Blake made the call to Sally and a meeting was set up with Marci for late morning the next day. Blake planned to spend some time with her in the office and then possibly pop out for some lunch if things looked favourable. The nice plush contemporary offices were located in Threadneedle Street in the City of London. This made it easy for Blake when he was doing the early morning starts and the late evenings at work. It was a shared office building with a posh legal firm. The reception and some other common areas were also shared. It was an arrangement that worked well for everybody. Marci pitched up at the front reception desk the next day at 11.00 am as arranged.

She introduced herself to the reception team.

"Hello, my name is Marci Watkins and I have an appointment with Blake Brown of Energy Consulting."

A smartly dressed man in what could be described broadly as something that resembled an army parade uniform acknowledged and greeted her. He then passed her an A4 sheet of paper which was attached to a clipboard and asked her to sign. After signing she took a seat and waited while he phoned Blake. The call came through and Blake picked up.

"Thanks Stan, can you please put her in the lift and send

her up to this floor?"

"Very well Blake, will do."

Stan did as was requested and ushered Marci towards the lift. "Would you please follow me, Miss Watkins. Please take this lift to the fourth floor where Mr Brown will meet you."

"Thank you for your help." Marci entered the lift, smiled at Stan and pressed the button for the fourth floor as advised. The lift doors closed and the journey was over in a flash.

Blake counted exactly thirty five seconds on his wristwatch – he anticipated this was enough time to allow for Stan to put Marci in the lift and for the lift to arrive at the designated spot. He straightened his tie before leaving the office and making his way to the lift where he stood, waiting politely for Marci. Momentarily, as per schedule, there was a ping of a bell and the lift light brightened, the shiny steel doors slid open and out walked Marci. Blake reached out with a welcome hand.

"Hi you must be Marci. Hello, I am Blake, good to meet you."

It was Marci's turn. "G'day Mr Brown – whoops, sorry, force of habit, what I meant to say was hello, and yes I am Marci."

"That's OK, and please – just call me Blake."

Blake led her to the office where he immediately offered her a seat and something to drink. Marci took a glass of water. The interview got underway. Marci sat with her back to the internal office window facing Blake.

"So Marci, thank you for coming at such short notice as well."

"That's fine Blake, no worries. I only recently arrived in London and am keen to get life here off to a good start."

"Oh good. I expect the agency have briefed you regarding the job."

"Yes they did. I understand that you are a small energy consultancy in need of an accounting and administrative system to manage your daily business."

"Yes, that's about it in a nutshell other than the fact that we have run things, or indeed I have run things should I say, in quite a haphazard way for far too long now, so there will be some tidy up of what we have already."

Marci looked around at the evidence which supported Blake's statement. Paper was stacked absolutely everywhere. At first glance there was no way of telling if there was any logic to it or if it was just randomly stacked but either way she could see that the task was going to be a bit of a challenge.

"I can see quite a bit of paperwork here which I presume is part of the problem."

Blake replied, "Yes it is, sadly. But things are not in as bad a shape as they may appear. The piles are representative of monthly accounts and stuff so it's not too bad. It's organised, it's just that there are lots of it. I would like to think that most of it could be simply filed away without too much difficulty." Filing, that was another one of Blake's hates.

Marci listened and looked on disbelievingly. Blake's story was about the only thing in the room which wasn't stacking up.

Blake took Marci's CV from his drawer and they went over it together. Blake asked lots of smart questions and, pleasingly, got sensible answers. Since he had little knowledge of accounting systems he did wonder at times if his questions were sensible or ridiculous but the main task at hand was to discover what level of dedication he might expect. It wasn't long into the interview that he realised he did quite like her. She appeared to be very honest and straight. It looked like she was what it said on the tin: the real deal. He asked her about her previous experiences, Sydney in particular. Marci opened up and began to tell him everything, starting with the size of the company, the size of the accounting and admin team, her role within the team, who she reported to, how the team performed and how she was rewarded, bonus systems, and so on. It meandered on a bit during which Blake allowed his mind to wander off the subject slightly. He found himself beginning to stare at her which he was a bit embarrassed about.

They seemed to have been talking for hours and it was more than obvious to Blake that Marci was the right person for the job – everything seemed perfect. The clock had reached 12.20 and it was time to get her out of the office for possibly a more relaxed conversation.

"Do you have time for some lunch?" Blake asked. "I know a nice little place nearby."

"That would be great, but only if you have the time, thank you."

"Sure I do, wouldn't have asked otherwise, come on."

Blake grabbed his coat and they headed for a small bistro not too far from the office that did the most wonderful pasta and salads – plus the macchiato was to die for.

They chatted as they walked to the bistro. Blake was interested in what Marci had done on her travels, the places she had been to. It all helped him to get a fuller picture. Later he assured the team back at the office that it had absolutely nothing to do with him fancying her.

Once in the restaurant Blake ordered a salad of crayfish

and avocado and Marci had the pasta special of the day, a salmon ravioli. Neither wanted any wine, just mineral water. It looked like one of those 'who is kidding who' lunches but as it was their first time out together both of them were being cautious. Blake really liked her but decided to play it cool. It was far too early to be showing his hand regarding that sort of thing. Anyway she hadn't been hired – yet. Marci on the other hand was loving all of the attention. She sensed that maybe Blake liked her but didn't want to be too obvious about it so she just flirted outrageously when she got the chance.

Blake stared across the table at Marci with those besotted puppy eyes while she told him everything about her life in New Zealand. All about her parents, her sister and her best friend 'Shooter' the dog. Blake just continued to dribble down his shirt. She could have had his hands in a vice and was tightening the handle and he wouldn't have noticed.

As she talked he was scanning every bit of her face. Her eyes, her hair, her eyebrows, everything was being registered in the 'I am falling in love' section of his brain. He noticed that her face was peppered with these lovely cornflake type freckles which had been liberally scattered around her nose and eyes. It was as though they had fallen gently from a spilt box of breakfast cereal. Her hair like golden straw must have been a shapeless frazzled bush when she was a child, but that didn't matter to Blake although it was clearly still giving her problems now. It was probably a nightmare when it got wet. But when she smiled; as far as Blake was concerned, it would effortlessly light up Brighton seafront on a dank late summer afternoon. Her eyes were crystal blue and they sparkled and danced when she stared. Her mouth was just as wonderful, framed with attention-seeking lips, soft looking and slightly plump, subtly shaped, they looked so kissable, they looked like they were made with the texture and sweetness of cherry flavoured marzipan. Then there were the dimples on either side of her mouth which appeared every time she smiled. The dimples reminded Blake of that little soft bit that you get on the top of a perfectly fresh soufflé as it is removed from the oven. This was all too good to be true.

Blake had fallen for her hook, line and sinker. Told himself that he never wanted to look at another woman again; Marci was perfect in every way, a sort of love enigma. From that moment he knew that if she ever threw her heart away he would be there on garbage day.

Once he had come back down to earth Blake's next big task was to decide if she was the right person for the job or not. Of course she was, wasn't she?

Chapter 6

It was Monday morning on the 17th of September 2012 and Marci arrived for work at 8.50 am on the dot. She looked absolutely radiant. Her frizzy hair was made of summer and her curls were made of spring. Her smile was as playful as a glass of pink bubbly on a warm summer's afternoon. She wore a short sleeved cotton blouse of light duck-egg blue with a shortish petrol blue skirt that hugged her hips and sat just above her knees, fitting her and looking perfect. Her shoes were a definite flat standard office issue but that didn't stop her legs from looking good. When she entered the office Blake stared agog momentarily; he couldn't believe his eyes, she looked amazing. Even better than how he had remembered her. Trying desperately hard not to make it too obvious to everybody that he was crazy about her, he made out that he hadn't taken any notice at all.

Blake politely welcomed her to the office. "Morning Marci, nice to see you. Is everything OK?"

"Morning Blake. Yes, I am good thanks."

Blake shook her hand. "I will show you to your desk and once settled in there it would be good if I can whizz you around the office and introduce you to everybody."

"That's fine Blake, thank you. If you can help me out with where things are like kitchen and bathrooms, oh, and if I can get some stationery that would be great."

"Yup no problem. OK follow me." He drew a deep breath as he turned away from her. She oozed the fragrance of fresh spring flowers and looked equally as new.

Marci's office was just two doors down the corridor from Blake's. The small print room and the kitchen area would keep them apart while they were working. Blake showed Marci where things were and helped her to load up with essential stationery. After the usual round of introductions in the office to meet the other people in the team Marci was led to Blake's office so that she could set about the task that she had been hired to do, which was sorting out the accounts and development of an auditable accounting and admin system. Blake introduced her more formally this time to the paper pile in his office.

Blake tried to make light of the mess that surrounded him. "I did have a little tidy up since you were here last week Marci."

"Oh I can see that," Marci said as she took one look at the paper mountain range which had been building week by week on the corner of Blake's desk as well as on top of some filing cabinets and of course the floor. Blake tried once more to point out that it probably wasn't as bad as it looked but somehow he wasn't very convincing. Well it was something that she could get her teeth into for sure but she soon realised that she had her work cut out for her.

And so it began. Marci got stuck in to her work and Blake got stuck in to his. During the next four weeks or so Blake would often bump into Marci if he passed her in the corridor, the kitchen area or in the lift. Once or twice he had managed a brief chat with her as to how things were going but by and large he had decided it was best to let Marci just get on with things in her own way. He himself had become a bit busier and had also been out of the office as a result of all of this. The piles of paper were noticeably disappearing from his office and so he worked out that some progress was being made. One morning he came into the office and every piece of paper had been taken away and presumably filed or whatever, maybe even shredded for all he knew. It looked impressive and such a luxury for him to have his office back to how it used to be all of those moons ago. It hadn't looked so good in a long, long time. Maybe the time had come when he needed to catch up with Marci and get a feel for how the system was progressing overall.

Marci was at her desk working studiously when Blake popped his head in around the door.

"Hi Marci."

"Oh, hello Blake, I didn't see you come in this morning."

"You looked so locked onto it when I came in that I didn't have the heart to disturb you, until now that is."

"Oh, sounds ominous."

"No, not at all. For the first time I noticed that all of the paper had gone from my office which meant that it had probably come to your office for processing which means some sort of system is up and running. So then I thought to myself that I had left you alone for far too long and I should come and see you to find out how things are."

"OK then, that's easy. Should we meet in say fifteen minutes or so, it'll give me time to print out some summary tables for you."

"OK that's good, I will be back then with some coffee."

"Can you make mine a macchiato please?"

Blake wondered if she suspected that he would do absolutely anything for her. If so was this the first test of how far she could take him. He smiled back. "Not a problem Marci, I will get you a macchiato."

Blake realised then that he was faced with a problem. The coffee machine in the office was a good one; it made just about everything that the team needed but for sure it didn't make macchiatos. This meant that Blake was going to have to put his jacket on and get down to Mario's café and he would also have to get back in fifteen minutes. It would be a close call, but still, when you are in love anything is possible isn't it – well most things anyway.

Apart from secretly fancying the pants off Marci, Blake was also impressed with the progress that seemed to have been made so far with her work. However this triggered another thought in his mind that he had not seen an invoice from World Temp for some time. He wasn't sure if that was a good thing or a bad thing. Unless it had come in of course and the system had simply paid it, imagine that. He had arrived at Mario's and anyway he needed to concentrate on ordering the right coffee otherwise life wouldn't be worth living. He would speak to Marci about it all when he got back up to the office. She sat in his office waiting. Finally some time alone with Marci. Just what the doctor ordered.

Using the accounting and admin system soon became the norm around the office and once it had been introduced to everybody things did indeed run much more smoothly; it was pretty much routine. Efficient invoice processing and cash calls all added up to better managed cash flow which is the cornerstone to sweet operations of any business. The admin side was going well with a traceable document system in place; Energy Consulting was purring along nicely. As the business grew Marci expanded her team to include a couple of junior accountants. Things were working out very comfortably for everybody.

Marci was fitting in well around the office. She was well liked by her colleagues in the team which is always good. As for Blake, well he really liked her too but in a slightly different way from the others, which for some crazy reason he was still keeping to himself.

Blake came in to the office early one morning as he needed to work on some presentation material for a development solution for a client. He had a deadline to finish it by mid-morning. Blake always felt that it was a bit odd being in the office on his own early in the mornings with nobody else around. As spooky as it was it at least always gave him the time he needed to think things through and critique his work. It was invaluable really and sometimes he needed to take the opportunity. It was time that he wouldn't have once the rest of the team pitched up for work. Blake had been in the office only for about forty-five minutes when he thought he heard somebody else unexpectedly coming along the corridor. He could hear a bit of a commotion in the kitchen area. He decided to investigate and wandered out of his office to see what was going on. To his total surprise it was Marci, the last person he expected to see.

"Morning Marci, how are you?"

Marci was equally surprised by Blake's presence. "Oh Blake, you made me jump, I wasn't expecting anybody else here quite so early."

She looked upset.

"Marci, are you OK?"

Blake couldn't help thinking to himself '"why was she here so early." Her hair looked a bit of a mess but he figured he had not better mention it, so he called out, "Marci, what's up, are you OK?"

Marci walked across the open kitchen area very slowly towards Blake. She was wearing her gym gear and as sexy as she looked to him, the reality was that she was more like a badly wounded and seriously defeated athlete. She also looked very upset. Her face was red, her eyes were a bit bloodshot and her usually free style and relaxed hair had a distinctly stressed look about it which was very unusual. It had started to sort of self-express itself which was generally a bit dangerous with hair of that texture, resembling similar shapes to industrial chimneys that blow spiral smoke upwards and beyond to some distant stratosphere. It was in need of work basically.

Her head down, Marci limped over towards him. As she stood right in front of him she dropped her gym bag on the floor, looked up at Blake and, standing very still, she started to cry. She was hurt and upset. Blake held her arms, quickly catching her as she tipped forwards as though she was going to fall over. Sobbing uncontrollably by now, she wrapped her arms around Blake and buried her face into his shoulder.

Blake pulled his head back slightly from her face and spoke softly. "Hey, what's up now? Have you hurt yourself? Are you OK?"

Marci looked up to face Blake and for the first time he could see a nasty bruise on the side of her face and around her right eye. He felt upset for her and also angry at the same time.

"What the hell has happened to you? Did somebody do this to you?"

In between the bouts of sobbing Marci started to explain that the only person who had done anything to her was her. She went on to say that she had in fact done this to herself having had an accident at the gym.

Blake was still in a bit of shock. "In an accident, what sort of accident?"

A partially angry and frustrated Marci blurted out, "I walked into a bloody plate glass door at the gym, for Christ's sake!"

Blake, with an appeasing sigh, "ah I see," he soon realised that in addition to him getting a soaking wet shoulder the tears were possibly being provided by a few things – meeting a glass door, maybe a bit of stress, homesickness, possibly boyfriend trouble (that one could be good news for him) or any number of things for somebody like Marci who was miles from home and in a foreign country.

"Look Marci, let's get somebody to take a look at you and then make you a cup of tea. How does that sound?"

Marci, still a bit frosty, replied, "I don't want any more of your English tea - it doesn't cure everything you know."

Blake, tried to calm her, "OK so I guess it's a macchiato then."

Marci squeezed a bit of a smile from the corner of her mouth and nodded her head. "OK macchiato it is." Not that this cures everything either of course, but he wasn't going to fight her over it.

As much as he was enjoying consoling Marci he figured it may look a bit suspect once the others started to arrive at the office. So a quick plan was needed to change this potentially awkward situation, plus of course he needed to get the macchiato as agreed.

One of the technical assistants in the office was a woman called Marion. She was always in nice and early, mainly to avoid any overcrowding commuter issues on trains and buses. Blake could see her through the glass doors to the office and he waved and called her over. Marion noticed his frantic distress signalling and came quickly over.

"Morning Marion, it's Marci: she has hurt herself in an accident at the gym. Could you do the honours please?"

As he spoke he kept one arm around Marci and gestured towards Marion. Twisting and pointing his first finger, he drew lots of different little shapes in the air which were designed to adequately describe Marci's injuries as well as show clearly how upset she was. It was a typical man thing and quite useless to anybody other than a man. He thought it was all perfectly clear and that the message was conveyed accurately to leave no doubt in Marion's mind. Naturally Marion didn't understand any of it.

Blake thought he should just leave her with Marion. Marion, being a woman, would probably know how to look after her better than him and would be able to diagnose any injury damage quicker since she was also a trained first aid person. After a bit of a look-see by Marion the diagnosis was that there were no serious injuries, just some physical bruising and a battered ego. For sure Marci was both hurt and upset but then plate glass doors do not yield easily. In the end thankfully it wasn't anything too serious. As far as Blake was concerned she still looked peachy.

He hadn't really noticed before but now, for some reason, as he walked away to fetch the macchiato he realised that he actually might care for her more than he first thought. It became more obvious to him as he walked away from her and Marion. Leaving her with Marion wasn't such an easy thing to do; it didn't feel instinctively right, even though she was in the capable hands of somebody else. If he was honest he didn't really want to leave her. He couldn't believe it but he began the process of questioning if he had really started to fall in love.

Logic kicked in again and the tug of war commenced between heart and mind. He didn't believe this was happening to him at first and so to settle this once and for all, well, Blake being Blake, he decided to take a logical approach of trying to dissect his emotions and then test them against all of the little practical steps of what had just happened. OK it sounds like a mistake and a mess that most of us can never really navigate through since it throws up more and more unanswerable questions, but for Blake – well, he was the sort of guy that just worked that way, he needed to work stuff out like that. It was a genetic thing with him. Problem for Blake was that it would probably go on for longer than it was really good to do. But that was Blake. Anyway, whatever the result, she probably didn't like him very much anyway, so the outcome wouldn't matter. After all she had been around the office for several weeks now and they had hardly spoken more than ten words to each other socially. She may even have a boyfriend for all he knew; maybe this was partly why she was crying. He told himself he had to analyse the situation just a bit longer to be perfectly sure.

Blake stared at Marci from across the office for a while assessing how he felt about her. Even though she was in safe hands with Marion he couldn't stop staring at her. His head spun continuously; he continued to ask questions and search to understand why he felt like he did. His overactive and slightly schizophrenic mind teased and tortured him in his search for a logical solution. He also had this irritating habit of talking to himself. It's good that nobody could hear him as it probably would have sounded like no more than childish gibberish. Not what you would expect from the owner of the

Company.

He continued to diagnose:

'OK the facts are that she had hurt herself, but she is beautiful." "That's got nothing to do with it."

"Why not?"

"Stick to the script."

"OK so she hurt herself."

"Yup."

"Then why do I care?"

"Oh you care, do you?"

"That just slipped out."

"Well then, isn't that a sign?"

"A sign of what?"

"A sign that you care?"

"Yes I care but why should I be emotionally engaged; she is after all just a colleague, somebody that I work with."

"No, she is more than that."

"What sort of more than that?"

Finally after near exhaustion he realised that it was simple. This continual debate he was having with himself was stupid. He just had to be honest with her and tell her how he felt.

Finally he agreed with himself that he should tell her, but tell her what exactly? Should it be that he loved her, liked her a lot, or that she was everything a lonely bloke needed? What he really wanted to say was that he realised when she was upset he got upset too. That must mean something. He looked across at her one more time. She was still upset; mind you she even looked great when she was upset and all he really wanted to do was cuddle her. If it wasn't for the fact that the door was about to get broken down by his team pouring in to the office for work he would probably be there right now cuddling her and wiping the tiny pearl shaped tears from her fluffy little cheeks. He was getting these feelings for her that made him ask himself if he was crossing the line with Marci; she was no longer just a colleague.

Truth was he was crazy about her. It was like he was being sixteen all over again. He was awash with feelings for her. Feelings that he had not experienced in a very long time. In a way he felt relieved to have had actually stepped over the line and he hadn't realised – it was on the journey back that it hit him. Before this he had always fancied her, of course – she was gorgeous so who wouldn't? But all of a sudden it was obvious to him why he always wanted to be able to smile when he got close enough to her, constantly wanting to make sure she had all she needed: he had fallen in love. He made his mind up that he would tell her how he felt.

So what happens now, that was the big question. What should his next move be, how would he tell her exactly how he was feeling? After all he was the boss of the company so he had that to think about. If he wasn't careful he could end up embarrassing himself by doing something really stupid in front of everybody. Then on the other hand he didn't want to do anything to scare her off or to make him – or her for that matter – look silly. God, what a dilemma.

Blake decided that it was a delicate situation which needed to be handled with the utmost care. One thing was for sure – he needed to tell her how he felt, he just needed to find the right moment. He asked himself how he would know when it was the right moment though. Then the penny dropped. It was obvious; of course, it was staring him in the face. Being an engineer he would simply need to engineer something. It shouldn't be difficult; he was confident that he should be able to do that. He hoped not, but maybe though the moment had already passed. He should have seized the moment when he was letting her soak his shirt with her tears. Blake was pretty useless when it came to dealing with anything involving emotions; he would just have to go away and work it out.

He thought he could start by asking her out to lunch. Not really the most original of ideas but it was a start. He remembered the last time they went out she had salmon so perhaps he should try and find somewhere nice with a good fish choice on the menu. In fact, it wouldn't be a bad idea for him to learn to enjoy some fish a bit more often. Stay off the meat for the day, or even a little while longer, it could help, he thought. He agreed with himself. "That was easy, OK then that's that settled." He would ask her out for lunch later in the day when she was probably feeling a bit better.

The building overall was quite trendy with each office being constructed mainly of nice large glass panels which also acted as partitioning walls. The open plan areas were spacious, bright and airy. As Blake walked towards Marci's office with the promised macchiato cupped tightly close to him, he could see Marci sitting at her desk. She sat quietly with her head in her hands and slouched over the desk. Her hair had fallen forward resting on her goose-flesh covered arms which stretched forward across the desk and supported her head. Although she had been patched up by Marion, Blake suspected that her pride still remained in tatters, so he should be extra sensitive when he talked to her.

Blake knocked gently on the door. Marci didn't seem to hear him. He stared for a moment at this vulnerable but gorgeous creature. He couldn't believe how stunning she was. She was as hot as a glass blower's lip and everybody knew it. It bothered him as to why he hadn't noticed and made his mind up about all of this before. She even looked stunning despite being beaten up by a glass door. Fortunately for him Marci hadn't responded to his first knock which now gave him some time to look at her for just a bit longer. He hoped nobody in the office had spotted the trance that he had gone into. He knocked again, this time just a little harder. She slowly lifted her head and sort of squinted at him.

"Marci, are you OK? I brought you your coffee thing, the marchy whatever."

Marci raised her head up a bit higher, she wiped her cheeks and sorted her hair out with her hands, brushing it aside her face.

"Oh sure Blake, I am sorry, I must look a mess. I just feel so stupid letting this accident happen to me in the first place. You know earlier I was a bit confused. I probably soaked your shirt an all. I didn't mean to. I certainly don't want to give you more problems. I came here to help you for Christ sake. You must think I am a real wuss."

"Marci, it's OK, really it's OK. I am just glad I was here when you came in this morning."

"Really? Thanks Blake." Marci reached out for the coffee which Blake handed over.

"Yes really, it's not often that I get the chance to wash my shirts while still wearing them!"

Marci grinned, at the same time blushing just a little bit. "You English guys really love to tease a woman all the time, don't you? I've seen it in the movies as well."

Blake didn't have the foggiest what brought this on.

Marci took a sip of the macchiato. "That Grant fella, oh, what was his name…"

"Do you mean Grant Mitchell maybe? He was in a TV programme over here called EastEnders, was on telly years ago, maybe it still is, I don't know. Did you get that in New Zealand, though?"

"No not him, the other one. God, who is it? You see this bang on the head has done a bit of permanent damage." Then from nowhere she remembered: "Hugh Grant, yup that's him, Hugh Grant. He was in that romantic comedy movie with the American actress who can change her size at the drop of a hat."

"Oh him, the Bridget Jones guy."

Marci giggled, "Yes, him."

'That's better, come on just a little bit more,' Blake thought to himself.

As they chatted Marci showed signs of slowly warming and possibly getting a bit more relaxed; maybe this was Blake's moment to move things on a bit. Why wait until later – he decided to seize the moment.

"Marci, can I ask you something?"

"Yes, Blake," staring at him with sore puppy eyes, "of course you can, as long as you are quick because I need to visit the girls' room and clean myself up a little."

Blake at that exact moment struggled to pop the question and began to mumble in true and typical of him, tongue-tied meaningless gobbledygook. A language unique to him which only he had mastered. "Well I wondered if you might like to, eh chat about any other, eh, mmm domestic skills that you have, (oh my god he couldn't believe he just said that, where the hell did that come from) over lunch one day – yes one day

71

of course."

The rapid invitation for lunch at the end of this totally messed up conversation did little to make up for his huge blunder or reinstate his dignity.

Marci bemused at his awkwardness wondered if by chance he was trying to ask her out, for lunch of course. Surely he wasn't really interested in her domestic skills? Anyway she didn't have a clue what domestic skills were.

Marci looked bewildered. "Sorry Blake, do you mean we should have lunch one day, with you – just you and I?"

Blake replied awkwardly, "Yes Marci, lunch, just you and me; if that's OK."

"And what about my domestic skills, whatever they are, what have they got to do with it?"

"Domestic skills, did I mention domestic skills? If I did then I'm sorry. My tongue must have got caught in my–"

Marci interrupted him while he was trying to explain himself, "Shoelace?"

"Shoelace, yup maybe shoelace."

At this point Marci smiled even more and Blake looked even more ridiculous. Finally it was all a bit clearer from the coy and boyish look on his face that he was trying to ask her out on a date rather than anything else. He just cocked it all up. Marci was relieved and grateful for the offer. Blake felt and must have looked like such a muppet – domestic skills, what the hell was that all about? He may as well have asked her if she fancied coming round to empty his cat litter tray. It was terrible, he knew it and even worse he knew that she knew it.

There was a moment's very awkward silence between them but Blake being a true pro tried to pick the conversation up again. "I know a nice little vegetarian restaurant nearby."

Marci was surprised to hear that. Firstly she had Blake down as a pork chop kind-of-a-guy and secondly she never expected an invite anyway.

"Thanks but I didn't have you down as a vegetarian,

He explained, "Well sometimes it's a nice alternative isn't it. Don't have to eat pork chop every day."

"Blake, it's a lovely idea but I don't particularly look that good or feel that great right now. I have a sore eye and my shoulder aches."

Blake was always ready for rejection but this answer was one he didn't particularly want to hear. Although thinking about it he wasn't sure if this was a total knockback or something else? He started to feel awkward and could feel himself clamming up. Then his senses immediately flagged up "rejection" – "that's two yellow cards and a red, off you go". He had blown it, asking her out so soon after her trauma was a stupid thing to do and even worse in the way that he did it. Panic was setting in and the tussle between his head and his heart kicked off. His head was telling him to give her space, but his heart just didn't want to give up quite yet. For the first time in a long time Blake decided to follow his heart.

He stammered, "Look Marci, to me you, well, you look fantastic. You really do, but as you say if you are not feeling so good then I suppose we can do it some other time. Take a rain check as they say."

Marci smiled and shook her head approvingly. "Sure Blake, when I am doing a bit better, perhaps in a day or so that would be nice. Thanks Blake, I look forward to it."

Blake awkwardly backed up a step or two towards the office door, clasping his hands in front of him and not taking his eyes off Marci at all as he reversed to the door. Trying not to sound down or totally put out he replied, "Sure Marci, that's great, whenever you are feeling better."

At that moment he could hear voices in his head again and he could feel the intense pain of a bright powerful light being shone into his eyes. This coupled with the repeating words 'Muppet! Muppet! Muppet! You blew it, you blew it!'

He had just turned to face the door and was about to walk out of the office when the flashing light and the voices were extinguished. Coincidently just at the same time Marci spoke. "Well, if you think I look OK then we can go today – it might be really nice actually."

Blake couldn't believe what he was hearing. He turned to Marci. "You're sure – honestly?"

"Well they say that you can't play on broken strings, so the sooner we get them fixed the better."

"That's brilliant. I will go and arrange something."

All of a sudden Blake felt as though his final steps to the office door were unexpectedly being lifted, they felt almost cushioned like he was walking on new thick pile carpet or something. He felt like he was possibly going where no man had gone before. All of a sudden (while he was up there in the clouds) he realised that he felt very different, almost smug and spoiled. Believe it or not this girl had just put a very big curl in his world. He wasn't expecting the sudden elevation but it felt good and he didn't want it to change.

As he reached the door he was still pinching himself. He turned to Marci. "By the way, if you are not so keen on vegetarian I do know this really nice little Italian nearby."

"It's up to you totally Blake. I like Italian food, so it sounds good if that is what you think."

"OK, Italian it is, 12.30. Shall I see you in reception?"
Marci nodded. "See you then."

She wasn't sure if she had done the right thing or not. He was a nice guy but was he her type? She wasn't so sure. Being from New Zealand she kind of liked guys who were a bit more rugged, a bit more bohemian maybe, Blake wasn't quite there. But one thing was true for sure: he had a lovely smile and he was a very caring bloke which could be a good place to start. On the other hand she thought maybe it wouldn't be an issue – after all it was probably just lunch and nothing more.

Blake scampered quickly back to his office and booked the table. He watched the clock for the rest of the morning and when the moment came to meet Marci he made sure that he was in the reception area waiting tentatively for her, on the button at 12.30 pm. He was so excited he couldn't keep still; he shook like a little nervous jelly that was about to be served up at a children's birthday party when Marci arrived. She had managed to dry her eyes, clean her face and sort her hair out a little. She looked wonderful.

They left the building and made their way to the restaurant. Blake had asked for a courtyard table since it was such a lovely warm day. The restaurant was just around the corner and within moments they were there and being welcomed by the owner and shown to the table. Once they were seated, menus were ceremoniously passed to both of them. Blake ordered olives and mineral waters to have while they decided what they would have to eat.

Blake looked at Marci. "Marci, I have a confession to make."

"Really Blake, so early in our relationship – is that such a good idea?"

"Well I like to get the awkward stuff out of the way as early as I can."

"It's a bit risky isn't it? It could ruin everything."

"Well it could do, but on the basis that nobody likes surprises then I tend to face up as soon as."

"Oh sounds shady, but go ahead, confess."

"Well OK, I love spag bog."

"Is that it? That's the sum of the awkward stuff: you love spag bog?"

"Well, sort of. Actually it's worse than that."

Marci was beginning to think being there wasn't such a good idea after all. "Go on, that's if you think I should know everything."

"Well, I am actually a bit of a spag bog nut in that I try it wherever I go and keep a league table so that I can constantly assess where the best spag bog that I have ever eaten is."

Marci figured this was probably a bit childish but decided to go with it a little longer. "You're kidding me, aren't you?"

Blake's lips twisted and squirmed momentarily in auto-nervous mode. Marci knew that this subconscious gesture could only mean one thing. She leaned forward across the table and whispered to Blake, "You're not kidding me, are you? You're serious."

Blake replied, "Afraid so Marci. It sounds a bit childish but I try the spag bog in most places that I go to."

Marci, thinking 'at least he admits it' said, "So tell me then cos I know you are dying to, where is the best spag bog that you have ever eaten in your weird pasta world?"

"Well, it's funny that you should ask. The best spag bog that I have ever eaten, absolutely ever, was at the restaurant in Antwerp airport, or Antwerpen if you want to use a local tongue."

"No way is that true. An airport restaurant where food is almost always notoriously poor?"

"Yup, it's true."

"Is that weird or what? It's so unexpected but also the last place I would have said." She urged him on although it wasn't difficult. "So how good was it exactly?"

"Well, if you really want to know, it was the best ever anywhere in the world."

Marci continued the teasing: "In the world?"

Blake, as gullible as ever, replied, "Yup, in the whole wide world."

"That's some accolade Blake. I mean how much of this stuff do you eat and how much travelling do you do in pursuance of the best spag bog in the world? Are you sure that you haven't just made this up?"

"Sadly not, it's true. I know it makes me sound a bit like a saddo but when you are on your own most of the time it's the sort of stupid thing that you do."

The penny dropped with Marci and for the first time she realised how potentially vulnerable and lonely a person Blake really was. She said, "But you haven't tasted mine as yet, have you?"

Blake got even more excited. "Well no, I haven't. I still have that pleasure to come, hopefully."

The waiter stood tentatively by the side of the table with pad and pen in hand. "Are you ready to order please, Madam, Sir?"

Marci looked up at Blake. "So Blake, what do you fancy, other than me of course?"

She had managed to do it again. Blake immediately turned a nice light pinkish colour in front of the waiter and anybody else within earshot of Marci's light-hearted mickey taking.

They ordered lunch and the waiter left them to it.

Blake said, "Bloody hell Marci, are you Kiwi ladies always so direct? Have you not heard of romance down under?"

"Of course we have romance and I didn't mean for it to be unromantic, I just wanted to get the situation clear, that is all. As I said earlier, you can't play on broken strings."

"So what does that mean in your mind?"

"Well you need to know if I am OK with it, don't you? And if I hadn't mentioned it how long would it have taken you to mention it then?"

"You are just teasing me now aren't you, just like you said that I was teasing you?"

Marci noticed a slight disappointment on Blake's face. She tried to make light of it: "There, got you, serves you right for teasing me. I didn't mean any of it; I was just fooling around. Sorry if it bothered you."

It didn't matter, fooling or not, the truth was that Blake was on the hook. He wanted to tell her but now that she had brought the subject up, albeit jokingly, he figured the ice was broken. All he had to do now was to keep being nice to her and show her how he felt; that was the tactic he would pursue.

Her fish and salad and his pasta dish with sun dried tomatoes and chillies arrived along with a nice chilled bottle of Pinot Grigio.

Marci decided that perhaps it would be better to try more normal conversation. "Antwerp doesn't sound like it should be the best place in the world for spag bog Blake. How do you reckon that came about?"

"Well, that's the strange thing. You know the basics of all good food travels well and what with people keen on experimenting and taking much more pride in their cooking it comes as no real surprise to me that even in such an unsuspecting place as Antwerp you can find the perfect spaghetti bolognaise. Why not! More and more people strive in life for that perfect dish than you realise. It puts them on the map I guess. Makes them feel good. And as for the Italians, well they did a good job in introducing good solid and very simple basic foods that have been screaming out to be personalised for years. Spag bog is a good example of that, more so than say 'fish and chips', if you know what I mean."

He continued, "What I think is so funny is that all of a sudden you have everybody's secret recipes popping up as well, which always makes me laugh, but that said don't stop it; it's great eating these gastronomic secrets."

Blake added: "Have you ever noticed how sometimes from the corner of your eye you can see somebody from the restaurant staff hanging around and waiting for you to take your first mouthful?. They want to see how you will react to what has just been dished up. That's because they feel it when you eat it. It warms them when they know you like it. They are not usually Michelin star chefs and it just gives these people the chance to have a bit of pride and at the same time tell everybody that it was their grandmother's secret recipe – which is mostly cobblers of course."

"So it's a dish that is very bespoke to its maker."

"Yup, it can be something like that."

"And here, how is the spag bog here?" Marci elegantly slipped a bite of some fish from her plate into her mouth.

"Pretty good, I would say 7 out of 10."

"Interesting – so not as good as Antwerp?"

"No, not as good. You know, over there they cook and cut the pasta so perfectly that I can twist it on my fork and make little animal shapes out of it." Blake grinned.

Marci couldn't believe what she had just heard Blake say, 'he could make little animals out of his pasta?' The guy was obviously nuts, really lovely nuts but nuts just the same. She couldn't see this relationship really getting off the ground. He just wasn't her type at all, cute but , no not her type.

With the taste of lunch still hanging on the pallet and the warm afternoon sun helping to make life a bit more intoxicatingly dreamy, they strolled back to the office for the last bit of the afternoon shift.

"Blake, thanks for that, it was really nice and it did me good to get out after my near death experience this morning. I appreciate that."

"It was a pleasure Marci and OK maybe a bit self-indulgent with all of that pasta story stuff but I haven't had the chance to have a lovely lady on my arm in a while so thank you too and I am glad that you are feeling better."

They reached the office reception; Blake leaned forward and kissed Marci softly on the cheek. God, she smelt good. Could it have been a bit of that fish sauce on her cheek that did it? Hopefully not.

The afternoon was a breeze for both of them.Blake found himself being wrapped in an almost gooey, sticky marshmallow world. Marci, on the other hand, developed some weird sort of meerkat habits where she periodically popped up to look across the office towards Blake, presumably just to see if he was looking at her. It wasn't clear in her mind at first but now she had decided that she really did fancy Blake after all and his stories about his stupid spaghetti animals. As far as Blake was concerned Marci was hotter than a dragon's nostrils and his feelings for her were not in any doubt. Marci knew that office romances were not normally successful and it probably wouldn't last that long. Once you had both tested the comfort of the copy machine and the boardroom table then that was pretty much it. Subconsciously perhaps that was what she needed right now, just to be a bit crazy for a while. Somehow though she didn't think that Blake would be that kind of a guy.

So slowly and surely the romance, albeit a bit awkward at times, began to blossom between them. Blake and Marci continued to have lunch together now and again and meet for chats after work to share the odd glass of wine. Truth is that they were starting to get on great together. This ritual of courtship went on for some weeks but for some reason there was nothing that you could describe as physical happening between them. He was learning a lot about her and she was learning a lot about him; they kissed and cuddled but for some reason unbeknown to both of them things were not really moving on past first base. Too scared of commitment maybe?

Part of the problem may have been because they hadn't triggered a physical relationship immediately. Maybe it was because Blake was the boss and Marci couldn't get her head around actually shagging him. Because things were not moving along with each other they both began to question the sincerity of their own feelings, wondering if they had both been reading the messages from each other in the wrong way. Although a very open one it became a confusing relationship emotionally. Neither of them knew what to do next. Neither Blake nor Marci wanted to offend or hurt the other and run the risk of possibly losing each other, so basically they were in a bit of a difficult spot. As much as he wanted her and she wanted him sadly it didn't look as though it was destined to be.

During the course of one of their lunches Marci had explained to Blake about the demons in her life and how she finally felt as though she was strong and brave enough to tackle them face on. It all sounded very serious and there was a bit of Blake that was quite saddened by what Marci was telling him. As desperate as he was to tell her how he felt about her the more time went on, it became more obvious to him that maybe it wasn't a good idea. He didn't want to mess with her head any more than it was being messed with. As time went on and Blake became closer to Marci sadly he realised that he couldn't tell her anything about how he felt as it wouldn't help matters.

As the days rolled on Blake watched as Marci became more distant from her work and seemed to be more saturated with talk of these demons. It was becoming obvious to him that he was clearly set on a course to put all of this behind her and to her this was far more important than anything else in her life at that moment. It was becoming obvious to Blake, and he could see that Marci had already made up her mind as to how both of their futures were going to turn out, and he didn't like what he was starting to sense. Sadly he knew that there was very little he could do about it.

It wasn't quite what Blake wanted but he knew that Marci must do whatever it would take to sort herself out. Above all if he loved her then he must respect that and not interfere.

That said Blake couldn't believe his luck, good or bad. It seemed unbelievable to him that he could let somebody who meant so much to him to just simply get loose like that and disappear from his life. It was a bit like gripping a dandelion as tightly as he could in his hand while knowing that he was going to have to stand back and watch as the breeze unlaced each of the tiny delicate stems and, like his love for Marci, bit by bit it would be torn from him and taken. He was basically helpless to stop it and he hated himself for being so inadequate and powerless. He tried to console himself by accepting that the right thing to do was to let her go free, soak up the pain and wait for her to come back, hopefully.

The desire to scrub her life of these so called demons had become so overpowering for Marci that she had decided it was imperative that she left London. In a short time the obsession became stronger and stronger and it was clear to Marci and Blake that nothing else mattered. Marci knew that it would take time to gather the inner strength that she needed if she was going to turn all of this negativity around. Her heart and soul needed to be strong, prepared for anything. In her mind there was only one place where she could go to find the time and sanctuary within her mind that would give her the inner peace where she could build the energy levels she desperately needed to win the fight; that was Kerala in India.

Chapter 7

It was July 2013 and Marci had only joined the team some ten months before but she had made her mind up that she was already moving on. It was a huge disappointment to Blake. He had no idea as to how he was going to deal with it. She was everything to him. Perhaps it would have helped if he had actually told her at some point how he really felt instead of just skirting around the edges. As disappointed as he was with Marci he was also really disappointed with himself. He just needed another chance and he promised himself that he wouldn't waste it if it ever materialised.

Eventually the day had arrived when Marci would leave. This was it. The woman that had put the curl in Blake's world was just about to straighten it all back out again. This part wasn't in the script, well not in Blake's script anyway. As hard as he tried he didn't fully understand the reason behind the decision to go, but he accepted that whatever was driving her must have been a big deal for Marci. Marci had told Blake that she needed to leave so that she could 'find herself'. That she was being tormented by the fact that she had not followed her dream. The voices in her head constantly nagged her and reminded her of this. These demons as she called them just wouldn't go away and the only way she could silence them forever would be to follow the path they had set for her. Blake couldn't help thinking that it was all a bit late in her life for that sort of thing anyway. Normally by the age of 42 people have figured out who they are at least, what they want out of life and how they are going to get it.

The whole issue with Marci leaving didn't sit well with Blake. He was tormented by it. It continued to raise more and more questions and issues in his mind than was good for him. It bothered him that he had probably contributed somehow to all of this. Was it him that had driven her away? Were these gremlins she talked about just conveniently constructed and being used as a vehicle to get her away from him? He didn't know the answers; he wasn't sure that he ever would know either. Every time he thought he had answered one there would just be another question. The situation was hopeless. There were just more and more questions. The bottom line was that Marci was about to leave her job, her life in London and of course Blake, and she was going to travel to India.

It was hard for Blake as he didn't want his emotions to be on show for Marci and all to see. He made a pact with himself that outwardly he would put on a brave face and not quiver whenever the moment came. He wanted desperately to be excited for her but as hard as he tried it was always going to be a hollow effort in many ways. He promised himself that while this was OK he wouldn't let anybody else see that.

Yes, he wanted her to be safe and well, he wanted her to get things straight in her head with herself for sure, but obviously what he wanted more than anything was for her to either change her mind or promise that when this was all over she would come back to him. As simple as that was, and the more he ran this around in his head, somehow he couldn't see either of those two things being on her agenda.

The last thing however that he wanted from Marci was an invitation for a celebratory drink as part of her send off, but he got one anyway. He sat in his office and stared at the e-mail invitation in total bewilderment; filled with sadness he hit the delete key with an abrupt "NO!", as if that was going to make any difference to her decision and maybe cleanse him of this agony he was in. After all, what was to celebrate anyway? She was leaving – so absolutely nothing. It didn't take a moment before he realised that he had made a huge mistake and he ran around to Marci's office apologising profusely, saying that he was a complete muppet and had hit the delete button by mistake when he really meant to hit the 'YES' button on the invitation and of course he would love to be at her leaving drinks. He hated himself sometimes.

The pub where everybody had congregated for the leaving party was called the Red Lion, a smallish place just off Bishopsgate. Most people in the office had used it as their local now for a number of years. As expected it was a good turnout. Marci was really well liked by her colleagues, plus there was the incentive of some free booze and nibbles which, for most if we are honest, was the biggest incentive of all. Well, let's face it, it's polite and the least they could all do was be there to wish her well before she set off on this fabulously described crazy adventure of endless Pilates, yoga type of ritual indulgence and wellbeing for the soul as she put it. Who couldn't be a tad turned on by that lot?

Things were meant to kick off in the Red Lion at around 12.30 pm but not everybody could make it exactly on time. They came in gradually, arriving in dribs and drabs for about the first fifteen to twenty minutes. By about 12.50 pm everybody was there and had a drink in their hands. Because of the amount of regular business that the office did in the pub the landlord had set an area aside for the special occasion as was the way in most London boozers. They all sat around the four or five allocated tables that were positioned towards the corner of the pub. It was as far away as they could get from the real ale drinkers at the bar, although there weren't really many of those supping that day. The overpowering scent from well-worn waxy jackets could put a girl off her Pinot Grigio all too easily when wafting in the wrong direction. Only those people that had put in the training to develop the much needed rigid constitution and poor sense of smell were able to drink and enjoy what was termed as real ale. By most others it was seen as nothing more than a continuous and failing experiment in trying to offer an alternative to perfectly good beer that was already available. Trouble was that it was called lager, but there is nothing wrong with a healthy bone of contention as was usually the case between lager and real ale drinkers.

As the farewell gathering got into full swing the table slowly filled up with used empty wine glasses and bottles, stacks of empty beer glasses and scrunched empty crisp packets. This was usual on these occasions and indicated that things were going well. Oh and not forgetting the empty plates that were once full of sizzling hot chips, traces of smeared tomato ketchup around the rims and not a single chip remaining says it all really. Yup, people will eat anything after a few drinks.

The small talk gathered pace and was now more like the continuous heady drumming that you get at a morning marketplace as they all tried to outbid each other for attention. All control was soon abandoned and it wasn't long before frantic gesticulation became the order of the day, finger waging at will. Now you see the influence of alcohol – it brings the best and the worst out in people as well as a lot of noise. Underlying all of this was a sadness that quite probably only Blake was aware of, possibly Marci herself as well but to Blake it wasn't obvious in her eyes. The feeling of gut wrenching emptiness vibrated and bounced around in a sad corner of Blake's head – his heart was free-falling and there was nothing he could do to stop it. It didn't matter if he tried to be happy or if he just rolled with it all; nothing changed inside for him; he was sick to the stomach. His girl was leaving and he didn't want her to go.

He looked at her from across the crowd as she chatted with some of her soon to be ex-colleagues. It was probable that Marci had no idea of what Blake was going through. The question in Blake's head went round and round relentlessly. Should he ask her to stay, would she stay if he asked? He knew that it was probably a stupid question and one that he already knew the answer to even though he hadn't actually asked her himself; there was no need. He was an emotional train wreck, confused and shocked and basically he didn't know what to do for the best. He just had to face up to the truth that Marci was on her way. Out of the door and out of his life. If she wanted to stay he needed to hear it from her first. It was all pretty pointless. Blake knew that it was a very simple answer to an extremely difficult question that he sought. In the end he couldn't handle the physical pain of it all and decided that he would do what was best for Marci and not complicate life for her any more than it already was. He would simply have to let her go in the most dignified way he could. No fuss, a peck on the cheek and just say goodbye.

Blake sat at the opposite end of the table to Marci. He wasn't really mixing in with the crowd and the spirit of the celebration. After all it was a form of celebration – wasn't it? He watched as Marci chatted and laughed with the rest of the group. Occasionally she would glance over in his general direction and then quickly back again. Embarrassingly he caught himself starring at her a couple of times which was not what he wanted. Although he had reluctantly made his mind up about not asking her to stay he wondered if he would ever see her again. And if he did when would it be? Neither of them was getting any younger. Why was he already missing her when she stood no more than three metres away from him?

What followed next was one of those crazy and frantic moments that grown up desperate people have sometimes. They resort back to their childhood and make the most impractical and impossible wish of all time, so idiotic that even a miracle would struggle to make it reality. Blake's wish was very simple, that they could both extend their lives say from one hundred to two hundred years, yes that would be the perfect solution to this problem, the answer to everything. They could do it all again. Marci could go off and fight her demons, and when she was mended they could still have a long and happy life together. How daft a wish was that? Blake scrubbed the thought from his mind almost as quickly as it appeared. It was a really stupid idea. He had to surrender and let her go, he was beaten.

It wasn't long before the group started to break up. For most the extra-long lunch break was over and they had to think about going back to work. The group started to say goodbye to each other as they donned their coats, at the same time making lukewarm promises to 'stay in touch'. This was followed by the tradition of giving a series of fake kisses. You know the type – where you suck your cheeks in hard and pucker your lips forward like you are poised to blow a big fat raspberry, hold it, and then rubbing a cheek of your choice on to the opposite side of the opponent's face you utter, 'mwah', 'mwah', 'mwah' – followed by a "Let me know how it's going, won't you?". Then you smile and leave. How's that for sincerity? We all do it of course and I am sure some will mean well at the time but most of the time it's purely habitual.

The heavy wooden and stained glass doors creaked and clattered as people made their way through them and onto the street. It didn't take long before all that was left were tables strewn with empty glasses and remnants of plates of food – as well as Marci and Blake of course who just sat there looking at each other.

Blake said, "So, just you and me."

Marci steadied herself up and got out of her seat. "Yup looks like it." She reached for her coat and putting her bag down on the littered table she stretched her left arm so as to be able to thread it through the sleeve.

Blake could see her struggling a little; it must have been the wine that she had drunk. "Here, let me help you with that." Blake lifted the coat, taking the weight, easing her ability to slip it on.

"That seemed to go well," Marci said. "Nice people – I will miss them, well some of them." Her right arm outstretched to receive the coat, she looked at Blake. "You were quiet. What was up with you?"

Blake wanted to stay true to his promise to let her go but at the same time he didn't see anything wrong with letting her know that she would be missed. "Oh just thinking, just wondering if you will be OK and if you will find what it is you are looking for over there in India."

Marci turned to him. "The thing is Blake, I don't know what it is I am really looking for. The chances are it may already have slipped through my grip, or maybe I will never know what it is I am looking for, or maybe it will come and find me, who knows."

Blake was confused. He had heard her but he didn't really follow what she said. By now her coat was now fully on and she had started to do up a couple of the buttons. "I just have to do this journey, Blake. I don't know how long it will be, how easy, or anything, I just need to go. I know how you feel about me but I would be useless to you without doing what I have got to do first; I am sorry, Blake."

The door opened and Blake and Marci moved outside onto the street, slowly distancing themselves from the Red Lion as they made their way in an unrushed fashion back towards the office. Blake realised that it was a difficult walk for both of them, full of sadness and of course unfinished business. It was made worse by the necessity of dodging people traffic as they went – those that had spilled from the nearby West End shops and were hurrying back to work or to the underground stations nearby.

All of a sudden, with the office still a couple of streets away, unexpectedly Marci stopped and grabbed Blake's shoulder. "Blake, this is it for me, I'm not going any further. I'm not going back to the office. I said my goodbyes already to everybody, there is nothing there for me now. This is it, it's as far as I go."

She raised her arm and pointed across the street. "I am going to go this way and you go that way," pointing back towards the high glass-fronted, very corporate-looking building at the end of the street. "So long Blake, see you in heaven."

In a flash Marci gave him a peck on the cheek, said her

goodbyes and turned and ran across the road, into the crowd beyond. Blake watched on helplessly; it was though he had been mugged. He was stunned. Blake was speechless. That was it, like the shining glorious end of some magician's party trick. It was over. She had disappeared in front of his eyes, simply vanished and he didn't even have the chance to say goodbye. He had wanted to tell her how he felt and that he was okay with her leaving; he wanted to know when she would be back, would she write to him, how could they stay in touch while she was not there. Now he couldn't, she had just gone.

That seriously hurt like hell. He wasn't ready for Christ sake, he wasn't prepared for an ending like this, but there was nothing he could do. He just stood and watched with kaleidoscope eyes as Marci twisted and filtered amongst the colourful yet busy crowd of shoppers into the direction of Cheapside. Then in the blink of an eye she had been consumed entirely. It was all meant to be very different. It certainly wasn't meant to be him standing like a condemned man on tiptoe and craning his neck trying to catch a last glimpse of her before she disappeared before his very eyes.

Blake was both sad and also at the same time really angry. The problem was that he didn't know who he was angry with – was it Marci for leaving like that or was it himself for not trying to stop her?

He mumbled to himself. "Bollocks, what a total prat I am. Why did I let her go without telling her how much she meant to me? Damn, damn, damn." He felt like punching himself.

He hoped that if he waited a while she might come back but after twenty minutes or so it was obvious that that wasn't going to happen. All he could do was to turn and head for the office. As Blake, devoid of pace, meandered along the remaining two streets to the office the induced and unavoidable process of analysing the whole situation had automatically kicked in. While he continuously told himself that it was all too early for this process at the same time he couldn't help himself either. He tried unsuccessfully to shut it out of his head but since the bad side was stronger than the good side it just got back up and dug its claws in even tighter.

In the past these sorts of moments usually needed to be shared with the bottom of a wine glass. It's common knowledge that to analyse a problem of such painful and romantic enormity, in order to get the best results you really do need to be tipping a half full wine glass away from you at about 45 degrees. Then at the same time as gently rolling and twisting the stem between your thumb and forefinger you stare hard into it with such an evil force as though you are attempting to actually boil the wine in the glass in order to get it to evaporate. OK, so he needed a drink.

Blake had decided that the traditional way was best and so he resolved to delay all the deliberating, pontificating and analysis until he had a drink in his hand. At this moment in time the only thing that made sense to him was that nothing actually made sense. He continued on to the office. He would give Joseph a call later and see if he was able to act as an agony aunt for him. He was a sensible guy and would know what to do at times like this.

When he arrived back at the office people seemed to be going about their work all quite normally as though nothing had happened. Was nobody feeling the seismic proportions of the gap that had been left by Marci's absence? He most certainly was. Was he alone in this, as from the way they were going about their business nobody else seemed to be bothered? Maybe this could be a good thing; it might help speed up the whole healing process for him. Then came the biggest test of all. Blake needed to get past Marci's old office in order to get to his own. He approached, determined not to let it upset him anymore than he was already. He noticed that the light was still on in her office and through the glass walls he could see her computer. It was still running, displaying one of her 'down under' screen savers; he recognised it as a photo from one of her trips to the Franz Josef Glacier region on South Island that she had enjoyed a couple of years back. Papers seemed to be liberally scattered on the desk. The calendar on the wall was running about two weeks late behind today's date. None of which really mattered. The biggest and most hurtful visual difference was that her seat was empty, pushed back from the desk and at the exit angle towards the door. For Blake this image cut the deepest. Although for all intents and purposes it looked as though everything had been left as though she had just popped out and would be back soon the reality was that she wouldn't.

Blake stared in but it was all a bit hazy. He saw her everywhere but then again nowhere at all. He just couldn't believe she was never coming back. As he hovered by the door of her office he did, for a nanosecond, think about going in and maybe turning everything off and tidying up. This soon became more complicated as he then realised he would possibly be able to smell her as well. That sweet subtle perfume that she wore. Piling on the misery wasn't Blake's thing so to avoid torturing himself any more he just kept walking. It semed to be the best idea. In fact he decided that an even more sensible thing to do was to put his coat back on and go back to the pub for that drink. He would call Joseph when he got home to see if he needed a drink as well.

Chapter 8

It's December 2013, it was now some five months after Marci had left London. Blake had not heard from Marci at all in that time. He had no idea what had happened to her. He always hoped that things were OK with her but not knowing just gave him the stomach cramps most of the time. One evening when he was at home and in the study sorting out his Christmas card listing he noticed that an e-mail had been delivered to his mail box; surprise it was from Kerala in India. There was only one person whom he knew in India – it just had to be Marci. His pulse raced as he frantically wiggled the mouse around and clicked fast and furiously, sounding like a cricket in mating season. Finally the mail box flew open and indeed he could see that Marci was alive and well and hopefully missing him; she had made it that far at least. He hadn't heard from her in such a long time, this was great.

Keen to get to the part where she says she misses him Blake started to speed read the first few lines of the e-mail, such was his hunger. Sadly the message didn't quite go that way. She had found some old friends in a coastal village called Kovalam. Apparently, according to Marci, it is a place made up of three small beaches (all sounded wonderful). Perfect for the study of Pilates and massage. It is located not a million miles away from the capital, Thiruvananthapuram (blimey how could anybody say that without hours of practice?). She had visited there a couple of years back and was now rebonding with some old friends from her previous visit, or "shacking up with them" as she put it. This obviously saved her some money but also she had some company which was more important since she "definitely would have needed

96

to offload on to somebody. I guess if you have demons, even little tiny ones, then Kerala is as good a place as any to try and bury them. The sand is soft which makes the digging easier I suppose'.

He wondered what was behind that statement.

Blake relaxed into the back of his chair and read the remainder out loud; he thought it might be more therapeutic. *"Blake, it's all going well over here. I am getting bloated on love and everything is good. I am finding myself. Also taking up Yoga and Pilates, can you believe that? I should have done this years ago. Kovalam Beach is a series of three crescent shaped beaches. I can swim in the Arabian Sea and have an Ayurvedic Massage on the clean sands. It's wonderful. Follow your heart Blake; fulfill your dreams, it's good for the soul. If you ever want to find me just follow my footsteps in the sand. I now realise I must have been born into the arms of an imaginary friend. Catch you later, lots of love - Marci xx."*

And then it ended. Much to Blake's disappointment there was nothing in the e-mail about how much she missed him, nothing to say 'could he get over to see her', nothing about how she missed him at night time, how she wanted to put her arms around him or how she wondered what he was up to. In fact she hadn't asked about him or expressed any affection for him at all. She didn't mention any of the things that were on his lips, the things that he wanted to say to her. Blake didn't take this very well. Consequently as a result he had mixed emotions about what was written in the e-mail.

At first Blake went down the route of making light of it all, telling himself that none of it made sense. Possibly at the time of writing it she was a bit high on something, or a bit drunk maybe. Blake looked at the text again searching

THE EDGE OF FOREVER

for some rationale behind what was written, perhaps the drugs or drink route was a logical explanation, could be – he supposed. But taking drugs or even drinking excessively didn't seem to be something that Marci would do. Well she never used to anyway. Yet somehow in the mail she sounded like a completely different person, not the Marci he had been used to; he didn't recognise her from this. Whatever it was she definitely seemed to have thrown those metaphoric shackles off and must have been certainly enjoying her time there.

Unsatisfied with his own explanation Blake continued to stare and ponder for a while longer at the computer screen, looking for a clue that was probably not going to be there. A clue that would basically explain to him why she hadn't said anything about missing him. He was desperate for an answer and just needed to know. Marci had told him lots of good things about how life was for her in India but had failed to say what Blake ultimately wanted her to say and that was what was really wrong, nothing else. Then there was always the possibility that it was just the new found peace that had provided the energy for this brief and in some ways disappointing e-mail. What was all that stuff about being 'born into the arms of an imaginary friend'? He had no idea; she must have been hallucinating or something, he pondered: most definitely. Blake was obviously hoping to find some sort of hidden or encrypted message in the e-mail from Marci that he could broadly translate to say "help me Blake I have been kidnapped, I need help, come and rescue me". He read the e-mail time and time again but it wasn't there. The more he read the only thing that really came across was that Marci was clearly getting on with what she set out to do, which was to take these demons on and beat them.

Eventually Blake took some comfort in the realisation that Marci appeared to be very happy at last, she seemed to be making progress with getting her life back on track. He didn't understand everything about it all but then that wasn't so important. Basically she seemed to be coming out of whatever crisis she was once in. As far as Blake was concerned it could only be a good thing. If drugs or drink had played any part in the construction of this e-mail then it was comforting to be able to believe that he was the first thing she would think of when she was stoned. As for Blake he knew that Marci was the only drug he needed; she was etched on his mind day and night. No matter how many miles there were between them Blake could see her face in minute detail as though she stood right there in front of him. It was as though she was tattooed under his eyelids. And to smell her he only had to shut his eyes softly and imagine his favourite flower, a single stemmed 'Norma Jean' rose, nuzzled teasingly against his nose, it was simply divine. For Blake this was all a rather serious case of heartbreak warfare. He missed her: it was as simple as that.

After the first mail others came quite frequently to start with, maybe one each week which surprised him. They were all saying the same message, that Marci was enjoying herself, that life was fine and as always they never asked how Blake was nor did she ever confess in any way that he was being missed at all – though for Blake they were all he had of her now and he had to be content with that. At least he knew that she was in good spirits. He wasn't so sure though if Marci saw it the same way. Eventually though the steady e-mail stream started to dry up a little to the point where Blake would only hear from Marci once each month if he was lucky. It got so that she would only write every now and again to update him of her latest exploits. Things like places she had visited and the sights and sounds. Gradually the e-mails told less and less of her real reason for going to India in the first place which was a good thing as far as Blake was concerned. He hoped that it was a sign that she was doing well emotionally. Her progress didn't seem so good to start with. By now the beach must have been a cemetery for demons as Marci seemed to be shedding them faster than the coconuts fell from the trees, the symbolic headstones randomly lining the beaches where they fall.

No matter how infrequent the e-mails became he always looked forward to hearing from her and wrote back promptly. Of course deep down he was hoping that one day the issues she had had, along with all of those demons, would get put to bed forever and that they might be able to talk more openly about how they felt for each other. Would it ever happen? Reality was that there was probably more chance of getting struck by lightning twice in one day. Deep down though he knew that winning the lottery would probably be an easier thing to do.

It was now July 2014 and communication with Marci had almost ceased. Marci hadn't been in touch as frequently as she was at first. For a while now the mail trail had only been one way with Blake sending her mails which were hardly ever answered; in fact he had not heard from her now in over three months.

One Saturday afternoon Blake had been taking life easy just sitting in a deck chair in the garden. He had played a round of golf that morning with Joseph and was ready to simply sip a nice glass of ice cold beer in the warmth of the summer sun. It was getting a bit late and he was on his way to the bathroom and passed by the study only to notice a flashing light on his computer. He had a message waiting for him. His money was on a message from Joseph probably praising Blake for how well he had taken the thrashing dished out to him at their recent golf game. Blake logged on to check; as it turned out the message wasn't from Joseph at all.

Blake dragged the cursor and clicked on the mouse to open and read the message. Out of the blue he was greeted by and slightly surprised by a message from Marci. Goodness he had not heard from her in a while. It was nice and made him feel good even before he had read anything.

The e-mail read, *"Dear Blake, I hope you are well. I wanted to write to you to tell you that I have decided to leave India and head home. I will pack up and leave Kerala soon. It is all a bit sudden but that's life. There is nothing to worry about, it's all down to a personal decision of mine. I will forward you details of where I am in New Zealand once I get back. Take care and I will be in touch soon. Love Marci."*

Blake scratched his head – whatever was going on now with Marci? It all seemed very sudden and unexpected, but then she had been there for a while now. He thought that Kerala represented a new life for her, new beginnings. He had at one point thought that she may never come back to what he called normality. To Blake the fact that she was leaving indicated one of two things: either that things had not worked out for her with whatever it was she had been pursuing, or just that it must have been at least three or four years now since she had seen her mother and her sister. Obviously something had happened with somebody somewhere; whatever it was it was important enough to drag her back home. For sure a lot would have happened outside of Marci's world in the time that she had been away and who knows maybe the penny had dropped and she just simply decided to give it up and go home? Who knows, but for Blake it was more confusion; he didn't understand everything about every choice Marci had made during her mission to go and 'find herself' and this was no exception. He just needed to accept it as part of the overall deal which he made with himself and that 'leap of faith' when he let her run out of his life. Anyway one thing was still very obvious: she wasn't intending on returning to London to be with him; in fact she was heading further away. Once he had realised this it made him feel even worse than he did already.

For an hour or two he chewed the whole thing over in his head, analysing why she would do this. First the golf and now this, he was driving himself insane with it all. He was hopeless at this sort of thing and didn't quite know why he couldn't just accept what was written and get on with things – but no, not Blake, everything had to be fully and forensically screened; dissected and pulled apart until he was convinced that he knew what was really going on. He developed a theory. Blake knew that Marci had a sister called Bronwyn who once lived and probably still lived in New Zealand. She had told him about her during one of their lunches together. But that was way back then and what Blake didn't know was that Bronwyn had been living with a guy called Gordon for some three years since, in Wellington. They were married, deeply in love and as far as Marci could see they were simply devoted to each other. More importantly Bronwyn was pregnant and expecting a baby in August.

Bronwyn was a couple of years younger than Marci; she had met Gordon in the year 2011 during a rugby tournament. They had been together for so long it was as though they were almost childhood sweethearts. It was strange how they met. Bronwyn had been helping a friend run a small tea shop near the harbour area in Auckland and Gordon, an Australian, had just popped in for a flat white after watching a rugby match and bingo, that was it; one flat white leads to another as they say and it didn't take much for Gordon to follow Bronwyn home when the tournament came to an end, all the way to Wellington. Their relationship was a total success story, they set up home together, remained dizzily in love and to put the icing on the cake Lucy was born in the August of 2014. They seemed to be made for each other and were blissfully happy. Lucy was a beautiful little girl with little chubby cherub like legs and a mop of golden curly hair. She had long slender fingers which suggested that she might play piano when she got older. In every way she was simply adorable and her parents were very proud of her.

So with nothing else to go on Blake figured that Marci's decision to leave Kerala simply had to be based on the fact that things were moving on back home and she was missing it all and didn't want to anymore.

Blake didn't reply to Marci's mail immediately for some reason. He had meant to but never knew quite what to write. A bit of him was fed up with continuingly telling her how pleased he was for her, how well she had done and so on, always wishing her luck when what he really wanted was to tell her that he just wanted to throw his arms around her and never let her go, no matter what. How much longer was it all going to go on for? Surely once the demons have gone then life can resume as normal can't it? Then of course the trouble with this was that after she had shaken off the demons, he wasn't there. And somebody else probably was. All in all it was really messing with Blake's head. He was in total turmoil with this torture and he found it all very difficult to deal with. None of this would have mattered of course if he didn't feel for her the way he did. So, since he couldn't bring himself to answer from his heart and say what he really wanted to say, then he figured that he wouldn't answer Marci at all; for a while at least.

Some weeks later on a Saturday evening in mid-September another e-mail unexpectedly arrived, again from Kerala. It was clear to Blake that things were now moving along at a faster pace as Marci had some decisive news that she needed to tell him. This time she included a couple of photos of Lucy which her sister Bronwyn had sent her and explained fully what was going on.

"*Blake, You need to know that I am going home in a few days, well three to be precise. I have made my mind up and have booked my air tickets back to Wellington. My time here is done. It was fun while it lasted but now it's over. I have completed my Yoga and Pilates courses and have also managed to get my head straight, so there is nothing much to stay for now. You may as well know that I sort of fell for a guy while I was out here but it didn't work out. I should have had my head screwed on a bit better. Basically I made a bit of a fool of myself but live and learn I suppose. It's over now (thank goodness) and it should never have really happened anyway.*

My sister Bronwyn has had a baby girl; they called her Lucy and I want to go home as I am desperate to see her. I have attached a couple of photos for you; I hope you agree that she is simply adorable.

I hope you are not too put out that I have decided to go home rather than come back to London to see you. I think of you all of the time Blake but to be honest I have never thought that it was our time. To be honest I don't know if it will ever be our time. It's like we should have been together many, many years ago and somehow we have missed the moment. Maybe we can meet again in the next life. I know you are the type of person that I could love and it isn't quite clear to me why I didn't let that happen. I often wondered how you were feeling about me and I was worried that I may be rejected if I let the cat out of the bag regarding my feelings so to speak. So, Blake, fate is taking me across the ocean back home again. Who knows – maybe there will be a moment in time somewhere which is reserved for us. A bit of me hopes so.

I also miss my mum. Haven't seen her in ages. You would like her Blake – she's a really nice lady.

So if you are ever in Wellington look me up; we can always chat about the old days. Love Marci xx"

Blake rubbed his hands over his face, kind of massaging his cheeks and pushing his fingers up in to his eyebrows in a circular movement. His eyes shut tightly as he worked his hands around and around rubbing harder and harder with each revolution. He wasn't thinking because he didn't know what to think. He couldn't get his head around the fact that Marci had had a boyfriend while she was in India. She had actually been with another man. He was devastated and shivering at the thought of it. His senses had often told him that if she ever got back to feeling normal and he wasn't there then somebody else would be and that had proven to be the case. But even worse than that it was obvious that if the pair of them had been a bit more open and honest with each other in the first place all of this may have been avoided. All of these wasted years, all of this pain and heartache. Why did it have to be like this? He felt sick to the core of his stomach like he had been lanced unexpectedly and was now pinned hopelessly to the floor, agonizing but resolute that the killer blow was about to follow. God it was a mess, his life was a mess. At that point he realised that witholding love would bring the worst pain and suffering that he would ever carry throughout his life.

Blake loosened his grip on his face and looked up to see nothing but an empty study. Life had seemed to suspend itself for a brief moment while he stared only at the wall. He soon realised that in fact he hadn't been lanced, that there was no battle going on around him and indeed feeling sorry for himself probably wasn't going to get him anywhere. With a judder of instant realism he snapped back into the real world. It was time to think a little bit more pragmatically and grow up. Time to do something about all of this before it was really too late.

He clicked on his mouse to open the attached photos of Lucy. It was not difficult to understand how all of this had made Marci feel homesick. A relationship going wrong on top of a cry from her family to come home, plus the photos sent by Bronwyn were bound to tip the scales between staying or not staying and in the end her blood compass steered her home.

Blake gazed at the two photos of Lucy; it was obvious that she was a lovely little girl in every sense. A mop of golden hair and a happy smiling face made him think that she looked a bit like Marci.

Again the paranoia kicked in momentarily and Blake started to wonder if her message was encrypted somehow.

Was it possible that there was something in it for only Blake to see? His focus adjusted to the closing line which read "*so if you are ever in Wellington look me up; we can always chat about the old days*". What did this really mean?

Was it possible to think that maybe seeing photos of Lucy had triggered some maternal need in Marci and perhaps inviting him down to New Zealand for a short break was possibly a code for something completely different, maybe to start a family!

Blake was often guilty of self-delusion, especially where Marci was concerned. This would probably more than likely prove to be just another case of the same. He thought about it for a while and eventually common sense prevailed. No, it was just a simple case of homesickness; she had now of course grown strong enough and wise enough to have worked out some plans for herself. She would put all of the Yoga and Pilates skills that she had learned to good use, find a studio back home and start her own classes. It was all upbeat and Blake realised he should try to find a way to be happy for her.

In his return mail he should wish her well and say that he was glad that she was free from everything that had upset her all of those years ago and was finally able to find herself. All that good stuff about if you love somebody you will set them free wasn't really working for Blake at the moment. Even though he knew it was the right thing to do at the time it still seemed like a bad idea right now and one he may well regret for the rest of his life as there was little sign of Marci ever coming back.

He decided that as hard as it was he *should* reply to her. He told himself "just don't mention that boyfriend incident".

"*Hi Marci, it really is lovely to hear from you and I am glad that things seem to have worked out. I was shocked that you are heading home even though I fully understand the reasons why. Lucy looks so beautiful – I bet you are so looking forward to giving her a cuddle. With your training now finished I hope you have all you need to get your own Yoga workshops going, so good luck with that.*

London is much the same as always, so you are not missing much. I have kept busy as usual. The other week I took a boat ride from a small place nearby called Woodbridge. It was great. So don't worry too much about me. I am still having fun.

Your mum and sister Bronwyn will also be glad to get you home; it's been a few years now totally that you have been travelling. Do you remember how the accent goes after such a long time away? Whatever you do, make sure you don't sound like an Aussie or they may throw you out. Okay I will sign off now, I am meeting my friend Joseph tonight for a glass of wine at our local pub so got to dash. If I haven't said, Joseph is an old friend whom I met at St Thomas' Hospital; in fact he was the Interventional Cardiologist who operated on me when I was admitted with my heart attack. Turns out he only lives up the road. Small world isn't it?

In terms of visiting I am happy to come down to Wellington at any time as it would be really lovely to see you. Maybe hear from you once you have settled back in and have done plenty of bonding with Lucy. Take care and safe travels. Love Blake x"

He could have said more. There was plenty that he felt he wanted to say but decided not to. It could so easily have been one of those e-mails that rambled on and on aimlessly blurting out all of his sorrows and woes, but the truth is it wouldn't have sounded or done the situation any good. In fact it would probably have been the worst thing he could have done. The good thing about modern communication is that when you get muddled with your words or lost on some intoxicating and hedonistic rant you don't have to rip the piece of paper out of the typewriter only to throw it into a basket and start all over again – no you can just hit delete; it's brilliant.

Fortunately for Blake though he didn't have to do much in the way of editing. He had kind of made his peace with it all. To be different wouldn't have helped. If he was ever going to win Marci's heart he needed to stay calm and just be patient. After so long now a few more years wouldn't really matter, he would just wait for the right moment. I guess at heart he was a romantic. He believed that if it was meant to be then it would. If it was forced then it wouldn't be so valuable; nothing ever is. What did somebody once say "If it passes you by then it's not meant to be"? That's how Blake was beginning to feel at times. Although he believed it to be true saying it left a slightly bitter taste. He was, at the same time though, almost consoled by its logic.

Chapter 9

Blake had arranged to meet Joseph for a drink in the pub later that evening. It wasn't the usual thing for them to do on a Saturday but Joseph had another one of his long weekends and putting his feet up was part of it, plus he enjoyed Blake's company. Blake wandered into the Queens Head craning his neck and looking for Joseph. He had seen Joseph's car outside in the car park so he knew that he was in there somewhere. The pub was a bit of a rabbit warren but eventually after a bit of running around he found him seated in a small quiet booth near to where the wine is stored. Blake approached him.

"Hi Joseph, how are you?" They shook hands.

"Good thanks and you?"

"So so. Can I get you a drink?"

"Only so so, doesn't sound that brilliant. What's up – and yes I will have another glass of this fabulous Argentinian Malbec that they have."

"OK just give me a moment. How good is fabulous?"

"Well about as fabulous as I have ever had. This stuff just gets better and better. I like it."

Blake turned towards the bar. "OK let's make that two of those then shall we." He set off to the bar to order the wine.

A few minutes later he was back holding two large glasses aloft, he placed them on the wooden table. "There you go, Argentinian Malbec, certainly looks a good colour."

"Thanks Blake," Joseph smiled as he raised his glass towards Blake. "Cheers, good health."

Blake reciprocated, "Cheers Joseph, and thanks for the good health." He took a rather large sip in a quick gulp. "Oh that is good."

"You're supposed to play with it, sniff it, treat it like a lady before finishing it off, not downing it nearly in one go. It's not tequila and this isn't Mexico!"

"Treat it like a woman you say. Well I will keep the way that I treat my women and the way that I treat my wine totally different if you don't mind, since I have no luck with women."

"Oh dear, so what's gone wrong now? Anyway I didn't even know that you had a woman in your life."

"That's just it, I haven't. Well I have but I haven't if you know what I mean."

"You're confusing me now Blake. Do you want to start again?"

"OK, from the beginning?"

Joseph replied, "Yes if you like, from the beginning."

"Don't be so patronizing! OK a few years ago I met a woman called Marci. She came to work for me at the office. We went out a few times, just lunchy stuff, nothing heavy and anyway I couldn't help falling in love with her, she was and still is all I ever think about." Blake stopped abruptly, took a small sip of his wine followed by a brief sigh.

Joseph prompted: "Go on, this sounds interesting."

"Well after a while she left London and went to Kerala in India to study Pilates and stuff, and now she has left Kerala and is heading back home."

"So what's wrong with that?"

"Whats wrong with it is that she isn't heading here to see me."

"Oh I see, and does she know how you feel about her?"

"No, not exactly, I don't think so anyway, well probably she might, I'm just not sure."

"What do you mean you are just not sure; probably. How can that be?"

"Well I never quite told her how I felt."

"Christ Blake if you are that crazy about her why didn't you tell her?"

Blake thought hard. "I wanted to, god knows I tried, but the right moment never really presented itself."

Joseph had him on the ropes. "Aha, now I see. Well OK, all is not lost, Blake: why don't you pop round and see her and just explain. Shouldn't be too hard, she will understand."

"That's the point: it is hard – she lives in New Zealand, Wellington, so no it isn't easy. Plus just before she left Kerala she got herself a boyfriend. Apparently she says it's all over now but, well, you know what women are like."

Joseph said, "Oh, didn't realise; it's starting to sound complicated to me."

Blake's wine glass was empty by now; he had downed the lot in about two and a half mouthfuls.

"I will get another couple of glasses of wine. It's probably going to be a long night." Joseph headed for the bar.

And so the evening was spent with Blake telling Joseph all about him and Marci, how much he adored her and where it all probably went wrong. Joseph was a good friend and he had a very good listening side which came in useful for both his patients and his friends. Sometimes there was little between them. It was some two bottles of Malbec later and very late when they both decided to leave the pub. Joseph phoned for a taxi which dropped Blake home before taking him on to his house. From the way that Blake spoke of Marci Joseph had a feeling that this would not be the last he heard of her.

Several weeks passed by. Blake had tried to throw himself

into his work as a way of helping him get over Marci. He had little faith in the hope that he would ever hear from her or ever see her again. As difficult as it was at times he decided to just get on with his life.

It was now 2018. Joseph and Blake had still remained very good friends and sometimes when they were both working in London they would meet for a drink of an evening, usually close to the hospital in Westminster. This particular evening in October they had agreed to meet at the usual pub as Joseph wanted to discuss with Blake an ambitious project that he had been 'playing with' as he put it.

Blake was intrigued and he was keen to hear more about it all from Joseph. He would never have imagined in a million years what Joseph was going to propose. Blake knew that Joseph was serious about his work and would never discuss anything that he saw as being impossible. His initial consensus was that it would at least be something straightforward like opening a private medical centre maybe?

Joseph on the other hand knew that 'pure folly' would probably be the reaction of many people he approached but because of their special friendship he had some confidence that Blake may see the opportunity a bit differently. After all this was not a skittish idea dreamt up on a fanciful whim after a glass or two of red wine. No, Joseph had been preparing these ambitious plans for some time now, continually researching in order to get it right. What Joseph was proposing was to develop a life changing gene rejuvenating drug – it would be the path to transhumanisation, the holy grail of medicine.

"Blake, do you remember all of those years ago when we first met?"

"Who could forget that? I was in agony and you saved my life."

"After that bit, you stood by the window that day looking out at the trains coming and going."

"Oh that conversation."

"Well, yes, we had a brief conversation about what it might be like to live a much longer and fuller life, beyond our generation's normal expectation."

"Yes, I remember you said something or other about, what was it; gene rejuvenation?"

Joseph nodded, "Yes that's right, I did."

"I thought it was quite fascinating at the time."

"It was and still is. Well, that's what I want to talk to you about again, now, this evening."

"Really? So not a private medical clinic idea then." Blake leaned towards Joseph. "Has somebody been dabbling with the black arts?"

"I suppose you could say that, yes, but that somebody is me."

"You? Oh goodness what have you done now?"

"Basically I have been doing some homework that has involved research into how we could possibly make all of this happen."

"Now you are scaring me, Joseph, but go on, it sounds intriguing."

"Well, I looked at the history and evolution if you like of medical science, what impacted the big changes, how was the inspiration and desire fed with the people that did it, where does it come from and why. Also I needed to know why some things failed of course. Basically after years of digging around I have what I believe to be the basis for scientific trial which could prove that our genetic structure can reproduce itself thus providing the transhumanisation process."

"You are kidding of course."

"No, not kidding. I wouldn't be saying it if I didn't believe it to be true."

"OK Joseph, it all sounds brilliant, but I need to understand it better; please just start again if you don't mind. One more time. Oh don't start yet, wait, wait, please wait, I need to get us both another drink."

Blake got up from his worn leather padded seat, turned and headed off to the bar to order another two glasses of the Argentinian Malbec. As he returned, steadily approaching the table with the two glasses Joseph, unable to contain himself, blurted out, "Look I know it sounds crazy but I can do this. I have researched and researched and I am convinced. The pieces of the puzzle are there now in front of me. All I have to do is start to piece it together. I know what I am looking for."

"When you say pieces of the puzzle – how many pieces are there?"

"Well my research suggests that we will get the results we need from merging two different genetic sources to create a hybrid."

Blake put down the two glasses of wine on the table.

"The long and short of it Blake is that I need somebody to back me financially."

"How much do we need for all of this, Joseph?"

"Not exactly sure, but six hundred thousand to seven hundred thousand pounds should do it." Joseph shuddered at the ease with which the numbers just rolled off his tongue. About thirty seconds of silence followed. Joseph was waiting for Blake to say something. Blake sipped more wine.

Blake looked square on to Joseph, he looked him straight in the eye and said, "Joseph, as far as I am concerned, you are a brilliant doctor, physician and top bloke. You saved my life, for that I am eternally grateful, you are passionate about life and this reflects in everything you do, I know that. OK you are always skint, but then doctors don't really worry about not having money, do they? But Joseph what I am trying to say is that all of this adds up to me believing in you. I trust you, albeit subconsciously, when I didn't even know anything about you. Now that I do know you I don't trust you any less. God it's difficult. Look Joseph, if what you are saying will help the world as we know it and make you a wealthy man in the meantime then it's the least I can do. Why not, yup, why not? I have some money from the sale of the shares in the business, so OK, let's go for it."

It was as easy as that, decision made. Blake raised a glass towards a stunned Joseph who all of a sudden felt like a lottery winner. Sporting a grin as wide as the bar in the pub was long, Joseph lifted his glass; he subtly tipped the edge of Blake's wine glass in a toast.

"Seriously you will not regret this, I mean it Blake, I mean it."

"I know that otherwise I wouldn't agree to help. OK Joseph, tell me once more about this crazy hybrid gene thing and this time slowly please."

"OK, we produce the hybrid gene from only two sources. Both of these sources independently show extensive longevity characteristics. I believe that combining them will produce all of the characteristics needed for the full transhumanisation process. Basically we create a serum which, once injected

116

into the body, will automatically and continually stimulate gene rejuvenation in our bodies to a number of years that is currently unimaginable. As genes die off they will automatically be replaced."

"So what are we talking about in terms of how long you could expect to live for? What, an extra fifty, one hundred or a thousand years?"

"I am not sure but one hundred to two hundred years shouldn't be an issue, eventually."

Blake was astonished and slumped back in his chair. "Bloody hell Joseph, sounds almost too good to be true. The holy grail of how to live forever, the eternal fountain of youth. Sounds like I need to get some shares in a birthday card manufacturing company."

"Look, OK so it sounds ridiculous but I know this can work."

"Joseph, I don't doubt you for a moment but from where I am sitting it just seems a bit, well 'Walt Disney', that's all. So what are the gene sources, where do they come from?"

"Some years ago there was a woman called Henrietta Lacks, she died on October 4th, 1951 of cervical cancer. Nothing odd about that you might say. But her contribution to medical science is arguably greater than any other in medical science, ever."

"Why, what was so special about Henrietta?"

"OK so she died of cervical cancer at the age of 31 at the Johns Hopkins University Hospital in Baltimore. Blake, her cells were the first to have their DNA mapped and not only that they were even shot into space in 1960 to test their effects on astronauts."

"Joseph, somebody had to be the first. It's fascinating but I don't see the link. Is there something else?"

"Okay, it just so happens that there is. When she was near death a small sample of her tissue was taken from the malignant tissue – standard practice of that time. A research team led by a Dr George Gey were astonished though to see that the cells grew at an alarming rate and further more they did not die. Blake, they did not die. Dr Gey also discovered that the cells, while cancerous, also had the characteristics of healthy human cells. They were easy to grow, simple to use and were classified as the first immortal cell lines in science."

"My god, so if they are immortal…" Blake paused momentarily to let the enormity of what he was being told sink in, "and this is only half of the story… so what are the cells doing now?"

"They are still growing, that's what they are doing, some sixty odd years later they are still growing. They are the most widely used cells in scientific research against stuff like Polio, Aids, IVF, they helped develop the Cervical Cancer vaccine a way back, they shed light on TB, Salmonella, are helping to combat cancers and more, much, much more. This is where it gets more interesting for us, as I believe they are pushing open the door to gene therapy. I believe that they hold a part of the key to gene rejuvenation."

"OK Joseph, but now what, what happens now? It's all fascinating stuff but it's history, very grateful history but history nonetheless. Everybody in the world of medical science knows about it presumably so as brilliant as it all is it must have its limitations."

"You know Blake, if all of Henrietta's grown cells were bundled together they would weigh an estimated 50 million tonnes; lay them down end to end and they would stretch around the world three times – three times, Blake. If you could create that amount of repetition in a person it would treble or quadruple their life expectancy. From one hundred to two hundred easily, easily. So history here is important Blake, very important."

"So how do we get hold of some of these cells? And why do we need something else, why another cell to blend if these ones can already reproduce themselves?"

"Well, since the Henrietta cells, or HeLa cells as they are called, are used in nearly every lab in the world we can access them easily through the hospital. The other cells we need are a bit more difficult to get."

"But why do we need them?"

"The HeLa cells, while surviving and invaluable, are not necessarily the key to total longevity on their own. They survive well but are doing so under almost protected conditions, Blake. The world is not a pure place to be in, and we need to make a gene that can rejuvenate under more hostile conditions. I believe that by blending the two types of cells we will have a more robust gene that will survive whatever is thrown at it."

"Christ Joseph, you really have thought about all of this haven't you?"

"Yup, I have, and I have found what I believe is the perfect match."

Blake said eagerly, "Spill, come on, tell me then."

"We introduce the gene from the Bowhead whale."

Blake was miffed by this. "Why on earth a fish?"

Joseph looked down his nose at Blake. "It's a mammal for starters, and there is evidence to support the fact that its life span may exceed one hundred and eighty years."

"Crikey, so let me guess: we just mix the two together and there you have it, the miracle of eternal life. It all sounds a bit too simple, Joseph."

"Yes Blake, it is simple and I believe that's why it hasn't happened yet. If we can get these cells to blend then I don't see why it won't work. All of my research points to it being a very strong possibility. Under the right conditions I believe we will be able to produce a gene which stimulates perpetual rejuvenation to offer immortality – possibly."

Blake stared at Joseph in total wonderment; his jaw dropped lower than a limbo dancer's ass. His face was virtually expressionless, all sort of cold, white and clammy, like he had just seen a ghost. He looked totally washed over.

Joseph leaned toward this solidified and stone faced figure and gazing into Blake's pupils waved his right hand in front of Blake's face. "A state of shock I think they call it."

"Joseph, slap me please, I can't believe what I have just heard. It is just too blue sky to take it in; it's almost indigo, it's so radical and simple and yet so crazy, so improbable and yet so doable, it contradicts and teases satanically as well as being an emotional cocktail of the sweetest kind; Joseph, it's huge, it's brilliant."

A very cool Joseph nodded his head in agreement and proceeded to knock back the remains of the Malbec.

Blake, with the colour returning to his cheeks, now chomping for reconfirmation from Joseph, said, "So let's just get this thing right, you believe that by blending these two sets of cells you can make people live potentially forever, or whatever, maybe two hundred years?"

Joseph confidently replied, "In simple terms – yes."

"Christ almighty, Joseph, Christ all bloody mighty. I need

another drink." Blake summonsed both of his wobbly legs and got to his feet and started to make his way to the bar.

"Sit down Blake please it's my round I think, I will get these. You don't look well enough to make it to the bar anyway!"

Blake conceded the diagnosis was a good one yet again and surrendered his wine glass. Joseph took it from him and disappeared through the small crowd of after work drinkers towards the bar.

Blake tried desperately to go into some sort of deep thought process mode during Joseph's absence which would allow him to come up with some clever questions or profound statements in readiness for when Joseph returned – but he failed miserably. All he could do was get warmer and warmer from the heat generating inside him as he thought more deeply about the value to the world from such a discovery. By the time Joseph got back to the table with the refreshed glasses of wine Blake was still in a state of shock.

Joseph said, "OK Blake, what do you think? It will cost a bit of money, but it will be worth it I assure you."

"I have thought and I don't doubt it on both of those scores. Problem I see is that you have got to get a bloody Bowhead whale from somewhere, but I suppose you have already worked that one out as well. Oh, don't tell me – they sell them at Billingsgate market."

"I asked already Blake and no they don't have one!"

"Doesn't surprise me. So how much are we talking about and what's the timeframe for having the drug ready?"

Joseph smiled wryly. "So we are down to business now, are we?"

"Looks like it."

"Well in money terms I reckon six to seven hundred thousand pounds or so ought to do it. It would get us to the point of having a blended solution tested and ready to market. Of course producing the supporting data would cost a bit more, so totally around seven hundred and fifty thousand pounds. Not a lot more. In terms of schedule, it could take me around six to eight months."

"So six to eight months and about three quarters of a million pounds or more. And will you still carry on at the hospital in the meantime or do you intend to leave, or what?"

"No Blake, I intend to take some leave of absence, so some time out basically. So once I have the HeLa cells then I will make arrangements to leave the hospital for a while which shouldn't be a problem, I already mentioned it to them. We will need to develop my basic lab facilities at home. We will need extra tight security systems in place, specialist instruments and so on, plus I will need to work in total isolation and secrecy."

Blake, still a bit dumb struck by the suggestion, said: "So what we will end up with is a gene that is robust enough to rejuvenate itself for an unknown extended period of time. Limitless transhumanisation Joseph, that's what you are on the threshold of creating. Potentially an indefinite existence. And this is strictly between you and me. Nobody else knows, cross your heart and all of that stuff."

"Blake, I swear, nobody else knows. Just you and me."

"So why me, Joseph, why me?"

"I thought about that Blake. Both of us owe something to medical science, Blake. It's time to put something back. Without it you wouldn't be here today. To give this gift will take time, expertise and money. Between us we can give those things. To get it to work we will need ultimate trust and a strong relationship; we have that, Blake. So it's the right time and we are the right team. I know it's right."

Blake felt honoured that Joseph felt that way about him and that he wanted to include him in this ride of a lifetime. There was an overwhelming sense of pride that he should be included in such a potentially great medical breakthrough. The thought of the implications that would impact his personal life were likely to be nothing short of amazing if it worked out, even if he was only funding it. It was a small price to pay back to something and somebody who had saved his life and whom he admired greatly. Blake had little hesitation, "OK Joseph, count me in. Let's do it. By the way, where do we get this whale from?"

"Alaska."

"Why Alaska?"

"Cos that's where the Bowhead whale lives."

"Really, all the way up there?"

"Yup, it lives entirely in fertile arctic and sub-arctic waters. Unlike other whales it doesn't migrate to feed or reproduce."

"OK, forgive me for being stupid, but why the Bowhead whale? How do you know that it lives for so long?"

"Good question Blake. Well the Bowhead whale was once thought to live for sixty to seventy years, a similar life expectancy to many other whales. However, discoveries of very old ivory spearheads have been found in a few living whales. Such a discovery happened back in 1993 and again in 2007. It triggered research which was based on structures in the eye of the whale. Results suggested that some whales could be one hundred and fifty to two hundred years old."

"So how were the spearheads found?"

"In May 2007 a fifty ton Bowhead whale was found off the Alaskan coast with the head of a harpoon embedded deep under its neck blubber. The arrow shaped object was found to have been manufactured in New Bedford, Massachusetts; it was once a major whaling centre, around 1890. Just this alone suggests to us that this little beauty must have survived a similar hunt from whalers of more than at least a century before. Now do you see?"

"It's all a bit crazy, Joseph, to be honest. To think that cells from this whale and Henrietta could be blended to produce a gene that reproduces itself, so we can live again and again and again. It's pure science fiction, the stuff dreams are made of. How come nobody has even thought of doing this before?"

"Well, sometimes the simplest things are the least obvious. Just look at it as science and nature getting along – science sort of helping or maybe enhancing nature, that's all we are doing. It sounds too simple I know. I don't know how best to explain it."

"I don't know about simple; it's intoxicating for sure, that's what it is, bloody intoxicating. It's on par with a cosmic event."

"Well you may think so but not me. It's big all right, or will be big when it works. As for cosmic… I have learned that you cannot ascribe great cosmic significance to things that are fate, and this surely must be a fate of sorts for medical science. I never thought that it would be mine though, but it is."

"Now you are sounding like a doctor; myself I don't believe in fate; nothing is meant to be, nothing, we make it all happen; there are no miracles unless we make them. You know, unless you are the lead dog the view never changes; it's always the ass of the dog in front."

Leaning towards Joseph, Blake added, "and who really wants that?"

A delighted Joseph held out his hand to Blake. "You are like me Blake; I always suspected that you would rather sit alone on a pumpkin than with a crowd on a velvet cushion."

Blake reciprocated. "Very profound Joseph, now sip up and then get us both another glass of this fabulous red wine."

Another round it was then.

Chapter 10

Blake had managed to provide the funding needed to support Joseph by selling some shares in his business to a wealthy entrepreneurial friend. While the sale took a chunk of Blake's business, it still left him with some capital and a handsome pension from the company that he hoped one day would come in useful.

Having the money meant that Joseph was finally able to plan the trip to Alaska in more detail and by the following year, 2020, he was basically ready to go.

So in April 2020 Joseph travelled to Point Barrow in Alaska. Point Barrow sits at the top of the United States, alone and a long, long way from anywhere. To get there you basically have to do another 725 miles or so from Anchorage. So from the UK it's a bit of a trip. Joseph knew that the journey was going to be tiring and uncomfortable at times and that he was almost guaranteed to get a sore butt. In order to combat some of these things he packed all of the usual common travel aids like neck rests and so on that would hopefully make it all a bit more comfortable.

For Joseph though it was the planning of the trip that was the most important part. Get it wrong and essentially the whole journey could so easily be wasted. It was crucial that he had access to the expertise that would help him get enough of the sample material that he needed. In order to do this he needed to have healthy sections of tissue that contained lots of blood samples. Joseph knew that once he arrived in Point Barrow he would also need help on the ground as he had not ventured much beyond Manchester until now. He would need somewhere to stay as well as transportation, and maybe at times a friend. He needed all of this as well as local knowledge and at times, well, a good friend who wouldn't go amiss when he needed help. Finding the right person or persons was an important selection process that took him some time to complete. Initially through the internet and later followed up by some telephone conversations Joseph eventually made a contact with a local Inupiaq guy called Brad Hastings. From what he learned Joseph felt he would be able to trust Brad as he was an Inupiaq. After all the word Inupiaq translates to mean real or genuine; so he must be. For the purist amongst us it is actually made up of two words: 'Inuk' meaning person or human and 'Piaq' meaning real. From this Joseph felt there was a good basis to trust Brad. After all Joseph was the kind of guy that needed a basis for everything.

The planning of Joseph's trip had to provide the optimum opportunity for when the access to the whales would be at its best. So it was important that Joseph arrived in the spring as it's only in Spring and Autumn that the Inupiat people are allowed to carry out the practice of what the system calls 'subsistence whaling'. Subsistence whaling means that rural communities who traditionally hunt whales can continue to practise this under controlled conditions.

Joseph had arranged to meet Brad at the airport in Point Barrow. The flight had touched down pretty much on time and Joseph had picked up his luggage. Brad stood in the arrivals hall waiting for Joseph. Up until now Brad had only been introduced to Joseph through the computer conversations; in fact this was a completely different sort of Indian for him. He was more used to the features of the North American Indian who had feathers on their heads as opposed to turbans. He wondered how much more complicated it could be. He waited patiently, holding up a tatty piece of fish chopping board at chest height in the general direction of the crowd of new arrivals coming towards him. He had managed to paint over the remnants of fish scales the words 'Dr Joseph Singh' across it in nice big letters. The font type remains a mystery to this day but Joseph saw the board and worked out that it must be Brad Hastings. He looked remarkably similar to what Joseph had remembered from their satellite video communications a couple of months earlier.

Brad Hastings had the typical features of a native from Barrow. They were clearly evident once he had removed the hood on his jacket from his head. His face was a crimson red, deeply etched with the life scars of a hunter and engrained hardship draped below his thick black wiry hair.

Joseph approached, held out his hand and in his plum English accent said, "Mr Hastings, it's me Joseph, Joseph Singh, god am I pleased to see you. Boy this place is a long way from somewhere."

Brad smiled, put down the weighty sign and took Joseph's hand, "That's why we love it here. Call me Brad, come on, this way, my truck is out front."

They talked like old friends as they made their way across the small fluorescent arrivals hall towards the glass doors.

Joseph said, "I am really pleased to meet you at last. I didn't think I would ever get here." He couldn't help noticing Brad's thickly padded coat. "You are dressed like it is cold outside, but I thought it was spring."

Brad replied, "Yes, probably it seems that way to you, but I am quite used to it. Spring is not so bad, probably around -4 to -22 deg Fahrenheit – for this time of year that's OK."

"Really? I wasn't expecting it to be quite so … cold!"

"I can understand that. You probably read that the average high here is around 17 deg Fahrenheit, that's about 8 deg C where you come from. Well Mr Singh, sorry Joseph, up here we have been below freezing temperatures for around 324 days now which is kinda normal in any year."

"So if I do see palm trees they are likely to be plastic?"

Brad liked his sense of fun. "Something like that."

Joseph chatted to Brad about the journey from London as they walked through the main arrival hall doors and outside to the set down point where people were being dropped off.

Brad said, "I hope you don't mind but I think we should load up and go; no point in hanging around." The night air had already started to bite deeply into Joseph's skin so he wasn't going to disagree.

"OK that's fine, don't want you getting a parking ticket on my account."

"That ain't what I meant. Anyway parking tickets are for city folk. It's not something we are familiar with up here."

"Gee that's lucky. I guess it's not pleasant being a parking warden working in temperatures like this anyway; must be hard to get somebody to do the job."

"Oh that ain't the problem. We love standing around and doing jack, especially in spring. No, the problem is that you can't write the ticket cos you can't get the damn pens to work!"

"Really? Why's that?"

"Simply too damn cold."

Brad gestured towards a black Nissan Navarra parked under a badly earthed and flickering street light. "It's over there."

He pulled the keys from his coat pocket and pointing to the truck he hit the key fob. The orange and red tail lights flashed a couple of times. He said, "OK Joseph dump your bags on the back seat and climb on in. Be careful and mind you don't slip on the side steps, they can still be a bit icy."

An unprepared and gloveless Joseph reached out for the door handle. He grabbed the handle and pulled it towards him to open the door. He didn't quite have hold of the handle and his fingers lost their grip. It wasn't a mistake he would make a second time. The pain seared through him as a thin layer of skin parted from the tips of his fingers on his right hand. The remnants of skin were still stuck to the door handle. He would always remember it, and the sight of blood, wouldn't forget that. Joseph shrieked, "Ouch, shit, that bloody hurt." The door flung open.

He clenched his hand tightly and quickly thrust his fist into the inside of his coat, up towards the underside of his left arm for some instant warmth. It should have provided some swift comfort which he hoped would eventually start to ease the pain. Unfortunately for Joseph that didn't happen this time. It smarted badly to the point where he almost cried.

It was good that Brad wasn't there to witness the first basic error. He was busy scraping ice from the opposite side windows at the time. Joseph reached up for the grab handle in the cab and standing on the kick plate he managed to pull himself up with his left hand and climb into the truck.

Brad was in the cab now and looked across towards an injured Joseph who was still smarting with pain and sheltering his damaged hand under his coat. "Sorry about that, I guess I just take it all for granted. The cold and its side effects are something you soon get used to in these parts. I can fix it up for you when we get back to the house. We have special stuff."

Joseph couldn't wait to see what that would be. He grinned and nodded his head in appreciation. "Thanks Brad, I appreciate that. Anyway no need to apologise, it wasn't your fault. I should have realised."

Joseph just had to try and forget the pain in his hand and concentrate on the main reason as to why he was there: the cells. He was confident that he would get the cells he needed as Alaskan natives had during the hunting season continued to kill small numbers of whales for subsistence purposes. During the journey to Brad's home Joseph quizzed Brad as to how this system of subsistence worked. Brad explained that they were allowed to catch up to 21 whales in spring and another 21 in the fall and that was it; beyond this it was illegal.

Joseph asked, "So how many have you caught so far this spring?"

Brad had an instant response. "Oh we are just getting started, so just a couple so far."

Curious of the world outside him Joseph wiped the side window in order to be able to see out as they drove. Sparse wooden framed houses lined the muddy streets as they made their way across town to where Brad lived with his family.

"So Brad, how long have you lived in Point Barrow?"

"Well I have lived here since late 1965 I guess."

Joseph had guessed that Brad would be approximately in his mid-fifties by his rugged features.

"My wife is a teacher here in the government operated school. Back in the 60s when I was a kid it was a much smaller community. Dog teams and skin covered canoes were the main ways of transportation around here in those days. During my childhood I used to hunt and travel with the village men by dog team and umiak. When I first met my wife we lived for a while nearer to the village of Wainright; we lived there for about two and a half years or so before coming back to Barrow in 1990."

"What's an umiak, if you don't mind me asking?"

"It's what we call the skin covered canoe. Hunting and whaling have always been the most important aspects of our lives. It's our main cultural activity, but equally as important to us is the harvesting of seals, walrus and caribou."

"And I notice the wooden houses are all built on stilts. Why is that, is that something to do with the cold?"

"Well, they are on stilts because of the permafrost which covers the ground from about below 2.5 feet to 350 feet in some parts. There is a danger that if you built your house directly on the ground you would melt some of the permafrost and the house could basically shift and your house shifts with it. You know in Barrow it even affects how people are buried. Bodies are usually sent down to Anchorage for embalming, and then brought back to Barrow where they are buried about 15 feet below in the permafrost. You will see that the cemeteries around here have only wooden crosses. It ain't cos we are mean, it's just that you can't install the sort of monuments that you are more used to in your country."

Joseph, while fascinated by all of this, couldn't help thinking that even in death this wasn't a straightforward place to be living in, if that makes sense.

Brad eventually turned the truck off the road towards

a track which unbeknown to Joseph led up to his home. As the truck turned the headlights gave a brief glimpse of the place where Brad and his family lived. It was, again, like all of the other houses that Joseph had seen during his ride, built of wood and sitting on stilts. Difficult to tell exactly but it looked like it was painted white, with a porch. If it wasn't for the balcony it would have looked almost Georgian style with those tiny square windows. Gingham curtains and slatted shutters at the ground floor windows closed off the view into the main living room from outside. Smoke belched from the chimney curling high into the crystal night sky. Joseph stood by the side of the truck and took in a deep breath of the razor sharp air. It felt like his lungs were being sliced and diced.

Brad slammed the door to the truck closed and ushered to Joseph, "Come on Joseph, grab your stuff and let's get you in the house before you go solid on me."

Joseph had heard the command loud and clear. As fascinating as the night sky was he wasn't going to argue and he headed directly for the front door. The house was constructed to keep the maximum heat possible inside. So the front door that Joseph was heading for actually turned out to be only one of the front doors. Because the houses were constructed with additional outer wooden lapped timber walls that were kept apart by blocks of insulation the walls could be up to two feet apart. Consequently this meant that you had an outer and an inner front door.

Brad was greeted by his wife Anne-Marie. They had two sons but they were older now and were not at home, probably out getting drunk somewhere. She turned towards Joseph and awaited the introduction from Brad which was politely given.

"Joseph, this is my wife Anne-Marie."

Joseph, his right hand being a bit tender due to the skin missing from his fingertips, offered his left hand, "Hello Anne-Marie, it's lovely to meet you."

Anne-Marie noticed his awkwardness. "You too Mr Singh."

"Please call me Joseph."

Anne-Marie said, "But I see you have hurt yourself. You must have a seat and let me take a look at it. I will first put your bags away for you; give them here."

Anne-Marie took Joseph's bags and headed towards a distant room somewhere in the dark back of the house.

Joseph called after her, playing down his injury, "I am sure it is nothing, but if you wouldn't mind I would appreciate it very much."

"No trouble," Anne-Marie shouted back as she disappeared into what was Joseph's allocated room. She reappeared momentarily, "I have just the stuff. Us Inupiat have used it for centuries; it has very good healing powers. We make it from whale blubber. We rub it on and in hours the pain and swelling will go and in a day the skin is replaced." Joseph couldn't quite believe what Anne-Marie had just said. This was chocolate to his ears. Could it actually be true?

Brad asked, "Coffee Joseph? I can get you that while Anne-Marie is patching you up."

"Fantastic, thanks."

Brad made his way to a range type of stove where a large blue enamel coffee pot had been standing, almost long enough to weld itself to its metal plates. He lifted the heavy pot and poured the coffee into two enamel mugs of similar colour that were warming beside the pot.

Joseph inquisitively and keen to know more, asked, "This

cream stuff that you have sounds fascinating. Do you get the ingredient from all types of whale or one in particular?"

Anne-Marie had just re-entered the room and answered, "It comes mainly from the Bowhead whale, so it's very special. But while it has fantastic healing powers I do have to apologise for its pungent, eggy smell. Yup, it really stinks."

Anne-Marie took the top off the pot and she wasn't wrong; as soon as the lid came off Joseph thought he was going to be sick. For somebody who had worked in hospitals most of his adult life that sort of reaction doesn't come easily.

Joseph exclaimed, "Oh my god, it smells like shit." Instantly he realised what he had said. He hoped he had not offended Brad and Anne-Marie and quickly apologised. "Oh I am sorry, I am really sorry, that just slipped out, it wasn't meant to, I do apologise."

Anne-Marie replied, "That's OK. Anyway it's about right – it does smell like shit!"

Joseph realised he was in good hands as a combination of grinning and chuckling blew into the room. They were all going to get on just fine.

Anne-Marie applied the cream and wrapped his fingers in some gauze and tape to protect them while he slept. Proud of her nursing skills she said, "There you go Blake, keep it on through the night and it should be OK to take off sometime during the morning. But then being a doctor you would know all about that."

Blake smiled back at her. "Thanks Anne-Marie, it feels better already."

Brad had sipped his coffee cup dry and to be honest was now ready for his bed. "OK Joseph, we should get some sleep. It's been a long day for everybody and tomorrow we will

need to be up reasonably early. We have to get down to the
harbour to the boat and out onto the water at first light."

"So when is first light then?"

Brad grinned. "As for first light well that's just an
expression around here. Sometimes we never see daylight."

Joseph nodded accepting his latest challenge. "Now, let's
get this right Brad, will we be heading for the Beaufort Sea or
the Chukchi Sea?"

"We can do both seas if you like Joseph. In fact we may
have to depending on how much sea we have due to the
forming ice."

"Oh really, it gets that bad?"

"Well this is the time of year when there is less ice but we
still may see some; it wouldn't surprise me."

Joseph watched as Brad turned and headed towards a
door in the far corner of the room which presumably led to
his bedroom.

He called out, "OK, goodnight Joseph."

"Yup, goodnight Brad. I may need you to give me a call if
that's OK."

"No worries, I can do that," Brad replied and waved his
hand in the air again.

Joseph finished the last mouthful of his coffee and Anne-
Marie led him to his bedroom.

"Goodnight Joseph, see you in the morning." With that
Anne-Marie disappeared through a door which Joseph
presumed to be the bathroom. So no traditional Eskimo
customs here then. Joseph was absolutely shattered; he closed
the bedroom door and made his way across the room to the
bed. The bed was quite high from the floor, presumably to
offer some protection from the cold floor and it was made

of chunky timber legs and frame. Thick blankets and skins covered a single sheet. Joseph wasn't sure if he would even sleep as he was so excited about being there. He finally felt as though the real journey had just begun and the next few days would probably be the most exciting days of his life.

It seemed as though Joseph had only had his eyes shut for a split second when there was a loud and crisp bang on the door.

It was Brad. "Joseph, you awake? We need to get ready to go, 15 mins out front."

Joseph was in a daze; he was disorientated and still tired from the travelling. In some sort of autopilot mode he managed to spring from the bed, and rubbing his eyes with clenched fists he shouted back, "OK Brad, I will be ready."

Brad shouted back, "Coffee is on the stove – grab what you want."

Joseph dressed. He just hoped that he had remembered how to layer his clothes to maximum effect. He had remembered that it's multi layers to keep warm, that's the secret. First he put on his long johns, then a vest, trousers, followed by a T shirt and a sweatshirt with a hood. He told himself that he mustn't forget his waterproof and windproof coat as well as gloves – and the hat, probably most important due to the amount of heat loss from the head. He quickly threw the hat, gloves and binoculars into a small rucksack and moved to make his exit from the bedroom – 6.5 minutes flat: not bad.

He looked down to check out his damaged hand. It certainly felt much better; the pain appeared to have gone, anyway. The swelling had also gone down and he could move it with hardly any discomfort. This was better progress than he had expected.

A quick cup of scalding hot coffee from a seriously well used enamel mug and Joseph headed in the direction of the revving engine. Brad was already in the truck, getting things warmed up. Joseph expected to see about one foot of solid ice totally blanketing the windscreen. But in fact there wasn't any.

"No ice on the screen, Brad?" asked Joseph. The hot air he exhaled was evaporating in the form of a fine mist from his mouth and nose, being swiftly absorbed into the clear frosty morning air.

"No, I put animal skin over the glass at night; it helps mostly. OK hop in, we have to go, bring your coffee."

Joseph threw the rucksack into the cab and quickly followed it. He barely had time to close the door before Brad had slipped the gears and the truck was reversing away from the house as he clipped in his seat belt. As cold as it was Anne-Marie stood by the door in her thickly padded dressing gown and fur lined boots, silhouetted against the porch lamp; she waved them both goodbye.

As the truck swung around and the headlights swept across the front of the house Anne-Marie was seen still standing there waving.

Brad muttered, "Stupid woman, she will get her death."

Joseph waved back at her. "She is a brave woman all right."

They drove a few more short metres to the end of the road and the truck turned right onto the main street.

Joseph asked, "So what happens when we get to the boat?"

"Oh we will meet the crew and set off, nothing fancy. These guys are just fishermen. As far as they are concerned you are here only to witness the ways of life of the Inupiat people. How we live, how we work. They think you may do a bit of fishing if the weather allows. They don't know nothing about your science thing going on back in England and your samples or stuff."

"OK, I guess that's for the best, best for everybody I suppose."

Brad drove the truck towards the harbour. It was dark but Joseph could make out sparsely spread wooden houses of various designs and colours. The roads in Barrow are unpaved and its first come first served in terms of their use. Superiority in this duel usually fell to the trucks on the road of which there were many. Most people appeared to drive pick-up trucks, albeit fairly well battered ones, in comparison to the Chelsea tractor that Joseph was more familiar with back in London.

Brad's truck twisted and turned in the muddy slushy road, occasionally sliding side to side as they approached their destination. As the harbour came into clearer view Joseph could make out clusters of densely packed sheds and jetties with a few boats moored up alongside. They passed large piles of used nets which lay frozen on the ground. God it was dark. That said Barrow sees around 80 days from May to early August when the sun never drops below the horizon. Joseph grinned to himself, so there is a chance that the day will brighten up somewhat.

"So Brad, what's your boat called again?"

"She is called Annie 2."

"Great name. Does it have anything to do with Anne-Marie?"

"Sure does, especially since I get to see more of Annie 2."

"Oh I get it: does it help to keep the levels of jealousy to a manageable level?"

"Most of the time, yes, but for me it's straightforward – I just love fishing, which is just as well since it's mostly what we eat. But Annie 1 gets a bit tired of hearing about Annie 2 sometimes. The name helps to keep things a bit sweet between us."

The truck approached the edge of the quay where Annie 2 was tied up. The vessel's mate and crew for the day were other local guys called Leon and Lee. Leon and Lee, like Brad, were also fishing fanatics. This was evident from the deep entrenched scars to their legs, arms and hands that Joseph would later get the pleasure of seeing as part of his look into the lives of an Inupiat. They had both been onboard a short while before Brad and Joseph arrived and had got the engine started, so Annie 2 was nicely warmed up when Brad and Joseph got there. Leon and Lee stood on the deck and welcomed both Joseph and Brad onboard, as was the custom.

Annie 2 was a nice fishing boat of steel constructed hull. She was about 60 feet long and fitted with a single winch located on deck below the wheelhouse. The winch could lift some ten tonnes so it was able to drag in a decent haul. Most fish would be caught using a net launched off the side and hauled back onboard using the winch; otherwise, at the bow end, she had an extended walkway that was used for firing spears at much larger fish. The wheelhouse was warm, cozy and functional with controls and communication systems. The kitchen was small but well fitted out with a top cooker and a microwave. Bunks and shower facilities were there but looked brand new which made Joseph suspect that they were probably hardly ever used. Brad, Lee and Leon didn't exactly look the types who would worry too much about dressing for dinner whilst on the boat anyway.

After the quick tour around the vessel came the introduction to some important safety rules, which included the whereabouts of the fire extinguishers, the life craft and life jackets. Joseph was pleased to see that they were still in pristine condition.

Once all of the formalities were concluded the ropes were released from the quay and Annie 2 headed out to sea. The ship's course was set towards the fishing grounds of the Beaufort Sea, while the sounds drifting from the intercom were set to something completely different – the album Café Buddha, a mix of tranquil and lifting jazz music, apparently. Joseph thought it sounded very nice but wasn't sure how it inspired the hunter in this band of great Inupiat seafaring warriors. Signs of such a culture were something that Joseph definitely didn't expect from Brad, Leon or Lee but then life was full of surprises. On the other hand it could have been just for his benefit; he wasn't sure at first but decided just to listen to the music and not mention it. Anyway he didn't want to hurt anybody's feelings either way.

The bow of Annie 2 seemed to be perpetually under water as she crashed through the high rolling seas on her way out to her destination. To Joseph her nose seemed to be feeding from the thrill of the challenge that faced her; it was an unquivering and stoic performance that any vessel captain would have been proud of. She looked as though she was gloating with every wave she broke. Like a fighter delivering a series of knockout blows. Until now Joseph's sailing exploits had been no more than a few hours in local estuaries and rivers so he wasn't particularly well prepared for what he was now facing. The reality of this trip was that it was definitely hardcore in comparison to any previous sailing. The boat felt safe enough to Joseph; his confidence was also high both in the ship and the captain's ability, so no need to worry there then. It didn't want to make him take his lifejacket off though. No, wherever Joseph went his lifejacket went too.

After a couple of hours Joseph decided that he would get some rest and headed down below to find a comfortable chair in the galley area. It must have been the combination of the early morning start, his bit of jet lag and the warm fire from the galley kitchen but it didn't take much for Joseph to fall soundly asleep. They had been sailing probably for approximately three and a half hours when Brad rushed below to find and wake Joseph. Annie 2 had been heading due north on her plotted course when a small pod of three Bowhead whales had been spotted at about half a mile off the port side in the 10 o'clock position. The pod appeared to be heading straight across the bow of the ship. Brad adjusted the speed so that they would cross each other's paths in about twenty minutes or so. This bit of time would give Brad and the team time to prepare nets that could be shot into the path of the passing pod. The idea was then to scoop one of the passing whales in the net and drag it to the side of the ship where it would be held while Joseph could hopefully get all of the sample tissue that he needed.

Brad had little time to waste so he shook Joseph quite firmly on the shoulders. "Joseph, Joseph, wake up, come on, we have a siting already of a pod of Bowhead whales."

Joseph, dazed and a bit confused with his unfamiliar surroundings, said, "Brad, what's up, what's wrong?"

"Nothing wrong Joseph. You must come up to the

wheelhouse: we have a siting of a pod of Bowhead whales."

Joseph leapt from the comfort of the chair. "Goodness, so soon? Great, that's good news."

Brad was already making his way to the galley door. Arms outstretched he held both sides of the bulkhead as he turned to check on Joseph's progress, who by now was only a couple of paces behind him. They both quickly made their way along the internal deck area and up the stairs to the wheelhouse.

By this time Annie 2 had been slowed to approximately five knots which meant that if the whales stayed on course their paths would cross in about fifteen minutes from then. Brad handed Joseph the binoculars.

"Look over there", said Brad, pointing just to the left of the bow of the ship. Joseph, still adjusting slightly to being awake, put the binoculars up to his eyes and scanned the area as gestured by Brad. Initially he didn't see the pod of whales as some large pieces of ice were also drifting in the general area which looked absolutely magnificent. Then, just entering from the far left of his field of vision, he saw the first of the pod. The whales were skimming the water with their large mouths open, searching for food. His heart leapt like a child who had just been given his first new bicycle. He couldn't believe it as he witnessed what was probably a mother and her two calves, just a few hundred metres away from the ship and heading in their direction.

"Oh my god Brad, there they are, you little beauties, oh how fantastic, I can't believe this. Are you sure they are Bowhead whales?"

"Yes Joseph, we can tell because Bowhead whales breathe air at the surface of the water through two blowholes located near the top of the head. If you look you will see that they

143

spout or breathe about one to two times per minute. If they are preparing to dive then they spout four to six times per minute. In addition the Bowhead whale's skin is usually black with a white spot on the lower snout. Calves though are blue to grey coloured, so these two messing around on the inside are still quite young. Also, they have no dorsal fin and no throat grooves. So we are pretty sure. We have been quite lucky today Joseph – sometimes we sail for six or seven hours before we see anything at all."

"So why do you think they are closer this time?"

"Who knows? It's a big ocean. They can go where they want when it comes to feeding I suppose."

"I guess you are right." Joseph put the binoculars down. "So what do we do now?"

"Well Leon and Lee have prepared to shoot the net," Brad pointed to the deck, "and we are getting ready to intercept the path of the whales and we will try to scoop one as it passes by. As long as they don't change course we can do this probably in about five minutes or so, although they look like they have slowed down a little bit now, so maybe a bit longer."

It was all trial and error based on experience; you might as well throw any handbook away at this moment in time.

Joseph said frantically, "Five minutes, OK, right, I should get my things ready."

"No need to panic. Let's see if we can scoop a young one first and if we do the plan is to simply drag it to the side of the ship and get it into a position so that you can get what you need before we release it back into the ocean. So you have plenty of time. We should be able to keep her alongside for about 20 odd minutes or so if necessary."

"That's great Brad, fingers crossed that it all goes to plan."

Joseph decided to go below and prepare himself should the crew be successful in their catch.

Brad grabbed the tannoy from the cradle and issued the instructions to the deck crew instructing them to prepare the net for launch while he switched the course slightly to ensure that the interception was still doable. The net was attached to a long boom which was affixed to a central mast on the ship. The boom would be launched and swung through ninety degrees to the boat so it acted like a keep net which they would use to scoop the whale. It would probably mean some additional manoeuvring since the whale could still change course in the sea at any moment. Leon and Lee got ready to launch. It was important that they got the timing right otherwise the nets in the water would create some unwanted drag should they have to give chase.

Moments later an excited Joseph joined Brad in the wheelhouse. Panting from running up the stairs he grabbed the binoculars again to look at the whales once more.

Brad said, "You probably don't need them anymore." Again he pointed towards the front of the ship, only this time to the starboard side. The pod had passed by the bow of Annie 2 and they were on course as was hoped. "Look, they have just nudged around our bow to the starboard side and are making their way nicely alongside us. With a bit of smart manoeuvring we can probably scoop one."

Joseph, clearly ecstatic about the prospect of the catch couldn't contain himself. "Wow, this is incredible. OK, well I am as ready as I can ever be. Just bring those babies home Brad, bring those babies home."

Brad looked on bemused at Joseph's change in behaviour. No longer the demure English manner, it had instantly flipped to something that resembled more of a deliriously excited big game fisherman with something large like a Marlin on his line. Grinning widely at Joseph's change of character, Brad swung Annie 2 around to line up the angle of the net and gave the order to launch.

The net rolled off the boom and dropped into the rolling sea. Standing in the wheelhouse, Joseph watched every single detail as the path of the ship and the pod came closer and closer together. There was clearly a lot of skill in this sort of manoeuvre as Brad fought to keep control of the ship as she rolled with the waves. The sea state was still throwing waves at around a height of 2.5 metres at this stage but she was a stable boat for her size and handled well. It was obvious to Joseph that Brad was well experienced in this type of thing and as desperate as he was for nothing to go wrong he could only put all of his faith in Brad. There was nothing else he could do – well, apart from pray and that probably wouldn't help much.

Leon signalled up to Brad that the net was successfully in the water. Tag lines at the sides had been fixed to the main mast; everything was in place. It was just now a matter of time. The next two or three minutes would be crucial. The point of impact seemed to last an eternity.

All of a sudden a scream of jubilation went up as one of the baby Bowhead whales crashed into the net. The free line was pulled and the net closed in to prevent the catch from escaping. Once this was made safe the boom would retract enough and the net raised sufficiently to give Joseph the access that he needed. It looked like this was the bit where Joseph was going to get wet, but he didn't care one bit. Here it was: the greatest moment that he had experienced so far in this journey. He didn't want to blow it now. He simply needed to think and act like the fine doctor and surgeon that he was, even though he had never been this close to a Bowhead whale before. He needed to take his time and get the samples and do it right. He braced himself for the big moment and made his way out onto the deck. He stepped into a harness that was laid out for him and once it was fully strapped onto him it was then clipped to a permanent fixing on the deck.

The young Bowhead whale seemed reasonably calm as it was gently ushered towards the side of the ship in the net. This one was just about twenty feet long and since they are approximately seventeen feet long when born this one was still quite young. Joseph watched on completely dazzled by the magnitude of this amazing creature. Closer and closer the boom brought the whale to the side of the ship and eventually lifted it gently so that most of it sat out of the water. Joseph needed to be able to reach his target zone through the thick blubber between the back and flippers of the whale. The main problem for him was that the blubber can be up to twenty inches thick which could take a while to penetrate while not upsetting the whale in the process.

The whale lay motionless but seemingly comfortable, caught and restrained in the scoop net. Close up it appeared bigger and more beautiful than Joseph had ever imagined. It was huge and thankfully seemed to be quite relaxed. It was easily three times longer and four or five times bigger than Joseph overall. It had a large bow-shaped head that took up about 40% of its body length. It seemed disproportionate in size but clearly this would allow the whale to penetrate ice should it need to surface and breathe. Such power was hard to visualise. Its eyes were very small and not fully open so it was difficult for Joseph to strike up any relationship with it, no matter how brief. This was the way for most surgeons before operating commenced. Its lips were noticeably huge which would help with the gathering of all of that plankton that they lived on.

Joseph slowly ran his hand over the wet, cold back of the whale for a moment. The cold and scaly skin felt alien under the palm of his hand. He felt privileged, humbled and also overwhelmed to be in the presence of this great creature. He took his time with the visual examination as he needed to convince himself that it wasn't stressed in any way before he would commit to taking the samples. When taking the samples he needed to be quick and concise with what he had to do; the last thing he wanted was to cause any more suffering to this fantastic and noble creature than was absolutely necessary. Leon and Lee continued to pour pumped sea water from a hose on the parts of the whale that were not naturally covered. This would help to keep it calm.

So, once Joseph had convinced himself that it was good to go ahead, he placed the long syringe into the body of the whale approximately ten inches above its short narrow flipper. Gently he eased the plunger down, very carefully at about five millimetres at a time and watched as the blood sample entered the cylinder and filled it up. He had it, he actually had it.

Chapter 11

Joseph's laboratory was a smallish, purpose built room at the back of his house. It had been designed for one reason only and since it didn't need to cater for a fuller range of experiments it was exactly what it needed to be – and no more. To get to it you first had to go through the existing utility area at the back of the kitchen and then through a door which led in to a converted boot room. All the doors were very secure with digitised locks. The only person other than Joseph who knew the codes to the locks on these two doors was Blake – that was if he could remember them, which was doubtful. There were no direct outside doors or windows to the laboratory. This was due to security reasons. Access was strictly from the front of the house only. OK so it wasn't the biggest lab in the world but after all one doesn't need much space for what was basically a molecular biology based task, does one? From the outside there was absolutely no hint of the room being used as a 'home lab' for scientific purpose which was just the way that Joseph wanted it. Albeit a bit on the small side, the lab was perfectly able to function. The former boot room had been converted by Joseph in order to improve the much needed sterile environment which was key to his work. The way that the door mechanism worked also kept others out while he was working since it had internal locks that could only be operated by the occupier. It was, then, perfect for keeping Blake at bay when he needed to.

The lab itself was fitted with a sealed floor, walls and work surfaces so that everything could be easily cleaned. Sanitisation was the key to everything that Joseph did. The rubberised flooring had been fitted to extend to some eight inches above the edges of the floor. It also sealed the floor totally to each of the four corners of the room. This would help with containing any spills and of course when cleaning down. The walls were tiled white and rose to three quarters of the way up the wall towards the ceiling. The remaining part of the exposed wall from the top of the tiles to the ceiling was painted white. Spotlights were mounted on each of the four walls for maximum brightness when needed. The ceiling itself, also painted white, was home to three independent banks of twelve neatly recessed spotlights that could be adjusted as necessary to provide the much needed precise lighting levels in the lab. A lighting control panel was mounted on the wall by the door entrance so as to allow Joseph to set the lighting as he entered and exited the room. Joseph was able to control every one of the thirty six lights in the ceiling from this panel. The work surfaces were grey granite; it was cleverly lipped ever so slightly around the edge to help prevent anything rolling off onto the floor. The only hint of a connection to the humdrum day to day urban life beyond those walls was a small air exchanger unit fitted to the wall. The unit was especially designed and fitted with tiny filters to make sure that any smells and particles were captured and dealt with before they reached the outside world. It was all important stuff if the lab was to go undetected from any neighbours or passing nosy-parkers. This was after all a very normal neighbourhood but Joseph couldn't afford to take the risk. Joseph had applied a high level of detail to the lab but also the internal facilities needed to be able to provide the results he needed. There was a long list of what you and I may call tools, but to Joseph they were his instruments. This instrument collection consisted of things like analysers, pipettes, micro tubes, micro plates, various calibration units, storage racks and of course a refrigerator for storage of samples and bloods, solutions and serums. There was also the much needed sanitation and safety protection equipment. The Institute for Molecular Medicine would have been proud of the set up there; Blake was, at least. Every time he visited he was more than convinced that the invested money was being well spent.

Blake hadn't visited the laboratory for some months now, since well before Joseph went to Alaska and he was keen to see the place fully fitted out and ready to go. He had planned to go there with Joseph at the weekend.

Blake arrived about 2.30 pm on the Saturday afternoon. It was quiet outside and the sun was shining. He was greeted by Joseph who was sitting in the garden at the back of the house.

Joseph heard his knocks at the door. He shouted out over the Yew tree hedging, "Hey Blake, I'm round the back, come on round."

Blake made his way across the gravel path to the gate that accessed the garden. "Joseph, great to see you again." A firm handshake was always the order of the day between them as they were very close friends by now.

Joseph replied, "Good to see you too. How have you been?"

"You sound just like my doctor."

"Well I suppose I am in a way. So how have you been?"

"Good, just busy as usual, haven't been doing anything nearly as exciting as you, bobbing around in the ocean off Alaska, messing about with whales and stuff."

"Well it was pretty exciting I can tell you, in fact one of the most surreal experiences for me so far. The Bowhead whale really was a magnificent creature."

"You have plenty of photographs, I hope."

"Of course. I plan to bore you to tears with those pretty soon."

"And so how is the lab coming along?"

"It's done, all finished. In fact yesterday was my last day of cleaning, sterilising, setting out and getting organised in there. You want to take a look?"

"Damn right I do, I can't wait!"

"Come on then, let's go."

Both of them made their way across the nicely trimmed lawn towards the back door. Joseph said, "We have to go in through the house – did it that way as you can't be too careful."

"Can I see the samples as well?"

Joseph replied, "Maybe, if you are a good boy!"

Joseph led and Blake followed through the house to the kitchen, then the utility room and boot room, passing through all of the double locked doors before reaching the laboratory.

Blake was impressed by the level of security; the attention to detail was so high that he wondered if Joseph's talent wasn't wasted and he should probably be consulting with the local constabulary for crime prevention. The final door opened and Joseph ran his right hand index finger over the sensor pad on the light switch. The light would always initially turn on to the last level of brightness until adjusted.

"Oh nice lights, Joseph. I never had you down as much of a gadget man – you surprise me."

"Then you are easily surprised, my friend. Put these shoe covers on and come here and look at the real toys."

With a wave of the arm he introduced Blake to the small mass of equipment that was neatly placed around the shelves and work surfaces.

Blake was taken aback by the professionalism that it oozed. "How on earth do you get hold of all of this stuff?"

"It's not so difficult when you are a doctor and working in a hospital, Blake. There is always a rep from one medical supplier or another that is keen to do some business. At the NHS we are bombarded with enquiries all of the time for this sort of stuff."

"I suppose you are right; never really thought about it I suppose." Blake pointed. "So what's that gadget over there, Joseph? It looks important."

"It is a haematology product which helps in transfusions, blood grouping controls and cell counting reagents, which is important if we are to be successful in blending the samples we have."

Blake was just like a child in a toy shop. He pointed at another object that he had no knowledge of. "And this one over here?"

Joseph replied patiently, "It's a centrifuge."

"Oh yes, of course it is. I see now."

Joseph could sense that it would be better for both of them if the question and answer session was not dragged out. "So you like it all then, Blake?"

"Yes I do, actually. It certainly looks the part. So when will you start work in here proper, you know on the blending thing?"

"I really want to start straight away."

"Oh really, so soon? I thought we might have a glass of wine or something to celebrate achieving the first milestone of our epic journey. I brought a bottle of Malbec, a real nice one."

"Better not open that just yet Blake. Why don't you keep it for the next time we are together – I really want to crack on. And believe me, Blake, there will be plenty of opportunities for us to have that drink."

"OK, I understand. So will it be OK for me to hang around and watch the master at work? I promise that I won't get in your way."

"Look Blake, while it's always lovely to have you around I really do need to get on and to do that I simply need better than normal concentration, and room to work. Can you please understand that?"

"Of course – room to work."

Peering over the top of his glasses Joseph spoke authoritatively to Blake, "Would you mind closing the door on your way out Blake, thanks. I could be here a while."

"OK, fair enough, I am being a bit of a nuisance. But I am just pleased to see you, Joseph. It's all so exciting for you. I am just left on the sidelines babysitting a bottle of Malbec. But I know my place."

Blake turned to leave. "But if you need anything, well, give me a call, OK?"

"I will and thank you." Feeling a little guilty for bullying Blake to the door, Joseph added, "I will walk with you and make sure the doors lock properly."

Blake was already heading for the door. He answered, "Oh no problem, I will make sure they are closed, thanks Joseph. See you in a day or so I suppose; I hope it goes well."

Joseph shouted out, "Thanks Blake, a debrief yeah, over that bottle of Malbec that you are saving." He paused, he was worried that he may have hurt Blake's feelings which was the last thing he wanted to do, so he turned again and craning his neck in Blake's direction shouted a bit louder this time, "Don't forget, Tuesday evening for the debrief."

The door clunked shut. Blake had waved goodbye; he was on the street and heading for the car. The bright sunlight tore at his eyes. He squinted as it dazzled him; they watered a little. His emotions were mixed. He felt elated and excited to think that Joseph could be on the final chapter of creating a method for continuous gene rejuvenation. He just wished that he could have been more involved but deep down he knew Joseph was right and respected that. Transhumanisation: could it work, could it become real? Who the hell would have believed it if you tried to tell them? It was too bizarre to comprehend. But then so was flying to the moon once upon a time. You just have to believe; remember the power is in the believer. What was probably more unbelievable was that Joseph was on the fringe of achieving just that in his converted outhouse, such a tiny room as well, with no windows – gosh.

Joseph got to work. He had sterilized everything very thoroughly. This was a familiar routine for him. Standard stuff. It was as though he was preparing for another heart operation.

Joseph was particularly concerned that the samples could have become infected. This was always his biggest worry. He had taken all the precautions standard to transportation and storage of the cells but sometimes for no obvious reason things can go wrong. He didn't want to spend time blending cells that stood no or little chance of success due to being infected. He set out to test each one initially for infection and any autoimmune illness, either of which would not be good for the success of transhumanisation. The ultimate care would be necessary.

The success of this whole exercise would depend upon Joseph ultimately being able to produce a genetic hybrid from the samples from the HeLa and Bowhead whale cells. The hybrid is the result of combining the two different samples to produce the desired gene. In terms of a genetic hybrid a good illustration would be a mule. This is where a combination of two variant genes from two variant parents, in this case a horse and a donkey, results in the development of an offspring; the mating will produce a mule. This genetic pudding if you will is common enough in some animals and even in plants. Joseph's philosophy was that if they could achieve perfect blending results from differing types of grapes to produce excellent wines then why not between human cells and those of a whale. After all, both are mammals but just from different vines that's all.

It was essential to the results that neither sample would dominate the other. The blend had to go smoothly. It had to be as easy as if they were falling in love, like being effortlessly zipped together. It may take a bit of time to get the right result as once the cells had been introduced to each other they then had to take the necessary time to get to know each other before going on to make vows to stay together and maybe get married. So in a way it needed to be a sort of genetic match made in heaven. Once both samples were mixed they needed to demonstrate that they wanted to be together. The hope was that they would form a blend that would prove genetic probability. This was the key to success and it was ultimately what Joseph was looking for. While

Joseph's studies gave him indication and high expectation that these cells may be compatible he didn't know for sure and so since the process with these samples had never knowingly been tried a positive result would be based on pure luck, at best a miracle. So fingers crossed.

Once satisfied that the samples were free of contaminants Joseph carefully mixed a small amount from each in the test bottle and placed them on to the orbital shaker for gentle mixing. All in all Joseph carried out this process for eight sets of blended samples. Once they were all completed the eight sets of new blended cells were transferred into a cradle for storage in the refrigerator. Once in the refrigerator the samples would effectively be incubated and their contents examined regularly over the next few days for signs of compatibility and growth. Joseph would be able to see this from changes in the blood layer.

While the whole process from mixing the samples to incubation took only about one and a half hours, Joseph was totally exhausted by the end of it. The stoic mental concentration needed to ensure that every delicate step was carried out with immaculate precision and careful notes made during the process was extremely tiring. Joseph kissed the last of the samples before placing it in the cradle and closing the door to the refrigerator.

The next thing to do was to babysit. He had decided that he wouldn't leave the house for the next few days or indeed have anybody over. His full focus and concentration was still needed. Even simple things had been prepared for such as having a standby power system available should he lose his mains supply. The kitchen was well stocked with food and drink; his hologramatic entertainment system was fully loaded with his favourite movies.

Like a very proud young dad with his newborn baby
Joseph was tempted to look into the crib every five seconds
but he knew that it wouldn't change anything. Like the
mating system for the panda bears he knew that he had to
give those cells time to get to know each other and then work
things out for themselves.

It was actually day three before Joseph decided now
may be a good time to take a peep at his new creation and
examine the results of his hard work and Blake's cash. He
made his way to the lab, carefully opening and securing the
doors behind him as he went. Once in the lab he opened the
door to the refrigerator and simply stared in at the cradle
inside which housed the tubes. Eventually Joseph worked up
enough courage to reach into the refrigerator and take hold
of the cradle. He very carefully manoeuvered it so as not to
hit anything which may shake up the contents and brought it
out sitting it gently down on the worktop. It was such a relief
that this part of the task went without any incident. He gently
removed one of the tubes and held it up to the light to see if
it was showing any signs of separation or maybe even growth.
Joseph was relieved to see that things looked promising; at
least the mix looked as though it was coagulating nicely.

Joseph had prepared two glass examination plates
that would go under the microscope for full examination.
The adrenaline in him was pumping hard as he carefully
unscrewed the cap from the tube and using a capillary
pipette he removed a small sample. The tiniest of drops from
the sample were placed on the plates which were put under
the microscope. Now the real moment of truth; Joseph placed
his eye over the microscope lens. He wasn't disappointed. The

cell pattern had changed and was showing signs of bonding. It looked like a marriage could definitely be on the cards between the HeLa and the Bowhead whale cells. Joseph was ecstatic; in his wildest dreams he couldn't believe that things looked like they would go so well. The dream he had had for so long, the holy grail of genetics was possibly on the cusp of being realised.

Would life ever be the same? Quite probably not. Joseph felt as though he was now standing on the edge of forever. As feelings go he didn't expect that it would ever get any better than this.

He now needed to put everything carefully back into the refrigerator where it had come from, hopefully with the same level of success that he had when he removed it. Once the tested tubes had their lids back on and were safely stored in the cradle he opened the door to the refrigerator and put them on the shelf. He took an age to close the door. It was agonizing for him, slowly pushing it shut with his right hand and at the same time pushing his face closer and closer into the ever reducing gap. At one point he actually had his nose almost jammed between the door and the side wall of the fridge, distorting it so as to make it difficult for him to breathe properly. He simply didn't want to let go. It was a bit like parting from a loved one at an airport; that continual forever standing on tip-toes that you do to get above everybody else, the stretching of the arm and frantic waving, never wanting to lose eye contact until the absolute last moment when he or she is nothing more than a small dot in the distance, and then in a flash they are nothing more than a blur of a dot in the quicksand of the crowd, until finally swallowed up.

It was about another millimetre to go and Joseph knew that the light would go out. Even when the door was finally closed Joseph still did not take his face away from the shiny surface, as though he was suspended in a trance like state, offering himself as some sort of spiritual gargoyle guarding over this very precious creation. Eventually his knees started to hurt so he had to get up, straighten himself and dust down his trousers. He turned towards the sink and with his elbow flicked the arm of the tap and ran some warm water. His hands were cupped and filled with antiseptic soap as he put them under the tap and rubbed them together to clean himself from any trace of blood or possible bacteria from the tests he had just carried out.

While things looked really promising Joseph decided that the programme needed a few more days so that the cells could get to know each other just a little bit more, just to be really certain.

He had carefully prepared some labels for each of the storage tubes which he would put on the next time that he examined them in the lab. The labels had been printed in big letters 'TRANSHUMANISATION CELLS' so that anybody who saw them could easily identify their contents, even Blake (who by self-admission can sometimes find it difficult to tell the difference between a rough red wine and a blood sample).

The next two days couldn't go fast enough for Joseph. He ate, he slept, he pondered, he reminisced and twiddled his thumbs, he did everything apart from relax. He drove himself crazy with anticipation, tossing and turning at night with nothing other than the whole process dominating his every thought and breath. He was so totally consumed; every moment was being devoured by this exercise.

Although Joseph was tempted to peep at the samples even sooner, he somehow found the inner strength to resist; he had been ardent in desire but now, all of a sudden, the non-stop arm wrestling and tormenting between his head and his heart was finally over.

It was the morning of day three. Joseph decided that he needed to start the day in a calm manner and so he set the table and prepared to boil two eggs for breakfast. With granary toast and oodles of butter this was one of his favourites.

Once the eggs were boiled he stood them up almost sacrificially in the egg cups and using a sharp knife he swiftly sliced the tops off. First the brown one and then the lighter one. As the yolk from both ran towards the sides of the egg cups he quickly added a pinch of salt to each. The next thing to do was to cut the toast into soldiers so that he could dip them into the runny egg yolks. All of this ceremonious protocol was meant to get him into a relaxed frame of mind which in theory should be beneficial for his wellbeing, helping him with the tricky task that he had ahead of him.

Joseph was really the consummate professional when it came to cooking; he was extremely skilled and accomplished at what he did but while the eggs and the toast tasted superb they didn't do much more than that.

He made his way to the homemade theatre, scrubbed up, donned his theatre blues and proceeded to sterilize the glass micro-plates. This time he planned to examine the contents of all eight of the storage tubes and so cleaned enough micro-plates to do this. Again everything had to be handled with care and precision. His notepad and his labels were ready;

everything was set to go. Eventually he was ready to open the door to the refrigerator. He carefully removed the cradle holding the storage tubes and sat them down on the worktop.

The next three hours passed almost without notice for Joseph as he industriously went about examining one sample after another. To his relief seven out of the eight mixed samples appeared to be successful with the cells blending seamlessly together. He put the one failure case down to potential contamination somewhere along the line but couldn't be exactly sure from where or what. Although this was sad news the very good news was that this gave him just under one hundred millilitres of useable plasma.

A sense of relief, excitement, pure joy and elevation swept over him. Of course until the mix was introduced to the human body there would be no real proof that it would work but for now everything was looking very, very positive indeed.

So it was nearly all over now; all he had to do was wash his hands, hang up his white coat in unceremonious fashion for the last time, switch out the lights, lock the door and leave. The next step was to meet up with Blake and discuss who would be the guinea pig for the Transhumanisation process; why not both of them?

Chapter 12

It was Sunday morning and when Joseph wasn't working one of his passions was cycling. He liked nothing better than the feel of the Lycra shorts and a headwind on his hairy knees. Living in Essex gave Joseph lots of opportunities for good cycling. The countryside in the north of the county was gloriously picturesque. It was packed to the rafters with small, unblemished Georgian villages and market towns which were originally born out of the wealth generated during the 16th and 17th centuries. A period of extensive and profitable wool and linen trading years which had carved out a never-ending legacy of charm and unique living which is not to be found in newer areas.

Joseph had decided that fresh air and exercise would be his reward for the success of the hybrid gene construction and so set about preparing his racer touring bicycle. For a moment he had thought about calling Blake to see what he was up to and of course give him the good news but decided not to. After being cooped up for the last few days he felt he just wanted to be on his own for a bit. As usual he would leave the keys in a place where only those special in his life would know how to find them. He thought for a moment though just as he was mounting the bike that it would be an unbelievable irony that the discovery of the 'Holy Grail' of medical science could possibly lie undetected should anything ever happen to him and the keys to the theatre were never to be found.

On most Sundays Joseph could be seen out on his bike. Whizzing around country lanes and creating havoc with the bog standard British Sunday motorist who was unfamiliar with the local custom of giving way to folk who are brightly dressed in sporty cycling attire. It was nearing the back end of lunchtime at about 2.00 pm. Joseph had been out for a while and had decided that he would stop off for a drink at the local pub in Boxford on his way back. It would be a kind of a personal mini celebration for himself. He figured he had earned that much. He had worked out that the best route would be to go through Hadleigh and head towards Stoke-by-Nayland and then cut through to Langham as the last leg of his ride back before heading home. In many ways this Sunday was little different from the others except that what happened next would deeply sadden all those that knew and loved him.

Joseph approached the picturesque little high street in Hadleigh. It was a well serviced, busy street with a number of shops, restaurants, banks and pubs so as usual a few cars lined both sides of the main road. Smallish, happy, family crowds sat outside the pubs and cafes of this pleasant and friendly market town taking drink and some form of lunch. Most shops were closed as was still a tradition on a Sunday in this part of the world. Joseph was still on a bit of a high, singing the potential of his huge success to the world as he cycled. He looked and made some sort of visual contact with every face that he saw, whispering words to each of them as he cycled past, "would you like to live forever" or "come to tea, I have something in my fridge that can give you life everlasting". It was silly but he was having some innocent fun and why not – he had worked very hard for a long time. He pictured the same groups of faces some 200 years or so on, still sitting in the sun and taking a drink on the Sunday lunchtime. It was an unbelievable vision. He grinned and pedalled harder.

Hadleigh, like a lot of other towns, does have some modern conveniences, like cash machines for example, or ATMs as they are more formally referred to. There were a couple of these cash dispensing devices dotted along the High Street, for the convenience of shoppers.

Simon Davidson was also going out for lunch on that Sunday with his new girlfriend. The area was awash with numerous gastro pubs and on such a glorious day this was his big chance to try and impress this new sexy Boho styled beauty in his life. He just needed to get some cash to do it with and had pulled in to the side of the road just in front of the building society ATM.

Simon, his car parked at the side of the road. "OK babe, just need some cash. I won't be a moment." She blew him a kiss. Without a single glance to his wing or rearview mirror he flung open the door of his sporty hatchback. Joseph didn't stand a chance.

It was Monday and Blake had phoned Joseph at home and on his mobile phone to see how things were progressing. He wanted to make sure that they were still on to meet up on the Tuesday evening as agreed. He hadn't heard from his friend since he'd left his house the previous weekend; it was a long time without contact between them. He just wanted some reassurance that things were OK; that would have been sufficient for now. But Joseph wasn't answering any of his phones. Blake left messages and figured that he must still be pre-occupied with his work and since they were meeting up shortly anyway he decided that he would leave him alone to get on with things. It wasn't like him though to ignore Blake for such a long time. Joseph was also due to be at work that Monday morning but he didn't make it.

It was Tuesday August 17th. The main story in the local newspaper read – "A cyclist was killed by a single 'hard punch' to the face on a Hadleigh street in the early afternoon on Sunday. Dr Joseph Singh, 49, who was knocked from his bicycle by a motorist, never regained consciousness after hitting his head as he fell to the ground in The High Street, Hadleigh, at around 2.00 pm on Sunday afternoon. Simon Davidson, aged 31, of Farm Lane, Billdeston has been arrested by the police. The police have said that the incident looks like an accident but they are investigating. Dr Joseph Singh had been struck with such force that his jaw was broken. The blow to the jaw pole-axed him to the ground and it was when falling to the ground as a result of this he sustained the injury which caused his death. Dr Joseph Singh, a keen rugby player who worked at St Thomas' hospital in London, was rushed by air ambulance to Addenbrooke's Hospital, but never regained consciousness and died early the following day".

It was now late afternoon on Tuesday. The news of Joseph's death was spreading quickly throughout St Thomas' Hospital. His colleagues and friends were in disbelief and stunned at the loss of a brilliant doctor and a good friend. He would be seriously missed, both professionally and personally.

It was 8.30 pm that Tuesday evening. It had been another warm, sunny day. A bit muggy possibly but Blake was still looking forward to that celebratory drink and meeting again with his friend Joseph so that they could jointly plan the next 'what to do steps' with the gene rejuvenation cells that Joseph had developed. Exciting times lay ahead for both of them.

Blake was in the Kings Head pub as usual. He had arranged to meet Joseph there at 8.30 pm but as of yet he had not heard from him which was a bit unusual. Anyway, his switched-on Blackberry lay on the table beside the two glasses of Malbec that were poured and ready. Blake checked his wristwatch probably every two minutes in anticipation of Joseph walking through the door any moment now. After about fifteen minutes Blake had still resisted calling him; anyway it was always possible that Joseph could be working late, some sort of emergency operation, you never know. If needed Joseph could call, text or mail to say he would be running late, which wasn't the norm, but anyway things do sometimes deviate from the best made plans, don't they?

Out of the blue Blake's Blackberry burst into life, lights and buzzing noises orchestrated in unison to tell him somebody was trying to get in touch. Blake looked at the screen expecting to see confirmation that it was Joseph calling but it wasn't. For some reason the message was coming in from somebody else, the Blackberry confirmed that it wasn't Joseph. It was a good colleague and friend of Joseph's who also worked at the hospital, Nurse Jackson. Blake picked it up and answered. "Hi Nurse Jackson how are you? I don't get calls from you very often. I guess you are calling on Joseph's behalf to tell me that he can't get away. What is it this time, an emergency heart operation again or something more exciting and less routine like he has to pick up his laundry from the launderette – or something else just as daring?"

"If only it could be that simple, Blake. If only. I don't know how to tell you this but Joseph died yesterday in hospital at Addenbrooke's; he was involved in a cycling accident on Sunday and never recovered. It's all very tragic and we are all totally shocked here, the team are stunned."

Blake was taken aback. He blubbered, "How, what, I can't believe this. God no, not Joseph, it can't be true, I mean I am meeting him for a drink here, in the pub, tonight."

"I am really sorry Blake, but it's true."

"Oh my god no, no, not Joseph, how did it happen?"

"It was Sunday early afternoon, he was in a place called Hadleigh, cycling. The police have told us that a guy opened a car door as Joseph approached and he hit his head on the car door." She paused, "he was knocked off his bike, he hit the road with such force, didn't stand much of a chance. He was unconscious immediately and never recovered. I really am sorry to bring bad news, Blake; I know you two were very close. We are all in such a state of shock here."

Blake was lost. He was in quicksand again and watching his world disappear. He felt his mouth dry up, his lips and tongue seemed to instantly swell. He struggled to get his words out. He could feel water trickle down the small of his back as he broke out into an instant cold sweat. Wet and cold like a stone his shirt had become soaked as he sat holding his Blackberry close to his ear.

"So what, what are you telling me, Joseph is, is dead? Oh my god, no this just can't be true. We have a meeting here, in the pub for Christ sake." Blake stared at the glass of Malbec that had become their tipple of choice when celebrating or not; he stared at the ceiling, then at the bar, and the crowd watching the cricket on the television, anything but stare at reality, real life.

Blake continued, "Where, Hadleigh? How, god this is terrible, terrible, are you sure, are you sure." There was nothing but silence from the other end of the line – Nurse Jackson had done all she could.

The silence was eventually punctured by Nurse Jackson; she spoke softly and sadly, "Blake, he didn't show for work yesterday. We were worried. He was expected back in after his extended break; it's not like him to just not turn up like that. In the end it was Addenbrooke's that advised us. They found some ID on him and then of course realised who he was from medical records. He was such a good man. Now he has gone. We are all very, very upset. I am sorry but I can't tell you more Blake. I know you two were very good friends."

Blake didn't like the reality of the situation. The dark place he was in slowly begun to turn darker and darker as he progressively started to accept that this wasn't a sick joke but in fact it was all very, very real. The harsh reality of what had happened was now rapidly sinking in. The next thing he was going to do was just cry.

In the background to this emotional trauma that he was suffering was Nurse Jackson; she was still listening. "Blake, Blake are you there?"

Blake wiped some tears from his face. "Eh yup, I am here, sorry Jackson, sorry I mean Nurse Jackson, I just need a minute."

"Look Blake, I have to go now but can I ask a small favour?"

"Eh yes, sure, ask away."

"Is there any way that you can get in touch with people who knew him such as the family, in due course obviously it doesn't have to be immediately, and could you find out about the funeral arrangements, who is making them and then please let me know. I can tell the others at the hospital. All we can do now is pray and pay our last respects. Please let us know as soon as you find out anything."

"Eh yes of course, of course. I will try and track down his family as soon as I can."

Blake could not take in what he had just been told. His head was spinning and he was in deep shock, nothing made sense. Stunned, he replied for a second time, "Yes, yes of course, sorry, yup sure. God, I can't believe this. I just can't take it all in. Thanks for calling." He hung up long after Nurse Jackson had hung up.

Finding out about family and funeral arrangements would be easier said than done as, other than a distant girlfriend who lived in London somewhere, Blake didn't know of Joseph having any real relatives in the UK that he spoke of, other than his sister. Surely the hospital would have records, the police even? Hopefully Joseph would have had a will or instructions with a solicitor in the event that something like this happened. Then there was the police, surely they would already have tracked down a next of kin, wouldn't they? Blake didn't know what to do next, he was in a daze and couldn't think straight at all. He asked himself 'where to start', not that starting even mattered at all, now that Joseph was gone. He sat and gazed in a hypnotic state at the bottle of Malbec still left on the table. Half of it was meant for his friend and only half of it was for him.

Blake felt totally helpless and he wasn't sure if he could do anything at all. He was still far too numb. He decided to sit down for a moment, he needed to take it all in, compose himself and figure things out. He must spend some time simply thinking of his good friend and not worry about anything else at all. It was only a couple of seconds into this thought process that he became overwhelmed by grief and sobbed quietly, racked in pain from the loss of this great man and friend. The numerous images of Joseph rotated round and round in his mind playing constantly as a backdrop to the humdrum from the pub, flickering away to remind him of every minute that he knew and shared with Joseph. He owed Joseph so much; he had repaid him so little. The man who had saved his life and became his best friend was gone. He had been taken in some crazy stupid accident; OK so he was doing one of the things he loved the most, but it didn't help, it didn't make it any better or easier to understand or accept.

He could only tell himself repeatedly 'it just doesn't make sense, it's not right, there just can't be a God, no justice, it just wasn't fair'.

Blake's eyes had glazed over by now, he looked towards the crowd that had gathered in the moments that all of this had been going on; he knew that nobody in that pub right now was hurting as much as he was. He stared up towards the ceiling of the pub again, his emotional grief turning slowly to anger and bitterness. Gradually with the anger in his eyes he drilled beyond the pub to the heavens far, far away. He stared and stared, continuously demanding answers as justification for what had happened. No answer was given, not even a simple one, nothing to help him understand. Blake wanted some kind of signal that Joseph was going to be taken proper care of in his death. His cries were neither acknowledged nor replied to. As time wore on the strain and tension in his mind eased and he sank further, deep into his chair, oblivious to all that surrounded him.

He desperately wanted to talk to his friend. He muttered words uneasily from his constantly dry lips. "Oh Joseph, Joseph, what has happened." Another tear fell, this time into the Malbec that sat patiently waiting for its never coming recipient, then another and another. Blake's life was about to be turned upside down. They were once a team, but not anymore.

After drinking only his half of the bottle of wine he stood and put on his jacket, picked up the bottle and made his way on autopilot to the bar. On his approach he caught the attention of the barman; he nodded his head but didn't have the stomach for the usual good time gesture. He gripped the bottle tightly by the neck with his left hand; traces of wine which had slipped as he poured it stained his palm. Reaching out with the half full bottle towards the barman he placed it gently on the shiny dark oak surface of the bar. This was the exact same place where Joseph had stood on many an occasion to order such a bottle of wine. Looking into the eyes of the barman Blake muttered, "My friend didn't make it in tonight; this is his half."

No other words were said. The barman could tell from Blake's blotchy red face and very painful looking eyes that he was clearly and deeply upset about something. "OK sir, thanks very much and I will look after it for him."

"Aye, you do that, you do that."

It turned out that Joseph had an aunt and a couple of cousins who lived in North London. With information from the police and some help from friends at the Hospital they were able to organise the funeral. It was a simple but very sad affair but fortunately all over quite quickly. Joseph was a Christian and so was buried at St Mary's Church at Langham in Essex. It was one of his favourite places to walk and cycle around. St Mary's sits on the brow of the Stour Valley on the Essex-Suffolk border, looking towards the beautiful, undulating and serine Suffolk countryside. Blake was resolute that if Joseph could have chosen a place to rest this would surely have been it. He was confident that Joseph would be very happy there. Since there were no other close relatives to advise otherwise Blake arranged everything to be there. It was the right choice for his friend; it was his friend's choice.

After the funeral a small gathering was held at the village pub. It wasn't a fancy affair. The landlord had laid on some food and drink which everyone enjoyed. There was little to say between the family and Blake since they knew nothing about each other. His work colleagues were very respectful but at the same time busy and so only stayed a short while before heading back to London. It wasn't long before the family did the same thing, leaving Blake on his own. He knew now that a gaping hole had appeared at his side and it would be an extremely difficult one to refill.

The day after the funeral Blake realised that he had better get around to Joseph's house and rescue the samples as well as any reports or notes before it was too late. It wasn't going to be particularly nice but nonetheless it was what Joseph would have wanted. It was imperative that nothing was either thrown away in error or taken by somebody.

Blake checked his watch: it was 6.30 am, he couldn't sleep. He decided that there was no time like the present and so he threw on some old warm clothes and jumped into his car and drove over to Joseph's house. It was the first time he had been back there since the day that he was with Joseph when he said he would start work in the lab. It was, in fact, almost two weeks ago but so much had happened in the meantime and Blake had kind of lost track.

Blake was at Joseph's house within fifteen minutes of

getting in the car. He pulled up by the side of the road and turned off the engine. At first he was more comfortable just sitting outside the house, not really wanting to do much more as it was all so very painful for him. He sat quietly listening to the birds twittering in the trees and hedgerows while building up his strength for the next move.

After some ten minutes of hesitation Blake opened the car door and got out. He closed it respectfully behind him. The serene tranquillity of the surroundings washed over him like a bucket of feathers. It was as though when Joseph died a lot of other things died at the same time. Would he ever be able to adjust and get over this? He didn't think so but knew he needed to try for Joseph's sake.

There was a coal bunker to the side of the house. It was dark and grubby inside and according to Joseph a great place to put house keys in when you wanted to leave a spare set lying around. Blake walked up to the house and could see the coal bunker on his approach.

It saddened Blake when he lifted the lid and found the keys hanging there. In a small plastic bag tied to the keys was a note from Joseph. It was as though Joseph realised that something would happen. He had diligently prepared for it, but then he prepared for everything with the same amount of attention to detail, leaving no stone unturned. Blake opened the plastic bag, unfolded the note inside and read it. He couldn't help but shed another very large tear from the corner of his eye.

It read 'firstly to whoever finds these keys, apologies that I am not here to greet you, secondly well done (as it's a bit dark in there) but please put them back when you have finished with them. Blake, if it's you, when you get in please don't

174

drink all of the wine – you can have some but save at least half a bottle for me. Take note I am your doctor after all'.

Blake's mind ran back to that Tuesday evening in the pub when he had been told of Joseph's death; he thought that it was quite poignant that he had saved half a bottle for him too. Was it some kind of code from the afterlife?

Blake unlocked the door and entered the house. He didn't want to spend a moment longer in the house than was necessary. His plans were to get across the sitting room, kitchen and utility room and out to the lab as quickly as he could. As much as he loved Joseph he wasn't ready for any trip down memory lane quite yet. Blake got to the door of the lab and put the code into the digital locking device. He could hear the clunking of the locking device mechanism and the door unlocked for him.

He went straight to the refrigerator and opened the door. Inside there were a number of bottles of this and cases of that but right there on the second shelf was a cradle containing seven storage tubes which looked like they had blood in them, each one marked up in big letters 'TRANSHUMANISATION CELLS'.

Careful not to drop or spill anything Blake nervously eased the cradle from the refrigerator and set it down on the worktop. He closed the door and turned to stare at the tubes. Was this it, was this the stuff that Joseph had been working relentlessly for? He was as sure as he could be.

Blake started to panic as he realised that the cradle would need to be transported properly so as not to damage anything and he didn't have anything suitable. He was angry with himself that he wasn't prepared. Why couldn't he be like Joseph and think of everything? He wondered how he was going to do this. Then he thought that maybe Joseph would have had a cooler bag or box in the house somewhere.

He needed to find one and quick, probably pack it with ice to keep the temperature nice and cool. Also he figured he should get some tea towels so that he could wrap everything to stop anything getting bashed around during the journey. He ran back into the kitchen and opened some of Joseph's cupboards until he found what he needed. The fridge in the kitchen was still running and Blake opened the freezer section and reached for a bag of ice inside.

So cooler bag, tea towels and ice: he had all he needed. He wrapped the tea towels around the outside of the cradle. Once this was done he filled the inside with some ice, as much as he could fit in. He then placed the wrapped cradle into the cooler box and then packed in the rest of the ice. It was a snug fit which he was pleased about. Once this was done he looked around for anything else that looked as though it may be of use, things like needles, syringes, sterile swabs etc. He gathered as much together as he could and put it all into a plastic carrier bag.

Joseph's reports and any test results were most likely to be in the study safe which was across from the sitting room; he would go there on the way out and pick up as much as he could. He knew the code to the safe.

During all of this Blake was trying hard not to engage in any sentimental thought process. He missed his friend terribly but he figured now wasn't the time to go to pieces; right now he needed some Dunkirk spirit. He was on a mission to get what was important out of there before it was seized by anybody else and probably destroyed and possibly lost forever. It was about twenty minutes after entering the house that Blake was ready to leave. He dared himself one last look over his shoulder as he reached the threshold of the front door. He glanced in momentarily and all he could see was a lifeless and soulless space. His gaze lasted no more than five seconds after which he turned off the lights, closed and locked the door and left. He didn't replace the key in the coal bunker but kept it in his pocket, figuring that Joseph's relatives or anybody else for that matter would call back again when they had run out of ideas.

All that was left was to gently put the cool box and other things in the boot of the car. As Blake approached the car he triggered the boot lock and the boot popped open offering oodles of space for him. He put everything down to one side and moved his sports bag and some emergency tools closer to the cool box to act as packing for the ride home. He pressed the lock button in the boot and it automatically closed itself and locked. Blake headed home.

It was about a week after this that Blake had started to receive calls from Joseph's relatives about the house. There must have been some contact with a solicitor or something in the meantime as they were asking about a will and did Blake know anything about the possibility of some keys. Blake was still in shock and wasn't much help. He was still in mourning but these guys hadn't wasted much time in getting started with their claim to a small piece of him – well his estate anyway. Initially Blake wasn't particularly interested in helping them. He figured that they probably wouldn't come up from London on some sort of a wild mission to find the house and try to get into it; no, it would have to be organised and proper – they were probably too lazy or too busy to do otherwise. So he figured that he had some time on his side.

The phone calls came about once every two weeks in the beginning. After six weeks or so later the frequency changed to one each week and the comments on the other end of the line became more demanding. Solicitors' names were mentioned. Blake would have preferred not to have been mixed up in all of this. After all Joseph was his friend, he knew nothing about family stuff and quite frankly didn't want to get involved. It was just because he lived nearby and was good friends with Joseph that he was being dragged into it.

In the beginning Blake wasn't too bothered about all of this; he followed the logic that if they were entitled to anything then so be it, they would get it eventually. He figured that ultimately he would probably need to help them anyway as painful as it would be.

Chapter 13

It is now 2027 and both Blake and Marci were each getting on with their lives. Marci was now fifty six years old and had settled nicely back at home in Wellington and, as planned, she was now running her own Yoga and Pilates school as well as spending time with her family – especially Lucy of course whom she loved and adored; they were all very close. Blake who was now sixty three did what Blake did which was work. After Joseph's death he just fell to pieces and working was his way of trying to get over it. The busy days helped him.

The years had continued to roll on almost unnoticeably in fact and for a period of about seven years both Marci and Blake had hardly mailed each other. The communication between them, while still nice, had become a bit all too infrequent and the conversation felt like it was beginning to dry up a little. It was usually around Christmas time and the New Year when they would get in touch and wish each other well.

Running her own Yoga and Pilates workshops had helped Marci to stay slim and trim; she was always fit and continued to look fabulous. Wellington was a fun place to live; there were always lots of interesting things going on there which brought people from far and wide to the city. Regular events were always being organised by the local community which attracted many to its sometimes steep streets. Marci liked to visit the artist's quarter of Wellington up in the area of Te Aro whenever she could. It gave her the chance to relax in a different environment from what she was used to as part of her daily routine. Usually the order of the day was to hang out after lunch for a while in a couple of her favourite trendy cafes that lined the craggy and hilly streets there. It was always a great and exciting atmosphere created by the bohemian and free style of mainly the artists and gallery owners that lived in the area. So with so many people continually milling around it wasn't long before Marci met Dylan. Dylan was from Auckland; he was of similar age to Marci. He was a tallish man with wavy hair and a weathered complexion which suggested that he may like sailing or lots of outdoor sporty stuff. He was casually dressed in linen trousers and cotton shirt when he entered the coffee shop.

He ordered his Lapsang Souchong tea at the counter.

The waitress said, "I'll bring it over to you sir. Where are you sitting?"

Dylan looked around the crowded room and there wasn't really much choice. He pointed towards a table near the window where an attractive lady sat all on her own and told the waitress, "I'll sit over there by the window, thanks."

Dylan made his way to the table where Marci was sitting. Oblivious to the pending disruption Marci, as elegant as ever was taking her time browsing through her glossy interior magazine as she simply sipped her macchiato.

Dylan approached and asked, "Excuse me, is this seat free?"

Marci looked up from her read and replied, "Yes of course, sorry, I will move some of my rubbish for you." She tidied the table a little.

"Thank you, no need to worry too much – I don't take up a lot of space."

Dylan pulled the chair out and sat down.

The waitress arrived with his tea. "One Lapsang Souchong tea," putting it down on the table. "There you go."

Dylan looked up. "Thanks very much."

Marci couldn't help noticing the strong smoked flavours of the tea wafting from the pot.

Marci said, "Hope you don't mind me asking but the tea smells interesting – what is it?"

"It's Lapsang Souchong, you either love it or hate it I suppose, me – I love it."

"So what is it again, Lapsang Souchong tea?"

"Yes, it's a black tea from China, I think and please don't quote me on this the Fujian province of China, wherever that is. My Chinese geography isn't that brilliant I am afraid. I drink it quite a bit; it has a fantastic smoky aroma and lovely woody flavours. I love it, one of my favourites."

Marci smiled, "I'm Marci by the way", and she offered her hand across the table.

Dylan promptly reciprocated and did the same. "Dylan, pleased to meet you."

"So you seem to know a bit about this tea Dylan or is it tea in general?"

"Well if I am honest it's tea in general. Sounds nerdy I know. This one though I particularly like but I am keen on a range of tea especially Japanese tea."

"Sounds fascinating. With all of this interest in tea you must have an English background."

"No, not at all, I am a Kiwi, from a small place called Davenport, just outside Auckland. I just love tea, no other reason. I suppose we all have our hang-ups." Dylan smiled politely. "And you, I see you are drinking a coffee."

"Yes it's my poison I am afraid, it's a macchiato. I discovered them in London of all places, some years ago."

"Well would you like another?" Dylan raised his eyebrows

teasingly.

Marci wasn't sure where this was going to go but she felt a little warm rush of blood to the head. If her instincts were good then she should accept the offer – after all he was an attractive man and seemed quite friendly.

Dylan broke the short silence, "Unless you have to be somewhere else that is."

"OK that would be nice, since I don't have to be somewhere else that is."

"I'll just go and order it then." Dylan stood and made his way to the counter; he ordered the macchiato and returned to his seat.

"So Dylan, tell me: Wellington is a long way from Auckland – are you just passing through or are you here for anything in particular?"

"Well actually I am just passing through. I am on my way to get the ferry to Picton and then I plan to drive down to Franz Josef and do some climbing."

"That sounds fun."

"Well fingers crossed, it should be. I have some friends that are already there and I plan to meet them and stay for a few days. And you?"

"Oh that's easy, I live here in Wellington, not so far from here and I just like the area and pop in now and then to chill out."

And so the conversation continued. Both showed an interest in one another and they were starting to enjoy sharing each other's company over casual stories and day to day humdrum. The playful and sometimes flirtatious sparring between them continued for about two hours or so with one macchiato leading to another. It was clear that neither one of them wanted to be the first to leave when Dylan asked Marci, "So what now, the place is nearly closing, we have sat here chatting away for most of the afternoon – do you fancy doing anything later, that's if you are free I mean?"

Marci wasn't surprised by the invitation but didn't want to seem too keen and immediately accept. She hoped her response wasn't too obvious. "Can I check a couple of things first and call you in an hour or so?"

"OK if that's good for you, here is my number." He removed a pen from his pocket and scribbled the number down on a paper napkin and handed it to Marci. "I am staying at the Museum hotel down by the harbour there."

"Oh I know the one, they have a great collection of weird and wonderful artefacts, some paintings, sculptures and stuff like that."

"Yes, that's right, the rooms are very nice, it's all quite contemporary."

"I've never stayed there, only had dinner once. Well OK, I will give you a buzz in about an hour or so, thanks."

Marci stood up from the table and again shook hands with Dylan before she left the coffee shop. Her car was parked a couple of streets away in Epuni Street; it was as close as she could get without being inside the shoppers' parking zone.

The journey back to the car went in a flash as she skipped up the road being high on the octane of meeting somebody new, not noticing anybody or anything as she went. 'Finally' she thought as she approached the car, 'have I just met somebody whom I like who may just be able to help me get over and forget all about Blake?' It was a tall ask but worth a try.

Marci made the call as was expected just before the agreed hour. She was so excited she couldn't hang on for the full sixty minutes and caved in after three quarters of an hour. Dylan, quietly confident, expected as much. He was delighted she had called as it was the first time in his three night stay in Wellington that he would have some company in the evening.

"Hi Dylan, it's Marci. Dinner tonight is fine by me if you can still make it."

Dylan replied, "Yes of course Marci, that's brilliant. Do you want to meet here at the hotel, in the reception of course, not in my room; I wasn't suggesting anything inappropriate?"

Dylan could imagine that Marci might blush even if ever so slightly at the other end of the phone with the mere suggestion of such a thing. Marcy, ignoring his jokey maybe even suggestive remarks, replied demurely, "Yes Dylan that's fine. What time works for you?"

"Let's say seven thirty."

"OK see you then."

Dylan and Marci had a lovely evening out together. Dylan explained why he was doing the trip to Franz Josef and how he came to love tea. Marci talked endlessly about Yoga, Pilates and her experiences in India. They both indulged one another like playful kittens hitting it off so well. There was something very serendipitous about the whole affair that intrigued and excited Marci; it was the perfect way to meet somebody. Dylan was so hungry to wrap his arms around Marci that for a moment he thought about staying in Wellington for a few more days – but regretfully his long-standing arrangements were cast in stone.

Dylan was begrudgingly by now leaving the next day for

Picton, his ferry sailing was around mid-morning. They had both had such a good time that they agreed to keep in touch and meet up again when Dylan was crossing back from Picton to Wellington, which was in about ten days' time, all being well. Secretly neither of them could wait for the time to come when they would be back together. It appeared as though Marci wasn't missing Blake quite so much anymore – or so she thought.

As for Blake, well the loss of his friend hurt him really badly. Their dreams of unveiling the 'holy grail' of medical science to the world were clearly not going to happen now. While Blake still had the samples he didn't really know what to do with them; the enthusiasm seemed to have died along with his friend Joseph. He wasn't sure if it was what Joseph would have wanted though; he was confused; it was difficult for him, so he just chose to ignore it.

Work was busy and showing little sign of easing up; they had picked up more contracts and increased the number of employees but it meant very little to Blake. Even though he didn't own so much of the business as he once did it didn't stop him from dedicating most of his day time and some of his night time hours to his job. He hadn't taken much holiday in a while, just a few long weekends here and there; there was one time when he had a complete week off and went to Split in Croatia but that was the longest break in some seven years now so it didn't really count. While he was there he conveniently latched onto a group of walkers who went out to various historical sites and places of interest and followed them around. He made a couple of friends within the group but it wasn't anything that was going to change his life dramatically. He was at this terrible time in his life grateful

185

for the company.

While some things in his life seemed to work out, others didn't for some reason. He wasn't quite sure why he seemed to lose everything that became dear to him. Work was going well but that didn't matter so much; his marriage had been very important to him once and now that had evaporated; his dear friend Joseph had died, being taken when things looked to be going so well; and then there was Marci.

Blake remembered that when he met Marci she just fast tracked to the top of the pile, he lost sleep and went off his food just thinking about her, she lit up his life and now she was gone, well just about gone. He hadn't heard from her in a long time anyway. She probably had a new boyfriend by now and didn't like to tell him. So the big question was 'what was a guy like Blake supposed to do now?'. He had no idea. The problem he had was that he was a complete and utter romantic, so if it was meant to happen then it would and subsequently if it wasn't then it wouldn't.

Well that was one way of looking at it. Or you could take the other which was that it wasn't happening because he wasn't making enough of an effort. He blamed himself for not telling Marci how he really felt all those years ago. Deep down he knew that he loved her and perhaps in his subconscious he wouldn't let himself be with another person – could that be what it was? He wasn't sure. He often wondered, though, what Marci would look like now that she was a little bit older. He hadn't seen her now for several years. Would she still have her fantastic, crazy, curly hair that was stronger and wilder than a windy Wellington winter afternoon, and her figure which was always trim, the way she smiled, could these things all be the same? He reminisced, yes of course they were. He missed her now more than ever. It had all been far too long and he realised that he had been stupid in the way that he handled it all. If only he had been more positive when he had the chance.

Lucy was born in August 2014 and today, August 2027, was her birthday: she was thirteen. She had grown into a proper little lady; she was bright and adventurous as well as being adored by her Aunt Marci. She liked all of the things that girls of her age loved which, summing up, was anything sweet or noisy. The family had all been to dinner at a local pizza restaurant on Willis Street to celebrate her birthday. Afterwards Lucy wanted a special sleepover at Aunt Marci's as the icing on the cake.

Lucy asked, "Aunt Marci, can I stay at your house tonight please, as it's my birthday?"

Marci was easy with the request from Lucy but it really was not her decision ultimately. "If it's OK with your mum and dad Lucy then it's OK with me, sure."

Marci and Lucy frequently spent a lot of time together at Marci's house. Since Marci had moved from Warren Street to just off Oriental Parade, not far from the Botanical Gardens, Lucy had virtually been living at Marci's there. The house was bigger than before and Lucy had her own room there, with wardrobes and drawers where she could put and keep her own things. It really was a home from home for her with the added bonus of some fantastic views over the bay.

Marci's sister Bronwyn and her husband Gordon agreed that it would be fine for Lucy to stay over as long as it was OK with Marci and also only if Marci was able to take Lucy to school the next day. Marci agreed with everything; she would enjoy the company, especially since her very short romance with Dylan hadn't worked out; the company would be nice.

At thirteen Lucy was a curious young lady, she never stopped asking questions and wanted to know everything that there was to know. She found the whole aspect of her Aunt Marci being on her own quite curious. It was a totally different concept from that of her mum and dad. She had just naturally assumed that it was always the same way for everybody, and now she had discovered that it wasn't. It bothered her as to why Aunt Marci didn't have anybody. She couldn't figure it out. Aunt Marci was very pretty, good fun to be with and could bake seriously good cookies, so what was the problem?

Once they got back to the house Lucy took a long warm soak in the bath and then changed into her PJs and dressing gown. She liked to chill out and laze around the house like this. Aunt Marci was still taking her shower by the time that Lucy had finished and dressed and so she was on her own for a short time. Lucy decided to take a bit of an excursion around the house, enjoying the time on her own to snoop at Aunt Marci's things. She had though seen most of the bits and pieces that made home more like home for Aunt Marci but there was a new photo on the hall table that caught her eye as she wandered around and killed time before Aunt Marci finished her shower and got dressed. She approached the hall table and picked up the framed photograph for a closer look. Lucy didn't recognise the person so she turned it around to see if anything was written on the back of it. The name Blake was written in black ink. Lucy figured that Aunt Marci must have put it away once upon a time just to unpack it again when she moved home. She thought that it was a funny thing to do but she must have had her reasons.

At that moment Marci came in to the sitting room, adjusting the buttons on her blouse as she approached. Lucy stood staring at the photo of the man called Blake which was positioned at the far end of the table under the lamp.

Marci wondered what was going on. "Hi Lucy, are you OK? How was your bath honey?"

"Great thanks, I feel much better now."

"Good, come on over and I will read to you for a while if you like or we can stream a movie."

"Yup, OK, there in a minute."

"So what has got your attention then, do you like my new lamp?"

"I didn't realise that it was new, yes it's nice." Lucy walked over to sit next to Marci.

Lucy sat down and asked curiously, "Aunt Marci, who is the man in the photo?" pointing over to the table. "It says Blake on the back of it; who is he? I haven't seen him before."

Marci, not really expecting the question and struggling for an immediate and sensible answer, replied, "Which photo, Lucy?"

"The one on the end of the hall table silly, near your new lamp, remember?"

Marci turned her head to look. "Oh him, well his name is Blake."

"Yes I know, it is written on the back of the frame. But who is he? Why do you have a photo of him in your new house when I didn't see a photo of him in your old house?"

"Well it's a long story honey and one that you wouldn't fully understand, but in short he is a lovely guy that I met a long time ago when I was working in London. He is a real friend who has been there for me ever since then."

"So where is he now?"

"Oh he is still working in London I expect, we haven't seen each other for a very long time now, years and years." She shrugged, "More's the pity. I have some e-mails from him now and again, in fact I heard from him just recently. Well I say recently, must have been ten or so weeks ago. He is doing fine, or so he says. It's about time he came here to see me. I miss him Lucy, really I do."

"Why, because he's your friend, or is he your best friend?"

"Well that, but also because he has been a bit more than that. You know how you are always asking me where *my* Gordon is, well that's him – or if I had a Gordon it would be him. It's a bit different between your mummy and daddy but if I had a Gordon – which I don't – then it would be him. Sorry if that's hard to follow."

"A bit but I think I understand."

Marci took Lucy by the hand and they both made their way to the sofa and sat down.

"OK honey, enough of that. What should we do?"

Lucy stretched her legs across Marci's lap and prepared to deliver more searching questions. "Do you love him? Mummy and Daddy love each other."

"That's a bit heavy for a thirteen year old, but since you ask, we never really talked about it."

"Did he love you?"

"Now come on Lucy, let's drop the story now; there isn't any more that I can really tell you. Let's stream a movie and have some popcorn or something."

Lucy was not deterred and dug in even though she sensed that Aunt Marci was a bit uncomfortable with the questions. "Only if you tell me, Aunt Marci."

"Oh Lucy you can be such a nuisance at times."

Lucy grinned and nuzzled her head into her aunt's shoulder in readiness for the full blown story.

"Well the truth is at the time of meeting and falling for Blake I didn't want to know. The timing wasn't good and I had other things to do and figured that I didn't need the distraction. I went off to India to do my Yoga and Pilates thing and basically left Blake behind. Sure he was very upset; I was upset but it didn't stop me from following a dream of mine. Sometimes you just have to pay the price and he was my price I suppose. Anyway that was a long time ago."

"If you love him why haven't you tried to tell him since then?"

"Well it isn't that easy. I don't know how he really feels about me now. He could have another woman in his life for all I know; it's just not how grown-ups do these things."

"So you haven't tried."

"No I haven't. Sometimes I wished I had but that was then, and maybe now I am simply too scared to ask."

"But why not try again?"

"I thought about it a few times but I don't think there is anything there now Lucy. I look for clues in his e-mails sometimes so that I can sort of judge how he may be feeling but nothing is obvious. I just don't want to push it. I am too old for that now."

"No you are not. Look at that man you met a while back called Dylan – he liked you, didn't he?"

"Well he seemed to at first but that was before his wife kind of complicated things."

"His wife, gee, I had no idea."

"No nor did I, but anyway he wasn't right for me either."

191

"Don't say that, you make it sound as though there is a list of people that aren't right for you. I bet Blake still loves you, it's just not obvious to him because of how you are."

Marci sighed gently. "If only it were that simple Lucy, well we will probably never know, so come on you, let's stream the movie and have some fun."

Lucy stared for a moment longer at Blake's photo. She wanted to help Aunt Marci but at the same time didn't want to upset her by prodding too much or getting in the way. If only there was a way that she might be able to get these two people speaking to each other again. It would be difficult. May be she could just try e-mailing Blake, introduce herself and simply ask him straight out how he feels about her, and tell him how Aunt Marci feels about him. You never know – it may just work.

Lucy eventually fell asleep while the movie was on and Marci gently lifted her and put her to bed.

It was nearing the end of October 2027 when Marci woke one morning not feeling too well. At first she thought it may be simply because she was getting a little bit older and so she didn't take too much notice. What was certain was that it was a sensation that she had not experienced before. She was feeling a bit heady and also a bit wobbly on her feet. Her vision was a bit swimmy which again was a new thing for her. She tried not to let it distract her at first and went about fixing breakfast as usual. To take her mind off things she would spend a little time smartening up the house but things were not getting better, it didn't help a jot and after half an hour or so she decided that she would probably be better off just sitting on the porch for a bit – after all it was a nice spring day. This meant that her usual daily walk along to the Greta

Point Café would have to be put on hold.

As she passed along the hallway she picked up a blanket and a cushion that were always kept near the door for times when she ventured outside. The framed photo of Blake caught her eye for some reason as she passed the hall table. A shiver momentarily shot down her spine as they exchanged the briefest of glances; acknowledging this she reached out and gently touched the frame. She felt that she just needed to be as close to him as she could at that moment in time, didn't know why really and the photo was actually all she had. She picked up the framed photo, took it outside with her and sat down in her favourite woven seat on the porch and tried to relax. The music played softly from the sound system which she had flicked on as she exited the house. It certainly helped with the meditation; after all she was a professional when it came to chilling out and within a short space of time her eyes were closed and the rhythm of her heart was drifting along in some deep sort of cruise control mode. She must have been sitting there for almost an hour when her passing neighbour and friend Izzy called to the house to pick up a bunch of old glossy magazines that Marci had promised she would get ready for recycling.

Izzy approached the porch and could see Marci clearly in the seat as she walked up the path. She noticed that Marci didn't appear to be moving. At first she thought that Marci was most probably just asleep but as she got nearer to her it was more obvious that her body seemed to be too limp, just a bit too relaxed. It was evident to Izzy that Marci didn't look, and probably wasn't very well. Her face was pale and while her breathing was regular it was very faint. She seemed to be in a very deep sleep or possibly even fainted, but Izzy was no medical expert. Rather than try and wake her to ask if she felt OK, Izzy decided that the best thing to do was just call first an ambulance and then Marci's doctor.

Within ten minutes the ambulance had arrived. The paramedics quickly rushed towards the front porch to examine Marci. Even during the initial examination she still didn't wake up. Once the examination was over one of the paramedics ran back to the ambulance to get a stretcher. From the initial diagnosis it was thought that maybe Marci had had some sort of a stroke but it wasn't 100% certain. The symptoms baffled the paramedics slightly and since Marci wasn't well enough to explain how she was feeling then they wouldn't take any chances. Still clasping the framed photo she was lifted and manoeuvred gently onto the stretcher and put into the waiting ambulance.

Within moments the stretcher was secured in the ambulance, the doors were closed and they set off to Wellington General Hospital.

Chapter 14

Sadly the results of the scans taken when Marci was admitted to the hospital showed that she was cancer-stricken, with aggressive tumours on her brain. It was a certainty to all of the doctors that Marci would probably be dead within a few days, maybe one or two weeks at the most. The aggressiveness of the tumours had taken all of the specialists by surprise and indeed they and her family were in great shock as a result.

Marci was on the ward and had been there for six hours or so before she slowly opened her eyes only to realise that she was lying in a bed that wasn't hers and in some strange place that wasn't anything like home. She was hooked up to an army of various machines and monitors that were definitely not there earlier in the day. Her sister Bronwyn had been keeping an observational vigil by her bedside since she was admitted. Marci slightly turned her head and she could see Bronwyn in the chair beside her but she was confused, dazed and tired and couldn't summon the strength needed to call out her name even though she tried. Bronwyn on the other hand had not taken her eyes off Marci for the last hour and as soon as she saw her sister flinch with some signs of life she immediately raised the alarm with the nursing staff.

Bronwyn reached and clasped Marci's hand. "How are you feeling honey? Don't worry, you are in good hands here."

Marci managed to produce enough energy to whisper, "Where am I and what's going on?"

Bronwyn leant forward to be close to her sister and spoke softly in her ear. "You're in hospital Marci, you had a funny turn and the ambulance brought you here. Now rest up and don't worry about anything." Bronwyn wiped a small tear from her face as Marci relaxed again and buried her head back into the pillow. Bronwyn looked on with saddened eyes; somebody was going to have to give Marci the very bad news of the diagnosis at some point and it wasn't going to be easy.

Nurse O'Docherty who had just come on shift appeared by her bedside. "So she stirred, did she? Let's take a look at her." She made her way closer to the monitors that reported on Marci's heart rate and pulse. "She is still very weak but the fact that she came around even momentarily is good news. We will keep our fingers crossed for the next four to five hours as they are critical."

"Is it OK if I take a break now? I am going to get a coffee and speak to my daughter Lucy, give her some good news that her aunt did wake up at least."

"Sure, you go ahead and we will keep an eye on her. I will let you know immediately if anything changes."

Bronwyn eased the pressure and relaxed her grip on Marci's hand and got up from the chair. She picked up her bag, leaned over and kissed Marci on the forehead. She was both saddened and devastated at the thought of potentially losing her sister. It was too unbearable to even think about. Reluctantly she left her sister to the team of doctors and nurses on the ward as she made her way to the break out area where she could call Lucy and Gordon.

Bronwyn spoke to the auto dial on her hand phone instructing it to dial home. It was a really nice evening and Lucy was sitting in the garden. When she heard the phone ring she ran immediately to answer it.

"Hello Mum, is that you?"

"Hello Lucy, yup it's me, how are you?"

"I am OK, but how is Aunt Marci, how is she doing?"

"Well Lucy the good news is that she awoke for a very short period earlier this evening, so we should just pray that she can do more of that first."

"But beyond that, is she going to pull through? What is wrong with her, Mum?"

"It's hard to say, Lucy." A lump appeared in Bronwyn's throat, choking her slightly as she spoke. "Lucy, I can't mask this situation at all. Your Aunt Marci is very, very ill and may not wake up again; we don't know." She wanted to slam the handset down on the floor and scream into space; it was probably the hardest thing she had ever had to say to anybody. It was very upsetting for her. Bronwyn was greeted by total silence from the other end of the phone.

Lucy wanted to cry, scream the house down but for some reason she couldn't. Once she had worked out and accepted that the grieving wouldn't really help she figured the best way forward was to do something positive, something that may produce some more energy – who knows it could help. The only thing she could think of was to get in touch with Blake; he needed to know. How was that going to help exactly? Well she wasn't sure but it just felt like the right thing to do and wild horses were not going to stop her. She raced up the stairs to her room, logged on and wrote her mail to Blake.

Marci was placed in the intensive care section of the Cancer Ward at Wellington General Hospital where she could be monitored carefully. Most of the time Marci was oblivious to her surroundings or where she was. Later that same evening Marci did come round for a short time but wasn't really strong enough to have any useful conversation at all.

It wasn't until mid-morning on the next day that Marci was in a position where she may understand and was told the terrible and distressing news of her diagnosis. Marci couldn't believe the news and the thought that she may only have a few days to live seemed to be the cruelest of tricks that could have been played on her. She was only 56 years old and just wasn't ready to die. At the same time, from the way she was feeling, Marci couldn't see how she could fight it all either as time was not on her side and the tumours were such aggressive opponents. All she could do was pray for some form of divine intervention.

After the fourth day Marci was put onto the ward for terminal cancer patients. It wasn't a happy place to be. To make things more comfortable for the patients the visiting hours were totally relaxed; people could come and go day or night. Marci had regular visitors every day from her close friends, her sister and of course Lucy.

Marci of course had no idea that Lucy had made contact with Blake. Lucy had no idea if Blake had even received the e-mail since she had no reply from him, let alone that he might just turn up and do something, which was what she had basically asked of him. What Lucy had, though, was faith, and in copious amounts. It was now day five and Bronwyn and Lucy were visiting Marci in the hospital. Marci was more awake than ever before.

"Aunt Marci, are you feeling different today, a bit better maybe?"

Marci, physically straining to talk, replied, '"Lucy darling, while every day is a blessing for me because I get to see you, I am very weak sweetheart and am not really going to get better. Mummy probably broke that bad news to you already."

Lucy who was full of faith and forever the optimist seemed unfazed or daunted in any way by it; she burst out, "Yes, and that's what they are all saying but I don't believe them; there has to be something that can be done. It just can't end like this." Small water droplets hung affectionately to the side of Lucy's soft facial skin. As they ran down towards her neckline the collar of her pretty white blouse became damp from soaking up the tears.

"Lucy, come on, be brave for me, try not to cry. It will only start me off and I have to save all of my strength for tomorrow."

Sniffling into her hand carefully and slightly embarrassed so that Marci didn't see, Lucy asked, "Why? What is happening tomorrow?"

"Well you are coming back to see me, aren't you? For me, Lucy, it's just one day at a time. Every day is a blessing because I get to see you Lucy."

"Can't you even try to look two days ahead Aunt Marci, just two days; for me? And then when you have mastered that maybe three and then four days and so on?"

Marci was instantly cheered by her niece's enthusiasm and grit when faced with such a mammoth task as this. "Wouldn't that be a great thing Lucy, it really would. Come and give your favourite aunty a big hug."

"Aunt Marci, you have to promise me that you will at least try because I have a surprise for you."

"Oh really? That sounds nice. I could do with a surprise right now." Marci mustered a bit of grin from the side of her frail mouth.

"I mean it Aunt Marci."

As Marci very quickly fell into another one of her deep sleeps clearly exhausted from all of this chit-chat Lucy clasped her hands together in a vice-like grip and once again muttered, "I mean it Aunt Marci, I really mean it, I am not playing." Lucy had visited the bank of faith for another withdrawal and frankly she didn't care if she was to go overdrawn by a country mile, it was worth it.

While Marci didn't show signs of deteriorating quite as fast as the specialists first thought she would, she wasn't getting any better. She just seemed to hang on to life by her mere fingertips; as frail as they were this stubborn woman wasn't letting go as yet. The days came and went and well basically it was nothing short of miraculous that she was still alive, albeit still very, very sick and for all intents and purposes terminally ill.

Some days she could not even muster enough strength to wake up and acknowledge her visitors. But for some inexplicable reason it seemed as though Marci's stubbornness and refusal to totally let go to the cancer was insatiable; she simply would not let it have the last word. Despite continued prognoses of little hope from the doctors and specialists that were treating Marci she still continued to defy them and the deadly illness.

It was a dry autumn evening in October. Blake was at home getting ready to entertain some friends. He was in his new home, well his latest home anyway. It was a neat timber framed thatched cottage with views across chocolate box countryside right on the edge of the village of Nayland in Suffolk. Blake wanted to show it off and at the same time show off his culinary skills. His friends had been moaning that he never cooks for them anymore (that's what friends were for) since he had in fact moved into the house some eight months previous. But Blake had work to do on his new home and he, being the patient type and a bit of a perfectionist, wanted to wait until all the work was finished and the place was looking its best plus some, before inviting anybody round. He felt sure the girls would understand once they saw the place; well he hoped they would. The men on the other hand tended to be more interested in the beer in the fridge rather than the decorations and fabrics.

Not only that but he wanted to spoil his friends gastronomically and he had only recently been able to get onto and complete the Thai cookery course at the Mistley Rose Hotel. It was a favourite with local foodies and wannabe chefs. He loved Thai food and it was an ambition of his for some time now to do the course and cook a fantastic Thai dinner for his friends. The trouble was that the course was only run once every five months. It was important that it was a success and that he was able to deliver the goods. He also knew that it was not just about the cooking. He had to be able to find the best fresh ingredients which may not be so straightforward in the area. As nice as the local shops were it wasn't exactly like living in Chinatown. So it was all a new experience and it took time and dedication, something he was sure that his friends, being good friends of course, would naturally appreciate come the big night.

The house was looking good; the cushions on the sofa nicely plumped, flowers in the vase and the soulful classic sounds of Labi Siffre meandered randomly from the in-built Bose sound system. Everything was ready. Blake was pleased. His guests were due in about an hour and since dinner was also cooking nicely he decided that since he hadn't checked his personal mail for a few days he would do it before the fun really got started. He went to the study, sat at the computer and switched it on. The 'you have mail' message popped up onto the screen. He saw that it was from Marci. He hadn't heard from her in quite a while. He was both excited and apprehensive about opening it as he didn't reply properly to her the last time – why should he anyway, it was all about some bloke called Dylan? He opened it.

The mail that he thought was from Marci turned out not to be from her at all; it read: "Dear Blake, my name is Lucy. I am writing because my Aunt Marci is sick. They took her to hospital yesterday. She is not just my aunt but also my best friend. I know all about you because she has told me everything. You need to know that Aunt Marci has cancer and is in a very bad way. She is very sick and I know you wanted to save her once and couldn't, can you please, please, please save her this time? She is in Wellington General Hospital. When she tells me stories about her life she always says that she loved you but never told you. Please help us urgently, lots of love Lucy".

Blake just reeled back in shock. This was really so unexpected and out of the blue, something he just hadn't counted on. Yes he had to admit that he had always loved Marci; likewise he had never told her. He had no idea how she felt about him. Now she needed him more than ever. He couldn't think straight for a moment. He had to take this chance, the chance he should have taken all of those years ago. Could he use Joseph's Transhumanisation gene? He wasn't sure. Would it save her life? He didn't know as it had never been trialled but at the end of the day it was what it had been produced for. He decided that ultimately he had no choice and just had to try it otherwise he was faced with losing Marci forever and he was certain that he didn't want that to happen.

He needed to think quickly, 'right flights direct to Wellington, 'em things to take, how do I pack the gene stuff, needles I will need needles....' His head was being bombarded with random and out loud instructions which was impacting on his ability to concentrate properly. He needed to sit down and take stock and get himself organised.

Within thirty minutes he had himself booked on a flight out of London for Wellington, leaving the very next morning at 7.30. It was on the latest airbus A 500-500 which would take fifteen hours direct. The next thing he had to do was call his guests and tell them that dinner was off, although when he checked the clock in the study he could see that it was all a bit late for that since they would be well on their way by now. He just hoped that it would all sort itself out; he had to pack.

Blake had been upstairs in the bedroom for only ten minutes when the doorbell rang for the first time. He dropped what he was doing and ran downstairs to answer it. It was Bill and Romney. Blake invited them in and they embraced each other as old friends do but Romney could see that Blake was a bit upset.

"Blake, what's up? I hope you are not upset because we are here."

Bill stood looking all concerned but said nothing.

Blake didn't know quite what to say. "Look, let's go and sit down. I can explain everything."

Bill and Romney followed Blake though to the lounge and sat down.

Bill said, "Are you OK Blake? You are making us a bit nervous now."

"No, it's nothing for you to worry about, I am fine, really. I am afraid though what has happened has thrown tonight totally into a spin."

Blake sat down in the armchair.

Romney said, "OK then, what's up? We are here to help if needed. Tell us what's going on."

"Well an old friend of mine, Marci, I may have mentioned her, she lives in Wellington, New Zealand, well she is in intensive care and has just days to live. I simply have to go and see her."

He couldn't contain his tears much longer and as embarrassing as it was in front of his friends he felt he needed to cry. Romney reacted first, "Hey Blake, come on now, don't worry. So, what are you going to do?" She put her arm around his shoulder, "What do you want us to do – anything?"

Blake tried to compose himself a little; in between the sniffling he said, "Well you could take care of dinner for me while I pack my bags."

Romney said, "Pack your bags? So you're going to Wellington then?"

Blake turned to look her in the eye. "Yes Romney, I am, tomorrow morning."

"OK, then, we will take you to the airport, OK?"

"But Romney it's…"

Blake wasn't allowed to finish. Romney interrupted, "Nonsense, we are taking you, simple as that and don't worry about anything tonight. You just get on with what you have to do, we will take care of the others when they arrive and will sort out dinner. Actually, I doubt you really want us around so once they have said hello and we have sorted them out with a Gin and Tonic those that want to can go to the pub for something to eat. So that's that sorted."

Blake was speechless. Romney seemed to have it all organised and it was such a relief.

Romney added, "So Blake, that's it, you take your time getting ready and don't worry about a thing."

Blake and Romney hugged, no words were needed between friends as good as these. He went back upstairs and threw a few more things in his bag leaving enough space for the medical kit and sample tubes. He could hear people arriving and being surprised at being greeted by Bill and Romney rather than himself, followed by the muffled sounds of small talk as people meandered round the downstairs part of the house to nose at what had occupied him for the last few months.

Eventually after checking and double checking that he had everything he was ready to go down and meet everybody. After a brief explanation about Marci and the initial awkwardness of it all was out of the way things eased very quickly and everybody was very supportive. They were all a bit disappointed of course as the evening was supposed to be different but at the same time understood totally. They wished Blake a safe trip to Wellington and offered love and support to his friend Marci.

It was dark the next morning when Blake left the house. He was nervous and anxious and a bit of him felt sick to the stomach. All he had to go on was an e-mail from a young girl whom he had heard a little about, but that was it. He told himself that if at the end of all of this Marci didn't or couldn't love him then it wouldn't matter; as long as he could save her life, this was, by far, the most important thing. For this he was totally reliant upon his dear friend Joseph; he prayed that everything would work out fine.

Some fifteen hours after leaving London Blake touched down in Wellington. He had not checked in any luggage and so got through the crowd at immigration and customs as quickly as he could and made his way outside to the taxi rank where he jumped into a cab.

Time wasn't really on Marci's side, Blake knew that. As anxious as he was to get to Marci he needed to wait until the day was virtually over. As painful as the wait would be he knew that the success of the reason for him being there would depend on fewer people being around to potentially stop him from doing what he needed to do.

He made his way to the hotel, checked in, dropped his bag and tried to rest as best he could for a few hours. He had prearranged for a taxi to pick him up that evening.

Chapter 15

Blake frantically pulled the taxi door open and before the driver even had a chance to ask his destination Blake had given him clear instructions for the General Hospital, "as soon as you can mate – thanks". He clutched his small holdall tightly into his lap as he sat on the back seat.

The taxi swiftly pulled out from the front of the hotel and sped off towards the centre of the city and on to Newtown. For the most part the journey was a blur. Blake took nothing in from the world outside as the taxi journey passed. No sights, no sounds, no ambience or feeling for this city. His gaze, set on repeat, flickered back and forth triangularly between his bag, the back of the taxi driver's head and the speedometer of the white sedan that he was sitting in. His instinct was to block out any potential distraction from what he was about to do. He didn't want his nerves to get the better of him. He had little idea as to the length of the ride from the hotel to the hospital. As the taxi neared the hospital and pulled up onto Riddiford Street he glanced up from the window and couldn't help noticing a small shop of sorts opposite the hospital called 'The Hope Centre'. It was run by the Salvation Army; aptly named he thought.

There was an ambulance just pulling out onto the road. Blake asked the taxi driver to drive slowly past and just pull over for a moment where the ambulance had just come from so that he could decide what to do next. There was a drop off place at the top of the ramp just out front of the main door but Blake decided against it, wanting to take some night air as well as make sure that he had his head on straight. He chose the underground car park as it offered him some much needed shelter from prying eyes so that he could pay the taxi driver and organise himself properly.

The taxi cautiously turned towards the visitor car park to the side of the hospital and then underneath as requested. Blake realised that he might only get a single chance at this and he couldn't afford to screw up. He paid the driver and the taxi sped off back out onto Riddiford Street and into the night.

Blake made his way from under the car park; he stared up at the tall glass building; nobody stared back. There were lights on but that was it, nobody to greet him. It was hard for him knowing that Marci was in there somewhere; now he had done the easy bit, all he had to do was simply go and find her. The woman he loved needed him more than ever before. This time he wasn't going to let her down.

Blake snapped at the handles of his bag, grabbing them tightly; with a deep breath he picked it up and was then ready to face the challenge that Lucy had set him. He drilled himself as he walked towards the door, "OK focus, don't do anything daft, just act normal and it will all be OK. Stay calm and if all else fails 'eat cake'."

He had every right to be nervous and apprehensive at this point since he knew that if the injection failed and Marci died he probably faced being charged with her murder. It was an enormous risk. He threw the holdall over his shoulder for a more leisurely sort of casual look as he approached, which funnily enough was the exact opposite of what he was feeling at that moment in time, and tried to stroll nonchalantly towards the main entrance door.

There were two sets of large, double, glass plated doors which opened automatically as he approached, one with a small time delay on the other, hopefully they wouldn't create any sort of noise which would draw attention in his direction – this was the last thing he wanted right now. His bones shook with every step as he crossed the door matting between the first and second doors. Finally he had made it onto the tiled floor, steadily making his way closer to the long main reception counter which was on his left hand side. He looked up and around and couldn't help noticing how vast and spacious the atrium was, brightly lit and well laid out with escalators leading to a mezzanine area above. He figured that there were bound to be cameras everywhere. The thought of this complicated things and just made him more and more nervous as he approached the front desk, the enormity of what he was about to attempt to do was becoming clearer with every step. He leant on the counter with splayed elbows, his heart pounding as he tried not to panic. Trying to maintain this calm and collected approach was hopeless really as he started to sweat like a race horse at the final furlong.

The reception looked like it was being managed by only a couple of staff; it was hard to tell exactly as one or two others seemed to be popping around, coming and going and intermittently fiddling with stacks of files and paper. He stood patiently it seemed without existence. Why hadn't anybody looked up to acknowledge him? Could he just slip past undetected? After all he was the only person on the visitors' side of the counter at that time of night. Trying desperately not to look like a condemned man he shuffled along and approached a receptionist, stood politely and waited to be addressed.

At last an elderly lady looked up. "Yes, can I help you sir?"

Blake was a bit shocked by the surprisingly authoritative tone of voice from the night receptionist's greeting which didn't really match her demure look at all. This was his first test and he had to stay calm and pass it with flying colours; there was no flunking this bit, it was important. His head was filled with imaginary, distracting voices from the baying gallery above, shouting loudly with instruction, telling him over and over again what to do and what to say. His focus nearly bolted for the door but he took stock momentarily; he told himself that he had visited hospitals many times before so surely he didn't need the advice of these unwanted visitors sent only to distract him. He took a deep breath and tried to rid them from his mind. Eventually the voices faded away.

A more composed Blake was able to continue and said, "Oh yes thanks, I am here to see a Marci Watkins. She was recently admitted and is being treated for cancer."

"OK sir, let's take a look, ah yes I have her details right here. Can I ask – are you a relative?"

Now this is such a simple question isn't it? But when it's asked in a way that demands the highest sincerity, honesty and integrity in its response it's difficult to lie. Blake loved Marci and, although he wasn't a relative, he cared for her more than life itself and he just prayed that this was evident enough to the receptionist from the look on his face when he answered, so much so that she wouldn't doubt his response.

"Yes I am."

"You are what sir?"

A slightly nervous Blake replied, "A relative, sorry, yes I mean I am her cousin from England, sorry I should have said. I am her cousin….eh yes, from England. My apologies I just arrived earlier today and I guess I am a bit tired and of course desperate to see her."

The receptionist was either obviously convinced or just too tired to challenge the conversation anymore and she lowered her guard. "That's OK sir. OK, please make your way to level three, ward two; the third floor is the home for most of the women cancer patientsTake the escalator right over there, at the top turn left and it's straight ahead, thank you." She pointed a finger towards the middle of the room.

Blake highly relieved at getting the green light turned and started to make his way to the escalator. He thanked the receptionist. "I appreciate your help, that's great." He told himself to stop jabbering.

He had taken no more than five or six steps when the receptionist's voice rang out in Blake's direction. This startled him and he stopped abruptly in his tracks. What was up now, had he been caught out already? He hardly dared turn around; his body had perspired to its maximum already and was recharging to perspire some more when she called out again, "Your bag sir, you forgot your bag."

Blake smiled. "Of course; so sorry, thank you."

The receptionist muttered to herself as Blake made his way to the escalator, "Nice guy but a bit forgetful and typically English with that apologising stuff all of the time."

Once safely at the top of the escalator Blake followed the directions he was given. The hospital was very modern, smart and airy, well laid out and everything was clearly signposted. As he made his way along the corridor he noticed a really nice looking painting that hung on the wall; it caught his eye. He briefly stopped to look at it and stared poignantly for a moment. The painting was called 'After the Rain' by an Alfred Memelink. Its message touched a nerve with Blake and made him realise that his task was nowhere near over and if he ever wanted Marci around after the rain then he had better be at more than his best tonight. Blake continued quickly along the corridor towards Ward two.

Just as he got within two metres of the door he was startled slightly as a man in his early sixties unexpectedly pushed the door open from the opposite side. He had only seen Blake at the last minute and held it open for him as Blake approached. Blake walked through and thanked the man; he could see there was a small reception desk along the corridor on the left hand side which was again manned but this time by a ward nurse. Blake made his way there and introduced himself. He explained that he had come to see Marci Watkins and that he was her cousin, 'Blake' from England.

The nurse acknowledged him and replied, "Yes, I was expecting you. Zoe on main reception had phoned to tell me that you were on your way up. What kept you?"

"Well it's my first time here and I wasn't so confident of the directions and, oh yes, I stopped to admire the painting on the wall on the way in; it's a great sentiment."

"You mean the Alfred whatshisname painting?"

Blake, feeling much more at ease now, replied, "Yes that one, Alfred Memelink is it?"

"I think so, now to business, you have come to see our Marci?"

"Yup, I came from England, got here earlier today, a few hours ago, just needed to brush up and make myself respectable before coming along. So can I see her please Nurse ..." looking over to her name badge, "Nurse O'Docherty?"

"It's not that you can't see her, Mr Brown, and I do understand that you have come a long way but it's just that she is sleeping right now. Marci tends to sleep a lot and so I couldn't say when it would be a good time to see her. Better come back in the morning perhaps."

Blake didn't like what he was being told but he couldn't let his emotions take over him now, he had to stay calm. He understood the issues of course but he needed to get to Marci in order to be able to inject her with the samples. He wasn't a medical man but even he knew that this stuff wouldn't stay useable forever without being kept in a controlled environment and the hotel fridge just may not cut it as a safe place. He convinced himself that it wouldn't wait until morning. He needed to find a way to do what he came for and to find it quickly.

Blake pleaded, "Could I at least look at her, please? With your supervision, of course. Like you say I have come such a long way." He tried to make light of the conversation, "Knowing my luck I will be asleep all day tomorrow myself, what with all this jet lag and so on."

"So where in England are you from?"

"Well from Suffolk originally. I moved to London for a while but recently moved back to the Essex Suffolk borders, long story but I have been renovating a house there for some time, recently got it finished."

"Sounds nice. I'm originally from Ireland myself."

"Oh lovely, whereabouts in Ireland?"

They chatted a bit more about life back home in general. Blake was hoping that she would eventually warm to his friendly manner and non-demanding behaviour, which just might get him where he wanted to be.

Nurse O'Docherty's parents were settled in New Zealand now for some thirty years and they were living in Auckland. She had inherited her father's beautiful dark raven hair and her eyes were as green as the Shamrock itself. Her accent was based on a good blend of Irish and Kiwi which made her sound a little bit like an east coast Australian at times.

"Dublin. Me and my parents set out years ago on our travels to get across Australia and New Zealand. I remember we had this big plan to try and reach Tahiti and unfortunately this was as far as we got."

"Sounds interesting, but why Tahiti?"

"Well another long story, but a distant relation of ours, Robert O'Docherty, married a French woman many years ago and after they married they went to Tahiti. He would have been my Great Great Great Great Grandfather; I think. Anyway apparently he was responsible for half of the population there at the time – they had about eighteen children."

"A busy man by the sounds of things!"

"If the stories they tell me are true yes, I suppose so, but that was a long time ago."

The mood was now much more relaxed. Blake figured that he had Nurse O'Docherty on side.

Blake asked, "So how far is Tahiti from New Zealand then? I know it's out in the Pacific somewhere."

"It's still about three hours flying with one of these new fandangled aeroplanes, so still a long way from what some people perceive as the end of the world."

"Mmm, I didn't actually realise it was that far."

"Okay Mr Brown, if you promise to be very good and very, very quiet I will take you to see Marci. However, please no touching, we really must not disturb her."

Blake's heart eventually stopped pounding like he had just completed a marathon (although it felt like he had) and he started to relax. Blake followed Nurse O'Docherty to the ward.

Blake knew that this was going to be a big moment for him. He was a sensitive man and the last time he had been with Marci was many years ago when she had walked out of his life back in London. She would be a different looking person now physically, wouldn't she? He wasn't sure how much damage the cancer would have done exactly, but he could imagine that it wasn't going to be good. He suspected not kindly, as it rarely does. He braced himself for the impact of the coming moment that he knew would be as painful to him as being in a high speed car crash. He was about to hate every moment of it. This would be the toughest test he would ever face.

The room itself was simple but functional. It contained the usual hospital survival equipment that we have become familiar with. A bedside cabinet with various containers placed here and there, some shelves with space for the smallest of personal effects. Two of the walls were decorated with some art by a local Maori artist; another of the walls had a TV with a built in communication system mounted on it.

As he was led by Nurse O'Docherty to Marci's bed he continually muttered to himself, "Stay on your legs Blake, for god's sake stay on your legs." He knew this was not a time to be drowning in emotion; it wouldn't help anybody. Emotion would just have to wait.

Nurse O'Docherty whispering, pointed to the furthest bed in the small ward. "This way Mr Brown, she is in the bed in the corner. Marci likes the window."

The room was quiet all right. Blake approached her bed with great care and caution. He could make out what was presumably only one other patient in the room. As he advanced towards her and passed the first bed he saw what resembled nothing more than a frail bundle of deteriorating skin and bone lying under the bed sheets. It looked like this was the only other patient in the room which was good for the task he had to perform.

After a few steps Nurse O'Docherty stopped. "I will wait just here and give you some privacy. Please remember sir what we have agreed, no disturbing her, and please just stay a moment."

With Nurse O'Docherty watching tentatively over his shoulder Blake stepped onto what he was about to treat as a floor made of rice paper and delicately stepped over towards Marci's bedside.

At first it didn't look much like Marci at all. As he got a bit closer he started to make out the medical notes and her name at the bottom of the bed – otherwise he would not have been certain. Mind you she was lying on her right shoulder facing the window which meant he could only see a bit of her, other than that she was covered to her neck by a thin cotton sheet. The tiny figure in front of him didn't move one bit as he got closer. It was clear even to an amateur such as Blake that she was not in good shape. Marci was petite, frail and emaciated to the point where her bones protruded from her skin threatening to puncture holes in it. She was bruised; large rouge blemishes covered her shoulders looking like pizzas. Her now visible left hand was skeletal, and any jewellery that was probably once there had more than likely fallen off, on the floor maybe. Her fingers resembled broken straw. Blake trembled uncontrollably for a moment; he wanted desperately to hold her. There was so much he wanted to tell her, what he had been up to over the years, and then all the little daft things like who had had a baby and who divorced who in the office as well as all about Joseph. Things that had happened to him that she wouldn't have had the foggiest as to what they were all about. But none of that really mattered right now. He had to focus on the job at hand; especially with Nurse O'Docherty watching. He wanted desperately to hold her, to pick her up and keep her tight to him. He knew that that moment would have to wait.

Sadly he could see and had to painfully accept she wasn't like the real Marci. He asked himself the question over and over, "where was the real Marci? Where was the curly blond hair that teased and irritated her all the time that he loved so much, the freckles on her face that he joked about with her? Where was that special and infectious spirit that oozed freely from Marci when nobody else had any left, where had it all gone?" It had to be there somewhere, maybe dormant and tired but it was there, he was sure of it. He reminded himself that he needed to pull himself together and stay on his legs. As upsetting as this all was, seeing her like this, it wasn't going to help Marci one bit if he collapsed right now. He couldn't let it happen. He needed to get a grip on the situation.

It was at this point that he decided that he wouldn't shed any more tears for her; in fact nobody would. He had to believe that the unyielding spirit in Marci was still there somewhere and with a little help from him and his very good friend Dr Joseph Singh they would be able to reawaken it.

As Blake looked at her frail body up and down in the bed he noticed a framed photograph on the bedside table. It looked familiar but he wasn't sure as the room was darkish. He walked around the bed and looked more closely. To his utter surprise it was a photograph of him, probably taken at the Italian Restaurant in London when they were together one lunchtime. He momentarily stared at the photo and then back at Marci, then again back at the photo. It raised an immediate question with him – had he always been more than a friend to her and she had never told him? After all this time, had she been keeping this secret to herself, all of these years, had she carried the pain of undeclared love, and now this, it had come to this.

This realisation triggered a cocktail of emotions that he had not experienced before. Lucy was right in her e-mail. Now Blake was more determined and driven to succeed. He couldn't screw this all up. She had to have the solution injected, now, tonight; every moment was precious. Looking at Marci it didn't look as though she would survive another day unaided. Once this was all overLucy was going to get a medal, maybe just for being Lucy – he wasn't sure what for exactly but whatever it was he was determined to make sure that she knew exactly how eternally grateful he was.

Nurse O'Docherty waved and in a soft but authoritative voice called him back from Marci's bedside.

"Mr Brown, that's enough now. Please allow her to rest, no more potential disturbance please."

Blake acknowledged Nurse O'Docherty's request and he raised his left hand so that she could see he understood. He then quickly leant over to Marci and whispered gently in her ear, "I love you Marci, I will save you, this isn't over, sleep tight angel."

So now he was faced with a big problem. If he was being asked to leave how was he going to get back in to the ward and inject Marci with the solution? He couldn't leave the hospital as they probably wouldn't let him back in until the next day and then there would be other visitors and family. He was bound to be rumbled if he left it until then. So somehow he was going to have to stay there until he could figure out how to get back on the ward. It appeared to be a difficult one.

Nurse O'Docherty ushered Blake towards the door. "Basically Mr Brown just follow the hallway and just on your right hand side you will see the escalator; just make your way back to reception and they will see you out. Nice to have met you and no doubt you will be back. I will tell Marci that you called when I see her." That was exactly what Blake didn't want to happen.

"Nurse, is there a bathroom I could use before I leave? I am really quite desperate."

"OK, if it's a crisis I suppose it will be OK." She pointed along the corridor. "You see by that illuminated sign over there, there is a bathroom there you can use. But hurry now as I am due a break in about three minutes and I would like you back here before I go."

"Understood nurse, I won't be long, scouts' honour."

He couldn't have been more grateful for this golden opportunity. Once inside the bathroom all he had to do was get the syringe loaded with a full solution and get back to Marci to inject her with it. Simple as that. He figured that if he waited long enough then there would be some sort of handover between the new nurse and Nurse O'Docherty which would hopefully allow him enough time to give Marci the injection. It took Blake a couple of minutes to prepare everything; he loaded the syringe and evacuated a bit of the solution to remove any possibility of trapped air. Once everything was prepared, he opened the bathroom door, listening carefully to hear the two nurses talking.

Nurse O'Docherty invited the new shift nurse to come into the ward sister's office to go over her evening's shift report and any particular patients' instructions. It was as though she had already forgotten about Blake being in the bathroom, perhaps assuming that he would have left the building immediately afterwards. This would clearly be the best chance that Blake would have. He listened for what he hoped to be the staffroom door shut, and quietly made his way from the bathroom towards the ward reception desk. His beating heart again seemed to be the noisiest thing in the hospital. He waited patiently in the corridor, hiding just out of sight and listening for a signal in the conversation between the two nurses that would indicate to him that it was safe to go. At last it came, and he heard Nurse O'Docherty say, "If you hold on a second I will get the chart from the file for Mrs Jennings and show you what I mean."

Blake knew that this was his going to be his best chance; he knew it and he took it.

Chapter 16

It was January 30th 2028 when what were expected to be Marci's last set of brain scans were taken. The results were startling to say the least. One of the tumours had completely changed direction and another had halved in size. It was nothing short of a miracle; all of a sudden it looked like surgery to remove them could be a viable option. After some discussion it was agreed though that perhaps they should wait a few more days and do one more scan before deciding upon an operation; if necessary seek a second opinion before making the final decision. At the moment it looked as though Marci was doing fine without their intervention. They informed the family of this decision who were obviously delighted with the news. They felt for the first time that time could be on their side.

Some ten days later Marci appeared to be doing better; it was a huge relief. Another brain and neck scan was carried out. This time the results showed that the tumour which had shrunk in size had now disappeared altogether; the larger tumour had also now reduced to half of the size it was originally and the tumour in her neck had now reduced to no more than a little lump of hard looking skin. While there were still signs of smaller spots here and there it could be seen that these had also shown signs of greatly reducing. Nobody could explain this remarkable phenomenon but believe it or not Marci was showing signs of not only beating the cancer but of having no symptoms at all. It was as though her genetic structure was being replaced almost cell by cell. It was the most amazing fightback ever known. It defied logic and confounded the unconfoundable amongst the doctors and specialists there; they had never seen anything like it.

Day by day Marci just got better and better. Doctors at the hospital continued to be amazed at the pace of her recovery. By the end of February Marci was sitting up in bed and welcoming her visitors in with open arms. She was also eating much better and had started to gain just a small amount of weight; more importantly she had started to get that sparkle back in her eyes.

The lost flesh on her once very thin legs and arms had started to reappear. She no longer looked like a coat hanger. By early March what turned out to be the last set of scans taken showed that the tumours, which such a short while ago threatened to take her life, had all but totally disappeared. Not only that but she was getting to be in good health. It was decided that Marci could probably start thinking about going home.

It was March 10th 2028 and Marci stood, arms crossed, in her PJs and dressing gown staring out of the window from her room on the 3rd floor of the general hospital in Wellington. It was very early morning, around 4.30 am, but Marci eagerly awaited the doctor who would hopefully give the all clear for her to be discharged from the hospital. The sun wasn't even up properly and the world was very peaceful from where she stood. The dawning of a new day was imminent and for Marci it was certainly going to be a special and long-awaited day for her. She had not prepared herself for disappointment.

In the distance she could just make out some distant engine noises, the odd taxi maybe doing an early morning airport run. The hospital was on the edge of town some fifteen minutes or so from where she lived in the Oriental Bay area. It would be a few hours as yet before she would be heading home but that didn't stop Marci wishing that every set of headlights that turned onto Riddiford Street was being driven by her sister, coming to get her. The overall view from the 3rd floor was OK at a stretch, especially in the direction towards Charles Plimmer Park but Marci was an ocean girl and she sorely missed being in the Bay area. Marci's house was just as she wanted it. When she first moved in it was considered by her friends and family to be a bit more than just a challenge but Marci thrived on this sort of thing. It wasn't long before she turned the delightful 1950s colonial style house with its sea views and terraced lawn into a very special home. She missed her regular walks down to Hataitai Beach where she usually constructed letters in her head to Blake before penning her e-mails, although not everything was sent. It was true to say that home had felt like a long way off until now and she had to admit that she really did miss it. She just couldn't wait.

The duty nurse, Bridgette O'Docherty, whose shift was due to come to an end soon noticed Marci was unexpectedly out of bed as she wandered around the ward on one of her rounds.

She approached Marci and gently put an arm very caringly around her favourite patient's shoulder. "Hi Marci, let me guess, can't sleep? Got the heeby-jeebies as my mother would probably say. To you and me that's butterflies in the tummy due to all of the excitement."

"It's been a tough and difficult time. I am just so relieved and excited about going home, I just can't stop thinking about it."

"I know Marci, it's a big step for you after such a long time here with us, it must be constantly on your mind."

"And then those all of those people that I haven't seen in such a long time, it's a massive change and it's constantly in my head at the moment."

"Yes, I saw from your notes that you could well be discharged today pending a couple of tests and a visit from the doctor."

"Yes I hope so, I feel so well. I just hope that the doctor's opinion is the same as mine."

"I am sure it will all be fine. Dr Turner is a good man. That said I really think you should go back to bed and try and get some rest until the medical staff get to you. It's still very early you know.".

"I wasn't sure exactly what the time was; I thought maybe 6 or 7 am."

"Not even close Marci, it's now only coming up to 5.00 am."

"Creeps! That explains why it's all so quiet out there. There is a bit of traffic about but not much. I thought it was odd. Well it looks like it's going to be a lovely day though, in my heart anyway." She turned and smiled at Nurse O'Docherty.

Nurse O'Docherty replied, "It sure is, and it will be an even better one if you get out of here. Apologies but I make it sound like a prison, don't I!"

Marci grinned, slowly turned away from the window and made her way back to her bed. She felt like dancing across the floor really but thought better of it. Nurse O'Docherty followed closely behind – just in case Marci did anything daft. Once she reached the side of the bed Marci sat on the edge, raised her legs and slipped in under the duvet.

Nurse O'Docherty waited while Marci had adjusted

herself and then decided to help with the pillows. "Just sit forward for me please Marci."

Nurse O'Docherty reached out for the pillows that needed to be arranged to better support her. Marci obliged by leaning forward slightly as Nurse O'Docherty plumped up the pillows.

It wasn't until Marci was sitting up and feeling much better that she noticed the small framed photograph of Blake on the bedside table. She had no recollection that it came with her in the ambulance; she figured that somebody, probably Lucy, had brought it from her house to the hospital during a recent visit and left it there as some sort of talisman – maybe? On seeing it Marci had placed it strategically behind the reading lamp on the bedside cabinet out of the way of most people's view so as to avoid the certain tirade of endless questions that she was sure to receive at some point. Its vision was obscured slightly, enough just to hide it out of the way from prying eyes, but allowing Marci to look at it whenever she felt that she wanted to.

Lucy's original thinking when had she brought it in was that it was probably not meant to be seen fully but at the same it should still have that all important talismanic effect. Marci couldn't be too cross with her as it seemed to have worked, and the photo had stood by largely undetected – until now that is. As Nurse O'Docherty was dusting down the duvet with her hand she glanced up towards the bedside cabinet and spotted the framed photo behind the lamp. She couldn't help but reach out and pick it up, staring at it intensely for a brief moment. Marci noticed this stare was developing into curiosity which in turn triggered interest from Marci.

Being keen to know what had caught her eye Marci asked,

"What's up Nurse Bridgette?"

"Oh it's nothing, it's just me being silly."

"Silly, what do you mean silly?"

"Well you never mentioned a husband or partner or whatever and so I naturally thought you didn't have one. I am sorry I shouldn't pry."

"Sorry, sorry about what. I never mentioned a partner or husband as yes, I don't have one."

Nurse Bridgette O'Docherty then turned to Marci holding the photo of Blake with both hands. She passed it to Marci.

"Oh that, that's an old friend, Blake, I am not sure how it got here. I suspect my niece Lucy probably brought it with her so that he could help me get better. So yes either Lucy or my sister would have put it there for some strange reason. It's the kind of thing they would do."

Nurse O'Docherty seemed slightly relieved that the puzzle looked like it could be explained. At least she now assumed she knew who he was.

Marci continued, "I haven't seen him for many, many years, and believe me it's a long, long story."

The bewildered look on Nurse O'Docherty's face had returned. "Are you sure that you haven't seen him for that length of time?"

"What do you mean, why are you asking?"

"It's nothing, it's just me being silly."

"Being silly? How? Come on you have to tell me, I am full of curiosity – spill."

"Well it's possibly nothing so I shouldn't mention it."

Marci wasn't prepared to let go. "Look we are all friends here. You have to tell me, don't leave me bungying like this; come on, what is behind all of this?"

"Bungying? That's a new one on me, but I think I know what you mean."

"So then, what is it?"

"Well OK, the man in the photo, you said his name is Blake. Well he looks kind of familiar to me, that's all."

"What do you mean familiar, and why would he? He is in London probably and we are in Wellington."

"Are you sure about that?"

"Well as sure as I can be. I had an e-mail from him about ten or more months ago; he said he was there. I suppose he could have gone somewhere else though."

"Boy, in London, that's a long way away. So on that basis it is highly improbable that he was here in the hospital."

Marci appeared shocked. "Here in the hospital? Where exactly? Was he hurt, what happened to him?"

"No nothing like that, he was here trying to see you. I should have mentioned it before. He said he was your cousin from England. He must have blagged his way past reception and then past me in order to get on to the ward. He came in one night several months ago now, as bold as brass he was, said he had been told of your illness and was desperate to see you. Mind you he is a bit older now than in the photo but I am sure it's the same guy; he said his name was Blake anyway; so he's not a total liar."

"Oh my god, I can't believe this." Marci was so shocked at the possibility of Blake being at her bedside. "So what did you do?"

"Hospital rules I am afraid. But he pleaded and well in the end I did accompany him onto the ward so that he could see you very briefly. I suggested that he may be better off coming back in the morning but I am not sure if he ever did."

"So you sent him away?"

"Yes I sent him away, sort of. It was in the middle of the night, he shouldn't have even been here really, it's not normal."

"So when was this exactly?"

"If my memory serves me right it was my last shift of nights before my birthday so it could have been sometime in October, yup four months or so ago possibly. Anyway it may not have been him. Even if it was him you said that he was just an old friend, so he doesn't mean that much to you then." Nurse O'Docherty smiled teasingly, causing Marci to blush slightly.

Marci, as stoic as ever, said, "Yes you are right, it could have been anybody, you did the right thing." She thought to herself 'It would be nice though to think that my angel had finally come to wrap his wings around me'.

"So who is being thrifty with the truth now then?"

"OK, fair is fair I suppose. He is a guy who I sort of loved, a long time ago. I never told him how I felt. It was stupid of me. At the time I thought that I was just too busy for love, I was confused and was chasing my own demons and stuff. I was too blind to see what was really important. In the end I just went off and left him in pursuit of my own to do list, which at the time I had down as being much more important. I guess also at the time I felt I was strong enough to get over him. Truth is I never have, he really is a lovely guy and I just wish I could do it all again, I really do."

"Maybe he is that angel after all, some reunion wasn't it."

Nurse O'Docherty reached out her hand and gave Marci the framed photo back. She took it gratefully and held it tightly in her hand, pausing just for a second to gaze at it again.

Nurse O'Docherty said, "Well I am convinced that he isn't in London now. I am sure it was him that was here that night. In fact I even spoke to him for a while – you are right he was real nice."

"So why would he really be here do you think?"

"Come on! There is no other reason, he came especially for you. Somebody must have contacted him, and he came here."

Marci was fuelled with curiosity and needed to know more. "So out of interest what did you talk about?"

"Well I remember he was standing by my desk having been sent up by reception. He said he was tired but he was desperate to see you; that was it really. He wasn't here long. I remember now; he asked if he could use the bathroom and then I didn't see him anymore after that. I went on my break and when I came back he wasn't here so I suppose he had long gone. Nothing looked wrong, I checked the equipment and you of course when I came back on shift and everything was fine. You were sleeping. Nothing was out of place. I didn't think any more of it really."

"So you are sure that you know when this was?"

"Yes as I said it was sometime in October."

"And he hasn't been back since?"

"Not that I know of. Well not on my shift. One of your family would have noticed him I suppose if he had been here during the day at all. At the time you were still quite ill and your family had sat through many a night time vigil here at your side. But somehow, Marci, you have pulled through. Technically you are too old to be called a miracle baby but that's what you are for all intents and purposes – a miracle baby. Maybe this guy Blake really was a bit of an angel or something."

Marci said jokingly, "Don't go there please. You are scaring me now with that theory."

"Well whatever he was he was here, simple as that. Now let's get you tucked up for a bit before the world and its wife wakes up and fractures this peaceful start to the day." Nurse O'Docherty finished tucking the duvet under the mattress. Straight away Marci put all of her years of yoga practice into full swing and started her breathing exercises to help her relax. Breathe in counting to seven, nice deep breaths and then slowly out for eleven seconds and repeat, and repeat. It was a basic relaxation technique she had practised for a number of years now. It had never let her down. Within two or three minutes Marci was again fast asleep. Nurse Bridgette moved quietly away from the bed, exhausted from her grilling.

It seemed as though Marci had been asleep for hours when she was woken by Dr Turner. He put a hand on Marci's shoulder; leaning towards her face he gently shook her and whispered into her ear. "Marci, it's Dr Turner. Can you hear me, Marci?"

Marci awoke abruptly; she was a bit startled. "Sorry Doctor, that was some catnap. It was the best bit of the whole night's sleep, to be honest with you." She composed herself a little. "Sorry, Dr Turner, isn't it?"

"No need to be sorry Marci, it's good to see you so relaxed. Oh and by the way you can call me Rex if you want to."

"OK I shall do if that's good for you."

"OK, so your notes tell me that if your bloods are OK then

we will be sending you home today from the hospital. How does that sound then?"

"Well that sounds just perfect to me, Dr Rex."

Dr Turner grinned at Marci's humour, "Good, well Nurse Morgan will take your blood and pop it down to the lab for screening. We should have the test results back in a couple of hours or so. I will then come back up to see you and all being well you should be out of here by lunchtime." He turned to Nurse Morgan and ushered her towards Marci, "OK nurse, if you could do what's necessary I would appreciate it."

Nurse Morgan, a native Kiwi, said, "No worries Doctor, it's as good as done. I am on the case."

"That's good – thanks." Dr Turner turned to Marci. "Oh one more thing, Marci, a dietitian will be along to see you shortly just to cover some dietary basics, I hope that's OK."

Marci smiled back. "Yes of course, not a problem." She tried to make light of things, waving her arms slightly. "I am here anyway."

Dr Turner smiled. "OK then, good." He then turned and walked away leaving Nurse Morgan and Marci to get on with things. The white coat left the room and all that could be heard were his fading footsteps down the hallway towards the other wards.

Nurse Morgan said, "OK Marci, this is totally painless, a procedure you are very familiar with I am sure." She was holding the blood test kit which consisted of what appeared to be a very long needle and a container with which to catch the blood in. "I just need to take a little blood from your arm, as soon as I can find a suitable place to take it from that is."

She rubbed and patted speculatively in a few different places along Marci's right arm trying to attract the attention of a voluntary source until one of her veins rose to the challenge.

"Ah here we are, that will do nicely." Before Marci knew what was happening the needle had been located in the exact spot and blood was being extracted via the syringe.

Marci hoped that Nurse Morgan was extracting just the right amount required as she didn't have much to spare. As quickly as the needle was placed in her arm the process was all over and it was swiftly removed. The sample was marked up and put into a plastic envelope. Nurse Morgan applied the small ball of cotton wool and plaster. "There, wasn't too bad, was it? I will just pop this down to the lab and then I will come straight back up and we can do your blood pressure."

Nurse Morgan turned and left the room making her way to the lab. Things were eerily silent for a while. The sun had come up and had filled the room. Each and every awkward corner was now lit up; there was nowhere to hide. Marci really wanted to get up and go to the bathroom but she figured that she should wait a bit until Nurse Morgan came back.

Within the hour Nurse Morgan had returned with the results. "That went better than I expected, a complete bill of health. In fact one of the guys commented that the blood was more like that of a twenty year old. They like to kid around at times."

Marci thought nothing of it. "That's good; hopefully the whole day will be like that."

"OK, let's get this blood pressure piece out of the way. Right, I need you to relax while I quickly do this, Marci." She reached forward and put the inflatable cuffs over Marci's right arm. She turned on the pressure monitoring machine which began to pump until the right pressure was reached.

Then looking at her watch she released the pressure in the cuffs. "Now, that wasn't too difficult, was it?"

"So how did I do?"

"All very normal, so everything is fine. Right, just relax, perhaps use the bathroom if you need to and the doctor will be back to see you shortly, with good news I reckon."

"OK Nurse, thanks."

"That's OK. By the way I had a word with the guys in the dietary section to make sure that they get up to see you pronto; we don't want them mucking things up, do we?"

"That's great and thank you. Mmm, the world is good, it looks like I am going home, I just can't believe it, after all these months, finally going home."

Nurse Morgan replied, "Nor can I or even the rest of the hospital for that matter – wonder woman!"

Marci's face shone, she was radiant like the breaking sun at the start of the day. Everything was beautiful, she felt beautiful, she felt so alive. The dietary nurse came to see Marci shortly after Nurse Morgan had left. Everything went well and so she was finally able to finish packing her bag in readiness for the final nod from Dr Turner. She had already set her day clothes at the bottom of the bed; she could officially get ready to leave the hospital.

It was 11.30 in the morning and her ride home was there to fetch her. Lucy was the first one in the room. She burst in running towards Marci with her arms open wide. Seconds later she was gripping Marci tightly around the waist as she buried her head lovingly into Marci's chest.

Marci gave the good news that she was officially well enough to leave the hospital as she soaked up the simple but self-indulgent pleasure of stroking Lucy's blond curly hair.

Lucy enjoying every second of the attention, said, "Brilliant, brilliant, can't wait to get you home. I have missed you so much." They continued to hug each other. They were gripped like a couple of Sumo wrestlers in a battle for supremacy, neither wanting to be the first to let go.

Marci, still not quite as strong as she used to be, eventually had to let go. "Phew, that was some hello!"

"It's because we all missed you so much."

"Well no need to worry anymore about missing me because I ain't going anywhere for a long, long time."

"You sure about that?"

"Oh yes I am sure, deadly sure."

They hugged again. The rest of the family had arrived by now and also joined in the big group hugging ceremony. Marci had her bags packed already and so it didn't take long to slip on the normal clothes that she had prepared, or demob clothes as she called them, and get ready to leave. As she left the ward she shook hands with Nurse Morgan and the other staff, people who were there to see her off, sometimes hugs and kisses were even dished out. She thanked them all from the bottom of her heart for everything they had done to help her. It felt like a bit of a royal send off. Everybody lined up by the door at the end of ward 3. After all she had become a bit of a celebrity to the hospital over the months as she defied all medical logic to get back on her feet and return to being so well again.

Marci said, "I just really appreciate everything you have all done for me, really I do."

Nurse Morgan replied, "Well that's what we are here for."

They smiled and a quick hug followed.

Lucy tugged at her arm and Marci knew that she was

already taking too long with her goodbyes. Gripping her aunt's hand Lucy gently supported her along the corridors towards the escalator through that fantastic atrium that everybody in Wellington loves to talk about and back to the outside world. Before she knew it she was being led outside by her niece and into the fresh air and a new beginning. Marci felt like she was being reborn. She felt new and fresh. Every sound and smell seemed to have been inexplicably purified and perfected in her absence. Like falling dominos, step by step her life was switched back on. The air was full of crystal clear fragrances and sounds that even Bose would find difficult to improve upon. Everything good seemed to have been amplified just for her.

Fortunately Wellington General was located just a few kilometres from where Marci lived in the Oriental Bay area. Marci's sister Bronwyn had decided since as it was such a lovely day they would drive Marci back home along the edge of town via Cambridge Terrace and onto Oriental Parade so that Marci could take in some of the view as part of her homecoming. The idea was to kind of reacquaint her with the world she had been pining for. Bronwyn knew that Marci loved this part of town. She could take in some sea air. It would do her good.

As long as the traffic was kind and the parking fairy was in a good mood then the trip home would be fine. Marci and Lucy sat in the back of the car and held hands throughout the entire journey. Most people would have been at work by now and so the streets were not very busy. Eventually the car pulled slowly on to Oriental Parade and Marci's pulse raced a little as she gripped Lucy's hand just a little bit tighter at the beauty of the bay.

Not only could she see the ocean now, she could smell it too, it was blanketing her mind and at the same time creeping back into her soul. The air was clear, crisp and pure as she plunged herself into it, indulgingly and almost greedily soaking it up like a piece of dry sponge in water. It energised and revitalised her like nothing else. Momentarily she closed her eyes and surrendered herself to the overpowering magic of it all.

Just a couple of hundred metres or so along the edge of the bay there was an ideal place to stop. There were benches where they could rest which would give Marci a real taste of freedom. It would allow her to walk a bit and get her feet wet again. Bronwyn knew that Marci enjoyed looking out onto Lambton Harbour and the Bay – and why not as it was such a nice day. It was an ideal place to stop, just perfect. They wouldn't stop for long, just for thirty minutes or so as Marci also longed to get home. Bronwyn pulled over and parked up.

Bronwyn leaned over to face the back seat and said, "OK Lucy, you take your Aunt Marci over to the bench over there," pointing to one nearest the water's edge, "while I get us all a cup of something from the tea shack."

They all stepped out of the car. Bronwyn ran her index finger gently across the locking plate and its sensors automatically locked the car. The later model of the car had voice command locking but Bronwyn was happy to make do with her older model. They had started to part and go in different directions: Bronwyn to the tea shack while Lucy arm in arm with Marci led her gently to the bench.

Marci called out to Bronwyn, "Lemon tea would be good sis, unless they have some jasmine tea of course, thanks."

Bronwyn shouted back, "OK Marci, and what about you

236

Lucy, what are you having?"

Lucy replied just as loudly, "Milkshake please, vanilla. Thanks ma."

Bronwyn waved her arm in the air to show that she got it all loud and clear. "OK honey, no worries."

Lucy said, "I thought you liked that funny tea, what's it called again – lapsong souchong tea."

"I do but I didn't think it was a good one to start with, I sort of figured I would break myself back in slowly. Anyway it goes down better after dinner or lunch."

"So what makes it so special then, is it a natural tea?"

"Well in simple terms it's tea from China which is smoked. But it is also known as the champagne of teas."

"Why champagne – does it have bubbles in it?"

"No silly, that's just a term to suggest that nothing can get any better. You know people talk of a champagne lifestyle, or champagne ideas and so on; this is the champagne of teas."

They finally made it to the wooden bench where they sat down. Marci gently eased herself into position and took a deep breath; she looked out onto the blue ocean of the bay and summed up in a moment how she was feeling. "Oh Lucy, this really is a beautiful day, the water is beautiful, in fact everything is beautiful. I never realised how much I just love it all. Being here, life, you and my sis. God I am one lucky woman to be able to get back into the garden of life once more."

"We are glad that you are here, Aunt Marci, especially me." Lucy, gave her a playful kiss on her cheek. "Do you mind if I ask you something about when you were in hospital?"

"Not at all, go ahead."

Lucy said coyly, "Well did anything kind of weird

happen?"

"Of course lots of things. I mean I wasn't supposed to survive but here I am, weird seems to happen to me virtually every day. Were you looking for special weird or just weird? What did you have in mind exactly?"

Why did Marci feel as though Lucy knew something that she didn't?

Lucy said, "Oh I don't know, I mean anything sort of unexpected…"

"Well OK then, there was this time when …"

She was about to reveal all when Bronwyn unexpectedly returned with the drinks. "OK one lemon tea and a milkshake." Bronwyn was back and they hadn't even noticed.

Bronwyn sat down on the bench at her sister's side. "So what were you two girls talking about? I didn't interrupt anything, did I?" She reached out and put her arm around her sister's shoulder and gave her a kiss on the cheek. "She isn't smothering you already is she? I did warn her to go easy on you."

Marci smiled. "No Bronwyn, she is fine, we just have a lot of catching up to do that's all." Marci turned to Lucy, "Don't we honey?"

Lucy puckered her lips and puffed her cheeks out and nodded in agreement.

Bronwyn said, "You two should have been sisters really."

Marci replied, "Oh that's nice, I kinda like the sister I have, thank you very much." Turning to Lucy Marci leant over "and I kind of like the niece I have as well. And that order is fine by me."

They all smiled and giggled in a girly sort of way and then in unison lifted their paper cups in celebration.

Marci said, "Just look at us, toasting with lemon tea and a milkshake – who would have thought it." She turned her head to look at the bay as she cupped her drink affectionately in both hands. With Lucy sat on one side and Bronwyn on the other surely this was a perfect moment. A lone scary looking sea bird circled overhead and swooped noisily past them a couple of times which brought some tiny distraction to the moment but other than that it was just flawless.

It was mid-April and the weather was cooling a little. Marci had been out of hospital for a few weeks and was still resting at home. Over the weeks she had had regular visits from a specialist nurse who kept an eye on her progress as she was also taking some prescribed medication.

The good news was that all the signs showed that Marci was still mending very nicely. She had started to feel really fine again, a bit like her younger self even. Marci had regained lots of her strength now and was able to get around reasonably well. There were no signs of any nasty after effects from treatment or the medication. It was, to the outside world, a miraculous recovery and totally unexpected. It baffled the hell out of her doctors but at the same time it was certainly good news and welcomed by all of her family as they all loved her very much. Marci had that sparkle back in her eyes again. Her skin was no longer grey and tired; it had returned to a shiny healthy glow. She was recharged, replenished and refreshed.

It was now early May. Summer was fading fast and there were some signs that autumn was just around the corner. Still, it was dry and with some thickish clothing and a jacket Marci was still happy to sit outside. To be on the porch and look out at the bay was one of her favourite pastimes of late.

It was a Saturday; the day had been busy with shopping in town in the morning and Marci returned home clutching a number of shopping bags, completely exhausted of course. She couldn't wait to put them down in the house and try and forget the shopping – definitely not her favourite activity. There was only one thing for it – a nice glass of Marlborough Sauvignon Blanc as a pat on the pack to celebrate continued independence and simply getting back onto the roundabout of life. Being able to shop in Wellington and carrying the bags to the house, if only from the car, was testimony to support the notion that things were virtually back to normal for Marci.

She decided to take the whole bottle from the fridge and put it in a cooler as she made her way to the seat outside on the porch. It was late in the afternoon and the sky was crystal clear but just starting to turn. She sat and gazed into the evening sky, just streaming her exhaustion into the vast absorbent emptiness. It was so peaceful and relaxing, just her, the stars and the crickets. She sat holding the wine glass by its stem and twisted it between her thumb and finger, making the wine playfully agitate in the glass.

Suddenly the tranquility of it all was broken as she heard the gate at the front of the house spring open. Marci looked up; she could see that somebody had entered the garden and was standing there. The shape was silhouetted against the few streetlights on the pavement. It looked like a man but she wasn't exactly sure. She wasn't expecting any visitors and so became a bit apprehensive but of course curious at the same time.

Marci called out, "Hello, can I help you, are you lost?"

The figure walked slowly towards Marci saying nothing.

By now Marci could see that it was surely a man from the dress, usual jacket and trousers. But since he had a hat on it still wasn't clear if she knew the person or not. Marci stood to her feet and put down her wine glass. Again she asked the question, "Hello, who are you and what do you want?"

Now only some three metres away and slowly approaching Marci, Blake removed his hat. He had no idea as to how she would react. It had been many years since they had last seen each other and on top of this she had been unwell, so he figured he would need to be a bit careful. In addition he was also very nervous which wasn't probably helping. She may not recognise him straight away as it had been a long, long time.

Blake lowered his arms to his side and stood up nice and straight; he was now standing within one metre of her. He could almost smell her skin. He was shaking like a pompom on a stick at a baseball game as he lifted his head slowly until he could look directly into Marci's eyes. There couldn't be any shadow of doubt in her mind at all as to who he was. He spoke softly, "Hello Marci, it's me, Blake."

Marci was dumfounded and went rigid with the sudden realisation that it was indeed Blake. She couldn't believe it and was instantly overwhelmed by what she saw. She tried to pinch herself but her fingers where too numb. She stared at Blake for a couple of seconds, maybe more, who knows, simply not knowing what to do, taking in all of the information in front of her and trying hard to work it out and make sense of it.

He spoke hesitantly and softly, "It's a shock I expect and I am sorry for that but here I am."

Marci flung her arms immediately around his neck and hugged Blake so tightly that his breath was instantly catapulted from his lungs into the sky above. Although gasping for air he really didn't mind as this also meant that his face was cushioned against her peach like skin. For a little while nothing was said; that's because nothing needed to be.

After a few seconds Marci broke the ice. "Blake, oh my god Blake, it's really you, I just can't believe this. Where the hell have you been?"

Blake dropped his hat on the floor of the porch and swiftly wrapped his arms round Marci's waist and clung on like his life depended on it. They were now both locked into something similar to a wrestling hold described as an 'elevated double chicken wing', neither wanting to or looking like they were prepared to put the other one down. And why not? It had been a long time coming.

Chapter 17

Throughout the time that Marci was in hospital Blake had decided to stay in Wellington so that he could be as close to her as possible. He didn't want to suffer the angst that comes with living on the other side of the world and wondering what the hell was going on. During her recovery time Blake had managed to secretly visit Marci in hospital but he wasn't able to get really close up to her due to the number of other visitors that were usually there at the time – plus also he didn't feel that he wanted to take the risk of being exposed quite yet. He wanted to make sure that she was clearly on the mend as he had no idea as to how the Transhumanisation solution would react with her. For the time being he just had to be happy to be close enough to see that Marci was making some progress which was all he needed at the time.

This watching brief, although he was glad of it, was very hard for him though, as deep in his heart all he wanted to do was hold her; he had waited what seemed to be an eternity. His sadness at not being able to do this was, though, slowly being eroded by the fact that he could see Marci getting better. It would just have to be enough for a while. Looking in from the outside Blake could see clear evidence that the gene rejuvenation serum was definitely working. The injection that he gave himself shortly after being with Marci on that first night was also working on him. So it looked like Dr Joseph Singh had probably found the holy grail of medical science after all.

He couldn't help thinking that the platform for this really warranted some Nobel Prize equivalent of a Knighthood from the King or even a new Bank Holiday or something.

Was it really fair that something so great was unleashed under such humble circumstances? No pomp, no big global ceremony? As ever grateful as Blake was, he couldn't help feeling that it was not quite fair on Joseph. But then maybe it was.

While Marci was in hospital Blake had managed to rent an apartment close to Wellington's waterfront on Kent Terrace. It was a bit bijou but did the trick and was good enough for what he wanted. He was able to walk to most of the things he needed and the hospital was just a shortish bus ride away. He grew to like the city as he wandered the streets. To him it was a city made up of a number of small villages, and he grew up in villages. Blake saw all of them bursting with their own character and DNA. You could pass from one area to the other and be continually entertained by their individual colour and vibrant culture.

Over the coming weeks Blake and Marci became virtually inseparable. Marci appeared to have springs in her steps everywhere she went. Blake kind of floated around on a cloud every day with a daft grin on his face most of the time. For all intents and purposes they were again and maybe even still very much in love. The strange thing though was that there were no long term commitments to each other but it was clear that neither wanted to really be parted from the other. Both seemed to be gloriously happy that they were together again, having lots of fun and catching up with what life had thrown at them over the years they were apart.

Blake, though, sensed that at some point the elephant in the room would have to be dealt with. Despite all that had happened recently the issue of how they felt for each other previously and why nothing was ever said had not really come

244

up. This played and provoked Blake to the point that it began to distract him a little bit. He didn't want to scare Marci away or hurt or upset her in any way but he knew that that things really needed to be transparent between him and Marci and he was going to have to deal with it. This being the case there were two things that he would have to get off the table; they were 1) why they never spoke about how they felt about each other in the past; and, 2) he would have to tell her what really happened in the hospital and what the implications of this were to both of them. After all, this was now after the rain.

It was a Friday evening, Marci and Blake were now five weeks into being back together. They had arranged to have dinner at a very nice restaurant in town. Marci looked stunning in her black cocktail dress and Blake did OK in his linen suit – he was no 'club book' model. Blake stood to greet her as she arrived in the restaurant; he couldn't help looking her up and down as she approached the table. Marci always had good legs and that hadn't changed. She was in great shape. He was besotted with her and it was all probably very obvious. They kissed on the lips and then sat down.

"Marci, you look wonderful as usual. Is it a new dress?"

"Why do men always ask that! No, I picked this up a couple of weeks ago from a nice boutique on Willis Street. I had been saving it for the right moment, which looks as though it has come along at last."

"Had I have known then we could have done this earlier. Well it looks really good on you."

"Thank you sir," she nodded and accepted his compliment. "And you don't scrub up too badly yourself."

Marci adjusted her seat and put down her small handbag. "This all takes me back a bit Blake, you and I sitting having dinner and stuff together."

"All of those happy times in London you mean?"

"Yes, something like that."

"They were happy days, weren't they, you and me. I mean, we could have made more of it, don't you think?"

The waiter arrived at the table to break the onset of slight awkwardness that was beginning to set in to the conversation.

"Should we just have some wine, Blake?"

"Good idea. I am sorry but I haven't looked at the wine list as yet." Blake picked up the wine list and had a quick thumb through, noticing an Argentinian Malbec listed. "You OK with a red, Marci?"

"Yes, no problem for me."

"Then we will take a bottle of the Malbec please, thank you."

The waiter nodded respectfully and left to fetch the wine.

"You said something about making more of our days in London."

"Oh it was nothing really, I didn't mean anything by it really."

"No Blake, we should talk about it, for what it's worth you are right."

Marci was glad in a way that this had come up; she sensed that it was something probably niggling away at Blake as well as it was with her and really they should speak about it. She remembered the promises that she had made to herself and Lucy should she ever get to see Blake again. This was that moment and she decided to be direct, take the bull by the horns. "Blake, I hold my hands up to this."

"What do you mean?"

"Well, when we were in London I behaved like a fool."

"But Marci please ..."

"No Blake, let me finish please. Yes I was distracted, yes I needed to sort out some things for myself but I shouldn't have done all of that without telling you how I felt about you. Truth is Blake I fell in love with you but at the same time I became so entangled, wrapped up and trapped in my own insecurities that I allowed our relationship to die. It's my fault."

"No Marci, no, it's not your fault." Blake reached across the table and cupped both of her hands in his. "Marci, I was as guilty as you. You needed me and I got it wrong, I thought that the best way to get you was to let you go and then wait for you to come back; trouble was that you went but you didn't come back; well not until now that is. I have waited all of these years to tell you how I feel about you. Christ I have virtually camped out on your doorstep for the last six months keeping some sort of talismanic vigil over you whilst you were in hospital, it's been driving me crazy. For years I have waited for you to be exactly where you are now. Here with me. I loved you then Marci and I love you now."

The waiter stood patiently at the edge of the table with the bottle of Malbec in his hands. Goodness knows how long he had been there but his presence had gone totally undetected by either Marci or Blake. Both of them were still holding hands across the table and in the thick of pledging a lifetime of love and roses to each other when they were interrupted by an ice breaker of a cough. It made no difference at all. Blake and Marci were so entangled in their own love knot which was so intertwined that wild horses wouldn't have dragged them apart at that moment in time. The waiter figured that probably the best thing to do was to leave the bottle of wine on the table and leave. So that's what he did.

With dinner over Marci and Blake strolled out into the cool evening air, hand in hand along the Boulevard.

Blake had planned to ask Marci if she would go away with him for a few days. For the first time he felt brave enough to ask her and confident enough that she would say yes. He just wanted to spend some time with her on her own. Just the two of them alone, somewhere nice and peaceful. It would give him the chance to rekindle things properly between them, as well as talk about all of the things that had happened in the world over the past few years. He also needed the opportunity to tell Marci all about Transhumanisation and the real reason that her recovery had been so remarkable. Plus, of course, what the future would likely hold.

He had always fancied one of those spa places where you couldn't fail to feel terribly guilty and also a bit smug about yourself after being treated to a sensuous rub down by a firm pair of well trained and professional hands. When he asked her if she would like to come there was little hesitation in saying yes which was brilliant news.

"So where will we go?" Marci asked.

Blake wanted her to put his trust in him and let him surprise her. "Do you mind if I don't let on quite yet, just want to make it a bit of a surprise, if that's OK."

"OK Blake, sounds great, I shall go home and pack."

Blake said flirtatiously, "Don't pack much though, will you!"

There was a place on the South Island which looked as though it wasn't too difficult to get to, near Greymouth. It meant a short ferry ride from Wellington to Picton and then a bit of a drive which hopefully would be fun. He hadn't seen anything of the South Island before but had been told by everybody that it was very beautiful.

The place he had in mind was called the Tamara Spa. He had read the brochure and it looked perfect. Sub-tropical Mexican style pampering at its best. For head to toe double indulgence this was the place and Blake was going to make sure that they got plenty of it. It included all of that weird stuff like rice and tropical fruit enzyme body scrubs, scalp massages, body nourishing Yucca flower and rice wraps, foot reflexology and to cap it all off an unsurpassed tea ritual taken on your own private water bed. If this couldn't stimulate the old 'joie de vivre' in both of them then nothing would.

The crossing on the Interislander ferry, as it's known, was very smooth and straightforward for the time of year and the car journey passed just the same. Once they landed in Picton they drove across the Marlborough wine country towards the west coast before heading down towards Greymouth. The coast road was rugged and windy in places and tightly patrolled by a mixture of tropical ferns and tall powerful looking trees which stood firm and uniformly upright like Maori warriors who guarded the way. The ever present twists and turns of the road provided occasional momentary glimpses of breathtaking coastline as dense woodland gave way to the infinity of the ocean from the cliff top road. The ocean was certainly beautiful and mesmerizing from up here, motionless and serene. The calm before the storm perhaps.

Just another 25 kilometres or so to go and they would be there. Marci who was totally relaxed throughout, had slept for the last hour or so of the drive which had given Blake the chance to snap staring glances across at her whenever he needed. She was a really beautiful woman and he was so glad that he had been given this second chance to be with her. He couldn't believe it. There were moments when he tried to see beyond her face and into her mind, almost penetrating the soft tissue with his curiosity and desire to emphasise how much she meant to him.

She looked so timeless, so gracious and so utterly feminine. Her elegance transcended her eternal appeal. He was falling in love with her all over again. He felt totally helpless as though he was strapped in to some sort of scary high speed rollercoaster ride with its unpredictable twists and turns. He was committed and once onboard and strapped in there was no getting off this time until it ended for both of them.

Another 15 minutes or so passed before Blake saw a white sign ahead which was fixed to a fence by the side of the road giving directions to turn left in 100mtrs for the Tamara Spa. He slowed and took the turning as instructed and followed the long gravel drive down to the front of the cream coloured Georgian house. Marci had woken as he took the turn off the road. She looked relaxed as they pulled up at the front of the house where they were greeted by a couple of young staff who offered to take their small cases to the reception area for them. Cases unloaded, Blake tossed the car keys to one of the eager young attendants who caught them instinctively and expertly like a native Golden Bell frog catches a passing fly (yes with his tongue) clasping it tightly. The attendant proceeded to take the car and park it round the back of the main house.

Holding hands Blake and Marci followed the awaiting porter to the reception area to check in. The reception area was based on a Mexican colonial style but presented sparsely to give a very contemporary feel to it. On the walls hung simple Picasso-esque sketches prepared by local artists. The fabrics were powerful in colour but again well spread out and arranged so as not to distract you for very long from the rest of the reception. The floors were laid in well-worn limestone flooring.

The receptionist greeted them. "Welcome to Tamara Spa. How was your trip?"

Blake replied, "It went well, thank you."

"That's good, well, here is your security pass, you are in room 22 on the first floor, Mr Brown. I hope you both enjoy your stay and if there is anything at all we can do, please let us know. The porter will show you to your room, thank you."

Blake noted that her name was Christine; he politely thanked her, turned and gently taking Marci's hand they both followed the porter.

Blake was seriously impressed by the effortless check-in and the warmness shown by the staff; at first he wondered how the receptionist even knew who they were but then he figured out that the porter must have tipped her off when he arrived in with the luggage, so it was no great mystery really.

Their room was spacious and bright with tall chalky ceilings, double balcony doors to a patio and a large set of windows joined on the opposite side that looked out towards distant tree top canopies which cut a rugged path towards the coastal route beyond. The Pacific Ocean could be seen briefly in the distance, a deep royal blue this time of year and demonstrating almost an eerie, motionless, very still character like it was covered with a thick impenetrable skin. Yuk blue custard.

Once in the room Marci turned to Blake. "So the sleeping

arrangements are…" looking at Blake for an immediate response which didn't come.

He stumbled. "Well there are two decent beds and I thought we could have one each. This would allow us to be together and chat and stuff." He paused for a moment and then coyly added, "Only if you are OK with this of course; if not I can easily get another room, no trouble."

"Hey I am a Kiwi and you know what they say about Kiwi girls."

"No, what do they say?"

"Well Kiwi girls have on average twenty two lovers in their lifetime."

Blake coloured up a nice shade of pink, being slightly surprised and embarrassed by this shock statistic as well as the awkward position that he found himself in over the sleeping arrangements. He pulled himself together and responded. "And how many lovers have you had then?"

"Twenty one so far – so tonight with any luck I might become Ms Average."

Blake wasn't really expecting an answer quite like that from Marci. It was nice in one way and then different and quite candid in another. He wondered even if it was true as Marci always liked to play pranks, tease him and mess around when she could.

He put on a shocked face as best he could to try and call her bluff.

Marci instantly noticed his jaw drop just a little and didn't want him to be disappointed; she moved towards Blake and stared at him closely in the face. Pinching both of the cheeks on his face slightly with the palms of her hands, she said, "Kidding silly, just kidding."

Blake showing signs of relief, gasped and grinned; clearly
Marci was getting better. "Phew that's a relief – I mean it's
none of my business anyhow and I would never have asked,
but Christ that's two football teams or thereabouts, that's
good going."

"Truth is Blake I suspect that the reality is that it was the
men who provided the stats for the article when interviewed
and like most Kiwi men they just added a bit on for good
measure." She laughed. "So what's the plan now then, Blake?"
kissing him playfully on the cheek.

"Well," he said, throwing open the balcony doors, "we take
a nice glass of bubbly and chill before going for some spa
treatment in an hour or so at around 5.00 o'clock if that's OK
with you."

"Sounds perfect. I can unpack later. Come on, let's have
that drink."

Marci stretched her arm and held out her hand to Blake
as she headed for the balcony. Outside the Veuve Clique, or
fizz if you prefer, was nicely chilled and the very comfortable
and sumptuous seats waited patiently for occupation. Blake
grabbed the bottle and with a quick twist of the cork it
eagerly flew out from the neck heading at speed for the lawn
just in front. The lively and spirited contents rapidly reached
the rim of the glass as he poured it. He put the bottle down
and both Marci and Blake raised the elegant and fully laden
glasses to each other for a toast. Staring at each other and
smiling Blake and Marci cemented their arrival at the Spa.
The glasses gently caressed, clink.

"Cheers Blake, here's to us."

Blake stretched and leaned over; he very softly and
sensually kissed her on the cheek. His lips lingered like a

humming bird hovers on its favourite fragranced flower.
It was perfectly weighted and effortless. Marci reacted by
smiling warmly towards Blake as he kissed her; she was very
happy.

The next hour, although very unrushed, seemed to flash
past almost unnoticeably as they sat outside unwinding from
the journey, simply relaxing and wallowing in each other's
affection.

There was a polite knock on the door reminding them
that the spa treatment was ready.

The spa treatment was fantastic: soothing, tranquil
and infectiously calming. The oils were zesty but light in
fragrance, with definite notes of citrus and jasmine. The real
talking point though for Blake was the Japanese tea which
was served on their very own private water bed. While it was
a kind of traditional way to wind down after your body had
been pummelled and abused slightly, Marci would rather
have had another glass of fizz. As pleasant as tea was, it wasn't
what she really wanted here and now.

It was now early evening and despite the fact that the sun
had nearly set the air was still quite warm. The area was very
peaceful, almost to the point where they began to believe
they were the last two people on the planet. Blake and Marci
decided to enjoy it all one more time and went back out on to
the balcony for the last of the Veuve Clique left from earlier
in the day. They relaxed and sat, gazing out over the well-
manicured gardens below. It was classily dressed in pretty
coloured tiny lights to try and emphasise that warm Mexican
hacienda feel. It worked: there was an instant satisfaction and
appetite for more as the lights shone and danced like jewels
in an aerial jewellery box. The distant sea ghosted as the sun

finally faded behind the horizon like some final curtain call. They sat close, held hands and chatted like new lovers often do.

Blake reached out to touch Marci's arm with the back of his index finger. Brushing upwards very gently against the fine blond silky almost invisible hair on her arm, slowly stroking her, he continued upwards to the base of her neck with the deftest of touches. It had been a long time since Marci had been touched this way and shown such affection. She began to feel very wanted and warm inside.

Blake eased himself from the chair slightly and leaned gently forward and kissed her uncovered shoulder. His right hand was now softly caressing the smooth and fragrant skin at the base of her neck between her tensed shoulders. Marci turned and kissed him passionately. The aroma of the pink pepper and wild raspberry oils from her skin gently blended and seduced the tension of the moment. It was the fragrance of pure femininity. A heightened sense of anticipation came over Blake as he unclipped her blouse. She was still a very beautiful woman in all aspects. Blake gently cupped her breasts. Marci motioned forward and they kissed again passionately. The movement of their lips was both synchronized and sensuous. All of those years he had waited for this moment – at long last he had her heart, it was his garbage day.

They woke early, Blake had arranged for breakfast to be served on their balcony. He needed to explain to Marci about the effects of the genetic solution he had injected her with and over breakfast seemed as good a time as any. They were both sat at the breakfast table in dressing gowns taking in the fresh warm air.

Blake looked at Marci and taking her hand clasped it tightly in his. "Marci, there is something I really do need to tell you."

"Oh that sounds exciting, what is it?"

"Well it's not easy and you may not like it; it's a bit hard to explain."

"Go on, try me. After all you are my knight in shining armour, you know, and at the moment I can't believe that anything you tell me would hurt."

"Well it's about how you recovered from the cancer, it's about me and what I did and a little bit about Lucy cos if it wasn't for Lucy then none of this would be happening." Blake looked nervously away towards the gardens.

"Now you have me worried; anything involving my favourite girl gets my attention."

"Look Marci, I may have done something bad. On the other hand it may have been something really, really good. I'm not sure, just not sure."

Marci tensed and frowned a little. "Then tell me what it is, why are you so afraid. Can it really be that bad? Just tell me – you didn't kill anybody, did you?"

"OK, OK, here goes." Blake took a deep breath and tried to compose himself. He was a bit afraid of Marci's reaction to what he was about to tell her since it was a fairly radical explanation and might scare her – that was if she believed it all.

"It was after my heart attack when I was recovering in hospital. One of the doctors there, in conversation, told me about the possibility of adding years onto your life through a medical process of gene rejuvenation; he called it transhumanisation. Basically the theory is that it will allow

256

you to live well beyond normal life expectancy. The feeling was that it may not be unreasonable to reach between one hundred to two hundred years old, but it's not exactly been tried and tested so he wasn't sure. The way things go with medical science, who knows, probably even longer than this. Anyway at first I didn't take much notice; I thought it was a mixture of science fiction and too much daydreaming. Then I became very friendly with the Doctor and a few years ago I funded some development work for this genetic blending programme between different gene sources. The studies showed that maybe, just maybe, they could provide the answer to longevity, or transhumanisation as we now know it. There was hope anyway. So basically Joseph, the Doctor, my friend, created a genetic solution that provides Transhumanisation."

Marci looking intrigued and also a bit fascinated, said, "It sounds brilliant, Blake, but what exactly does this have to do with me?"

"Well, everything in a way and then again only a bit of it, if you see what I mean?"

"No Blake, I don't, there is clearly something you are not telling me, so you had better get on with it."

Blake struggled to find the best place to start exactly. I mean how far back should he go? The bits about Joseph and Alaska and the HeLa cells, while historically important, he didn't think were particularly the best place to begin. Perhaps start with Lucy: anything to do with Lucy and Marci would be sure to find it interesting.

"I was preparing dinner for a few good friends one evening last year. I checked my mail box on my way from the kitchen up to the bathroom and I noticed what I thought was an e-mail from you. I hadn't heard from you in a long time and got quite excited, so I opened it and read it. It turned out that it was actually an e-mail from your niece Lucy who oddly enough seemed to know all about you and me and, well, she went on to tell me how sick you were. She told me that as I didn't save you before – I guess she meant when you were leaving London – and if I loved you I had to really prove it by saving you this time. I was shocked, scared and worried sick. She told me that you had cancer for Christ sake. I was petrified."

"Where is this all going, Blake? Have you done something illegal? Is this dream I'm having about to shatter in front of me? Are you about to confirm that what I have thought for most of my life is true – basically that life is just full of shit for most of us, and I know because I have had more than my fair share – is it true after all? God I thought seeing you and being with you had just changed all of that. I thought it was finally going to be different."

"No Marci, please no, don't get upset, nothing like that. It's going to be different I promise, but in a good way, nothing bad, I promise you."

"So, what then, Blake? Why can't you just tell me? You English are hopeless unless you have a cup of tea in your hands! Go on, have a cup of tea and let's get this over with."

Blake, slightly embarrassed by the very true observation made by Marci, carried on, "Joseph my doctor friend, completed his work and died soon afterwards, I got hold of the Transhumanisation genetic solution and, well, I brought some here with me to Wellington in response to Lucy's mail. I came to the hospital when you were sick and I injected you with it. Then later that night I injected myself."

Marci leapt to her feet. "You did what?"

With a sense of calm Blake tried to explain. "Yes, when you were in hospital I visited you one night and I injected you with that stuff. Marci, that's why I think you are better. The real reason for being well enough to come here. In fact I know that's why. That's why you are here Marci, that's why – if it keeps working – you, me, us, we can live our lives all over again, maybe another sixty, seventy or even one hundred and twenty years together – who knows."

There was an instant and tense silence. Marci sat stunned at what she had just heard. She stared with a glacial expression at Blake. He had a tear in his eye; he started to feel like his world was about to end, like a criminal on death row in his darkest moment. He stared back at her with a desperate worried look on his face. For a moment he was convinced he had seriously cocked up. Marci began to cry inconsolably.

"So it *was* you at the hospital. God Blake, what have you done?"

Blake was shocked. "How did you know it was me? Oh yes the nurse who was on shift and the photo."

"Yes Blake, something like that. At first I didn't quite believe it as I didn't see the link."

Blake pleaded his case some more as best he could. "Look Marci, all I did was take a chance; I took advantage of a breakthrough in medical science; I took a chance for Christ sake, what's wrong with that? What other chance did you have exactly? None, I seem to remember. And *why* did I? That's an easy one to answer: because I love you, that's why. Isn't that the best reason? OK so maybe it was an act of passion-driven lunacy, I know, but I would do anything for you. I would do it again tomorrow if it was necessary. Marci, if I had waited to ask you, well, you would have died. I couldn't bear that. Please believe me, I love you and just wanted to try and save you for as long as I could. I had to take the chance. Is that such a bad thing?"

Blake didn't know what else to do; he wasn't really prepared for such a strong reaction from Marci. Sure, he realised that it would be a shock, but if it had made the difference surely it wasn't all bad? He had done his best. He reached forward with his arms and waited for Marci to accept his apologetic plea of what was no more than an act of passion, even though a bit mad.

It took a moment or two but eventually she looked up and they hugged each other tightly, no talking, just holding each other, gripped in relief and also shock at what had happened and the whole uncertainty of what was possibly going to happen next. Momentarily they were uninformed together in fear, nervousness and apprehension; they had no idea as to the future and what life would throw at them. Marci, drying her eyes with the back of her hand, asked inquisitively, "So these drugs, you said they weren't properly tested but do they have any side effects that you know of?"

Blake had no idea. "Such as?"

"Well, when I get to 150 do my tits fall off, for example?"

Blake, relieved that Marci seemed to be back to her old humour, replied, "Not sure but we can blame Lucy if they do."

Marci could hear the start of faint pitter patter as sizeable globules of raindrops appeared from somewhere above and were starting to tap with some frequency on the small table top on the balcony. "Oh no, it's starting to rain," she said.

Blake replied, "Don't worry, it will stop – believe me, there is life after the rain."

Chapter 18

It was towards the end of November 2028. Blake had moved out of his apartment in town a few months before and was now living with Marci in her house on Ocean Parade. The sun was warm for a November afternoon. A few birds could be seen riding the thermals high in the sky. It was peaceful and serene. A few close friends and family had been invited for a barbecue lunch to help welcome Blake into the family fold and to also sort of cement their relationship in front of Marci's nearest and dearest. The white picket fence had been given a fresh coat of paint and so it looked even more welcoming as you pulled up out front of the house. A mixture of zesty colourful blooms covered the borders between the front gate and the Victorian styled metal porch.

Both Marci and Blake had worked hard to tidy the garden and make it look good, with hedges clipped and lawns with their edges trimmed; the place looked neat and well manicured. It certainly looked good enough to grace a page in any Country Life magazine. In addition the food was prepared. The BBQ was ready to rock and roll and Marci had lovingly chopped fresh mint to add to the mango salad, one of her favourites (well that along with avocado, tomato and cream cheese on a toasted bagel). She added some light wine vinegar and oil to the salad and lightly tossed it with her hands. A little bit of African jazz in the background to get things into the swing played from the sound system installed around the house and the garden.

Exhausted from all of the hard work Marci and Blake had barely sat down after preparing everything when the wind chimes at the side of the house suddenly burst into life.

This simple and early alarm system told them that their first guests had arrived, having brushed passed them as they made their way into the garden. On hearing this Marci reached for Blake's hand and squeezed it gently in order to give him some courage as this was the first time that he would have met some of the people that were going to be there today. She then followed this up with a quick and playful peck on the cheek.

Blake wondered what was going on. "What's that for?"

"Nothing, I'm just happy and I want you to know it, that's all. Anything wrong with that?"

Blake smiled back. "No, sounds good to me." With that Blake reached forward and lightly kissed her on the lips. "Now that's how to give a kiss."

Just at that very same moment Marci's sister Bronwyn, her husband Gordon and Lucy of course all appeared in the garden.

Bronwyn had sensed just a little bit of awkwardness in that moment that they caught the loving couple canoodling and couldn't resist exploiting it a little by saying something, "Oh hi guys, I know we are a bit early but we aren't interrupting anything, are we?"

Arms crossed she stood at the edge of the decking, grinning like a Cheshire cat. Bronwyn had a devilish sense of humour and had always teased Marci at every opportunity, in a very sisterly sort of way of course. Marci took all of her remarks as anecdotal and frivolous, most of the time not hurting her at all.

Marci, as was expected by Bronwyn, bit back, "No sis you weren't interrupting anything. It will keep until later anyway." Her eyes flashed towards Blake. "Won't it, Blake?"

Blake knew full well that he didn't need to say anything. Anyway this issue was in a territory confined between two sisters and Blake didn't want to go there. Blake's response was to jump to his feet and offer drinks to everybody. "I have, sorry, start again, we have some of that mojito cocktail drink that you guys all like so much, it's a slightly different recipe. Are you all going to have a glass?"

Gordon was a bit quieter and more laid back than his wife and being polite was habitual to him sometimes at the risk of being a bit boring according to Bronwyn. It was just the way he had been brought up; his parents had drummed it into him from an early age. He broke the silence. "Love one, Blake, thanks, don't mind if I do," turning to Bronwyn, "do we honey?"

Blake turned towards Lucy and crouching in front of her, said, "I have mixed something a bit special for you too young lady."

It wasn't immediate but Lucy had to admit that she had started to grow very fond of Blake. After all she had not really met him properly until recently so it was kind of understandable. She had heard all about him of course during the long sleepover evenings at Aunt Marci's house but it wasn't the same as physically seeing him and getting to know somebody first hand. For sure she was indebted to him for successfully saving her one and only Aunt Marci, although God knows what he had done to her exactly; probably nothing except show up and hold her hand. But if that helped then she would always be his friend.

Lucy though had other ideas about who might get all of the credit if awards were ever going to be given out. She put the remarkable recovery success down to that little bit of positive thinking that she installed in Aunt Marci's mind by getting her to count those extra days rather than just one day at a time. Maybe it wasn't all down to Blake; perhaps Lucy and her were just a perfect team.

Gordon offered to help Blake fetch the drinks and they both made their way in towards the kitchen. The jugs containing the readymade cocktails were in the fridge and ready to go.

This left the girls alone in the garden. Marci turned to Bronwyn. "Bronwyn, you are such a tease. Poor Blake, he isn't quite used to your satirical sense of humour. Go easy on him. I don't want to scare him off quite yet, or even at all. Goodness knows it has taken all of this time and my horrendous illness to get him back in my life. You know Bronwyn I have been given another chance; please don't trash it for me, be sensitive."

A repentant Bronwyn put her arm around her sister's shoulder. "Oh Marci, don't be silly, I really was joking and I guess I didn't realise he could take things like that to heart. I am sorry darling."

Marci reciprocated and with arms now wrapped around each other they hugged. Bronwyn lifted her head from Marci's shoulder "I never knew, Marci, that a certain little girl had a big hand to play in all of this."

Marci released her grip on Bronwyn. "Well somebody had to have tipped him off of course, I guessed as much; bless her. The nurse at the hospital told me that a guy who looked like Blake had visited me in there, mysteriously in the middle of the night and then Blake got round to telling me how he found out about me being sick, I couldn't believe it. He told me that he received a message from Lucy which at first he thought was from me. So it looks like some sort of a plan was concocted to try and save me. The rest is history. She really is a remarkable kid, I don't know where I would be without her. It doesn't bear thinking about."

Marci glanced across the garden towards Lucy who was now looking all grown up. She was a tall girl for her age. The hair on her head was full of curls, just like her aunts, and again with piercing blue eyes, just like her aunts. She was dressed in a lovely flowing cream summer dress with patterns of tiny apricot flowers decorating it all over. She looked elegant and lovely.

Bronwyn decided to dig a bit deeper. "But how did she know about you and Blake and all that stuff about how you felt about him? I mean, why would she?"

"Oh that bit's simple enough – we used to chat during our girly sleepovers and so she knew it all, plus I guess she just cares, simple as that."

Taking Bronwyn's hand Marci turned to look at Lucy again who was now playing with a tennis racket. "I know that I owe her a lot, more than she or anybody would ever know. Goodness knows how I could ever repay that. Whatever she did, or whatever she made happen, well it's a miracle."

"Look Marci, she adores you, you know that, so just be there for her Marci, like she was there for you. That's all."

"I will Bronwyn, always, I promise."

The two sisters hugged again. Bronwyn said, "God it feels good to have you back where you belong Marci, it really does."

Blake and Gordon returned from the kitchen to the garden with the tray of drinks. Gordon had carried the tray while Blake carried the cheeseboard and opened doors, gates and generally made sure that Gordon wouldn't trip over anything. Happy that they had safely completed a successful returning mission they put the drinks tray and cheeseboard down on the wooden garden table.

Gordon, with a reward-seeking grin on his face, said "There, we're just like a couple of professionals."

Blake said, "Thanks Gordon, now all you need to do is drink like a professional too."

"I'm certainly going to give it a go, Blake me old mate."

Blake warmed and was comfortable with the old mate stuff; it made him feel welcome, sort of accepted and part of the family which was important to him and Marci. The mojito proved to be as popular as was predicted and Blake was soon back in the kitchen chopping fruit and adding exotic flavors to make at least two more jugs before lunch. But who was counting?

More guests had arrived and the party was in as full a swing as it was ever going to be. Small clusters of people all around the garden laughed and chatted while the aroma of smouldering chicory from the fire which was cooking the marinated lamb steaks just drifted sweetly scenting the afternoon air. They had been marinated briefly in balsamic vinegar and it was just gently wafting from the back of the house over everybody. The aroma was lifted up and out in all directions stimulating everybody's appetite, its fragrances smelt delicious. Everybody enjoyed the imaginative and creative gastro effort that had been put into the food that was laid on.

Gordon said, "That was great food Blake, thank you. I see you didn't eat all of your goat's cheese though – what's going on there then?"

"Well I really only recently got the hang of goat's cheese if you know what I mean. Maybe I never grew up when it came to eating properly. My mother, God bless her, would always tell me off for leaving something on my plate when we were kids. It was usually the things that smelt or tasted strong that I didn't want."

Gordon replied, "Well I enjoyed it, especially with the figs and redcurrants, delicious. Anyway you must have been doing something right when you were young as you look pretty good on it Blake, that's for sure."

"Thanks Gordon, nice to hear, not too bad for an old timer, hey. But what about Marci, look at her, what a transformation from just a few months ago; she was on death's door at one point. The changes in her now are unbelievable."

Gordon couldn't agree more. "I can't believe it either, it's really a miracle. You are a lucky guy Blake, she is a stunning woman."

The talking, the sipping of mojitos and grazing the wonderful food that had been prepared and laid out seemed to meander on and on forever that day. The total moment became timeless. Lazy summer afternoons were made for times like this. It would go into the scrapbook along with many other memorable halcyon days of summer. This proved that it was entirely possible to domestically engineer paradise.

As the evening drew to a close people started to say their goodbyes and leave. Soon it was time for Bronwyn, Gordon and Lucy to head home as well. Marci and Blake stood at the end of the path and with their arms entwined around each other's waists. They stood at the fence and waved everybody goodbye as they left. They waved until the car pulled off the drive and headed up the road out of sight, homeward bound.

As was typical for that time of the year the stars began to sparkle as if they were being put on display for the very first time. Nice and bright as if shiny and new. They delivered that wow factor that you got when you were a child, lifting the lid off your old gran's jewellery box for the very first time to expose a collection of unseen gems that would shine and sparkle like glittering trapped fireflies in a jar if held to the light. They could illuminate both your heart and mind and at the same time provide a slosh of excitement that would run and tingle uncontrollably through your veins.

Marci looking up at the clear warm night sky, said, "It's beautiful, isn't it Blake? It just takes the meaning of life to a different place altogether." Totally relaxed she rested her head on Blake's shoulder and whispered, "Do you think love should have a colour and a name?"

Blake was mystified. "Mmm, have to think about that one, explain a little more please."

"Well if there is anything more beautiful than the night sky which we call the 'Milky Way', maybe the next thing so close to us that we can sort of understand is love. So I think it really deserves a colour and a name, doesn't it, just like the Milky Way. Each person can choose his or her own name or colour and just associate that with love – can't they?"

"So how many Mojitos did you have this afternoon exactly?"

"Oh I don't know, all I know is that when I see the night sky like this I realise that it is the most beautiful thing and I always want to be able to see it. If you know what I mean."

"Well sort of, we have to thank Joseph and Lucy for this of course."

He turned to kiss her on the forehead. "But what has this to do with love having a colour and a name thing?"

Blake knew that he would struggle to get a sensible and properly coherent answer by this time as Marci was showing signs of being pretty tired. He went for a compromise. "Well I see what you mean but I wouldn't know where to start really with that one. I suppose it's the view of a true romantic."

"One day we will find it Blake, our colour and our name. It will keep until then, no rush."

Blake and Marci decided to sit outside a bit longer, relax and take in the sweet evening air. It had been a very long and hard day for Blake and Marci but at the same time it was mission accomplished. She closed her soft pale blue eyes and rested her head on Blake's shoulder. He twisted his neck around to give her a gentle kiss on the top of her head. Blake gently and affectionately ran the back of his finger down the side of her face. He had seen it that day and could feel it now. Real life was beginning to return within Marci. The softness of her skin was as refreshing and as warm as fragrant tropical rain. (If you have ever been to one of those upmarket Spa resorts and tried the variable scented showers then you will know what I mean.)

The moment lasted only a few seconds. A shaken Marci woke abruptly. "Come on honey, time for bed, although you probably want to check your e-mails first."

Holding each other up they turned and walked back to the house. Marci said, "Maybe I can shower while you check your mail, how does that sound?"

"Oh the mail can wait, as can the clearing up. I will sort it all out in the morning." They reached the front door and went inside the house.

Marci asked, "Are you sure about the dishes?"

"Yup, absolutely, they can wait as well."

Marci said playfully, "Oh I see, it's now one of those nights is it?"

"Not sure, maybe I would just like to hold you for a change, you know an old fashioned cuddle."

"I like the sound of that, but maybe we could take it to a completely different level … what do you think?"

Blake was curious as Marci's teasing ability was endless. "What do you mean, a different level? It's a cuddle for heaven's sake."

Marci had other ideas. "Well, we hold each other and without saying anything we just think until we are thinking the same. Joined up thinking."

"Sounds good but you mean like joined up meditation?"

"That's it, joined up meditation, should we give it a go?"

"Is it the New Zealander in you that makes you so off the wall at times?"

"Maybe, but I like to think it's because I am a woman and am more sensitive to earthly things than you are. I see possibility where you simply struggle to see."

Blake smiled to himself; clearly this was now the mojito talking. "Look Marci, meditation isn't really my thing. Let's just get into bed and take it from there."

Marci started to undress and get ready to take a shower. She unclipped her bra and threw it towards Blake which he caught. "Oh so why isn't meditation your thing then? Is it because you are a stiff upper lipped-English bloke?"

Marci had the ability to bring out all that was good in Blake; he was happier than he had ever been even when she mocked him in this playful way.

He emphasised his English accent. "Marci, it's quite straightforward. I believe that meditation is the same as being in a perpetual state of near ejaculation – nobody really wants that now do they?"

There was a deathly silence as Marci tried to work out exactly what Blake had said. For once she seemed lost for words.

It took about two minutes for normal business to be resumed and Blake eventually heard the shower being turned on. Marci shouted back to him, "OK Blake, since you put it like that, you win, we will do it your way just for tonight, but remember honey, the hinge that squeaks gets the grease."

You would have thought that by now Blake was used to being shot at with humorous quips but in tennis terms it was now definitely 'advantage Marci' after that one.

Chapter 19

For Blake and Marci the next fifty years of life were good.
They doted on each other and as well as being lovers they
were also really the best of friends. Despite their ages
they both felt as though they were starting out in life and
everything was easy and cool; they were both very happy
together. There was little discussed anymore about the past
and the analysing of how they had gone their separate ways
just disappeared; the regret period seemed to be firmly
buried in yesterday. The conversation was now very much
about the future, their future. They had found each other
again and wanted to make the most of it all. Although they
showed no signs of aging or ill health neither was certain as
to how long it would all last. Historically bubbles would burst
at some point. It was probably this thought that kept them on
their toes more than anything else.

One of the first things that Blake needed to do was to
sell his business in London and move his life completely to
Wellington. At the beginning of 2029 he put the business on
the market and by the end of that year he had received an
offer which he accepted. Business was booming and the ever
growing turnover on the books helped him get a very good
price for it.

The forever yo-yoing of the housing market back in
England was now fruitful again and so he decided to sell the
house back in Langham and moved some personal pieces of
his across to Wellington. Marci described them as antiques
and didn't at first want them in the house as she said they
they clashed with her very no-fuss contemporary lifestyle.
Blake found this quite amusing but wouldn't give them up

as they were very much part of his past. He conceded that it was also probably a very English thing to do since we were more tied to our homes and our past than those in a lot of other countries. Eventually it was accepted that it was all a part of who he was and so the pieces were allowed to stay. It was mostly art work anyway consisting of paintings by local artists and some bronze statues that he had collected along the way from his visits to Suffolk and Norfolk. As it turned out nothing looked out of place; it was all in Marci's imagination.

Soon after, in 2031, Blake and Marci moved house from Oriental Parade to Evans Bay Parade. They needed a place which was more theirs rather than just Marci's. It was important to Blake to show that he had a stake in the relationship rather than just lodging there and so they took the step to move together to a spot which Blake was sure would make Marci deliriously happy. Blake knew that it was one of Marci's favourite areas in Wellington. She felt privileged to be living there. The house was a modest house but it had fantastic views, being just across the road from Hataitai Beach. It was the perfect place to live. It was close enough to family, Lucy in particular; the general amenities of life if needs be were a few minutes on the bicycle or a short walk; and then there was the beach of course which was just across the road. The lifestyle was intimate and rarely interrupted; they were able to share peaceful walks and slow breakfasts together as they looked out onto the bay. Life just couldn't have got any better.

It was during one of those late summer evenings as they both sat outside and after a couple of glasses of wine the conversation got around to childhood. It was a part of each other's lives which neither knew little about. It had been a long time ago now but these conversations were good as they got the early memory banks working and actually you realised that you could remember more than you first thought.

"Blake, what was life like for you when you were a little boy? I don't know anything about your roots, what school was like and if you had any friends, or did naughty things."

"Boy, that's a long time ago now Marci, I am not sure that I can even remember properly. God it's nearly 80 years ago now, let me see. Well I do though remember my first day at school, or at least I think it was my first day at school."

"Really? Crikes!"

"Yup, my mother forgot to tell me that there was a break for lunch, I thought when the bell rang that it was time to go home and so put on my things and went outside to wait for my mum. I stood and waited for at least an hour outside the school gates to be picked up by my mum who obviously didn't show up."

"I guess she came eventually."

"Oh yes, about 3.00 in the afternoon. Fortunately one of the teachers came looking for me. I was cold, thirsty and starving."

"Gee, all that time standing outside a school, so little and on your own. Weren't you scared?"

"No, not really scared. I guess I was worried because mum hadn't shown up but I wasn't scared. Things were different in those days."

"Different, how do you mean?"

"Well, different from the kids of today, or even in the last sixty years or so really."

"That's a bit wishy washy. Can't you be a bit more

accurate? You see, I know very little of the first part of your life; it would help me a lot."

"Life was more innocent, we didn't have much as a family, we were working class and happy. There was not as much health and safety or big brother as we see now. We survived being born to mothers who smoked and drank while they carried us – not that my mother ever did."

Blake was quick to differentiate between his mum and most other mums. "We could take aspirin in those days and eat blue cheese as well as egg products, loads of bacon and processed meat, tuna from a can and never got tested for diabetes or cervical cancer; it was brilliant. Today people just can't do that sort of thing. Life is more self regulated, some of the innocence and freedom has gone. We used to drink water from the garden hose; goodness me, I remember we always seemed to be messing around with hoses or water guns in the garden. It was pandemonium sometimes and somebody was always soaking wet. It was all just simple stuff, until electronic and video games appeared on the scene that is; after that the innocence just disappeared, sort of evaporated into space. I guess looking back it was all very exciting but at the time we didn't realise it. We were just kids."

"Sounds as though you enjoyed it all though, that's what childhood is all about."

"And you what was yours like, or should I guess?"

"If you want to, go on."

"Well, I reckon that you were spoilt rotten, always the best in the class and teacher's little pet."

"No that's not true. My dad died when I was a little girl and my mum raised us. Life was bloody tough I can tell you. Yes I was a little spoilt at times but we were close to each other and mum raised us as best she could."

"Well she did a very good job, if you don't mind me saying so, Marci." Blake reached forward and kissed her on the cheek. "A very good job."

It was 2042 and there was also a new king and queen on the throne in England. It had taken longer than the public would really have liked but eventually in the early forties a new wave of Royal jubilance swept the country and the few countries that remained as part of the old commonwealth. It was interesting to Blake that the people of New Zealand remained so loyal to the British monarchy throughout the years when the progressive way for other Commonwealth countries was more towards independence. Even though the public face of the Royal family had been in decline now for a number of years this couple were a nice couple and seemed to reignite a lot of interest in the Royal family. Blake even remembered their wedding back in 2011.

The one thing though that Blake had hoped he would see during his continuing and extended life was his beloved England win the football world cup again. It was way back in 1966 when England last achieved this success, despite coming close in 2034 and then again in 2050. It seemed unbelievable that in the final in Paris, exactly one hundred years later, in 2066 they were narrowly beaten again, 2-1, only this time by the Dutch. It was proving to be the most elusive of trophies for the nation, for some reason or another.

Generally Blake and Marci were having an absolute ball. Life was full of fun and enjoyment. It was full on, up to the brim with adventure, new and unusual experiences. Blake and Marci were very close and growing closer day by day. Being in good health would have obviously played a big part in this. As well as the relationship with Blake getting better each day, Marci was also able to watch Lucy grow up and get married which was something that at one time she could only have dreamed of. The wedding took place in Nelson on the South Island which is where her new husband, Taylor came from. The family was English and had settled in Nelson some fifteen years before, having sold their Kent fruit farm and decided that New Zealand was the place for them. As well as being a farmer Taylor's father was a very keen sailor and was now able to sail to his heart's content in the breezy and sometimes risky waters of the Tasman Sea.

The wedding was wonderful. It was held outside in the well-manicured grounds of their fruit farm home just on the outskirts of Nelson. From the grounds of the farm you could get a good look at the spectacular Dun Mountain with its reddish soiled summit against beautiful blue sky. The ceremonial area was capped by a strategically placed white sail that was being supported by a number of tall angular chrome posts. The sail provided shade for the guests against the hot sun. They overlapped each other to offer protection for all of the guests and the tables, which were elegantly set for the wedding breakfast and the evening's celebrations that followed. The food and wine had been prepared in a way that was simple, unfussy but full of delicate flavours. Obviously these were fiercely proud parents. The whole ceremony had a very English feel to it with a good twist of South Island simplicity, which added that bit of zest to the whole thing.

A few years into the marriage it was discovered that sadly Lucy could not have children and so Marci wasn't going to be the great aunt she would have delighted in being, which made her just a little sad. This sadness was probably understandable since she had no children of her own and subsequently no grandchildren of her own either.

Blake and Marci had a lot of time on their hands. It was an unbelievable extended retirement programme that didn't look like ending very soon. In order to fill their time they took up hobbies as well as travelled quite extensively to places that otherwise they probably wouldn't have. Blake learned to play the saxophone and Marci took up Thai cooking. It wasn't difficult to see who had the more appreciative results from the courses since there was never anything left on the plate once Marci had prepared one of her special noodle dishes. That said, a bit of smooth blues after dinner always went down well, even if it was a bit raw and scratchy.

In terms of their travels the good health they enjoyed still gave them the energy they needed to be able to walk, climb and just generally explore in a way that was more common to younger people, certainly not to anybody over one hundred years old, but it wasn't going to stop these two.

One thing they both shared was a love for wildlife and particularly big game. In 2065 they took a trip to South Africa exploring the well-trodden paths of the garden route with its luscious wineries and delightfully beautiful countryside. Plattenburg Bay and Neisner were their favourite Oceanside towns with their far reaching golden sandy beaches and friendly people. Marci always thought that it wasn't so dissimilar to some areas of New Zealand with its hazy summer days and mature sunsets that would regularly wash down the day in style. It was possibly an arguable case but since there were fewer lions and elephants in New Zealand Blake never really saw the similarity!

It was a mid-afternoon in April 2076 and Blake sat in the

garden just minding his own business. The day was warm with a crystal clear blue sky, not a single cloud to shatter the perfectly uniform colour on the canvas above. Marci could just about see Blake from the kitchen window. He was slouched in his favourite deck chair. She was curious as well as a bit concerned about him and so moved her head gently towards the open window and listened for any possible sound that might tell her if he was all right, but didn't hear anything. She figured he was possibly having another one of his deep thought days. These were on the increase, being a bit more frequent these days as he was getting that bit older. He was, after all, nearing one hundred and twelve years old and she thought that it could be possible he would be wondering just what to expect in the future. She wasn't of course experiencing the same sort of emotions as she was only one hundred and four years old – just a youngster in comparison! Marci decided to take a jug of lemonade outside and join him for a chat. It may help him. She took the lemonade from the cool box and picked up two glasses.

Marci approached Blake and put the glasses down on the small garden table. She leant over and kissed him gently on the cheek.

"What's up old timer, are you OK?"

Blake replied, "Yes I guess I am, I was just kind of looking up at the sky into nowhere, which frankly I never get bored with by the way, and was trying to place me, as a puzzle piece you understand, into the great universe."

"That sounds very dark and heavy going if you don't mind me saying so. Lemonade, honey?"

"Yes please, anyway what's with the old timer bit, cheeky? You are nearly as old as I am."

"Have you figured out that you are probably the oldest man in the world right now – is that what is bothering you?"

"No I hadn't and there is nothing really bothering me, I am just kind of apprehensive about it all, that's normal, I think. I have never been this age before. I don't know anybody my age who I can talk to about it so I am a bit stuck."

"So what do you want to do, go out and search through a bunch of small villages in Japan or somewhere, looking for somebody your age that you can buddy up to for chats? Blake you can't let this kind of thing get to you. God, when you injected the transhumanisation solution you had to be hoping that it would take us past a couple of Christmases, didn't you?"

"Sure, of course I did, and I am not panicking or starting to get jittery or anything, but Marci I am starting to find it hard to have normal conversations with people. They think I am a freak if I tell them how old I am. My birthday cake is going to have one hundred and twelve candles on it. In truth we should be getting a licence from the fire brigade to be able to light it, plus three people to volunteer to light it otherwise the first candle will have burnt out before we get to the last one. Look, most of the time I am OK but at the moment in a way I sort of miss people my own age. I find I have more in common with them, and there aren't so many around these days."

"So what should we do with the remaining four containers of the solution that we have frozen, then? Should we use it so that we can make our own little group of friends, somebody to go fishing with maybe when you are one hundred and eighty?"

"No Marci, no that's not it. Anyway we have to prove that the stuff we have left will work, and it probably doesn't. We could look stupid or even worse kill somebody in the process. We would have to offer it up to medical science and then we would just look silly. That's why we haven't offered it to any of our family, just can't take the risk. It could destroy our lives. Anyway why are we talking like this? You just popped out with some lemonade and now listen to us."

"Is this our very first row, Blake?"

"No Marci, I am not arguing, or rowing. Look, I am sorry, I am just a bit knotted up with it all right now. Come on, let's have that drink and chat about other things, about all of the good stuff we have done."

Marci poured the lemonade from the jug.

Marci handed Blake a glass. "I know it's weird to think, though, that you could be the oldest guy on the planet..."

Blake interrupted her. "Marci please, please don't ..."

"Hang on, I haven't finished yet, I was going to say as well as being the sexiest and sweetest."

Blake grinned. What was it about this woman that he found so irresistible? "Thanks Marci, I love you too."

"Are you sure or are you just saying that because I brought you some lemonade?"

"No, it's true and I can prove it."

"How exactly can you do that?"

"Well true tradition dictates that I make passionate love to you for hours until you are exhausted and begging me to stop."

"Oh I don't know, I could always just set the alarm and once awake I can ask you to stop."

Blake wasn't sure if he should even answer her as he

sensed he wasn't going to win the argument. "Mmmm, OK, let's beg to differ, should we?"

Marci replied, "Don't you want to put it to the test, then?"

Chapter 20

A few weeks later Blake was celebrating his one hundred and twelfth birthday. The day had started well with a nice breakfast in bed. Blake and Marci had planned to go sailing on the lake in their latest boat; it was a 30ft catamaran that sped across the water like a flying fish.

The picnic hamper was packed, the wine and water had been nicely cooled and was stored safely in the ice box, the emergency sweaters had been stowed as a just in case in to the day bag. They jumped into the car and opted to take the twisty coast road heading down towards the marina. They had been driving for about fifteen minutes when the phone rang. It was a call from England. Adam his grandson was on the line to break the bad news that Blake's daughter Sarah had sadly died during the night, quietly at home. It was not a long conversation. It came as a big shock to Blake as he had never ever considered that she was getting old and may die – and as for the day when he could possibly go to his daughter's funeral, well it was the last thing he thought he would ever be doing.

Sarah was eighty eight years old, a lovely woman, tall and slender; like her mother she was gentle in nature and passionate about the environment. She had had a nice life, hardly ever sick, and had raised two fantastic children, Adam and Tom. Seemingly she just died of old age which was something Blake had forgotten all about. Adam told him that funeral arrangements would be within about a week.

Blake and Marci didn't get out on to the boat that day after all; instead the rest of the morning was spent making travel plans for him and packing some winter clothes that he would need so that he could travel back to England almost immediately. There was a flight leaving Wellington the very next day for London and he would be on it. Blake loved Sarah very much and in addition to it being a very sad day it also felt quite surreal and disorienting in a hallucinatory sort of way. He was confused as well as being very sad. All of his thoughts seemed to spin slowly around in his head. Nothing would stop.

At the age of one hundred and twelve to be going to your eighty-eight year old daughter's funeral wasn't quite the normal thing to be doing for anybody. He knew that her children, who were now in their mid to late sixties, would also find it a bit strange that their very old grandfather, who should already be dead and buried a long time ago, could still show up at their mother's passing out parade. There were bound to be questions asked and eyebrows raised surrounding what would be seen by some as nothing short of miraculous or bizarre, even a freakish situation. All of which bothered Blake to be honest as he wasn't ready for it.

The fourteen hour direct flight to London gave him a lot of time to reflect. Blake had now lost the last of his immediate family, his daughter Sarah. His son James had died several years before at the age of seventy two. He was buried quickly and Blake wasn't given the chance to be there due to some misplaced contact details. More like the family didn't want him there. His first wife Rachael had died about thirty five years before; her life was cut short by cancer but she still outlived her new husband by some eight years.

This was all in contrast to his own lifestyle, where he was living on and on, transcending generations. The recent death of Sarah made him realise that the joyride though was

284

starting to get a little bit painful and the real price to pay was just starting to become clear. Blake had begun to feel a bit lonely in the world and he was uncomfortable with it. Obviously one day it all had to happen but he was in such a privileged position that he never had to think about it. He was with Marci and just enjoying his life. In the beginning his philosophy was that the future would only come one day at a time and so he felt he could deal with whatever it threw at him. For the first time he felt he may have been a little bit wrong and had underestimated it all.

He had some of the transhumanisation solution left; why then hadn't he passed it on to his family? Surely he owed them that much? He analysed this question for most of the flight without a successful conclusion. The obvious concern was that he wasn't sure of either the pros or cons. At the time of taking it and injecting Marci no trials had ever been done. He didn't want to pass on the potential risk of it failing and doing irreparable damage. It seemed a flaky argument now since they were both living proof that something was working out. Guilt was starting to wash over him and possibly rightly so. One thing was certain: the loss of Sarah in his life was significant and painful. It felt like having talons driven into and then ripped out of his chest.

There were also great grandchildren but Blake didn't know that much about them. The combination of living in New Zealand and being separated from the family for many years meant that he hardly knew them. It didn't make fostering a relationship with them as easy as if he had been around and lived in the same or next village. They had heard of him of course: he had sent cards at Christmas and birthdays, although none ever came back the other way.

All he could think about during the flight was his little girl. How they had played when she was young, her horse riding lessons, the time she grazed her knee when trying to ride her bicycle. That brilliant photo of her that he took when she was about ten years old, hanging upside down from her climbing frame with her fountain of golden hair cascading towards the ground like a mystical water feature. Her smile, it was infectious.

Growing through those school and young student years – OK he hadn't see as much of her as he would have liked due to his constant working but the time they had together was priceless to him. Oh and he must not forget the piano lessons, goodness me, they were bad. She played like she had broken fingers and they were bound together somehow. Needless to say there were not that many lessons overall. I guess some things are just not meant to be and Sarah being musical was one of them.

Probably though one of the most memorable things for him was when he had taken her on his motorbike to a piano lesson. Nothing abnormal or unusual in that maybe, except that on this particular evening she complained she was cold and so he sat her on his lap and buttoned her up inside his coat to keep her warm. Her happy little face popped out of the top of his coat like a little marsupial as they went along the road together. Well you could do that sort of thing in those days. Now of course it's only in places like Bangkok where you can go up the road on a motorbike in true circus style.

The flight from Wellington was quite smooth, no real turbulence issues to speak of. It was difficult to watch a movie with tear filled eyes as Blake soon found out. Sarah had been a wonderful daughter. In her adult life she had taught at both nursery and middle schools, painted some beautiful local scenes around the river Stour and of course raised two lovely children of her own. Her husband though, who had already passed away, had been a good father and husband as far as Blake was aware but he wasn't Blake's favourite person after all – but then nobody was ever going to be good enough for daddy's little girl.

Blake had no idea of the funeral arrangements. He figured he would get there first and ask questions later. His ticket was a flexible return so he could fit with whatever was needed when he arrived. He just needed to make sure that, along with his small piece of luggage, he arrived safely.

The food on aeroplanes had improved a lot over the last 60 years or so with separate restaurants now onboard and à la carte menus to choose from, offering exotic meal choices as well as good steaks and fish. Blake could see that it wouldn't be long before each flight grew its own vegetables. You know, a little onboard allotment in the hold producing lots of organic vegetables and exotic fruits. All climate-controlled to achieve perfection. The thought of being able to produce fresh strawberries and possibly micro bananas at 5,000ft, or even maybe have a fish tank or oyster farms onboard really excited him.

After dinner Blake went to the upper deck for a massage. He hadn't booked but after checking with one of the stewardesses he was told that they had a slot available. As instructed he slipped his clothes off down to his shorts and lay on the bed. The touch of those soft hands was heavenly and reminded him of the time he took Marci to the Tamara spa. It was just what he needed.

The plane touched down ahead of time at 5.45 in the evening at terminal nine Heathrow Airport. The flight time of 13 ½ hours from Wellington was a bit better than was scheduled. What he needed now was a smooth trip across London and a fast intercity train up to Manningtree. He bought a ticket and boarded the cross London monorail. The monorail trip to Liverpool Street would only be some 20 minutes so he should make it in time to buy one of those Cornish pasties from the train station before boarding the intercity to Norwich. Oh yes, some things never change except the price of course – they were now £22.00 each, but still good.

Cornish pasty in hand he ran to platform 32, which was on upper level 3, and jumped on the Norwich bound high speed intercity. It glided effortlessly all the way to Manningtree in just under 35 minutes. Fantastic – he never thought he would have seen the day. It was worth living all of these years just to experience this amazing change. My how things had improved; mind you it had taken many years to get there.

It was now around 7.00 pm and Blake had arrived at Manningtree Station. The place had changed a little since he was last here. The old station buffet had been extended up with another floor above it plus a roof terrace which cantilevered out over the track giving great views across the farm land. There was outside dining and live music coming from the roof area which created a happy, almost South American style carnival atmosphere.

A manmade cut in the river had been routed to the far end of the station which allowed sailing boats to come up and be moored on a purpose built jetty. Taxis now pulled up in a dedicated gravel drive area away from the station front. There was a small cluster of bespoke shops for hairdressing and beauty products, local crafts, specialist food outlets and florists. It was good; he liked it. Blake jumped a cab to Dedham for the last leg of the trip. It was only five minutes along the road.

Dedham hadn't changed much at all in the last 60 years or so. The Sun pub still stood there in the centre of the village and it looked as good as always. It would be his home for the next few days. It was located opposite the church where the funeral service was going to take place. He checked in and, once unpacked, made a call home to Marci.

The phone rang a couple of times before she picked up.

"Hi Marci, it's me Blake."

"Hi there, are you OK?"

"Yup I am fine. I arrived safely. It's spooky being back though the place hasn't changed much in all of these years. It feels strange, as you would expect. God, who would have thought that I would be here for my own daughter's funeral? OK believable enough for some people I know, but not when she is only eighty eight. I can't help feeling guilty now because I didn't share the transhumanisation solution with anybody else. It was just us."

Marci tried to avoid the awkward topic. "Look, I know those beds on the flight are comfortable but you must be tired. Please get some sleep, you must be shattered after such a trip. You will feel much better in the morning. I hope it all goes as well as can be expected and please get home safely. Call me anytime, I am always here for you. Take care Blake, love you." With that Marci hung up.

Blake held the handset still to his ear and listened as the

voice he had longed to hear was irritatingly replaced by a constant buzzing noise. He put the phone down and decided that he would go for a quick night cap before getting some sleep.

Blake wandered downstairs to the bar and lounge area. It was good to see that the lounge area hadn't changed much. He remembered all of those years ago when he and Rachael would meet up with friends in the pub and grab a seat in the corner where those big sofas would be. It was nice and they could all enjoy a drink on a Friday evening in front of the fire.

He ordered a cognac from the bar and knocked it back swirling it around his mouth as he searched for some form of comfort from it in this situation. But it was not forthcoming.

Blake needed to tell Adam that he had arrived as he had not heard from him since the phone conversation; also he needed confirmation of the funeral arrangements. This was a bit of a dilemma for Blake since he wasn't sure if he should go to the house or just give him a call. He ordered another cognac as part of the process to facilitate making up his mind. This was followed by another and then another which basically forced the decision to stay put and call Adam at the house instead.

Adam told Blake that the funeral was planned for the coming Friday, late morning at 11.30 am; that was three days away. This would give Blake the time to spend reminiscing and rewinding the clock from when he lived there all of those years ago. The other thing he would be able to do of course was to visit Sarah and spend a little time with her as well as pay his respects to other old friends already lost.

The Friday morning came and a small solemn and

mirthless group had gathered at the local church. People politely greeted each other, shaking hands and bowing heads in respect. The atmosphere in the front gardens of the church was eerie with an uneasiness about it. Blake was finding it difficult to relax. He stood as a lone and solitary figure barely recognised or acknowledged by anybody. He was sure that some thought he would already have been dead. The service was short and poignant as well as being a celebration of the life of a wonderful woman. They praised her for the tireless contribution to the community. Blake had planned to say a few words and when the time came for him to stand he made his way to the pulpit.

"I shouldn't be here today to witness the moment that my daughter is laid to rest. But in many ways I take comfort from the fact that I am here as I was when she came into the world. I was able to speak the first words to her that she would hear and am now able to speak the last as she leaves us. She had joy in her life in that she brought joy to the lives of many and also she felt joy herself. She was a much loved and special person to me and to her family and friends.

"When she was a little girl we would walk on the beach near our home town. Sometimes she would try to hide from me, a game we played, like many young fathers and their small children. I would always find her. Every time she would ask me 'Daddy how did you know where I was?' and I would say, 'when I need to find you I simply follow the footsteps in the sand'. Once again she has gone from me but once again I know exactly how to find her."

It was a hard delivery and Blake fought off tears of sadness as he spoke those last loving words to his daughter. He hoped that he could be understood by all of those in the congregation. Sarah's friends and family that had gathered now stood perfectly still in a moment of sad reflection. Images of Sarah flicked across their minds like an ever recurring old movie. Tears freely flowed the short but moving journey down the faces of her children, her father and her friends.

The church, white walled and beautifully decorated with her favourite flowers of Arum lilies, was picture perfect as the light shone through the delicate stained glass windows casting colourful creations across the whole congregation. It was almost as though Sarah's spirit danced and played before their very eyes in some sort of final curtain bow. Her coffin was gracefully lifted onto the shoulders of her surviving relatives and she was carefully carried out into the small churchyard where she would be laid to rest in the freshly dug soil. Blake was washed over with a cocktail of emotions: sadness, guilt, regret and love, all for Sarah. If they were meant to hurt and confuse him then they were certainly succeeding. He needed to see Marci; he needed to see her now more than ever. Outside the church Blake embraced and hugged his aged grandchildren tightly, wishing them well.

Once the service had finished people slowly and respectfully made their way back to what had been Sarah's home – a large Georgian house on the edge of the village called Dalethorpe. It was a beautiful and peaceful place, timeless and majestic. The back of the house ran down to the river Stour and from the front you could see up the hill towards the spire of St Mary's Church in Langham, the village which was once his home and the home of his great friend Dr Joseph Singh. It was indeed a very old house originating from the 16th century and given a modernised

Georgian look which was completed around the year 1800. Blake found it hard to believe that this sort of monument to the old empire would still be standing but obviously Sarah had given it many years of love and attention and devoted many hours of her precious time to maintaining its feeling of cozy grandeur. It was a fine English home and a testament to her life.

Friends and family had by now gathered informally in what was affectionately named as the 'River garden'. The garden was laid formally with symmetric pathways knitted together by neatly trimmed box hedging, framed around clusters of carefully placed crops of mature lavender. Central to it all was a large but simple water feature which gently trickled water over an ornate sculpture of angels. The scene was both very fitting and peaceful. The view from the river garden was of the paddock and beyond and the river itself meandering peacefully towards the village. Blake could sense Sarah everywhere as he slowly made his way over the crunchy gravel pathways trying desperately hard not to displace the finely positioned stones under his feet. He had little concept of what sort of reception he was about to receive.

Eventually he was greeted by Sarah's eldest son, Adam. Adam was a tall, well groomed and handsome man, smartly dressed and nicely spoken, with a very friendly smile. He didn't resemble the image portrayed from the recent telephone conversations.

Adam introduced himself with his outstretched hand, "So, what do I call you? Grandfather seems a waste of time, don't you think?"

Blake reciprocated and offered his hand also. "Blake, just call me Blake, Blake is fine, absolutely fine." He was still feeling a bit nervous and it probably showed.

"OK then, Blake it is then, grandpa."

"OK, you can call me grandpa if you want to, that's also fine by me. I don't have an issue with that."

Adam jumped in and cut Blake off in conversation slightly. "You know mum always talked of you. We have heard all of the stories about you with your heart trouble, divorcing gran and then disappearing mysteriously off to New Zealand. Oh and thanks for the Christmas cards by the way. I particularly liked the one with the sprouts on it one year."

"Thanks for yours."

"We never sent any."

"I know."

"Look mum talked fondly of you, you obviously meant a lot to her. I just wanted you to know that. You spoke well of her at the funeral and we thank you for that. Please don't get the impression that people here hate you; the problem is more likely to be that we just don't know you as well as we obviously should. And by the way, what the hell do they put in the water down there in whatever village it is you live in?"

Blake responded calmly although it was a bit of a struggle. Who the hell was he to patronize him about the way he felt for his daughter? "I live in Wellington Adam, Wellington. It's not a village, and as for what we put in the water, well, mostly water actually."

"Didn't mean to offend, it's just that you look so bloody good on it. What are you now? One hundred and twelve years old or something, how the hell can that be? You look and act more like a sixty year old."

"I agree, visually it may look slightly out of place but it doesn't make me a bad person."

"So what are you then, some sort of freak of nature? Well whatever it is let's hope you have passed it down in your genes because I could certainly use some of it. And mum could have done as well."

"Yup, I know and that saddens me Adam, more than you will ever know. I loved your mother dearly and I missed not seeing her in the later years of her life. I missed not having her around."

"So why did you not get in touch a bit more often, then? All it takes is a call, an e-mail or something – you know, Sarah @therivergarden.co.uk, it was as simple as that."

"I suppose I was avoiding a lot of questions I guess. I was a bit afraid and also didn't want to make the lives of others a misery. My ex-wife Rachael, your grandmother, was always good at poisoning the truth and on the couple of occasions I did make contact I understood that you guys had already sentenced me as a guilty man and didn't particularly want to hear from me anymore."

"That's not quite true. Sure, gran tried to make it look like that but mum was always there for you, always straightening the story out."

"I am really sorry Adam, I loved your mother and have missed her and always will. I can't undo what has been done. I can't get the river to flow back upstream."

They both turned to acknowledge the river.

Blake said, "Oh yes, that river and its famous Suffolk Mud."

Adam smiled. "It's a bit of a myth around here, the healing powers of the Suffolk mud; tastes good on salads though so shouldn't complain. Some people around here believe that the inspiration for everything can be provided by the mud from this river and since the North side belongs to Suffolk it has been translated over time to Suffolk Mud. You should go to the deli in the village before you go back; they sell a salad dressing named after the stuff. Been making it for 80 or 90 years now apparently."

"I'll do that thanks, I'll do that."

"But promise me one thing, Grandpa."

"Yes Adam anything, just ask."

"Don't disappear anymore, we need to know what the hell you are getting up to down there in Wellington. Who knows, maybe even come and visit you sometime, if you can live long enough."

"OK Adam, that's a deal, and I think I will live long enough for that, I promise."

"Good to hear that." Adam put an arm around Blake and hugged him tightly which Blake appreciated.

Blake asked, "So why this particular garden when there are other nice spots around the house?"

"That's an easy one. It was mum's favourite place to come, simple as that. She would come out to the garden every day and sit here for an eternity sometimes. She would gaze out over the paddock to the river; she loved it, she belonged here. She is in here with us right now if you look carefully."

Blake sensed this might actually be true and for a moment he wondered if he felt her brush past him. Just for a split second if he closed his eyes he could feel her presence. He ached to reach out and touch her, smell her, hear her. If he stared long and hard enough through the water spray from the fountain he could see shifting images of her dancing all around.

It wasn't long before people paid their respects again to

the family and made their way home. After speaking for the last time to Adam and Tom, Blake collected his things and politely left also. He wanted to take the fifteen minute walk across the paddock and along the footpath by the river back towards the village.

The next morning Blake woke early. His sleep pattern was still shot due to the combination of extensive travelling and the emotional rollercoaster he had been on since arriving back in Dedham. Arrangements were made for him to leave Dedham that same day in the afternoon and head back to Wellington. Before he left he wanted to have some time at the cemetery, alone with Sarah. He left the Sun Inn and walked across the road to the churchyard, entered the grounds and made his way across to her newly prepared grave at the back of the church. The grave was in a nice spot looking out towards the neatly groomed playing fields. The morning was sunny, dry and Spring like. This unusual warm weather had tricked the trees, hedgerows and wildlife as there were signs of plant and wildlife that weren't typical for the time of year.

Blake made his way through the graveyard to find Sarah's spot. The abundance of freshly laid flowers and wreaths heaped upon her grave was a stark and chilling landmark that made it easy to find. He stood numbly beside the place where she had been laid to rest. Silent sorrowful tears made their way from his cheek, periodically dripping down onto the freshly turned soil. For a very brief moment they formed the beginnings of a minute oasis before being absorbed by the earth below, just as his daughter had been only a few hours before.

Blake spoke to her emotionally, "Sarah, my lovely Sarah. In some ways I am happy and in others I am very, very sad.

I am happy because I knew you and happy for being your father of course. Why sad? Well because you are no longer here. In some ways I am also sad because I am still here. You have lovely sons, I met them yesterday and we talked a lot about you, your life and your garden, your work. I am sure that you are very proud of them. I want you to know that I will do whatever I can to be there for them as they get older, should they ever need me. You will always be in my heart. I never stopped thinking about you. Sadly your mother had tainted things slightly to make it seem as though I didn't love you or your brother very much but that simply isn't true. I loved you and your brother very much, I would say even before you were born. I can only pray that one day I will get the chance to put my arms around you again and tell you one more time for myself how much you mean to me. I loved the garden, by the way; for a moment I was sure I saw you there. Bye my love."

Blake took a step back, poignantly he bowed his head. With that he reached into his jacket pocket for his crisp white handkerchief, pulled it out and blew his nose. A crow sitting high above in a perfectly rounded horse chestnut tree broke the poignant silence with a high pitched shriek that interrupted Blake's moment with Sarah as he replaced the handkerchief into his pocket.

He then reached down and dug his fingers into the freshly dug soil, grabbing a handful which he slipped into a small plastic bag that he had brought with him from home. He folded it neatly and deposited it back into his jacket inside pocket. It wasn't much but it would always help him stay close to her even though he would be on the other side of the world. He stood next to her in silence for a few moments –

just remembering.

There was one last thing for Blake to do now before he left the village and that was to go to the Deli for a jar of that extraordinary salad dressing called 'Suffolk Mud'. The lady in the shop eagerly served him and packed it in some special protective wrapping to stop it being damaged during his long journey home.

This whirlwind trip had taught Blake a stark lesson. He realised that he had to plan his life better and use the gift of time that he was given for better use. He needed to plan more, if not for himself but for others. Up to now he had wallowed in it all with Marci and to a large degree had lost the important contact with his family. One day that would all be too late if he wasn't more careful about everything. He promised himself that he would talk to Marci about it when he got home and hoped that she would understand – after all her sister had died but she still had Lucy.

He checked out of the hotel and headed for the railway station in the taxi that was waiting outside as he appeared in the doorway. He stood and took one last lingering glance before getting in and closing the door behind him. It was a sad day.

The ride to the station was a short one with no problems at all en route. One thing that you could always count on was that this area of the Essex and Suffolk borders was always peaceful and unrushed. It was brilliant to think that despite continuing changes in the wide world this little patch of England with its divine tranquility remained unchanged.

Just an hour after leaving Manningtree Blake was glad to be checking in for his flight back to Wellington. He still hurt inside but his tears had started to dry and his focus was now on getting back to Marci. He wondered if one day Marci would ever come back to Dedham with him. That would be great, wouldn't it? He checked his wristwatch, just fourteen hours and he would be home where he belonged.

Chapter 21

Blake had been back from England now for a couple of weeks. Sarah's death weighed heavily upon him, especially since he still had transhumanisation solution in the freezer, albeit untested. Although even though it was untested it didn't make him feel any less guilty for failing to really help her. Could he have done, should he have done, it was torturous. He sat outside in the garden drinking some green tea. The morning was warm and the air fragrant with honeysuckle from the blooms that surrounded him. He heard the garden door swing open but couldn't be bothered to turn around to see who it was. There were faint almost girly shuffle sounds of soft footsteps on the wide mahogany boards that made up the veranda; it was Marci. She approached him from behind in her usual playful mood and put her arms around his neck, softly kissing the crown of his head and gently hugging him.

"Guess who?"

Blake said, "Absolutely no idea."

"Aha, you didn't even try! So how are you doing? Still a bit sad after the trip?"

"I guess I am, also I feel a bit tired from the journey but the whole experience is tiring in itself, as well as emotionally draining which doesn't help. It really was the most awful thing I ever had to do, even though Sarah lived a good life. We should have helped. I just feel terrible."

"Blake don't beat yourself up. We knew that this gene rejuvenation business was going to mean that we could outlive those we love, I know it's hard, God forbid I miss Bronwyn terribly so I know how you are feeling. But you shouldn't blame yourself this way, we agreed not to take chances on our loved ones, we need to stand by that decision or it's not fair on those we choose to help and those we don't. How do you decide these things?"

"I loved her though, Marci, very much. If it hadn't have been for her mother continually telling her otherwise then it may not have been quite so bad. She would have known that I loved her. It matters to me."

Marci loosened her arms and dropped them to his shoulders, she leaned in to his neck and whispered, "You're a good man Blake, Sarah knew that I am sure, she knew that you loved her. Believe me, she knew."

She felt the tea pot which was cold to touch. "Yuk, how about a top up of that green tea? Come on, I will make us a fresh pot, or maybe even some white tea, how about that?"

"No Marci, no more tea, please come and sit here for a moment."

He held out his hand as she walked around to the front of the garden chair and sat down beside him. Even at one hundred and five she still looked so lovely with her frizzy hair against the sweet smelling honeysuckle. Blake leaned forwards on to the edge of the seat and faced her. Clasping both of her hands with his he asked her the question that he had wanted to ask for more than sixty years, "Marci, will you marry me?"

Marci was in shock, she reacted badly and raised her voice. "Will I what? Will I marry you?"

Blake replied, "Yup, that's what I said."

Marci went a little berserk for some unknown reason. "That's what I thought you said. What has brought this on? Is it the fallout from the funeral, or are you still suffering jet lag or something or maybe it's your beta blockers doing the asking or do they put funny stuff into that Suffolk Mud that you bloody well rave about? Marry you, why would I? I am 104 years old going on 105 for Christ sake. Why now. And what colour wedding dress do I get to wear at my wedding, at this age? Some sort of psychedelic bloody rainbow coloured thing? And who do we invite? We hardly have any friends that are still alive, and as for our family well they are dieing all around us. "

Marci stood up from her seat, she ranted randomly some more at Blake before storming off back into the house; her footsteps on the veranda were not quite so soft as they were on her approach. In fact this time they sounded more like a a herd of cattle running loose. The back door clattered open in response to her slapping it with her hand. It swung to and fro at speed for a couple of minutes until it tired and became still.

Blake could hear plates and cutlery being banged on the kitchen table as Marci set things for some lunch. He thought he should probably let her have a few moments alone rather than going in to try to calm her down. After all he was in a bit of shock himself to the response, a simple 'oh that's nice but no thanks' would have done. On face value he couldn't see why not but just maybe his proposal wasn't such a good idea. It certainly looked that way.

About another half an hour had passed before Marci called Blake in for lunch. She had managed to prepare a simple salad with some grilled fish. They ate together inside but the atmosphere was a bit tense with barely a word spoken. This was the first time in all of the years they had been together that they had fallen out. There was a high probability that it wouldn't last and so Blake figured he would simply wait until the moment was right to tell Marci how much he loved her and that he meant well and meant what he said. That moment he hoped would come later that evening.

Marci and Blake had planned to take a walk down by the marina that evening, have a glass of wine and maybe something small to eat. Nothing had been said during the afternoon to change things so both of them assumed that the plans were still as they were. They would simply go about the afternoon in silence and meet up on the porch at 7.00 pm, dressed and ready to go.

Marci stood outside patiently waiting for Blake. She held out her hand as he appeared in the doorway. He took this as a sign that she had calmed down and was no longer cross with him. He gladly accepted the olive branch. He leaned forward and softly kissed her neck. God she smelled good, irresistible as always. What was it? That lime, jasmine and ginger body lotion she had always worn; ever since he first met her she had smelled that way. They strolled hand in hand to the car. Blake was ever so slightly relieved that they were both back in love again.

Things were still a bit quiet in the car as they travelled towards the marina. Marci would normally be jabbering away about her day and vice versa but this time there was some sort of awkwardness that had formed a bit of a barrier. More than once Blake wanted to break this and apologise but he didn't quite know how. He came close a couple of times but stayed silent as he didn't want to risk another upset. Marci on the other hand just drove; her focus was on the road ahead as usual.

They turned off the road and into a small parking lot

where they both got out of the car. It was a warm evening which was quickly darkening as the sun disappeared over the bay. Everywhere couples strolled hand in hand on to the boardwalks of the marina, clasping arms and hugging each other as they went. Blake smiled at Marci as she finished locking the car doors and made her way to the back of the car where Blake stood waiting patiently. He raised and held out his arm as Marci approached. She folded her arm in his, gave him a peck on the cheek and they set off to blend with the evening air and the beautiful people of Wellington.

They had been walking for only a short while when Blake couldn't stand the semi silence any longer.

Blake turned to her. "Look Marci, I just want to say how sorry I am for what I said earlier, the whole marry me stuff. It was ill timed and I hadn't really worked it all out. It was impulsive of me. I said it out of love, out of fear in a way. I never meant to hurt or upset you. I am happy for us to carry on like this for another 100 years if we want to. I really am very sorry."

Marci stopped and turned to Blake. "Blake, no need to say sorry. I accept – that is if the offer is still on the table."

"What do you mean you accept? Accept my proposal?"

"Of course, I would love to marry you, and I accept your apology as well, so long as you buy me a long glass of something very fizzy."

Blake's eyes lit like a beacon across the evening sky, one that could have been seen all the way to Auckland. "I can't believe it, I don't believe it. What has happened to make you change your mind?"

"Well I never said no, did I? OK I never said yes either but a girl can't rush into these kind of things – it took some working out, that's all."

"What do you mean, can't rush into things? You are 104 after all, so why not take your time? Take as much as you want to – after all you have all of the time in the world."

He reached forward and they kissed passionately.

"Christ Marci, you just made me a very happy old man. I can't believe it. I am 112 years old and am marrying the girl of my dreams."

They grabbed a table that had just become available at the Qui wine bar and ordered that bottle of bubbly.

Marci said, "So when should we do it, the big day that is?"

"No time like straight away, if that's OK with you. Perhaps we should go to one of those islands in the Indian Ocean and get married over there, unless you want a virtual Skype wedding."

"The Indian Ocean sounds better, the Maldives maybe, I always wanted to go there."

"Sounds perfect. Let's search for some options and see if we can get something booked up."

That night the sex was fantastic. They gyrated and creaked like a couple of old crickets hard at it in the long grass. In the morning after breakfast Marci logged on straightaway to a specialist Maldives wedding site called 'Married Bliss'. She searched through multiple electronic pages until they found something they liked and got to the point of booking.

Marci sighed. "It looks beautiful, Blake."

"It certainly does. It's strange how I never went there in all my years. That crystal turquoise ocean and the soft cream coloured sands; it's like some sort of paradise, quite stunning."

Marci, impatiently wanting to get on with it, said, "Well should we hit the button and instead of sitting here dreaming about it actually go there instead? That is if you still want to get hitched in say three weeks' time, that is."

"OK – do it."

One quick click was all it took. They then both just stared at the screen, waiting for confirmation when all of a sudden a message had popped up displaying those disappointing words, 'sorry but you timed out please try again later'.

Marci let rip, "Eeerrrrggggghhhh, this is crap, damn computers, they should make allowances for elderly people. So what now?"

"I know, let's go into town and speak to one of those specialist companies."

Within two to three minutes they were both jumping into the car and heading down town to a wedding arranger and travel agent that Marci knew of. Marci had seen them in a local magazine but couldn't remember exactly the street name, she thought it was near Willis Street somewhere. Blake drove as fast as he could, the car twisted and turned through downtown Wellington. Eventually they turned in to Willis Street and there it was, half way down, Cosmos Worldwide Travel and Wedding Arrangements. Marci put the palms of her hands together and started a quick prayer to the parking fairy. Fortunately she came up trumps immediately as a space became available as a couple in a convertible pulled out onto the street about 50 metres away.

Marci, finger wagging frantically, shouted, "Quick, quick, pull in over there, over there."

Blake steered the car in racing driver style into the just vacated space. He said, "Ah, ah a miracle, we got a space.

Never done that before. Usually I am running around the block for ages looking for a space."

Marci replied, "No miracle, all you have to do is ask and be nice to the parking fairy and hey presto."

Blake shook his head in disbelief. They got out of the car, shut and locked the doors and made their way back down the street towards Cosmos.

Blake pushed open the door and held it for Marci. The place was empty which surprised both of them. A young slender, rather gorgeous dark haired woman greeted them both. "Hello, my name is Miranda. Can I help you in any way today?"

"I am Blake and this is Marci. We want to get married and want to do it in the Maldives. We had messed around on the computer and filled out all of the online boxes and then pow – something crashed and we timed out and then we ..."

Miranda interrupted. "I'm sorry, did you say that you two lovely people want to get married?"

She stared at them in a peculiar way which gushed total surprise and bewilderment. Her mouth hung open slightly with no sound coming out of it whatsoever. It went on for far too long. Marci decided to break the silence.

"Why yes, is that so unusual? After all, you do arrange such things, don't you?"

Miranda was swiftly jolted to her senses by Marci's cutting tone. "Sorry well that's fantastic to see people of your age actually falling in love and getting married. You must both be in your seventies or thereabouts, I am guessing. I don't mean to be rude."

Marci fired back, "Then don't be, although it's an easy mistake to make, especially in our case," Marci added, swinging round and pointing to Blake. "Blake here, my husband to be, recently turned one hundred and twelve and I will be one hundred and five years old next month to be precise."

"You are kidding, right?"

"Nope, not kidding. Now, can we just get on with this before Blake reaches his next birthday – because we are busy people you know!"

Miranda was stunned. "Oh my God, I can't believe it, oh my God, I've never, never …"

Blake nodded politely. "If it helps we can't believe it either." Leaning over towards Miranda he added, "And we are still hard at it."

That comment killed any further excitement or curiosity from Miranda. Suddenly it all went very quiet and she finally got down to the business at hand.

All in all it took about half an hour and the booking was completed. It was official that Blake and Marci would marry on a beach on May 28th 2076 on a small island in the Maldives called Olihuvela. It was alleluia time.

That evening Marci sat on the sofa with her legs curled under and read from the traveller's guide:

"If anyone has ever tried to understand what paradise really is like but couldn't then they should just go to Olihuvela. It's one of those many islands that make up the Maldives with its crystal turquoise bays which are lined by spotless creamy coloured beaches to a backdrop of palm trees that stand proud like on duty grenadiers. Everyone and everything is friendly; the ocean is full of interesting and beautifully designed multi coloured fish and turtles – apparently there is even a chance that the sharks won't bite you. The skies, whether at night or by day, remain blemish free in untouchable perfection in every sense. Throw in a few indigenous highly scented plants oozing their captivating, sweet, pungent aroma all day long and all of your buttons are pushed at the same time. It's maddeningly fantastic. The sensitive seduction of it surpasses the finest chocolate money could buy. And believe it or not there is a bonus, yup really, each day is the same as the next on the basis that once perfection has been achieved then nothing else is an option".

"Blake, it sounds divine, I can't wait."

"Me neither Marci. Christ it's exciting, you and me, Mr and Mrs, I just can't believe it."

The day finally came when Blake and Marci had arrived on Olihuvela and were now preparing for the big wedding ceremony. Arrangements were made so that it was conducted by a specially flown in dignitary from the capital Malé. He had all of the necessary papers to join the two old love birds so that they would never fall apart; joined as tight as ever like some sort of love zip. Like sand and sea, that kind of thing. They waited patiently in their villa over the water each dressing in total silence. Both of them gliding around each other like well-choreographed dancing performers. It was all a bit surreal. The time now was 2.20 pm and the wedding ceremony was at 3.00 pm. Not long to go. All of this would be followed by a few images for the photo book before the wedding breakfast on the beach.

Marci wore a simple cream silk, sleeveless box dress. It was neatly embroidered with small silk roses around the shoulders and neckline. Blake wore a cream linen two piece suit from his favourite British designer from years ago called Paul Smith. It was a miracle that it was still in one piece since the moths in Wellington were some of the fiercest and hungriest he had ever come across. Marci carried a small and simple bouquet of local in season flowers that were put together by a young girl whom she had met on the beach just the previous day. She looked radiant. Blake sat on the edge of the bed and watched as Marci carried out the final touches of spraying herself with some soft perfume. He always liked it on her neck. The light bounced off the ocean below the villa and onto the walls casting playful shadows across Marci and her dress as she finished off putting on the perfume and playing with her hair. She looked stunning.

Blake couldn't help himself. "You really are beautiful, Marci. I am so glad we are here today and getting married. Doing this with you completes everything, this place, the stars in the sky and us. The final chocolate in the box. I love you so much."

"I love you too honey, now don't go all soft on me. Talking about going soft, do you have your special tablets with you for tonight? It is our wedding night, after all."

"What is it with you Kiwi girls?"

"Just can't get enough of you pommy guys I guess." Marci kissed him playfully. "Come on, let's get married."

It was difficult to choose a particular spot on the island where it was best to get hitched as every bit of it was just beautiful as the other. As tough as it was Marci and Blake had nominated a place in the garden between the lagoon bar and the beach. The reason for this was that on the morning when they had arrived and after checking in they passed this way to their water villa and a bird sang like crazy, entertaining them as they went. They laughed about it being trained to sing like that for all the new guests, some sort of welcoming tune. They later found out that the female bird had been guarding some younger birds in its nest and was more than likely sending a warning shot to anybody or anything within a range of about 25 metres. OK, it may be a bit dangerous as a location, since the bird was still there, but there was a very good chance that there could be birds singing on the wedding movie. It was worth the gamble.

The ceremony was sweet. Both Marci and Blake promised to love each other for ever and always, no matter what. That simple promise seemed to be enough in their eyes. All of this was witnessed by a small crowd of pure romantics who probably always gathered at these kind of things. The sort that just like to cry a lot for no reason at all. As it turned out this was just as well as Marci and Blake had not organised anybody for the task. When the ceremony was over Blake happily kissed the bride; they were pronounced husband and wife. The small crowd clapped limply as Marci threw her bouquet into the air. Powered by pure tradition and a bit of fortune it was eagerly caught by a very pretty young lady who had been standing there all on her own. She smiled back at Marci, giving her a faint wave of the hand followed by a muted thank you.

So that was it, they were married. It took about a full minute and a half for the on loan congregation and the rented dignitary to disappear. All that was left were Marci, Blake, the indefinitely twittering birds singing their heads off and of course all of that lovely sun, sand and sea. Oh a couple of nosey turtles wandered by but seemed totally unimpressed by it all – but then at their age it probably wasn't the first wedding they had seen on the island.

Marci and Blake stood alone holding each other in their

still and purified wedding vacuum; staring at each other
for a while, half grinning half smiling and doing that thing
where your bottom lip comes up hard against your top lip
making you look like a camel – yup that's the one. They
were oblivious to the fact that they had been abandoned
by everybody who moments before had clapped, cried and
thrown paper petals in the air. No words were needed; they
both knew exactly how they felt about each other. Guilty
pleasure – by far the best type if we are truly honest. It may
have been borrowed time for Marci and Blake but nobody in
the world would have been able to convince them that they
had not put it to good use.

Blake reached out both arms. "Come here wife, let me
give you a hug."

Now it was just the two of them and the bird singing above
in the trees as they held each other tightly for a few precious
moments more. All that was left to do now was to dance the
night away.

Marci lazed in a canvas sun lounger, one arm draped
across the top of her head, the other holding a glass of
bubbly. "So what now, husband?"

Blake leaned over and gently kissed her on the forehead.
"Well wife, I thought we could finish this bottle of champagne
and go for a stroll around the island, through the water's
edge, talk to the hermit crabs as we go and maybe find
somewhere to sit for a while. We can talk about the highs and
lows of being married before we go for dinner in about two
hours. How does that grab you?"

Marci thought he was joking but he wasn't. "Come on
Blake, do we have to? Can't we practise a few of those married
highs and lows instead, since it's all official now?"

Blake replied, "Would love to darling but it's a bit early for gymnastics Maldive style, anyway it would spoil the next little surprise."

"Mmm Blake, so are you saying that the sex isn't as exciting anymore now that we are married, is that it?"

"Marci please, no I didn't, I just want to wait, please, just a little bit."

Marci stretched out the fingers on her left hand and curled them upwards like some highly trained Thai finger dancer so that she could stare one more time at her wedding ring. She decided to relax her demands and said, "You mean there is something better than what has happened already? There's more?"

A relieved Blake replied, "There is always more, always. Come on let's stroll. Oh and leave the shoes, you won't need those."

Marci had no idea that just a hundred metres or so from where they were staying Blake had arranged for a very special private party for two. Marci picked up her bag and the camera and they wandered hand in hand across the sand towards the next stage of what was already a delightful afternoon. A simple table that had been set by the water's edge greeted them. It was draped in crisp white linen and centred with the same flowers that had been used for the wedding bouquet. The slightly mismatched silver cutlery looked like it had been cobbled together from treasure troves washed ashore onto the beaches from over the years but it fitted the bill perfectly. With their ivory handles they would have been graced by past rich and beautiful ancient mariners that drifted the Indian Ocean in schooners maybe more than four hundred years or more before. The table was circled by twelve tall oil lamps pushed into the sand that would light centre stage for the main event. It felt and looked very theatrical, like the nucleus of a big West End play.

The length of Marci's silk dress meant that she would be fine, it shouldn't get wet, but Blake would certainly have to roll up his trousers. Anyway it helped with the sexy castaway look that seemed to be all of the rage around here. It was almost therapeutic.

As they approached the table a very elegantly uniformed butler greeted them and offered to take Marci's shawl. Being pampered was one of her least guilt ridden pleasures. In fact she had always responded to it in quite a royal way which seems to ooze very naturally from her with ease. Blake sometimes thought this to be quite worrying really, especially for a Kiwi girl, when they are generally more famous for other things – apparently.

A very gracious Marci courteously took her seat. Blake sat opposite in his. The sun was beginning to set across the Indian Ocean and the warm seas gently motioned, swirled and bathed their feet in ceremonious style as though it was all part of the package. Each grain of diamante sand repeatedly soothed and caressed therapeutically. The sand shifted unyieldingly around their feet, like a bespoke Savile Row tailor would relentlessly work away, trimming and trimming constantly until there was nothing less than a perfect fit.

The sun had begun to set like a giant red glowing tomato in the distant sky, sending out shards of light dancing across the water; it really was the most gracious final curtain call of all. This must surely be paradise and heaven harmoniously rolled in to one.

The waiter approached the table as dinner was about to

be served. He carried a tray which was covered by a silver dome. He turned, faced Blake and offered him the tray.

A curious Blake asked, "What's this, a surprise?"

Marci smiled. "Well it's my wedding present to you, Blake. I had a funny feeling that you may organise something a bit special. To follow that would always be a very difficult act to follow. This dinner party for two idea, actually sitting in the ocean and having all of this, the wonderful food and the stunning beach all to ourselves, well it's got to be impossible to beat, hasn't it? It's the most romantic gesture ever; I can't think of anything that could top it and frankly I wouldn't even begin to try. So I needed to make sure that my gift for you could at least be on par with all of this or whatever you did, no matter what."

Blake was bemused and wondered what Marci had in mind. She was a seriously sensitive, aware and at times a complicated woman and he couldn't always work her out. This time though it had to be something she could carry easily, fit onto a silver tray and be manageable, so there was some kind of clue at least.

The waiter patiently faced Blake and with outstretched arms offered him the tray. His heart raced in anticipation. Blake was simply meant to lift the dome and accept whatever was underneath, what could be easier. He looked across at Marci, with a question poised on his lips but she got in first.

"So aren't you curious, aren't you going to lift the lid?"

"Yes of course, but knowing you as I do I am a bit, well apprehensive."

"It's my wedding present to you, Blake. How difficult can it be? Go on, lift the lid."

Blake finally did as he was told. He reached out and

grabbed the lid, much to the relief of the poor waiter who had stood there patiently for the last few minutes or so while Blake dithered. He raised it warily, half expecting a big bang that of course didn't happen. And there it was, Marci's gift, Blake couldn't believe it. It was a jar of Suffolk Mud. Only Marci could pull off something like this. Why did she always know exactly where and how to strike?

Blake was left with a dry mouth and finding it difficult to speak.

"Marci, I just, Marci…" Blake started to get a bit emotional as a small tear ran down his face.

Marci reached for a tissue from her bag and handed it to Blake. "Christ sake Blake, you are the only guy I know who cries over salad dressing."

"Marci, it's simply the best wedding present I could have had. You know what it all means to me."

"No Blake, today is the best wedding day a girl could have and I love you so very much. It will always be special; in fact I doubt my next wedding will be anywhere near as good. What I can't figure out though is that I wait over 100 years to marry my Mr Right and he cries over salad dressing."

Blake replied jokingly, "Will you shut up about that, it's emotional, I can cry if I want." They both laughed.

Marci leaned forward and took both of Blake's hands. "There is part two of the wedding present, Blake."

Blake's slightly sad face lifted a little. "Why doesn't that surprise me – so what is it then?"

"As part of this whole journey I believe we need to go to Suffolk. We need to go there – what do you say?"

"Marci, it's a beautiful idea, you're beautiful, but it's Dedham and it's in Essex. But I know what you mean."

"OK Dedham then, wherever it is. That place where they make Suffolk Mud."

"Anyway, how did you get …I mean how did you manage to…and a bottle that size, cos you are not meant to bring perishables onto the island?"

"Don't ask, it may spoil it all a little bit."

Marci smiled and blew him a kiss from the other side of the table. "Blake, it just occurred to me, this scene, it's almost as though we are sitting on top of our own wedding cake. The way the table is placed in a circle with the lamps, the creamy sands are like the icing on the cake. It's magical, you are magical. Suffolk Mud is magical."

A few days after Blake and Marci returned to Wellington they set the wheels in motion for the trip to Dedham.

Marci was on the phone busily organising, "Yes it's two tickets to London, direct of course, well we want to be there in June, early summer. We will need to keep the tickets open as we are not sure exactly how long we will stay. Sure I can wait a while for you to search something out and get back to me." Marci hung up and shut down the VDP (visual display phone).

She barely had time to make some tea when the travel company called back and the VDP lit up.

Marci answered, "Hi Marci here. Oh hi world travel, so you have some options for us already?"

"Yes Mrs Brown we do. We can get you out on June 30th, leaving Wellington at 09.00 am and arrive London that morning at 11.20 am. I have also searched a courtesy hotel at the airport so you can get some rest and a good night's sleep before your journey the following day. A car will be delivered to the hotel for you in the morning around 09.30 am. If that is OK with you I will go ahead and book all of this."

"Yup that's fine, just go ahead and book it all up, thanks so much. Blake my husband will be pleased. Oh, about the return…"

"Oh yes, it's open and up to you when you decide to head back. We just need twenty four hours' notice. We fly London to Wellington three times a day now so it's real easy."

"That's great thanks, and you have all of our travel data on the system, right?"

"Yes we do, I can see the biometric profile data is complete, so when you get to the airport just say hi to the voice recognition and do the DNA sample and that's it. Can I ask you a personal question though?"

"Sure, as long as it's not too rude."

"My biometric profile data says you are nearly 105 years old. Is that really true? I mean, I guess it is since it's your data but I don't know anybody that age, I mean…"

"Yes it's true. My birthday is coming up soon. I know, isn't it amazing? And my husband here, we just got married a few weeks ago, he is 112, isn't that brilliant?"

"So do you mind me asking; how do you do it?"

Marci wasn't in the mood for small chit chat. "Oh, plenty of beetroot juice and sex I suppose, it's all you need. Will that be all?"

Marci slid her finger across the visual display panel and the phone went off.

Blake had been out fishing for most of the day. It was one of his new pastimes that he had thrown himself into lately. There was a list of them as long as both of your arms which kicked off when he reached one hundred years old. First there was the saxophone – that started reasonably well but went downhill as he really struggled to read the music. This was followed by yoga, sailing, cricket, an array of water sports, wood turning, Spanish lessons, vegetarian cooking, Thai cooking and so on. He had done the lot, badly of course. One thing about getting old and not losing your mind or body strength is that it makes you fidgety and Blake was certainly that.

He was good at some of the things he took up and not so god at others but the main reason for stopping them was not that he lost interest it was just that one by one his tutors eventually died or retired and died later.

The car pulled up outside on the gravel drive. Marci took a quick look out of the window and confirmed to herself that it was Blake. It would take him a few minutes to put the fishing rods, basket and other things away in the garage before coming in with the 'catch of the day'. Just enough time for Marci to crack open a nice bottle of 2069 pinot noir from the aged old Marlborough Estate.

"Hi Marci, I'm home, where are you?" Blake stuck his head inside the kitchen door.

Marci called out, "I am out on the porch. I have wine, nibbles and good news."

"OK I will be right there."

Blake pushed through the garden door on to the porch, holding his red snapper in trophy fashion above his head.

"Look what I caught, it's called dinner – it must weigh 5 or 6 kg. Grilled with a bit of garlic butter and chopped shallots, sounds delicious, can't wait."

Marci couldn't believe that anybody could get so excited over a dead fish, but anyway… "Looks lovely honey, drop it in the fridge and then get yourself back out here, double fast."

"OK will do."

Blake returned outside a few moments later, hands washed and with dinner safely laid out in the cool box of the refrigerator.

"OK, so what's all the excitement about?"

Marci poured the wine. "Do you know, they have been making this wine for as long as I can remember, what since my 20s or 30s so that's about 90 years and it still tastes good today."

"Come on, stop stalling, get to the good news."

"Oh yes, nearly forgot, I booked the tickets."

"What tickets? Oh do you mean the Suffolk Mud express tickets?" (as they were affectionately labelled in the Brown household).

"Yes Blake, those tickets."

Blake said inquisitively, "And when are we heading out then?"

"June 30th leaving Wellington, we have a room at an airport hotel for the afternoon and evening when we arrive and the car will be delivered in the morning."

"That's perfect, it all sounds very relaxed, thanks. You certainly know how to make a guy very happy."

"Well, it isn't what I do but the way that I do it. It isn't what I say but the way that I say it and more importantly how I look when I say it – in case you don't recall I think that was a famous line from an actress who was around yonks ago called Mae West."

"I knew that."

"Liar!"

They filled the glasses one more time and Blake chatted about their dinner and how difficult it was to hook the fish. It seemed to have put up a bit of a fight as usual. Blake specialised in long drawn out stories with familiar endings. By some miracle Marci never tired of them. Sometimes she wondered why she loved him so much; it was a difficult one, not an easy one to answer. It was what happens when an unstoppable force meets an immovable object.

After a couple of glasses of wine Marci got a little melancholy and shifted her seat closer to Blake's. "How much do I mean to you?"

Blake, who had had a couple of glasses himself, replied, "If you got hit by a bus tomorrow, well, I would miss you."

Marci was immediately incensed and jumped up. "What, is that it? You would miss me, miss me, is that all?"

Blake giggled at seeing her rapidly catapult herself from her seat and getting herself in such a pickle over this. "OK Marci, if it makes things better, I love you. Now I have said it, are you happy now?"

Marci stood over him playfully. "But was that really you talking or was it your beta blockers?"

Blake grinned. "Well you will have to wait an hour or so to find out the answer to that one."

Marci, not able to get the instant reaction she was looking for, quipped, "Must have been the beta blockers then."

June 30th arrived and Blake and Marci headed to London and on to Dedham as was planned. She had finally been able to complete the pilgrimage to the home and source of Suffolk mud, the river Stour and the quaint old village that had occupied Blake's heart along with hers for all of these years. The cradle of all of his energy was evident for her to see and to feel.

Chapter 22

It was now 2096 and Blake had recently turned one hundred and thirty two years old. This year for his birthday they had decided to go bowling. Despite years of practice he still struggled for consistency in good scores, but he was still the fastest at bending down and doing his shoes up.

It was a Sunday morning and they trotted off into town to the newest 10 pin bowling facility that Wellington had to offer. The Diamond Bowl.

It was great fun.

Birthdays should always be fun but for Blake, of late, it was considered to be a bit of a sad time. It was that bit on the calendar when the summer was just starting to fade gracefully away towards a new hemisphere and the mood in the air would begin to ease itself into drifting towards a slightly different way of life. Sweaters and cardigans were the order of the evening, well for outside eating anyway. Oh, things would be good for a few weeks as yet but the seasonal writing was on the wall as they say. And would it be possible that this autumn could be their last together? It was a haunting question that both Blake and Marci had talked about many times over the past years, typically at this time of year for what seemed like the last twenty or thirty years or so at least. So it was no coincidence that it was usually a sweet *and* sour month.

While the wine helped it was of course also easier not to talk about it than actually talk about it. But to be honest living for one hundred and thirty two years was now starting to take its toll, not so much physically for Blake and Marci but more mentally and emotionally. Your heart breaks first with the constant loss of those you love, everything else follows on from that. It gets to the point where there isn't a lot that you haven't done, several times over in fact. This would always lead Blake to really question the true quality of living on to two hundred years old and potentially beyond. Which, over dinner, could sometimes become a heated and endless debate.

A big piece of Blake couldn't be more grateful than getting the chance to possibly live with Marci for a hundred and twenty years or thereabouts but the price that they had both paid for it all was more painful than they had ever thought possible – but inevitable of course. Naturally at the time when all of this was triggered it was a plan that was never thought through until afterwards and then for several years to come.

With greater intensity Blake found himself more and more often fighting with the question of all the associated moral issues. Overall he had generally convinced himself that he had always done the right thing of course. At the time it was no more than a selfish reaction to a cry for help. His reaction was instinctive, a knee jerk but one born out of the love he had for Marci. And under the circumstances he was convinced that ninety nine percent of people in his position would have done the same. So there was nothing at all wrong with that, was there? Also Blake knew that it would have put a huge smile on the face of his dear and seriously missed friend Joseph. So nothing wrong with that either. After all it was what he had been working towards for most of his adult life, God bless him.

What Blake had come to realise though, was that there was an ever extending list of issues that hadn't been thought through at all at the time of his heroic decision to save

Marci's life and at the same time extend his. Oh yes and the more he thought about it the longer the list would grow and grow. Apart from the very personal issues there were over the years the repeated witnessing of the Earth's continuous lashing out at humanity in one form or another didn't help matters on the grander scale of things.

Such incomprehensible, very random, inexplicable and mostly vile acts by Mother Earth would, with ferocious regularity, have no problem with killing and crippling vast swathes of people, splintering families, disassembling groups and ripping the heart mercilessly from helpless communities that mainly for historical or geographical reasons simply stood in the way. There were a number of ways this usually happened and Blake had seen more than he was happy with over the years. There were tsunamis, great floods as well as a few earthquakes and plenty of hurricanes. There had been what seemed like 'forever lasting droughts' and of course we must not forget the inexplicable fires which usually sprung up in areas that were eerily similar in size to some counties in parts of England.

Mostly those that suffered from this little lot would normally be poor and impoverished or very isolated and difficult to help. Many times the only sin of those people who suffered was to live in places which could arguably be described as being heaven on earth. So ironic, isn't it? What a heavenly price they continued to pay.

And then of course there were all of the other people, the ones that you loved, your family and friends. Some of this group would be the ones that you would have bet your house on not ever seeing them die during your natural life time. This understandably generated the toughest and most guilt ridden emotions of all. Having to stand idly by as your children and even their children died one by one in front of you wasn't a role that Blake had reckoned on playing and it was indeed especially painful to him. In fact it hurt like hell.

Blake often wondered what would have happened if Joseph had not been killed that day. Could the drug have ever gone to the open market and have reached mass production levels? Maybe the costs would have been so high that very few people could have afforded it, thus creating an elite race which would ultimately have led to some form of social anarchy and uncontrollable warfare. Would the government have intervened to prevent this? He doubted it.

Or would they have purchased the drug and provided everybody with it in a similar way that they handle flu prevention to the masses? Then there was the question of how you balance living for indefinite periods with reproduction – surely you can't let both of these run as normal?

The whole issue raised many questions in Blake's head. He would never have the answers of course but he did appreciate that quite probably most wise men would see that ultimately greed would eventually poison the human social structure and drive it ultimately to self-destruction. It all amounted to sheer devastation for the human race as far as Blake could see. On balance Blake thought it was for the best that the drug wasn't released to the rest of the world and that things turned out just the way they had. Regretfully Joseph had to lose his life for things to turn out this way.

Dr Joseph Singh being single handedly responsible for triggering the demise of the human race doesn't sound right or fair really. Especially since Joseph was such a caring and gentle man. Blake knew that in his heart that would not have been Joseph's intention. It would, though, have been difficult to sell that opinion to those that were in the here and now and suffering as a consequence.

Blake stood by Marci's side of the bed with a cup of jasmine tea in his hand. It had been the traditional wake up call for nearly 70 years in their house. They always started the day this way. He leaned over and whispered gently, "Marci, Marci, come on honey, wake up now."

She responded with an attempt at a soft groan, the type you get from somebody coming out of an anaesthetic. He placed the tea on the bedside table. I know, it's 2096 and we still have bedside tables, isn't that amazing? I suppose some things never change.

Blake pushed the wall mounted sensor for the play list. He remembered that an old British band from way back were always one of Marci's favourites. He struggled to think straight, 'goodness what was that hit they had around the end of 2011'.

He ran his fingers across the digital listing until he found the album, Mylo Xyloto, that was it. Coldplay, that was it how could he have forgotten. He searched for the track that she liked, he thought it was track three from memory. It had been probably ten years or so since it had been played last. He found it and hit play. He hoped it would get her stirring nicely.

The windows in the room were on light sensors and adjusted automatically as the sun gained ground on the day. The view from the bedroom was fantastic. Blake stood and just stared from the window with his mug of tea in his hand. You could see right across the bay with nothing interrupting the view. Blake and Marci were very lucky to be living at Hataitai Beach, in an area that had remained as it was all of those years ago when they moved in. It was the sort of view that would only cost you lots of time, which fortunately for Blake and Marci they had plenty of.

A partially awake Marci rolled over and stretched out for the jasmine tea. Blake standing at the window heard the commotion. He turned to speak to her. "Hi Marci, sleep well?"

Marci replied, "Yes sort of." She squinted at Blake through one eye as she wasn't properly awake as yet. "I see you have taken up your usual position on the bridge. So my Capitano what sort of a day is it looking like?"

"Well it looks like it has promise for an April day."

This non-committal sort of response always annoyed Marci. "What on earth is that supposed to mean: promise to be good or promise to be bad?"

Blake sensed he maybe didn't make it clear the first time but couldn't be bothered to try harder as it was too early in the morning. "Well promising to be good or promising to be bad is still a promise. Anyway it's hard to tell at the moment. The barometer shows it is a bit muggy out so it may be that there could be a storm later, but I don't know."

"Well fortunately you make a better cup of tea than you forecast the weather, dear." She placed her cup back on the saucer. "It was nice tea Blake and I didn't detect any little somethings in there that shouldn't have been."

Blake didn't like the reference to the 'little somethings' and he snapped at Marci. "Marci, for goodness sake woman, is this how it is always going to be with you? You know that I wouldn't do such a thing."

"Do I Blake, well I hope I do." Her eyebrows raised, she looked at him searching for a straight answer. Sometimes it just got to her. This whole continual question about how long they should go on for, why wasn't it right, it used to be, when did it become wrong. She hated herself for it, she hated Blake for it. She kind of knew that Blake's view was right but she didn't think she was ready. Certainly since her sister Bronwyn had died she had been very sad and it had caused her to think about what was worth living for, but she loved Blake and as long as he was there she would be there too, simple as that.

"OK Blake, I'm sorry, it's unthinkable of me, sorry."

"Marci OK I understand, I really do. It just means that you are not ready as yet."

"Ready, what do you mean ready?"

"Well ready to think about it seriously, not ready to talk about it or agree to it. You haven't been quite the same since Bronwyn died, it clearly upset you. It doesn't matter; we don't need to talk about it now."

Marci began to get emotional. Just a reminder about Bronwyn's death would usually bring her near to tears. "No Blake, I don't think that I am quite ready as you put it."

Marci threw back the cotton sheets on the bed and swung out her legs. She walked across the bedroom towards the shower room. Blake on the other hand continued to give the view from the window his undivided attention, his stare searching intensely for something to distract him. Marci slipped out of her nightdress, it dropped to the floor. She touched the shower control sensor and the silence was broken as the power pump for the shower kicked in. Marci's favourite setting for the shower was Tropical Rain. She said it was both

329

sensual and invigorating. Blake couldn't figure that one out as once when they were in the South Pacific together way back in 2080 on the island of Bora Bora they were caught in a tropical rain storm, sensual and invigorating it wasn't. If his recollection was right it was just and wet and coolish, more suited to a fish and not dissimilar to most rain that Marci never stopped moaning about. Ah Bora Bora, now there was a place to remember. Beautiful volcanic islands surrounded by coral reefs and turquoise lagoons inhabited by infectiously happy people. Happy, happy, happy.

Blake had been standing by the window for at least half an hour or so when Marci's return from the bathroom disturbed him. She put her arms around his tummy and nuzzled her forehead into the small of his back. She smelt delicious – just like tropical rain in fact.

Marci said, "OK honey, enough of all of that stuff, let's have some juice, go for walk on the beach and then figure out what we will do today. Then when we get home I can make us a nice brunch. What do you say?"

"Sounds like a plan to me. I will grab a shower and get dressed."

The beaches at Hataitai Bay were sandy and long, perfect for just wandering off and losing yourself on. Their routine was quite straightforward; they would walk for just over an hour in one direction, turn around and walk back. They did this most days of the week, sometimes before breakfast but mostly afterwards. The water today was gently rolling onto the sand and rushing up to the beach in small spills, only to be beaten by a slightly larger wave right behind it. Even though the tide was coming in it didn't matter much as the beach was easily wide enough to cope.

Only once, way back in 2022 did the water ever get near the top of the beach and look like it may threaten the local neighbourhood in any way and even then it was back to normal after twelve hours or so.

The pace of the walking always started out as a bit of a workout between them. The first half hour had just an edge of competitiveness about it – neither Blake nor Marci would admit to it though. This way of exercising was not unusual among Wellingtonians as for so long as Marci could remember the streets, beaches and promenades were always full of joggers, cyclists, skaters and walkers, religiously suited in their uniforms of ultra-light Lycra so that they could display the flat tummies and rippling biceps to anybody who may be remotely interested in viewing.

Marci and Blake passed the first half hour mark with little meaningful or creative discussion. The time seemed to be dedicated to the more trivial niceties of life such as agreeing when next to get the car serviced and for delivery of food essentials. As they walked they realised that the beach was quite empty. They had only seen another odd person bathing and a couple of young children paddling, even though it was warm enough. Usually more people would have turned out on a day such as this. They walked on a bit further, still not saying very much. Another fifteen minutes or so passed when the silence was broken by even more niceties.

Marci asked, "So how are your legs holding up?"

"Not bad for a one hundred and thirty two year old – thank you!"

Another five minutes passed when Marci chirped up again, "Still able to get your breath old man?" One thing that had been constant throughout their relationship was Marci's ability to tease Blake; she was relentless and seized every opportunity; she teased him with a passion. She also loved him with a passion though this time she would need all the love and strength she could get from Blake to help her across this very wobbly bridge that they both now faced.

Blake warmed to her cheeky remarks. "Marci, I am good and what about you? At one hundred and twenty four I suppose you are still a baby."

The bottom line was that the transhumanisation process appeared to be rolling on and on and every day was another miracle for Blake and Marci. On the rare occasions they were required to declare or advise their ages to people there would be a polite intake of breath usually followed by a 'really, well you don't look it' as if they knew what to expect because they saw people of that age regularly running around all over town. Even to this day they had escaped a scientific prodding and copious amounts of samples and tests by the medical fraternity. Goodness knows how but they were able to just get quietly on with life. That again in itself was another miracle. Blake suspected that one day his DNA would get collected for some minor random reason though and then the game would really be up. They would be viewed as freaks at best.

Blake decided to break the stuttering silence. "It's all so unnatural Marci, or at least that's how it feels to me now. I find each day more and more …"

Marci cut him off before he had finished; she knew what was coming next. "I know all of that Blake, I know. I also know deep down that you are right but I just can't accept that it will all end. That's where I get stuck. I just can't think of ending it all. I just can't do it. It doesn't seem right."

"So what do we do then? Just wait for a tragic accident or

something and hope that it wipes us both out? What exactly do you see as the alternatives Marci?"

Marci felt under pressure and reacted defensively. "Stop Blake, stop what you are doing to me, it isn't fair."

She stopped walking and stood there totally motionless. Head down and staring at the sand she said quietly, "Let's go home, I am going home."

Marci turned away from Blake and started to walk back across the beach. She knew this probably wouldn't resolve much but it didn't matter. It at least put a temporary halt to the discussion and that was good enough for now.

Blake knew that he would not physically be able to stop Marci and also it wasn't a good idea to try. Emotionally he was in a vacuum somewhere between his love for Marci and the fear of a tragic accident separating them. Feeling helpless and stranded he could only stand and watch as Marci powered her way back across the beach towards their home. He would have liked nothing more than to run after her but he knew she would need a lot more time to come to terms with it all.

For Blake the big dilemma now was: would he wait for Marci to come round to the idea that life couldn't go on any longer so that they could end things their way, or would he have to wait for that moment when they were struck by some sort of tragic accident which he would welcome with open arms as long as it took both of them at the same time? God it was becoming a mess.

Approximately two hours later Blake arrived home. Marci was in the house preparing the brunch. It was one of her famous avocado and shrimp salads. Of course sprinkled and freely tossed in some Suffolk Mud just to make it all that bit more special. The table was neatly set on the porch. A simple table dressed with a crisp white cloth sprinkled with pale blue crockery and extra shiny cutlery, the type that have those pistol shaped handles. Blake's favourite. A faint soft breeze gently greeted her as Marci emerged from the kitchen carrying a tray piled to the hilt with the main course and various assorted condiments. They sat to eat brunch.

Marci said, "I do love this time of year: the muggy heat has left the air and life is so comfortable now until we reach May of course and then God knows what after that. It's anybody's guess. We need to make the most of this time together, Blake."

Blake looked up. "You are right, we do. Wine? (silly question really) I'll get some."

Marci smiled. "A bit early isn't it, oh OK then please, you choose."

Blake pushed back the chair, dropped his napkin by his plate and got up from the table. He returned a couple of minutes later carrying a bottle of Malbec.

Marci noticed that it wasn't the usual New Zealand Pinot that they were drinking. "Oh, that does look special, Blake. Are we celebrating something? I am not pregnant you know."

Blake, with a sullen look on his face, sat back down at the table. "I shouldn't think so at the ripe old age of one hundred and twenty four."

Blake poured some wine for both of them.

Marci, passing over the salad bowl to Blake so that he could dish some food, said, "So what is it then, if it's not something I have done then it must be you? Come on, spill."

"Marci, we have been together many, many years and with all the things that we have been through, you should understand me like I understand you."

"Mmm sounds like a song I heard once many years ago, anyway what's love got to do with it, what's it got to do with anything?"

"Another song hey? You are always joking Marci but this time it's very serious."

Before he could say another word the penny dropped with Marci and she quickly interrupted him, "Oh of course it's April again isn't it? I should have guessed. You have got the blues again haven't you? Christ Blake, what are you trying to do to me, to us? I know that not everything has been easy but can we just try and enjoy each day as it comes and count ourselves as being very, very fortunate?"

"It's all so unnatural Marci, we know it is. In my head I don't want it to end, I don't want to be apart from you ever. In my heart though I don't know if I can continue to take the pain that we repeatedly go through. It's just too hard at times. It just can't last forever, it just can't, and I can't last forever either. We have to decide and agree to end this somehow, our way; it can't be left to fate. Let's not let some tragic global event blow us to smithereens or wash us away like we were in some sort of TV episode, just extras in some epic movie or something. It needs to be as important to us as every other day, every other thing we have done with each other."

Blake topped up Marci's rapidly emptying wine glass. His voice tempered, "You know Joseph and I would drink this stuff in the pub all of those years ago while plotting how to develop the gene which would continue to rejuvenate life, it was the holy grail of medical science. God it was going to change so much. It's our gene. A simple bottle of Malbec became the fuel for our entire decision making, well the important bits anyway. Who would have thought it?"

Marci wasn't surprised by this as in her experience many decisions are made while being coerced along the way by something soothing. "So how many bottles do you have?"

His mood changed, he lifted the bottle to about head height and tilted it toward Marci. "One more after this, so it's the second from last bottle. I doubt I will be getting any more."

"Very poignant, almost a bit penitent. So what are you saying – that when we get to the last bottle it will symbolise the end of the road for us, so what, we now need to make our last decision?" She screamed. "I fucking hate you. Don't make this decision for both of us, it's not fair. You know that if you go I go too."

"Marci, I love you more than living itself. I can't begin to describe how I feel about you, you know that. But we can't go on, and on, and on. I want us to end this on our terms, our way, loving each other as we always have."

A calmed and temperate Marci replied, "So your plan is that we take our own lives, is that it? Boy you really have all of this worked out, don't you? You've bloody well masterminded some sort of exit strategy with the Lord, a sort of road to retribution for the sin you feel you have committed – or what else have you done that I don't know about, are there more sins that you want to talk about you asshole?"

Marci started to get even more angry as she took control of the conversation, "So this done deal, what is it, two souls for the price of one? Die one get one free? Christ Blake, so what are you going to do, shoot me and then turn the gun on yourself, or is it something with a lot more razzamatazz like holding hands and swallow diving together off of the Sky Tower in Auckland?"

Blake as beaten as he was still tried to make light of it all, "No, you know I hate heights."

Marci didn't see the funny side. Blake tried again with a different tack.

"Look, please Marci, I know this isn't easy for you, nor is it easy for me. Yes it's a hard toffee to chew and believe me I can't bear the thought of it either but surely it has to be better than the potential alternatives. All I am asking is that we think about it. Let's not drink all of the wine. Let's please save some, just in case."

Chapter 23

Lucy had died in September 2095. Even without any assistance from the transhumanisation solution Lucy had managed to live to the ripe old age of eighty one before she passed away. Seeing her get quite old was a miracle in itself but when she finally left this earth it was as expected going to be very, very sad, especially for Marci. Marci missed her very much every day and found that her not being around left a huge gap in her life. Lucy had been her best friend for such a long time that it was going to be hard to lead a normal life again without her.

There was a distance appearing between Blake and Marci that wasn't there before. They were now both quite old themselves, although they did look much younger. The transhumanisation solution which promoted the gene rejuvenation theory had definitely proven itself to work. That Christmas, in fact most of the summer together was the worst ever. The void in their lives was opening wider and faster than they realised. Soon there would be nobody left at all whom they could speak to, visit or have anything to do with whatsoever. They became more reclusive themselves, hardly going out – they certainly were not interested in trying to make new friends at all.

One day in May 2096 Blake found Marci sobbing into a hammock as she lay in the garden. Blake had a really good idea as to what was on her mind but thought he should talk to her anyway.

"Hi Marci." He stroked her hair away from her damp cheeks. "What's up, you not feeling too good?"

Marci didn't answer straight away. Blake said nothing

and continued to stroke her hair. Eventually the silence evaporated. "Sorry Blake, I have been a complete arse, I know that now."

"What do you mean? Why? What's up?"

"Over us, over life and the whole issue of always wanting to be together, I didn't realise how much it was all going to hurt, I had no idea. Lucy's death has been the final nail for me and it has made me realise that you were right. Your way to go together, rather than leave it to fate."

"Hey Marci, come on, calm down don't go upset yourself now. It's OK. Some things in life are more difficult to get over and deal with than others, we know that. We have had some very difficult things to get over; it will be all right."

Marci wiped her eyes. "No Blake, it won't, not this time. I have made my mind up and I want to do it your way."

"Marci we don't have to do this, really we don't."

"Sorry Blake but we do. I just want you to promise me one thing and that is that you don't tell me when or how and please try to make it as painless as possible, and for Christ sake don't let me go on my bloody own or I will kill you, you understand."

"Marci, there is no need …"

She interrupted him. "Blake, you gave me back my life once and now I am giving it back to you. That's it."

Marci got up from the hammock and disappeared across the garden back into the house. Blake was a mess; he didn't know what to do or think and he just sat outside for the next hour or so. He wasn't sure if he should even go back into the house or even speak to Marci. What the hell would he say after that?

A few weeks rolled by and Blake had tried to get life back

on to an even keel as he researched and planned what to do next. He tried to look and act normally throughout, but he felt as though he was cheating on Marci in some way and it wasn't what he wanted but he respected Marci's wishes. After much researching he decided that he would use a poison. He obtained a quarter of a litre of strychnine from a farmer who lived in the Hutt Valley area.

Blake went to the garage by the side of the house, switched on the lights and closed and locked the door behind him. He had hidden the poison behind his tool box. Strychnine is used as a common pesticide and is relatively straightforward to get hold of from farmers and a number of specialised country stores. From what Blake had read and understood it offered the best solution. The biggest problem was that it is one of the bitterest substances known to man and so he would have to take care and blend it well. He didn't want Marci to be able to taste it at all. He had promised her there would be no awareness or pain involved.

Blake put on a pair of surgical gloves and reached for the poison from behind his toolbox. The poison was in a smallish glass bottle that was protected from damage or spillage by a hard plastic outer case. The case was fastened with plastic clips which Blake snapped open and he took the bottle of poison out and very carefully placed it upright on the worktop. He moved the plastic carrying case to one side and then reached out for the bottle of Malbec, a Luigi Bosca, Joseph's favourite, its quality he thought quite fitting for such an occasion. He was glad that the last remaining bottle was such a good one; it was how it should be. He told himself that Joseph would have approved.

Carefully he withdrew the cork and opened the bottle

of wine. God it was irresistible as he inhaled a large slug of
the beautiful and stunning bouquet. Fortunately for him he
needed to drink about a cup full in order to make space for
the strychnine. He left the bottle standing open for a moment
while he playfully twisted the cork around his nose, inhaling
the magical fragrances before drinking his allowance. Blake,
eyes closed, tipped the cup back and soaked up the full
flavours of Malbec from his last ever bottle. Next he needed
to empty about half of the remaining wine into a jug.

Blake had a clean glass measuring jug ready to pour the
poison and the wine into. Holding the measuring jug tightly
with his left hand he gripped the wine bottle with the other,
picked it up and steadily poured about half of the wine in. He
watched intensely as it splashed and swirled naturally around
the bottom of the jug for an instant until the level rose to
about thirty millimetres and then it slowed and eventually
stopped. He twisted the wine bottle away so as not to waste a
single drop. The plan was to put in about half of the bottle of
wine and then mix in all of the strychnine giving it maximum
blending before replacing the mix back into the bottle with
the wine that was left.

A very nervous and uneasy Blake proceeded to carefully
twist the top off the bottle of strychnine. The dark patches
of moisture on his skin produced by the cold sweat could be
seen through the thin latex material of the gloves. His hands
shaking, he carefully and slowly tipped the bottle of poison
so that it ran into the jug with the wine. He was naturally
nervous and started to feel sick in the stomach as he watched
the venomous cocktail blend in front of his eyes. His mind
was racing and he needed to take deep breaths to calm
himself down.

The problem was that he knew exactly what to expect once the mixture was swallowed, and it wasn't pretty. On the other hand it had to be powerful and quick enough to kill off the rejuvenating genes; God he hoped it would work. It was an emotionally draining and ironic situation to find himself in; it was difficult to deal with. He knew that after drinking one or maybe two glasses of the mixture at most it would be all over within ten to twenty minutes or so. He wasn't sure as to how much pain there would be or if they could slip into unconsciousness or not. The literature he found only explained how the head and neck muscles would begin to spasm and how intense convulsions would take over leading to asphyxiation before death.

There was more information available if he needed it but frankly what he had read already was more than he could stand to know about. He just couldn't stop thinking about Marci; her face went around and around in his head all of the time. And then there was the job at hand – had he overlooked anything, were they doing the right thing? Maybe they should wait another fifty years or so, why rush? Most importantly Blake had promised Marci that she would not feel any pain or discomfort, that she would not even be aware or realise that it was happening. What he had promised her was virtually a simulation of dying in her sleep. Blake was no expert and so all he could do was hope that he had chosen the best solution.

With all of the mix now back in the wine bottle Blake only had to replace the cork, wipe the bottle with a small towel and carefully put it back on the wine rack, all ready to pick up later that evening.

Blake decided that he wanted to leave a note to the world

which would explain everything as well as leave any personal messages. Since Marci wanted to be kept out of all of this he decided that he would write it as though it was from both of them. There was no point in any one person shouldering the blame for what was about to happen so he would word the letter to explain everything and leave it from both of them.

Blake never thought it would come to this. This was without doubt the most difficult thing he would ever have to do. How could he dignify such barbaric and tragic behaviour and yet celebrate their lives all in one note? The evidence was everywhere so surely people would realise that Blake and Marci had taken their own lives, wouldn't they? He was confused and bewildered and didn't know quite what to do other than let his heart do the talking.

Blake locked the garage and crept back into the house. He sat quietly in the study at the computer, fingers poised over his keyboard, his mind was blank and he struggled to find the words. He had sat for probably an hour in total silence with just the ticking clock for company, before being given some guidance, possibly by Joseph, he wasn't sure.

"To our extended family, friends and beyond.

By the time you find this note life will be all over for both Marci and myself but maybe it's not too late for some of you. More will be revealed but ultimately it's your decision if you wish to take the chance or not.

There are things that you will not know about Marci and me. We first met each other in the year 2012 some eighty four years ago when I was forty eight and Marci was forty one. We fell in love but didn't have what it takes to tell each other and ended up being apart for many years enduring excruciating pain and suffering as a consequence. We didn't know it then but later as we got older fortunately fate and a little girl called Lucy brought us together again. The truth is we were still madly in love with each other then and it stayed that way.

Due to some changes in medical science we were able to extend our lives through a gene rejuvenation process known as Transhumanisation. This genetic miracle was made possible by a man called Dr Joseph Singh in the year 2020; he sadly died without knowing if it would really work. We were just given a chance and we took that chance because we simply wanted to be together for as long as possible. Marci does and always will, whether in this life or the next, mean everything to me, I hope you understand. We have both learned that withholding love will bring the worst pain and suffering that you will ever carry throughout your life. My advice is then never to do it.

In the end we simply realised that we couldn't go on extending our lives indefinitely. The cost endured has been too great as we watched on and lost our friends and loved ones along the away.

Marci and I loved each other dearly and it was always important to both of us that we stay together right to the very end of this unbelievable and remarkable but beautiful rollercoaster ride. Sadly that's where we are now. For us it was time to get off, together we reached the end. Please forgive us for the selfishness and any pain we may have caused. Blake and Marci"

Blake printed the letter, folded it and put it in an envelope. Later that day he would put the envelope in the picnic basket that they were going to take to the beach with them that evening.

It was four in the afternoon and one of those wonderful autumn days that they see occasionally in the area where the day's forever persevering sunrays embrace the sand and rocky coastline and by night bright stars would invite the crisp dry air. It was perfect for a small picnic on the beach so long as you wore a good sweater.

Marci and Blake were both well wrapped up as they made the short trip across the road and along the beach a little bit. They liked to see the movement of the vessels that moved to and from Lambton Harbour. Blake hoped that since it was something that they did on a fairly regular basis Marci would not suspect anything. Blake carried the picnic basket and Marci carried one blanket for them to sit on and another to wrap around her shoulders just in case it was colder than she was expecting. At one hundred and twenty four years old she wasn't going to take any chances. The picnic prepared by Blake was a simple supper of Montgomery Cheddar, a few oatmeal biscuits and the bottle of Luigi Bosca Argentinian Malbec.

They held hands and walked, not saying much. Blake struggled emotionally and was finding it difficult to hold it together. But he had to. The promise he made to Marci was the only thing that kept him going at that moment.

Still hand in hand they wandered down to their usual spot on the beach in silence. Marci affectionately squeezed Blake's hand. "You OK, Blake?"

"Yup sure, just a bit sad that summer has left us and winter is approaching, but other than that I am OK."

"Blake, I know that since Lucy died I have been a bit off and I am sorry about that, really I am…"

Blake quickly interrupted. "Hey Marci, it doesn't matter, you were entitled to be, you were very close to her, she was a special person in your life."

"She was, but so are you. I kind of felt that if it hadn't been for her we wouldn't be here together now, and well I owed her a lot, plus of course we were very good friends."

"Marci, it's all understandable, it doesn't matter."

Marci seemed to have something that she wanted to get off her chest. "Blake, I know we have talked about the fact that we can't go on forever and I know now that it's not right…"

Blake stopped and turned towards her. "Marci, please don't say anything, there really isn't any need, let's just quietly enjoy the moments that we have together."

Marci conceded and softly pushed her head against his shoulder as a way of saying OK.

Eventually they reached their favourite spot. There were some small dunes which would protect them from any wind and also give them some support to lie against. Marci put out the rug while Blake removed his shoes, rolled up his jeans and slumped down with his hands behind his head. He stared out towards the sea. He tried to think straight but was in a bit of a mess to be honest.

The sea trickled up against the edge of the beach in a calming sombre sort of way, relentlessly but peacefully invading. Turning and unfolding constantly like nature's answer to industrial machinery.

Marci put her arm around Blake's shoulder and kissed him. "Oh Blake, evenings like this are just fantastic – just you and me on the beach, nobody or nothing for miles and miles."

"Yes, I agree, most of the time."

"Why most of the time? What's up?"

"Well most of the time I am happy of course but sometimes this bit saddens me as well."

Marci prompted, "Go on."

"Well lately I can't help thinking of Rachael and the kids, and you know..." He stopped abruptly. "God it is so complicated."

"No it isn't. You loved your family very much, you had the chance to do it all again. Who wouldn't, and I for one am glad you did. It's been the most beautiful time of my life. If somebody ever said to me that I would be snatched from near death and my life rejuvenated in the way that it has been I would never have believed them but I would have taken the chance, anybody would have done the same."

"I guess you are right, it's just at that time, well it was so bloody confusing, all of it. I just never in my wildest dreams thought we would get here."

"What, like those old commuter trains to London that you used to tell me about?"

"Yes, those old trains. Do you know that was over one hundred years ago now? God almighty, scary thought."

"So if you can go through that then this should be a piece of cake."

Blake started to feel uncomfortable with the way that the conversation was going. "Too much analysing. Come on let's have some supper."

He opened the lid of the picnic basket and they both unpacked what was inside and laid it out on the blanket. Blake had put in some crystal glasses for the wine. For the cheeses and oatmeal biscuits they had small china plates patterned in gold edging, all very English. As soon as he laid it out he realised that he may have made a big mistake.

"This all looks very nice Blake, are we celebrating something by any chance?"

"No not that I know of, I just thought we hadn't used them

for a long time and so, well, why not?"

"Sounds like a good idea to me."

Blake was relieved that Marci didn't dwell on his response and seemed to accept it. Blake cut some cheese. "Do you know a very old friend of mine introduced me to this cheese around about oh let's see, year 2000? I am amazed that you can still get it."

"So the perfect last meal then, is it Blake? Enjoying something from the past, it kind of rounds off the whole journey nicely and brings a sense of comfort maybe to it, don't you think? Some things will never change Blake, no matter how much transhumanisation there is in the world. Cheese will still be cheese."

Marci turned to Blake. "I love you Blake, you really are a lovely man but you can't keep secrets, can you?"

There was total silence as Blake was struck dumb, speechless at what Marci had just said.

Marci gazed into his eyes. "I know you made promises not to tell me and I don't want you to think that you failed, it's just that … well, it's OK Blake, it's OK."

Blake still in shock was freefalling. "I am so sorry Marci, oh God, it's a mess, I just wanted…"

"It's OK Blake, it's OK, really, I am ready."

Tears rolled helplessly down Blake's face as he listened to those words from the woman he loved more than life itself. There was nothing he could say, only hold her as tightly as he could. "I love you too, Marci."

"Come on, no more tears, you don't see me crying. Let's crack on with the picnic before tomorrow comes."

"OK, if you insist." He cut some cheese and put it on to the side of one of the plates along with some biscuits. He passed the small humble meal over to Marci.

"Thanks Blake, and the wine – were you going to share that or just keep it all to yourself?"

Blake said nothing. He opened the wine and poured himself and Marci a glass.

Marci thanked him and raised her glass towards Blake.

Blake did the same to Marci. Words didn't really cut it right then. They just sat looking at each other and penetrating deep into each other's souls for a few seconds. Marci then leaned forward and kissed Blake gently on the lips. "Blake, I don't mind what happens from here on in because we are together and that has always been the only thing that has ever mattered, just you and me."

With that Marci took a big gulp of the wine followed swiftly by another. Blake looked on in despair; he instinctively wanted to shout stop but it was too late. Now he needed the courage that Marci had; he just hoped that he wouldn't let her down.

"Tastes good Blake, you have to try it."

Blake raised the glass to his lips and after a brief moment of staring at Marci for courage he took two big mouthfuls of the wine.

Marci said, "So what do you think, any good?"

Blake replied, "Not bad, I have tasted worse."

Marci thought that was funny and grinned. "Really Blake? I didn't think it could be any worse."

Blake topped up the glass and together they took another large mouthful each.

Marci shuddered and shook her head as the bitterness of the wine hit the back of her throat. "Oh, that one was a bit strong. Christ, what have you put in this?"

"You don't want to know."

Marci decided to move closer to Blake and lay by his side. She put her head on his lap and pulled the blanket over herself. "Blake, it will be quick won't it, and you won't chicken out and let me go on my own will you?"

"Don't be daft, we have come so far now the last few steps are just another part of the jigsaw. I can't go through this process again, it just wouldn't be right and not only that I don't want to ever love anybody else."

"So what do we do next?"

"Talk Marci, we talk until we can't talk anymore."

"Blake, please hold me and don't let go."

Blake held her tight for what would be their last few moments together in this way. Blake nuzzled his face into the side of her neck and took in a deep breath just to smell her one last time. "God why do you always smell so good, even at 124 years old?"

"It's a secret and one that I shall keep to myself."

Blake had always admired her ability to make fun, she warmed him in so many different ways. He was indeed a very lucky man to have had the love of this woman.

Blake noticed that Marci had gone a bit quiet. He tried to keep her with him for as long as he could. "Marci look at the sky Marci, the stars are coming out tonight, almost like a parade, they are lighting up the path for us for our next journey, for us Marci, for us."

It was too late for Marci now. Blake felt a spasm in her neck, followed by another which was more ferocious and obviously more painful than the first. The sensation for him and obviously for Marci was simply unbearable. He pulled her closer to him trying to offer as much comfort and protection as he could and gripped her with all of his strength. Marci didn't speak, she made no noise at all, not even a whimper. The spasms soon became very aggressive and viciously violent. Blake rolled her over towards him so that he could see her face. Her eyes were tight shut, her skin had turned a purply blue colour with a map of tiny blood vessels protruding from her cheeks. It was a blessing that she had drifted off into unconsciousness.

Blake sobbed, "Marci don't close your eyes, please don't close your eyes, don't leave me now, please, please, I love you Marci."

Blake held on to her as tightly as he could. Moments later he felt a tightening of his chest and the spasms kicked in as his head started to shake uncontrollably. He put as much effort as he could into holding Marci as he gently motioned back and forth, rocking them to try and ease the symptoms of what they were experiencing.

Another violent spasm shot through his neck like he had been shot in the back at close range. Blake clutched Marci as tightly as he could in his arms. He could not have held her any tighter without snapping her bones. Their bodies were almost smudged together as one. In excruciating pain and despair Blake reached to the sky for his God, "Fuck, what have I done?"

His eyes streamed with tears and his heart ripped with pain as Marci lay dead in his arms. At this point every muscle and sinew in his body was racked with pain and the unrelenting aggressive spasms returned and tore sadistically through his body one more time just for kicks.

Blake lunged forward; he was desperate to kiss Marci just one last time. His partially closed eyes streamed with tears and his bloated mouth foamed slightly as he reached forward to kiss her gently on her face.

Blake cried out helplessly, He knew there would be no angel to greet him. At that moment he realised that he couldn't hold her any longer. The pain in his hands and throughout his body was running the show now and it demanded that he should let go of Marci's body. The convulsions and seizures that immediately followed consumed him in some ten seconds; he took his last breath.

Blake and Marci Brown took their own lives on May 28th
2096, it was their twentieth wedding anniversary. They had
known each other for eighty four years and had lived together
for sixty eight of those. They truly loved the bones of each
other but just took some time to be brave enough to deal
with that. Due to the length of time they spent together they
were exposed to a lot of suffering and pain from the loss of
their loved ones and family. The great sadness this caused
ultimately triggered their suicide. They died holding each
other for as long as they possibly could until, exhausted,
something else took over. Blake's hand prints could be found
in places on Marci's body, he had held her so tight, probably
he just couldn't bear to let her go.

Police Statement to the Press.

*Two bodies, that of a Mr Blake and Mrs Marci Brown were
found on the beach at Hataitai Bay in the early hours of the morning
of the 29th May. Their bodies were found slumped across each other
underneath a beach rug. The police were able to identify the bodies
from passports which were later found on the clothing of Mr Brown.
Data points to Mr Brown being one hundred and thirty two years of
age and Mrs Brown being one hundred and twenty four. Police also
discovered what is believed to be a suicide note written by the couple.
The couple are believed to have lived in the area of Hataitai Bay.
Police are not looking for any other person in connection with this
incident but would like to interview anybody who knew the couple.*